American Queer

50 Years of Stories and Poems

by

Richard Kitzman

Published in the United States by OFM Publishing LLC, dba Q Publishing House, 2101 Arapahoe St., Denver, CO 80205

All text by Richard Kitzman

Cover Art by Ivy Owens

Edited by Addison Herron-Wheeler

ISBN - 979-8-3485-2973-4

Dedication

I dedicate these stories, our stories,
to the women and men below, gone but never forgotten.

Archie	Lou
Boris	Marco
Brian	Max
Byrdman	Michael
Charles	Mitch
Craig	Paul
Dan	Richie
David McF.	Rodger McF.
Eric	Roman
George	Sara
Double Jeffrey	Terry
Little Jeff	Tim
Joe	Tom
Jonny V.	Tony
Kagey	Wes

May you all be dancing in a great disco under a glittering ball to
fabulous music! Save a dance for me.

Introduction

Recently, I turned 70, lucky to greet another decade with the joy of being a gay man. This awareness did not arrive overnight nor without pain. Nor without the love of many friends not so lucky; they died needlessly and painfully from the ungodly plague of AIDS.

Some of them had encouraged me to write about our experiences so our culture would endure in a world that wanted us dead and gone. Their challenge became this survivor's self-imposed

duty, but writing was an unproven offering to honor them. Until now.

In *American Queer*, early efforts from school days predict a goofy, passionate perspective and launch 50 years of compositions exploring humor and horror, fantasy and mystery, the erotic and the patriotic. Every tale is about love—getting it, losing it, experiencing it, searching for it—within relationships and circumstances of different kinds, not all of them queer.

For queers, coming out of their closets is a lifelong, daily declaration — I come out over and over in *American Queer*—but coming out isn't always about sexuality or gender. Everyone has a closet of fear. Everyone has the same difficult and strange task in common: making sense of being human. We all seek our place in this vast universe. *American Queer* examines our shared humanity and all its tragic and comedic weirdness. At the very least, I hope you are entertained.

But these stories are more than entertainment. Be careful where you read them because they could provide evidence to imprison, fine, torture, execute, or silence and deny you, me, anyone on every continent in over 60 countries with anti-queer laws. And though the U.S. Supreme Court ruled sodomy laws (criminal punishment of private, consensual, non-procreative, adult sexual activities) unconstitutional in 2003, be careful in which state you read the stories. Twelve still have anti-sodomy laws, not that you'd be arrested and prosecuted for engaging in those actions. But about 2 years ago, mothers and doctors were not arrested and prosecuted for having or conducting abortions. With the repeal of Roe v. Wade, strategies to attack and overturn the 2015 same-sex marriage case of Obergefell v. Hodges rumbled immediately. I have no doubt hard won queer rights and freedoms will be targeted in the near future.

American. Queer. Two powerful words that evoke a wide range of meaning, historically and presently. And I rescue them from those who have shamelessly warped and weaponized their definitions. The two fluid adjectives/nouns describe who I am—American since birth and queer (or different) since 4. In my 7 decades I've slid from one end of my comfort/discomfort spectrum to the other because they both come with privileges and problems.

Sadly, millions of so-called Americans still want us queers dead and gone, but they do not get to define what "American" means, certainly not as delusional, mean-spirited, bible-driven traitors. And I'm putting them on notice their pejorative use of "queer" is no longer an insult. It's a lavender badge of truth.

I'm also an OK, Boomer, a gay elder if you will. Declaring my queerness in the 70s was illegal and life-threatening. Today, billions of social media postings, all avenues of entertainment, and events of a global reach celebrate queerness. But despite hard-won legal protections and bursting cultural expressions, coming out is still life-threatening. Haters and hypocrites target the LGBTQ+ tribe in the sanctimonious disguises of moral legislation and religious righteousness. Even dancing is dangerous; at Pulse in Orlando and Club Q in Colorado Springs, people were just having fun. Which apparently is extremely threatening.

But we must not yield to fear. The murders feel like a massive insult and betrayal because dancing and fun—joyful, ecstatic fun!—have been a huge part of my gay life. Of course, I also remember the excruciating anxieties, but not like I remember having fun with my dancing buddies.

They thrive on these pages, not biographically, but in some sacred way I know but cannot express. On some weird cosmic plane by this ineffable means, their legacy remains relevant and helpful to those struggling with gender and sexuality, ensuring the achievements and sacrifices of my friends were not lived in vain. I'm grateful for what I learned from them, grateful for their love and encouragement, and grateful to honor them with *American Queer*.

AMERICAN QUEER:
50 Years of Stories and Poems
by Richard Kitzman

**Trauma Warning:*
Stories marked with an asterisk contain themes of sexual
violence and violence against the LGBTQ+ community.
Read with caution.

SCHOOL DAYS
1970-1975

The Noble Gallus Domesticus
(The Chicken)

1970

I wrote this piece to compete in high school Speech meets. Inspiration came from television's Laugh-In with loudmouth Joanne Worley's riff, "Is that a chicken joke?"; and Alfred Hitchcock's movie The Birds. Both provided the equivalent of water cooler chitchat at the drinking fountain for my high school buddies and me.

I delivered this melodramatic reading in the Original Essay category in my go-to get-up: a black-and-white paisley, poofy shirt (accented by a purple scarf) tucked into gray bell bottom slacks over calf-high lace-up boots. Fabulous! I never won anything with this silly piece; competitors agonized about nuclear war, famine, race. I got laughs.

* * *

Once there was a story written by Daphne du Maurier. Once there was a director who read it. His name: Alfred Hitchcock. The book: *The Birds*.

I saw this movie. (Pause, cringe, look away.) Suddenly and for no reason, pretty, plumy creatures attack unsuspecting humans. They swarm over their victims, pecking out eyes and biting legs and hands, ripping apart skin, in other words, death by beak. After the birds create havoc with their horrific avian assaults, the warning tale chillingly ends as a family, stranded in a boarded-up house, is held captive by thousands of flocks of feathered fowl, eerily still, patiently waiting to continue their revenge on the human race.

After the cinematic shock and the end credits rolled, I thought of the noble chicken. I don't know why; I just did. And I thought, what if we were given housing fit for ants it was so cramped? What if this housing was outside, exposed to every element of weather: boiling heat or freezing cold? What if we had to build nests in all types of hostile environments? What if the only foodstuffs to consume were crunchy insects or squishy worms or rock-hard corn kernels? What would we do? Why, just like fictional birds, we'd rebel, too!

So, humans, take warning. In the real world, to avoid its justified vengeance, we must end the immoral acts we commit every day on the *gallus domesticus*, commonly known as the chicken.

Join me and the brigade against killing the noble chicken!

You, yes you, right out there in the audience, use some portion of this innocent, cuddly fowl, in some horrible and hideously foul fashion. In the following few minutes, I will tell you about the abuses of today's chickens and their effects.

One horrendous abuse of so many is that humans kidnap—chicknap?—the unsuspecting mothers' unhatched eggs and then eat the yet unborn baby chicks. What is this world coming to when we go and steal the poor, helpless hens' children? You'd be angry, too, if someone stole your unborn baby and ate it. Picture yourself as a hen, watching your egg be cracked open, fried, boiled, or poached, and then devoured. You prefer your eggs scrambled? Has mankind invented a crueler instrument of torture than the egg beater? But the brave hens of America keep on laying eggs in hopes that someday they read the newspaper headline—or someone reads it to them: "CHICKEN MASSACRE STOPS!"

After eating the hens' eggs, you would think we would stop bothering our fine feathered friends, but no, we keep on with our massive killing by eating the chicken itself! I ask you, would you like it if someone bit into your drumstick, or broke your breastbone to make a selfish wish? I should think not. Slaughtered by the millions, these prisoners in coops have no choice.

And the different deaths which our friends go through to provide us with food are grisly, gruesome, and grim. One way is depicted in the following tale, worthy of Poe, because it's not for weak stomachs. I should know because once, I—I was forced to help with an avian slaughter.

    American Queer

First, the farmer grabbed a bird violently by its legs, stunned it by whacking its head on a wood block—THWAP!— then decapitated it with an axe—CHOP!—without the winged martyr putting up any fight in self-defense for fear of pecking or scratching its murderer. Of course, it's hard to peck and scratch when you're stunned and headless, but that's beside the point because we, the murderers, laugh as the chicken runs squawking and bumping into objects that it obviously cannot see like a, well, like a chicken with its head cut off. All this pain and humiliation just so we humans have something to sink our teeth in and fill our tummies with.

But there's more. To satisfy her (our) bloodthirst, the farmer boiled the bird to pluck its feathers so someone may have a soft pillow or mattress to sleep on.

The next humiliating injustice? The naked carcass is waved over a fire to singe what's called pinfeathers, teeny, tiny, baby feathers annoying to humans' sense of taste. But what's even more abominable is the slaughter of millions of our fine feathered friends at chicken factories worldwide—the horror, the inhumanity, the hell! But … I've got to finish. (To self: You can do it, you can do it.) Because you see, ladies and gentlemen, the farmer, the slaughterer was my mother. Yes, my mother. So there! I've admitted my shame. Care to make something of it? Pardon me, pardon me, this is stressful. My confession has lightened my guilt, but I—I must move on, up, and forward. For my sake, as well as for the sake of the chicken.

Through the ages, through some ironic twist of fate, this symbol for courage and bravery has become the symbol of paranoia and hysteria. Crying "The sky is falling, the sky is falling!" Chicken Little may be right some day, thereby saving humanity from getting clocked on its collective noggin. The fuzzy little guy may become that heroic symbol of courage and bravery instead of cowardice and scorn. In this twist of feathery fate, it must have been a twist of somebody's twisted, taunting, tyrannical mind, who had had a terrible, tormented, and terror-filled life, and promoted the character assassination. How else could people nutty as fruitcakes, bats, bonkers, bananas, cuckoo if you will, perpetuate such a dreadful, inaccurate accusation? How could any normal, sensible person come to the conclusion

                                        American Queer

that our noble chicken is chicken, or chickenhearted, in deed, as yellow in soul. Oh, the ironic injustice, so undeserved, so untrue.

We must face the real truth, the painful, agonizing truth. All of the preceding reasons that we use chickens for are escape hatches from reality, selfish and shameful. We should feel guilty when taking the life of a chicken or eating its unhatched eggs, never to hatch as cute, fuzzy, little chicks. Which reminds me of Easter, when so many babies, bought for kids to torment, then to abandon, are cast aside like a boring toy; and when so many eggs are bought. boiled, dyed, then left to rot like yesterday's omelet. We should feel humiliated to know that we have taken a defenseless chicken's feathers to sleep upon, to dream upon, when the cock or hen undoubtedly needs the plumage more than we do, and when there are plenty of other materials available.

Why do we pick on the chicken? Why! Would the chicken, if its claws were in our shoes, force those inhumane conditions on us? No, because it's not human! Or in this case, not chicken! Can you picture a chicken able to think, comprehend, and communicate? No, because we ignore the possibility! Some say the insects will dominate the earth next, but it might be the chicken. And then where will the human race be? Hitchcock and du Maurier answered. The future is terrifying.

You may be asking yourself, "Is this a chicken joke?" I assure you I am earnest in my love and concerns for the noble *gallus domesticus*.

The problems and prejudices against the chicken will never cease until, finally, the chicken flies—as best it can—out of its cage of bondage and forces humanity to pay for its debts and crimes! Think of that the next time you bite into a grilled breast covered in hot thick, gooey gravy or chomp a deep-fried drumstick with a delicate, spicy crunch.

Mmmm … yes, well, ahem, I see it's time for lunch.

And so, I leave you with this: At the very least, if I've touched some part of your heart, the next time you see a chicken crossing the road, don't insult it by asking the chicken why it's crossing the road. Let it cross. It's none of your beeswax. Just don't run over it.

Thank you so much, one and all, for your attention today. And please! I beg you to join my brigade to treat the

     American Queer

simple chicken kindly and with compassion. It's up to you to grow our flock. Members are as rare as hen's teeth, and that's no chicken joke.

On Patriotism

(Speech Contest sponsored by the Brighton Elks to write an
essay about patriotism)

1971

*I won the first-place prize of a $300 scholarship sponsored by
the Elks Lodge, and delivered the essay as a speech at an Elks
congratulatory luncheon. The money paid for almost a full
year's tuition at the University of Northern Colorado.*

* * *

Unless you're a veteran, how can American citizens
fully appreciate the services given to us by the members of the
armed forces? What these men and women have done for us
cannot be measured in terms of dollars or words. Attempts are
insufficient and lacking.

Participation in this contest of 1970 is my attempt to
show my appreciation. Though all of us high schoolers never
lived during World War I or World War II—times when our
shores were threatened with foreign invasion, our founding
ideals with destruction—we have all reaped the fruits of our
fellow Americans' actions. If not for veterans'
valorous convictions and performances, our laws, our
constitution, our basic freedoms may have been compromised or
lost. Too many times, the ideals they fought for, were crippled
for, died for, are taken for granted.

Because of a current unpopular war, too many times they
themselves are abused; too many times they are ridiculed and
slandered in spite of their courage and sacrifice. This lack of
gratitude and respect for our veterans threatens America's
economic, religious, social, and moral prominence unsurpassed
by any preceding or existing governments.

Our heroes and heroines are so often forgotten by the
general public, especially by younger people. They can't relate
to the frustration, the pain, the heartache, the despair, the loss of

life and limb, and the fear our former protectors experienced—all of which was to preserve an America that future generations could live in and be proud of. They have succeeded with flying colors: red, white, and blue.

When I look at our flag, I can almost visualize some battle scene—the confusion, noise, filth, its agony of injury or sadness of death, outcome unknown—and I think of how

many soldiers and officers went through all this over and over for me, for all Americans.

It must be a great feeling to know you have done something for your country, a feeling that must fill the heart of every veteran. And wouldn't it be astounding if that same feeling, that feeling of pride and love of country, could be generated through the heart of every American? One way would be to simply acknowledge the courage and service of these men and women by saying "Thank you."

Pages

1973

(To a poet from a would-be poet, February 1973)

Opening the volume from the shelves of my mind,
I read—once again—
where who was once a gentle, golden knock
became a booming beat.
The echoes I still hear.
The echoes I still retreat from.
The echoes I regret.
The pages on which the echoes reverberate,
  yellow like a dusty sunflower,
  worn and torn from being flipped—
  forward and backward,
  backward and forward—
a melodrama on fool's cap.

A minor character
(who is printing himself on my newest pages)
  had a part,
the traits of whom were telegraphed to me
  by yowls and howls
  snapped and barked
by tongues ignorant.
(But these newer pages reveal differently.)
And on other pages I read
where a friend we've shared,
you and I,
and so, perhaps, even more.
The volume I close shut
and put back—once again, time and time again—
  in hopes that dust and cobwebs collect
  and forever catch the pages

     American Queer

to their permanent place on the shelf.
It's no matter.
This new volume I dedicate to you.
It's no matter.
Because this is for you from me.

Your pages you read to me
are written deceivingly well—
        for your own sake I presume.
And what new decrees and rules and proclamations
        may be written on your pages,
I do not know.
I read you,
but like the words,
        am puzzled and unsure
        and at times, intimidated.
I see you rarely,
but take you home,
and pour over my pages of your words.
Our pages may be set in different type,
the words may mix and make no sense
        and challenge and hurt and contradict.
No matter.
I understand.

And these pages for you
I write for myself in part;
and because people publish their messages on reams and reams
        of onion skin—
        dry, crackly, easily shredded and creased—
        and then it's too late.
Mine is imprinted on vellum
        and give to you these words:
                I love you.

There.
I've said it in an ink of blue honey
and I've made an ass of myself
but I don't care!

                                        American Queer

It's just these words—three, airy, of eight easy letters—
        sound so simple, so silly, but fall like a balloon-rock
        on dull comfort.
I only wish … I only wish
        I was brave enough to print more.
Perhaps I wouldn't mean it
and I'm mad at myself
and my pages are getting in the wrong sequence
and I look in the mirror
and wonder who is looking back
and who would ever look with me
and I make sense of this insane confusion
        only by understanding, but—
        not enough, it's not enough,
        you're never near enough to touch.
I only hope there's time enough for time to tell me.
And this! This foolish epistle I should never have composed,
this, what a lovesick child would scribble, then giggle and sigh.
I sigh, but I cannot laugh.

I've written too much, too goddamn much—
and on lifeless paper!
But these words remain—
        my words.
If you care, put them in your own book.
Just don't crumple me up and throw me away.
No need to attempt a query,
I'll be reading you again, soon.
There.
Ink dry, sticky perhaps,
but on my mantelpiece I'll place this.

And so, I put down my pen,
anxious about the next time I'll pick it up
and just when the inkwell will run dry,
and shut my eyes …
and go to sleep …
and go to sleep and dream …
and dream pages upon pages, reams upon reams …

                                        American Queer

that will be shelved upon heaps …
upon heaps of other dreams …
different only in the thickness of their dust …
until the powder of their memories
            is blown away …

Pane

1975

His full-framed view
was gazed through
a web of twigs and branches,
and nothing began
or ever begins
as it should;
or rather,
something did begin.
Dreamt of kisses never kissed,
hands never held,
he did;
And from such a lover a lover's silence ensues:

> Come to me,
> come to me,
> my unknown lover,
> where friendly black forest-covered
> roving rocks
> do wiggle and heave and writhe.
> Non-physical transformation—
> and you are in my arms.
> Fervent limbs lift high,
> entwining twigs and branches of yours
> …

And so, the pane of this world
from his bed
is but a rock's toss.
And the phantasmagoria
builds to such extremes,
that he re-releases
and re-releases

American Queer

and re-releases …

        Come to me,
        come to me
        my unknown lover.
        Hydraulic my derrick,
        the geyser that gushes and belches a
        boiling oil
        that does scorch the skin and soul alike
        …

And so the rocket launched explodes,
the ignition that lit a jarting jet fuel
in full-framed view
of silver shadows
of the sky and street and stars
across so near,
yet so far …
so far …
And not only did it not begin,
but began and begins again …

        Come to me,
        come to me
        my unknown lover.
        Enter me here,
        enter me there,
        my unknown caverns
        where pointed porcelain peaks
        are guarded by a salivating snake
        to charm the coming of yours,
        re-entered
        slurped and gurgle-gargled
        retreating
        re-entered;
        or the puckered bud
        blossoming with moonlit blush,
        welcoming and enveloping your
        cylinder silo stinger,
        corpuscular red

and penetrating puce
and violent violet,
a pole-boring place
to be poured into and take shape of.
Oh imagined pain!
Perpetual long-lastingness …

But a kiss kissed
and a hand held,
these are the wishes across the way
where a shadow,
silvery, star and street lit,
sits and moves to the window of his world
webbed with limbs and twigs and branches.
And from such a lover,
a lover's silence ensues.
And as nothing ever began—
it begins again.

NEW YORK STORIES 1979-1984

There's Chocolate in Heaven!

a true & mysterious Yuletide Tale,
embellished, But only slightly;
the Veracity of Our Readers
being a Fact, Well-established!

1979

(Dedicated to my Patrick, Craig Kitt, wherever he may be)

After five rings: *"Hi, this is Daniel. I'm not here right now, but after the beep, leave your name, number, and a brief message. I'll get back to you when I can. Ciao!"* BEEEEEEP!

God, get this recording out of my head, thought Patrick, but it played again and again.

As flakes fell straight as strings on the dimly lit street, he staggered home from a Christmas Eve party, weaving a wake of meandering footprints through the white blanket. "Mounties always get their man," he said aloud, "but do they always get him back?"

Hi, this is Daniel ...

He moved out; he should call me. I should throw up. God, I hate throwing-up.

Protecting the quiet of this holy night from the din of the holiday, naked trees flocked white and tear-shaped lamps stood guard like silent sentries. A car rarely rolled by, and when one did, tires crept by with muffled crunches, mottled headlight beams lit a confetti of specks, and exhaust plumes tethered to a pipe floated behind. Festive store displays glowed soothingly through frosted windows. Reveler's cries echoed occasionally, but muted, as though every New Yorker had vowed not to disturb the tranquility of this moment.

Except one. "Not calling him. Not calling him. Not calling him!"

     American Queer

And another, from behind, odd sounding. "Shut up down there!"

"Shut up yourself!" Patrick swung around, wildly punching only air, slipped, and fell hard. Cursing and seeing nobody nearby, he picked himself up, but a ghostly, icy gust swept him sideways, and he fell again, smacking his head on concrete. "Ouch, ouchie, ouch."

Way too high and drunk. If only—the world stop spinning. God help me, need a little rest. Where am I?

Sprawled before a dilapidated brownstone, Patrick hoisted himself up its stairway, each step cause for a whine, and scooted into a corner of the porch. Dramatically thinking his shoulders ached from carrying the weight of the world, he grasped them and shivered, the cold air that enveloped him reviving cold memories of visits to Harlem and his fight with Daniel.

When was it? Just yesterday. After Daniel stormed out of his apartment, he had phoned him so many times, and, getting no live response, the recording had branded his brain. To leave a message, or not to leave a message—that was the quandary cleaving Patrick's worry. To do so implied apology, defeat. Not to mention no chance to truly apologize, to win back his lover. Plus, what if he left a message and Daniel did not reply? Or the living Daniel answered? He found comfort in the recorded voice with its melodic tone but never left a message.

My head hurts. How can I see—stars? It's snowing. Shouldn't have gone to Libby's party—or answered her call.

E arlier Christmas Eve, Patrick's best friend and agent Libby, had listened to his laments about his lover. She had searched a candy box, selected a chocolate, tasted it, made a face, and returned it to the box. "Sweetie," asked Libby, "how many times did you call him?"

"Not once."

… BEEEEEEP! …

   American Queer

"Liar," accused Libby. "I've been trying to call you, and your line's always busy."

"He wasn't home," said Patrick. He pulled pictures from a box and glanced at a photo of him and Daniel atop the World Trade Center.

"Leave a message?"

"God, no!"

"Darling, don't shout," said Libby, "I'm a very rich, three-time divorcé for good reason."

"Yes, you lure men," said Patrick, "then turn either their heart or bank account to stone. A modern Medusa."

"I am not a gorgon!" shouted Libby.

Patrick knew she was patting her French roll that reminded him of the Bride of Frankenstein's zebra style. It's how she regained her composure.

"I'm your art gallery owner. Speaking of—you know Rona, my most successful client? Last week, Bloomie's featured her edible, holiday crafts. I wheeled the old biddy in; she autographed these *objets d'art* in frosting, and we made a fortune."

"Goodie for Rona," said Patrick, sweeping up the broken remains of an angel figurine.

"What's all that noise?"

"I'm painting." Patrick stared at tubes of color, dry brushes, clean rags, and blank canvases.

"Liar."

"I smashed something, alright? Cleaning up the damages."

"Paint! I can't sell what I don't have."

"You can't sell the ones you do have."

"You haven't created the right picture. Yet. I can smell talent, and you stink to high heavens."

"Thanks?"

"Fame, fortune, New York will be at your feet.

"What should I do about Daniel?"

"Call him. Or work. Paint is one letter away from pain," answered Libby. "You're an artist, artists do, so do come tonight. It's Christmas Eve. Paddy, sweetie, I need you. Who else can meet my poor-starving-Irish-Catholic-homo-artist quota?"

          American Queer

"You forgot red-headed," said Patrick. "Forget the Catholic part, and your hoity-toities."

"Then come for the orgy of yum-yums," enticed Libby. "My place will simply reek of epicurean splendors."

"Why do you keep having Christmas parties? You're a heathen."

"To celebrate!" trumpeted Libby. "Otherwise, what's the point? That and all the glittery things. So pretty. So good for business. And don't change the subject because you have problems with money."

"Always sunny in a rich man's world."

"Sweetie, stop it," Libby fired back. "I can't help that my great-great grandfather was a robber baron."

"I know."

"And I know my clientele. The rich are the angels of artists, so drop this pissy attitude, and your angel will drop in like magic. Meanwhile, drop in here nine-ish. You could get a commission. Bring Daniel."

"I'm not calling him."

Hi, this is Daniel ...

Libby searched her candy box for another chocolate delight. "Please come. I simply must have amusing guests besides the tedious ones. And you two make such a beautiful couple. Red and Black. Like checkers. *Trés chic.*"

"Listen, Libby—"

But she would not listen. "Darling, if I could wave a wand and make it better, I would. Now stop mopping and moping, and start primping. You've only two hours." Click!

Patrick jerked. "What the—"

Ice. Slipping. Steps. Brownstone. "Oh, yeah." Now he remembered why he was sitting on a hard porch freezing and aching.

In the opposite corner, tennis shoes with a boomerang design peeked out from under clothes and rags. The large mound

American Queer

was loosely covered by a garbage bag held down by an odd hat. Snow dusted the heap like powdered sugar.

"Do I remember that?" He did not.

Above the mound of trash, plywood replaced the small window of a graffitied door, a lone bulb emitting low light. Patrick strained to read two notes taped to the inside of its frosty, fractured glass: one printed, *No Soliciting*; the other, scribbled, *Beware of God*. He blinked a couple times. *Beware of Dog*.

"That's better."

Not really, came a thought not his own.

"What?" For God's sake, I'm hallucinating.

For your sake, came another thought not his own.

Losing it, I'm losing it. Must sober up, get a grip. Wind so cold. Hope Fido's asleep. Me too—bit longer.

Patrick curled himself more tightly. Echoes of gaiety and a mild, fragrant aroma permeated the air. The hubbub of holiday cheer in a penthouse on Sutton Place drifted through his mind.

"God," he said, "when will the snow stop?"

The snow had started when Patrick arrived at Libby's.

After greeting his hostess, he rounded the buffet with several laps. Smeared evidence on his gold plate verified her promise of epicurean splendors: steaming lobster casseroles, baby quiches with baby spinach, prime rib, pastas, and pastries, the blintzes gorged with flown-in, fresh, white raspberries. ("Darling," the hostess had said, "anyone can get red raspberries.") Creamy desserts and bowls of Belgian chocolates abounded.

Patrick had claimed a comfortable niche in a small study with a blazing hearth, holly garland draping its mantelpiece. Anchored on oversized, red and green patterned pillows, he sat on a cushy sofa, observing the wealthy company and speaking little. As the string trio enchanted gabby guests, liquor flowed freely, marijuana mingled with evergreen, and candles by the gross blended with the fire to cast gradients of glow. Orchids sprouted copiously. Vermillion poinsettias lined walls like velvet hedgerows. Everything imbued the walnut-paneled room with a cozy haze and a spicy scent.

Viewed through his crystal goblet—empty of purple wine for the sixth time—the kaleidoscope of reflections mesmerized him, particularly a frilly, pink angel crowning the tall Christmas tree. It looked like the one he had smashed earlier in the day, a gift from Daniel.

… I'm not here right now …

Patrick was warm, full, high, and alone. Nevertheless, a black olive on each digit of his left hand diverted his discomfort. Patrick bit one off.

A dowager, wearing a sequined Santa Claus suit, occupied the dark green divan. Like an orange-haired hound, she wolfed down her food, and waving a forkful of crab cake—a small piece stuck to her chin—she babbled about civilization ending at the Hudson and America being a vast void of nothingness.

Another olive disappeared.

Standing and spreading her flabby arms before Libby's thirtieth floor vista of Manhattan, Ms. Claus proposed a toast to the communication dishes, spears and spires blinking through the white cascade as the crucifixes of the twentieth century.

"Mf–what?" gulped Patrick. While he sucked the black fruit on his thumb, a dozen people raised their glasses and twittered with glee. The pink angel seemed to wink at him. He ate another olive and decided to leave.

His hostess escorted him to her private foyer, its dome aglow from indirect lighting. As he swayed waiting for the private elevator, he thought Libby's expression—too tight from numerous nips and tucks—epitomized travel at Mach speed.

"Darling," she said, "you've an olive thingie on your finger."

"One for the road." Patrick gobbled his hand's last black thimble and put on his gloves.

"Very Freudian. Did you make any deals?"

"I drank, smoked, ate, snubbed your rootie-kazootie pals."

"Oh, how gauche."

"'S a wonderful life."

"You've barely a pot to piss in."

"Meant with a cheeky tongue."

"Merry Christmas anyway." From behind her back, Libby presented a gift, grinning with self-satisfaction. "Open it."

Patrick ripped at green-grid paper and red ribbon. The box revealed a small painting depicting a crèche. A lotus blossom graced the Madonna's Monroe-esque blond hair. She wore a mini-skirt and go-go boots, her earthly husband wore chains and studded leather. Pink pigs and flamingoes adored a baby Buddha—belly and smile intact—who napped in a crib of soup cans. Three drag queens replaced three kings, Shiva danced one-footed with multiple arms akimbo, and a Star of David shimmered above the hut. Vigilant from a hillside, his staff topped by a crescent moon and his head ringed by a Lifesaver candy halo, stood a Black shepherd with aviator shades and splayed wings.

Libby reveled in how the artist had owed her a favor and condescended to give her this small canvas, six inches square. "It's so quaint."

Patrick feigned delight. "Lucky me."

"You don't know how lucky," agreed Libby. "She'll be dead in a year, and her product will triple in value."

"Ah, commerce," said Patrick. He zipped up his parka, re-wrapped the Rona, and put it in a pocket. After thanking Libby, he explained his reason for giving her nothing. "I need 90 dollars for rent."

"Paint me a masterpiece," said Libby, pulling his scarf tighter round his neck.

Not the response he intended, Patrick said, "As soon as I get home."

"Then Paddy, darling, make up and make out with your beau. No more calls to pseudo-Daniel."

Hi, this is Daniel …

"And let's not waste the mistletoe." They stood underneath bound sprigs. Libby kissed Patrick on each cheek and promised to see his new work soon. "Then we'll lunch at the Plaza."

"Are you buying?"

 American Queer

"Don't I always."

"Someday, I will buy you lunch at the Plaza."

"Yes, you will, and I will love it, darling."

Patrick wondered what new work he would show her from his pitiful castle in the sky on the second floor. Right now, he felt suffocated, hot, and high. Hearing the arrival of the elevator, Patrick swiveled too quickly, and before the door opened completely, walked into it, bouncing back dazed. He rubbed his forehead and said, "I think I'm seeing heaven."

"Darling, how dreary."

"What?"

"All that perfection."

"Wouldn't you like to see heaven?"

"How would I know," said Libby, yawning. "I've never been there. Will there be chocolate?"

"I'll find out."

"Do, sweetie, do," said Libby, "then let me know." She offered to pay for a taxi, but her guest declined, needing fresh air. "Then watch out for drunk elves," warned the hostess, "and remember, darling—"

As the elevator door shut, Patrick heard Libby say something about Van Gogh and not losing an ear.

C an't hear ... can't hear ... God, I'm deaf!
Somewhere, a church bell bonged four times.

Ah, heard that. Wake up. Why didn't I take a taxi? This air—too damn fresh. Find me frozen. Daniel. Call Daniel. How? Couldn't stand listening to his stupid message again anyway, so businesslike, so like him. And what's with *Ciao?* Only Italian he speaks besides *spaghetti.* God knows he left me; he can get in touch with me. Ahm zo tahrd off playeeng zis game.

... I'll get back to you when I can ...

"God," he said, "I am so sorry."

                                        American Queer

I'm sorry!" Patrick had shouted. "Please stop packing."

"This isn't working." Daniel yanked ties out of their closet. "I haven't made quota in three months."

"Is that all you can think about?" said Patrick in Daniel's face. "Your quota?"

"It's what pays our bills."

"Implying my work doesn't."

Daniel strained to calm himself. "Paddy, I don't care about the money."

"I said I'd pay you back."

"I don't care." Daniel threw some clothes in his gym bag.

"I can take care of myself," said Patrick.

"But you don't take care of our home," said Daniel.

"Home. You crash here."

"You don't want to live at my place."

"I'm not welcome."

"What?" Daniel entered the bathroom, gathered his toiletries.

Patrick dogged him. "That's my nose trimmer."

"No, it's not."

"You may keep it," said Patrick. "When we stay at your apartment, we rarely go out or have your friends or family over. And when we do, they treat me like I've got donkey ears."

"Right now," said Daniel to Patrick's reflection in the mirror, "you do look like an ass."

"It's your mother, isn't it?" accused Patrick. "She hates me. All of Harlem hates me."

"You're crazy," declared Daniel. "and a master at changing the subject. And paranoid. You should be paranoid, but not because of that."

"Then what?"

"Do you want to end up like Archie or Tom? I don't."

"That's a low blow."

"Or Paul or Mitch—"

American Queer

"Why would a Black man be with a red-headed, white boy?"

"—or Jeff or Johnny—"

"You're embarrassed to be seen with me."

"—or Lou or Casey—"

"In Harlem, you can't hide."

"—or George or Tony—"

"Can you?"

"—or Marco or Michael—"

"Answer me!"

"It's not 1980!"

"It's not fair!" Patrick hurled a ceramic angel, shattering it against the wall.

Daniel jumped. "No," he said quietly, "it's not."

"Then God, how I hate it. Do you hear me, God? I hate this life!"

"Don't say that," said Daniel, rushing up to Patrick. "Don't you ever say that again!"

"Or what?" Patrick did not move.

Daniel moved a few shards with his foot, and deflated. "I gave that angel to you. A year ago, today."

"One less thing to remind me of you."

Daniel absorbed the sting with a forceful zip of his bag. "You don't get it," he said. "When you do, call me. I might pick up the phone."

"Too easy. Stay and fight like a man."

"Until then," said Daniel, putting on his coat and opening the front door, "you can do it every night with the doorman for all I care. *Ciao.*"

"HA!" yelled Patrick down the stairwell. "We don't have a doorman!" He slammed the door shut and cried.

"**D**AANNIIIEEEELL!"
Whether Patrick's wail on the brownstone stoop was audible or not, a voice sounded in his head: Hey.

"Daniel? Daniel!"

Suspended by night, shadows, and dark skin, the whites of eyes gazed at him from the opposite corner. Like a black Cheshire cat, a grin crawled, baring bright, white teeth.

"Merry Christmas."

Patrick pressed himself back into his corner and screamed. "AAHHHH!"

—which scared the man, who did likewise—

"AAHHHH!"

—both parrying the other's shrill riposte in their vocal duel—

"AAHHHH!"

"AAHHHH!"

"AAHHHH!"

"Stop your yowling!" shouted the man.

"You stop!" Patrick shouted back.

"You started it!"

"Get out of here!"

"I was here first!" asserted the man. "So you can move your butt—Lordy, are you crying?"

"I am not crying," lied Patrick. "Stay there; don't come near me!" Woozy and terrified, he slid down the icy steps, then ran as well as he could.

"Come back here!" called the man. "I'm talking to you! You're walking on thin ice, white boy!" The dark mass stood and shook its head. "Dammit, nobody listens, nobody, no how."

Looking like a down-and-out court jester, the man wore shoes with boomerangs, a hunter's cap with earflaps, scarves, and several coats, some buttoned, some over his shoulders. Like a cape, a garbage bag draped his costume.

"Minding my own business, cozy as a bedbug," resumed the man. "Now I have to get my sorry, Black ass up and after that stupid, white ass. But I'll get him," he snickered devilishly, "and he won't know what hit him until it's too late." In a second, the man trotted next to his target.

"AAHHHH!" screamed Patrick.

"Don't start that again."

"Stop following me."

"Tell me why you were crying."

"Mind your own business," snapped Patrick.

"You are my business." The man stopped running, then hollered, "See that big-ass, yellow taxi coming? If you don't come back here and talk to me, white boy, I'll run in front of it, and you'll have to pay."

"What?" Patrick wheeled around. "You're crazy."

"No, I'm an angel! Hiram's my name, saving your ass is my game," he proclaimed, then reached out to shake hands. "Pleased to meet you."

"Don't touch me."

"Are you always this cranky?"

"Help! Police! Help!"

"Jesus, Mary, and the Holy Saint Joseph," muttered Hiram. "OK, Paddy me boy," he announced in an Irish accent, "here I go!" Flapping his arms and squawking wildly, he dashed into the street and flew toward the taxi like a wild, black bird.

"This guy's higher than I am," said Patrick. "Hey, wait a minute. Don't. Don't do that!"

The taxi honked, braked, and slid sideways, heading toward the flailing maniac. Patrick ran to him and yanked his coats, tumbling over the curb and pulling the kook down on top of him. A horn blared, curses were yelled, and the taxi swerved, barely missing the two men. But for their panting little ghosts of cold breath, the street was still.

"Feeling frisky?" asked Hiram with a smirk and a wink.

"Get off me!" shouted Patrick. "What the hell did you do that for?"

"Because you're sad," said Hiram, rolling off his savior. "Because nobody listens to angels. Besides, I knew you wouldn't let old Hiram get hurt. Very lonesome and tiring, angel work is." He observed the rundown neighborhood that even in its urban blight revealed beauty. "I'll be sorry to leave this. But I want to go home."

"God knows, so do I."

"Amen, He does know, but first, He wants you to listen to me."

"Oh, get up." Patrick helped the man to his feet and thought, Thank God, I'm wearing gloves.

"You're welcome, white boy."

Patrick ignored the puzzling response. "Stop calling me *white boy*. I don't call you *Black man*, do I?"

"No." The man hung his head, then blurted, "Call me Hiram! That's my name, saving your ass is my game. Pleased to meet you."

Again, avoiding the offered hand, Patrick sighed, "Sweet Jesus,"

"Amen, brother."

"I'm going home."

"Why?"

"To get out of the wind."

"What wind?"

Patrick realized the air was motionless. "There's a freezing blizzard, or haven't you noticed?"

"It's a tad nippley."

"What the hell—" Patrick also realized he no longer exhaled puffs of vapor. Fog had replaced the falling snow, and the streetlamps reflected a delicate drape, fluffy and golden. "—is happening?"

"A conversation," said Hiram. He motioned politely and moved to the porch of the brownstone where they first met.

"Forget it." Patrick walked away.

"Ah!—" Hiram cried out and clutched his chest. "—my heart," and sat down hard on the steps.

"Are you for real?" exclaimed Patrick.

"No," moaned Hiram, "but you go on. I'll live."

Patrick rushed to his side and kneeled. "What? Are you having an attack?"

"Darn ticker." Hiram gasped for breath. "It comes and it goes."

"You need a doctor."

"No! I need you to stay with me, minute or two."

"You sure?"

"I'm sure.

"Rest for a while." Patrick sat next to Hiram. The cement step was not as cold as before.

"Mighty fine of you, boy, mighty fine."

"And don't run in front of any more cars."

"Nosirree, done with that." Hiram miraculously breathed normally. "You're a very intelligent boy."

After silence, Patrick asked, "I imagine this is a busy time of year for you?"

"What?"

"For angels, Christmas and everything."

"Oh Lordy, yes. But plenty of time for rest when I get home." Hiram's eyes followed something in the distance. "Duck!"

Instinctively, Patrick covered his head and recoiled from a sharp whack on the brownstone behind him. "What the hell was that?"

The men stood up and saw a bird lying lifeless before the entryway.

"A pigeon?" asked Patrick.

"Ain't a duck." Hiram delicately picked it up.

"It's all white. A dove?"

"Do I look like an ornithologist?"

Patrick frowned. "Wonder why it crashed?"

"Lost," said Hiram, "just trying to get home like all of us."

"Poor little guy. Is it dead?"

Hiram's sudden tears fell onto the bird, limp in his bare palms.

Patrick attempted a closer look. "Are you crying?"

"Leave us be."

Hiram cradled and swaddled the bird in one of his sleeves, shut his eyes, turned away, and murmured words Patrick could not hear except for the last: *Amen.* He glimpsed a faint, pinkish outline around Hiram's shape, but when Hiram turned around, the blush evaporated. The dove cooed, bobbed its head, and flew away.

As the bird soared, Patrick stared at it, then Hiram. "What did you—"

"Nothing," said Hiram. "Birdie was stunned."

"Makes two of us."

Hiram sat, sniffled, and cleared his throat with a hacking cough. "You got a cig?"

"What?"

"A cigarette."

"Don't smoke."

"What the hell is this world coming to?"

"You're unbelievable."

"That's your problem."

Patrick stared at the psycho and thought, how could I have touched this person? Filthy, smelly—I am not!—the voice inside his head contradicted. "Did you say something?"

"Nope."

This geezer's freaky, thought Patrick. Sick, the bird, suicidal, insane also—"Wait a minute. You called me *Paddy*?"

"Did I?"

"Before you ran into the street."

"Red hair, freckles. You've got to be Irish."

"That's presumptuous. I could say things about you."

"Me?" said Hiram, chuckling. "I'm Black Irish."

"Everyone is," said Patrick. "You couldn't have seen me that clearly."

"Oh, I see you."

"How'd you know my name?"

"Lucky guess. Look, don't argue with an angel."

"So, where's your halo and wings?"

"Do I look like a prissy greeting card?"

"And sweet disposition?"

"Someday, artists will answer to a real angel. C'mon, sit down, take a load off." Patrick complied, and as though talking to a two-year-old, Hiram explained, "See, there's exclusive ranks of angels. You got your cherubim, seraphim, and diaphragm. Ha!" Hiram hit Patrick on the back and convulsed in laughter, which progressed through another coughing fit. "God, I'm funny."

"Very droll, yes."

"Man, you one tight ass." Hiram pinched Patrick's cheek and leered.

Patrick slapped his hand away. "Knock it off." Lecherous old coot, he thought.

"I am not lecherous," said Hiram, sticking his nose in the air.

Again, Patrick ignored his uncanny remark.

                                    American Queer

"Merely excitable," continued Hiram.

"And presumptuous."

"I know my clientele," said Hiram. "Look, if angels flew around sporting wings and things, people would run the other way. *Eek! I saw a creature fly in the sky, wearing white robes and a gold ring round his noggin!* I look just fine, and you run the other way." Hiram held up his palm, stifling Patrick's impending disagreement. "This is my disguise. You'd pee your pants, little boy, if I showed you what I really look like."

"I've seen enough for one night."

"You haven't begun to really see."

"I don't really care."

"You think you carry the weight of the world on your shoulders," said Hiram. "Don't you know, it'd crush your skinny ass flatter than a roadkill squirrel. You still don't believe I'm an angel?"

"I believe you're Irish," said Daniel, "because you're full of blarney."

"Ah, you're crazy."

"That's the pot calling the kettle black, no offense intended."

"I confess, a little bit taken," said Hiram.

"But it's not the first time I've been called crazy today," admitted Patrick. "I'm lost in time. What is today?"

"Why, it's Christmas Day." Hiram grinned ear to ear. "Happy Birthday, Jesus!"

"You're feeling better," observed Patrick, rising to leave, "so I'm off."

"Ah!" Hiram clutched his chest again. "The big one! Help me!"

"I'm getting help."

"Wait! Don't leave ol' Hiram alone. It comes and it goes. Darn ticker."

"You've got to—"

"Thank the Lord? Grand idea, I do, and amen!"

"I mean—"

"See, it's gone, all better, ticker's OK. I'm OK now. Whew. That was close."

"How can you just blow off pain like that?"

"Pain's a sign of life," said Hiram matter-of-factly. "Nothing hurts more than a broken heart, and tomorrow isn't promised to anybody." He began rummaging through his pockets. "Tell you what, you stay with me, I'll pay you for your time, kind sir, yes sir, that I will do."

"A bribe?" Patrick eyeballed the madman, afraid of God-knows-what he would produce from his pockets.

"Greenback-a-dollar. You never see Lincolns nor Washingtons?"

"Never enough of them."

"That's the truth." Hiram laughed, continued his search, then mumbled, "Too many pockets. I know the loot's here somewhere, where'd I put it. That's not it. Whoa, Nelly. Not that either. Freak this boy right out of his lily-white mind. Amen, been looking for this." He entrusted Patrick with a half-eaten sandwich wrapped in paper. "And don't drop it! Dug it out near Zabars. Your folk sure is wasteful."

Patrick sat, gingerly holding garbage, feeling sorry for the guy and ashamed. "Are you hungry?"

"I have that snack," said Hiram, still burrowing among his pouches. "You?"

"No."

"Humph," grunted Hiram. "You're starving."

"I just came from pigging out at a party."

"Didn't say starving for what, did I? Found it, amen!" he exclaimed triumphantly and presented a clump of crinkled bills. "Feast your eyes on these, eh! Ninety-three dollars. Go ahead, count them. Your time worth ninety-three dollars?"

"More."

Hiram burst out a gruff, belly laugh. "Amen! Your time worth a hell of a lot more than ninety-three dollars. But this'll clean me out." He waved his fistful in front of Patrick's nose and said, "That be the smell of money, sonny."

Patrick looked around suspiciously. "Put it away," he whispered. "You want to get mugged?" Then he thought, What am I saying? Probably how he got it. I did not steal it! declared the same voice inside his head. "You said something."

"Did not."

"You did too."

　　　　　　　　　　　　　　　American Queer

"Take the money."

"I don't want it!"

"Is my money not good enough for a white boy?"

"No!"

"Afraid you'll catch a disease if you touch it? Might be maggots between the bills? Or roaches? Lord knows—and I do mean Lord knows—how many of His pesky little creatures are in this city." Hiram lowered his voice and leaned into Patrick, who abruptly became a confidant. "I know everything He creates is holy, but I do not care for those critters myself. Nosirree, not one iota. You won't tell God I said so, will you?"

"Your secret's safe," said Patrick. "And I'm not afraid of any disease or bug."

"Well, you should be, white boy. You should be."

"Shut up. You're nothing but a tramp."

"Some people would call you the same."

"That's it. I'm out of here." Patrick thought he had done his good deed and stood to leave the loon alone.

"Now don't get in a snit," said Hiram.

"Here's your snack," said Patrick, handing over the sandwich. "Merry crappy Christmas."

Hiram clamped onto Patrick's sleeve and pulled him back down. "Please don't go," he begged. "I'm sorry. I've got to give you this money, or else I won't get to go home, and oh Lordy, how I need to—"

"Let go!" shouted Patrick as he jerked away from the fanatic's grip.

"I'll buy something off you. What do you have to sell?"

"Nothing."

"You got a watch?"

"No."

"Rings or things?"

"No."

"You have less than I do and are stepping on my last petticoat."

Patrick thought, Like I'd tell you if I had any valuables. "I think I can run faster than you."

"You forget," smiled Hiram, "angels fly."

"On angel dust, maybe," said Patrick.

"Uh-huh, no way, no how. Horse crack's bad news. Haven't you got anything? Don't be holding out on old Hiram now."

"I'll give you my gloves."

"Gloves?" Hiram was disappointed. "My hands get cold, I stick them down my pants!" He butted shoulders with Patrick and giggled nastily in his face.

"Goodie for you." Patrick expected to shrink back from the stench of bad breath, but it smelled incredibly, weirdly, like cloves. A voice in his head said, I've never suffered from halitosis. "Hali—what? Never mind. I've got squat. Look in my—" He stuck his hands in his parka to pull out empty pockets but felt the Rona. "Here. Take this. Please."

"That'll do. Ha!" Hiram snatched the packet and offered his green wad.

"I can't take money from a bum."

"I'm an angel! Hiram's my name, saving your—"

"Yeah, yeah, yeah. Consider it a gift."

"I am not a charity case."

"It's Christmas, or have you forgotten?"

"Do not sass me, boy," said Hiram. "I am not your servant. I got rules to play by, and home you got to help me get. If you don't, I don't know what I'll do." He thrust the money onto Patrick's chest and shrieked, "Take it!"

"Alright! Relax."

"Hallelujah!" Tickled with his transaction, Hiram stood, danced a jig and kissed the Rona. "Going home, going home, thank you, sir, thank you."

Patrick stuffed the sticky wad of cash in his pocket, alert for insectile movement.

"Now you got to give me your ear."

"No." Patrick flashed on a vague memory about Van Gogh. "Now you can go home, and I can go home."

"What for? No one there."

"How do you know?"

"Well, is he?"

"Never you mind," said Patrick, miffed by the fluky guess. "You got what you wanted."

"Not your ear," wrangled Hiram. "A bargain's a bargain."

Angel man, thought Patrick, if you're a thief setting me up, you picked one poor victim. And whoever heard of taking money from a stinky bum?

"I do not stink," answered Hiram, "and I am not a bum nor a thief."

"Are you reading my mind?" accused Patrick.

"I read you like a book," said Hiram. "I'm no trickster. I'm an angel of the Lord, and I want to be with Him soon."

"Not soon enough for me."

Struck speechless by Patrick's rebuff—but only for a moment—Hiram sadly asked, "You really want me to go? Aren't we having fun?"

"Yes. No." Exasperated, Patrick said, "I mean—I'm sorry."

"Apology accepted." Hiram suffered his pique with dignity. "Angels have feelings, too, you know. Now, if you've got time," he said, "I'd like to see my purchase." He ripped off the green-grid, wrapping paper, then added, "But can't. Too dark."

Behind them as though on a dimmer, the entryway emitted more light.

"You didn't just—did you?"

"Faulty wiring," said Hiram. He squinted, looked at the picture, at Patrick, the picture, Patrick. "What is it?"

"A Rona."

"What's a Rona?"

"An artist," said Patrick. "It depicts your territory, Bethlehem, etcetera."

Hiram squinted again. "Why so it does. The birth of baby Jesus, amen! My, my, my. Mary wasn't a blonde, though."

"You're the expert."

"And she sure wasn't white," said Hiram. "Sort of looks like me, the handsome shepherd holding the staff."

Patrick glanced but chalked up the resemblance to his blurry eyesight.

"Colors are bright. It's quaint."

"It's hideous," disagreed Patrick. "I'm better."

"I swear," sighed Hiram, "there are more artists than dog turds in New York City. Seems anywhere I go, I'm stepping over an artist. What do you paint? Better not say angels."

"Portraits. Of humans."

"Faces, ah yes, wonderful faces. Want to paint my face?"

"You're not human."

"You will make an exception. Are you famous?"

"Only to myself."

"You don't want to be, I can tell. Fame melts," said Hiram, scooping up a handful of snow, "like this here nature's lace, amen." His other hand dug under his coats, found safekeeping for his treasure, and patted his side with self-satisfaction. "I like to get my money's worth. I am no fool."

"Then I'll give you back sixty," said Patrick. "Frame's worth thirty."

"Too late." Again, Hiram fumbled among the many folds of cloth that bundled him. "Got something else for you."

"No, please, I don't want—"

Hiram pulled out a shiny object; it caught the glint from the entryway light.

Patrick did not stick around to feel the stick of the knife. He saw headlights and bolted into the street, shrieking, and frantically waving his arms. A limousine slowed almost to a stop. Patrick knocked on its dark, rear window that rolled half-way down, and pleaded for help, but a face mouthed something and motioned hurriedly to the driver. Tires spun until hitting pavement, the black tank careening forward, Patrick imploring its occupants and pounding its trunk that fish-tailed down the street. Shockingly, the wacko stood next to him and shouted "Asshole!" at the limo, then flipped the bird.

"AAHHHH! How do you do that, you speed freak!" Patrick pivoted to flee once more, skidded on ice and fell hard.

Hiram stared at the red taillights, dying out like the eyes of a drunken devil running backwards. "Lord, with all due respect, you have made a crazy world with lots of crazy people in it." He shifted his gaze down to Patrick, and with hands on his hips and a shaking head, he clicked "Tsk, tsk, tsk. Child, what am I to do with you?"

  American Queer

"I hurt. Leave me alone, you wino."

"Pot calling the kettle black, no offense."

"You stink!" Patrick threatened with his fists, then whimpered as his fuzzy world spun.

Hiram roared, "I told you, I do not—I'll prove it." In a tick, he knelt next to Patrick and put him in an armlock under his coat of many layers. "Now what do you smell, huh? What do you smell now, white boy?"

Patrick's muffled cries and feeble struggles only tightened Hiram's head lock. He thought this was his end, but the choke felt more like determination than imminent suffocation. Needing to breathe, Patrick inhaled deeply, became silent and motionless, then bewildered.

Hiram whipped open his coats and released Patrick. "Told you so."

Patrick breathed evenly. "How—? You smell—I don't believe it. Old Spice?"

"That's your problem," said Hiram. "Humans, now they're stinky. You've got your snot and puke, and piss and poop, and then you sweat like pigs that don't sweat at all. Infections? Lordy, Almighty! Oozing doozies, pus all green and yellow. And if you don't floss—"

"Stop." A familiar sour taste formed in Patrick's mouth.

"Yep, being human is a very smelly business."

"Oh God, I think I'm going to—going to—" Patrick got up on his hands and knees, gagged, vomited.

"And I rest my case," said Hiram. "Proof right there in that pitiful pudding." He put his arm around Patrick, who spewed more of his overindulgence, and adopted a fatherly tone. "You did more than eat at that party, didn't you? That's OK, little boy, get it out. One more heave-ho? OK, good boy. My, but you look like crap."

"You're not exactly my type of sugar plum fairy."

"Looks are deceiving. You should take better care of yourself."

"I can take care of myself, no thanks to you."

"You will," predicted Hiram. "Here, wipe your mouth."

Skeptical of the rag held before him, but drained and needy, Patrick accepted it. He held his stomach and groaned. "I want to die."

"No, you don't," said Hiram, "but you do want to live bigger."

"No. Die."

"Now, now. You're feeling better already, I reckon. What got into you back there? Got to feed you with a long-handled spoon. I was about to offer you my spirits." Hiram held up a silver container. "And I do not do that for everybody."

"A flask?"

"Well what did you think it was?"

"I thought—I thought you were pulling a knife."

"A knife?" Hiram leaned back and laughed. "How many dumb ass pills did you take at that party? Uh-huh, no way. Knives are dangerously sharp. I might cut myself. We angels bleed too, you know. Bleed gold."

"Gold."

"True fact," said Hiram. "You'd have found out if that taxi had hit me. Now stop acting like a damn ninny. Come over to my parlor and have some Christmas cheer. Let's celebrate the coming of the Lord's baby boy. Amen, hallelujah!"

The man shouted with such unabashed joy, Patrick caught himself grinning.

"Today's not really His birthday, mind you," said Hiram, "but that's another story."

"A drink?"

"Nip of the pup that bit you."

Patrick grasped the extended palm. "That's it?"

"Lovely view from there."

Hiram indicated the brownstone. He supported Patrick under his arm, and together, they mounted the top step and sat. The night had nudged the fog aside, creating a hole that revealed a cluster of twinkling pinpricks.

"Would you look at them stars?" said Hiram. "Now this flask I've had since I was, oh, knee-high to a pixie, given to me by my father. It doesn't break like bottles." He took a quick swig, passed it, and cringed. "Hot-chaka-khan."

"I just heaved a lung," protested Patrick.

"Nectar of the gods," tempted Hiram.

Though his stomach rumbled, Patrick wiped the lip of the flask, thought, What the hell, drank, and choked.

Hiram cracked up and slapped his pal on the back, making him choke more. "*Muey delicioso*, isn't it?"

Patrick managed to rasp, "You said—nectar of the gods."

"A clever ruse."

"You don't even know what *ruse* means."

"Worked on you. A ruse by any other name—"

"Would still taste like rotgut." As Patrick handed back the flask, he noticed dents and scratches and tarnish, also the initials *F.S.H.G.* and *1619* engraved on a band. Father, Son, Holy Ghost, he thought. What a joke. Again, the voice inside his head said, *Is not!* "What are you doing to me?"

"Nothing, man."

"You are too."

"It's the liquor." Hiram held up his flask. "Liquor should taste like liquor. Make your lips curl up to your nose. None of that damn, namby-pamby, syrupy, crème de crap for Hiram. If I want chocolate, I go buy me a Hershey bar."

The lecture jarred Patrick, and he used the opportunity to satisfy a question. "Speaking of chocolate, and since you'd know," he asked, "is there chocolate in heaven?"

"Sweet Jesus, yes. Wouldn't be heaven without it." Hiram poked around his pockets. "Got some here somewhere."

"No, no."

"Suit yourself. Personally, I never met a piece of chocolate I didn't like. Nor human being."

"Hardly the same thing."

"People are a lot like chocolate," said Hiram. "Once you get inside, there's always a sweet surprise."

Astounded he felt better, Patrick thought for a minute, then asked, "After I gave you my painting—"

"Nobody gives me anything I don't pay for," said Hiram.

"Excuse me."

"In life, accuracy counts."

 American Queer

"OK. After you bought my painting," Patrick corrected himself, "what did you mean *with him soon*? Roommate?"

"More like a landlord. Home is a big place."

"Where?"

Hiram pointed up. "My castle in the sky."

Patrick thought he implied a distant, luxury high-rise that disappeared into the clouds. "Blarney Castle?" he quipped.

"Nope. I'd like to go back tonight. You'd be my very last one of a very long line."

"What do you mean?"

"I mean, have another drink," said Hiram, his guest complying with a grimace.

"Last what?"

"Why, to meet my quota."

"Quota." Patrick looked incredulously at the flask and laughed deliriously.

"It's not funny," said Hiram, "goes with the job." He swallowed another shot, "Hot-chaka-khan," and shuddered. "You know I've been on this continent a long time."

"Since 1619?" asked Patrick.

Hiram posed in profile. "And I remain giddily good looking."

"Head turning," indulged Patrick. "Where did you come from?"

"A long, sad story, break your heart it would, but it'll have to wait because we are not done yet."

"Oh, yes, we are."

"Hang on now. If I don't get you, I don't go home, not that this place is all bad." Hiram looked skyward and said, "But there's no home like my home. You'll see it someday, though not for many a year."

Patrick doubted that. "What happens if you don't get me?"

"Back to the old grind for old Hiram. If not you, somebody else. Down here, there's never a shortage who need saving. Swig?"

"No," said Patrick. "Let me get this straight. You, of all people, think I need saving."

                                    American Queer

"Don't patronize me, boy," said Hiram, "but amen, yes. As sure as Hiram's my name and saving your ass is my game."

"And you're the one to do it?"

"Takes a black sheep to save a black sheep."

"Save? From what?"

"Yourself."

"Myself?"

"Did I stutter?

"Lucky me."

"But you don't have sense enough to know it. Too damn cranky, always in a snit over nothing."

"Alright, alright."

"Let's just say, you're sad and afraid and don't need to be. Life is one BM after another."

"I'll bite," said Patrick, "*BM?*"

"Blessed moment. Life is one blessed moment after another. Every friend you miss? Paddy, me boy," said Hiram, "a gaggle of angels watches over you, not just old Hiram."

"How do you know about—?" But Patrick interrupted the track of his question—threatening memories of grief receding—shook his head and voiced a small laugh. "This is all a dream, isn't it?"

"If you mean this," replied Hiram, spreading his arms to encompass their surroundings, "yes, a dream of a kind, but not what your kind thinks a dream is. If you mean this here flask of jimmy-juice? No, spirits are real."

"Then pass the ambrosia."

"Like life. Dee-licious."

Patrick swallowed and squirmed. "More like gag-alicious."

"Have another," offered Hiram. "Don't stand on ceremony now."

"No," replied Patrick, then remembering his manners, repeated, "No, thank you. Hey, you're trying to get me drunk."

"Right," leered Hiram, "so I can take advantage of you."

The two drinking buddies laughed hysterically, but as their hilarity dissolved, Patrick disliked the look in Hiram's eyes. My God, he thought, he's not kidding. He's drugged me. Worse, poisoned me. No, he drank first. Diseases. He's spreading some plague. And me, so polite. Goddamn! *Don't use that word,* an outraged thought not his own decreed; *don't even think it!* Sparks seemed to fly from the lunatic's eyes. Patrick guiltily regretted breaking the third commandment, shut up, and calmed down. What a strange night, he thought. Wait until Daniel hears about this. If ever.

… so after the beep, leave your name and number …

Hiram puckered from another swig and put away the flask. Then, almost kissing Patrick's ear, he whispered, "You get one wish."

"Repeat that," said Patrick. "A little further away please."

Hiram cocked his head and glared. "Business is business. You get one wish."

"One what?"

"Pay attention, this is serious," said Hiram. "One wish, wished for three times. Not three different wishes, one time, so don't get greedy. I'm no fairy godmother—well, maybe in your case—but I'm no genie either."

"Tonight," said Patrick, appealing to heaven, "I've heard it all."

Hiram straightened up. "You haven't begun to hear it all, white boy."

"Stop calling me that," insisted Patrick. "This is ridiculous."

"I didn't make the rules," barked Hiram. "And you don't have a thing to lose except always being cranky in a snit." Patrick was about to bicker, but Hiram forewarned with a frown. "Now then," he spoke more softly, "roll it over in your mind real careful now, and when you're ready, say your wish three times."

"Right now?"

"No, next Tuesday. Yes, now." With no response from Patrick, Hiram commanded, "Do it!"

"I'm thinking." Better humor this old goat, thought Patrick. Definitely a screw loose.

"You know me, I get a little—" Hiram pointed a finger at his ear, spun it, stuck out his tongue and rolled his eyes.

"Get out of my head."

"What? I think you're the one with a screw loose."

                    American Queer

"Behave yourself," scolded Patrick. "Do you want to go home or not?"

"Point made," said Hiram, "but stop changing the subject. I don't have all night."

Patrick scowled and thought, I must be screwy to do this. But like the man said, I've got nothing to lose. So, what do I want … That's easy. A million dollars. Ten million dollars. A gazillion, bazillion dollars. Awfully big order for one angel. World peace. A million dollars would be easier. Rent. I need ninety bucks. Wait, there's ninety-three in my pocket. I can't keep this money. I'll give it to charity. I am a charity. No, this hobo bought my Rona fair and square. My own exhibition. Hmm, no paintings to show. Daniel. I'll wish for Daniel to come back. This is absurd. Then again …

"I know an angel."

"Thought you didn't believe in angels," said Hiram. "Somebody crowding in on my territory?"

Patrick smiled. "The angel I know is in this world."

"But not of it."

"Hmm?"

"Go on."

"No. It would take a miracle."

"'Tis the season."

"This angel," Patrick began again, "he left me. I pissed him off."

"Seems to happen more this time of year," said Hiram. "You'd think the opposite would happen. Joy to the world and all that. It doesn't make sense. The world shouldn't piss off people, but it does. People shouldn't stay pissed off, but they do. That's your way; it's in your nature, but your folk can forgive too. I can recommend a little book, if you like."

"You done?" asked Patrick.

"Sorry," said Hiram. "In this moment, tell old Hiram your wish. Nice and easy. Very important, three times."

Patrick breathed deeply and said, "I wish—" But as he was about to complete his hope, he gazed at the man. With growing intensity, an atmosphere of gold and silver and pink and violet light surrounded him. Patrick blinked several times; the man still shined brightly. The ravaged face of the vagrant transfigured into a luminous face, radiating trust and innocence and bliss, as smooth as a newborn … angel. Patrick looked into its peaceful eyes, then closing his own, said, "I wish—I wish for Daniel's happiness. I wish for Daniel's happiness. I wish for Daniel's happiness." He exhaled slowly and opened his eyes … the incandescence faded, and before him sat an intoxicated derelict, staring at him with a smirk.

The man stood, flipped the earflaps of his hunter's cap with a grin, said, "See you later, 'gator," then proceeded down the stairway.

"What?" Patrick was dumbfounded. "What's the matter? Did I say it wrong? Hiram, where are you going? That's it? *Later, 'gator?* OK, very funny. Ha, ha. Now what about my wish? Hey! Come back here. I'm talking to you. Who the hell do you think you are!"

From the sidewalk, the man answered, "Hiram's my—"

"SHUT UP!" screamed Patrick, rising like his anger as the man walked away. "God, I'm so stupid, so pathetic. I made mistakes, but I love Daniel so much, I give my dearest dream to a street drunk. A disgusting slug. I must be crazy. So, you're right. Daniel too. What did you put in that drink? Some potion to cast a spell? To hypnotize me? You some voodoo, black magic witch doctor? Who gets his kicks pulling hocus-pocus tricks on whiteys like me? Well, you got me. Got me good. So, you move along, little angel. You can go home now, anywhere as long as it's far away from me. But save me? I'll save myself from devils like you with your mumbo-jumbo wishes and twisted Jesus and God crap. Because there's no such thing as angels. You're living proof. You're not an angel. You hear me? Angel my ass. You're just a common, everyday ASSHOLE!"

The man rushed back, pointed up to Patrick, and cried, "I am an angel of the Lord!"

"Asshole of the Lord!"

"Hiram's my name, saving your ass is my game!" Again, he walked away.

"I'm a pissed off faggot! Patrick's my name, kicking your ass is my game!"

He tore down the steps and leaped onto the man's back, flinging them both oomphing to the ground. The man struggled

                 American Queer

to get away, but Patrick wrestled furiously and gripped tightly, yelling, "Damn you! Give me my wish!"

"Go home!" ordered the man.

"Go to hell!"

"He'll see what He can do!"

"He who?"

"Who do you think?"

"Jolly Saint Nick?"

"Go home!"

"Not until you give me my—!" The man crawled mightily and almost pulled away, but Patrick grabbed his ankle with both hands and held fast. "—my wish!"

"—is Her command! Now, let go!" A final, vehement jerk freed the man. "And go home."

The round ended. They both stood, wobbling, chests heaving. Suddenly, the man looked horribly perplexed, embraced himself, doubled over, and dropped as though a puppeteer had cut his strings.

Patrick gaped. "What the—oh, no. You get up," he demanded. "Darn ticker give out again? Probably because you don't have one. You think you can just flop over, that I'm a total sucker and I'll stop? No way. So, you get up. Get up and fight like a—like whatever you are. A sick bastard. Hiram! Whoever you are. Get up!"

The man did not move.

"Hey! I'm no fool either, you faker. I said get up. Hiram! Old man!" Patrick stood over him, "I am not falling for this," then knelt and rolled him over. "Hiram?"

"Darn ticker," wheezed the man. He found Patrick's hand and squeezed. "It comes and goes for good this time."

"Don't move."

"Pretty feisty—for—for a white boy."

"Hush," said Patrick, cradling the man's head. "We'll go to a hospital, and—"

"No. Going up," coughed the man, "castle—sky. With Him—soon."

"Tricksters don't die."

"Paddy, me boy, who said anything about dying?"

"Who are you?"

"I'm an angel, Hiram's my name—"

"But how do you know my name?"

"Remember," smiled the man, "I'm Black Irish." He choked on his chuckle.

"Everyone is," said Patrick. "I'm going for help, back in a minute, so hang on. God, I don't believe this is happening."

"Your problem." The man refused to release Patrick's hand. "Must—believe."

"OK, I believe. You got me, alright? I believe you're an angel. I believe—"

The man exhaled, "Home ..."

"Hiram, you hear me? I said I believe you're an ... angel." Patrick's sudden tears fell onto the man, head limp in his arm, hand slack in his own. "Hiram? God, no. Don't do this. Hiram!" Patrick looked but no one was around. He clambered up the stairs and beat on the door to the brownstone. "Hello? Anyone? There's an emergency! A man needs a doctor, an ambulance, quickly! His heart—can anyone hear me? God, please, hurry, there's a man—"

Patrick stopped—behind him, low laughter grew lusty— and he slowly turned around. As if the lid on a jack-in-the-box had sprung open, the man popped up from where he lay and unfurled his arms. A sudden, furious wind whistled through the air and danced a duet with his many coats and sleeves and scarves and capes that hung at various lengths and fluttered like ragged wings. The grotesque harlequin threw back his head and belched a cackle that electrified every atom in the air. He seemed to grow gigantic—not in size, but in sheer, infinite presence—to swiftly drift, to seemingly hover before Patrick, who, gaping up and backing away, slid down the wall of the porch, pressing into the corner like he wanted to push through the stone.

Through growling guffaws and scoffing snorts, the angel bellowed, "I AM AN ANGEL OF THE LORD, AMEN! Hiram is truly my name, and saving your ass is truly my game. I am an angel, just as sure as you are one of the saddest little boys I ever did see. You've been calling for God all night. God this and God that. The Lord God Almighty is always home to answer your calls. The Nameless knows and answers before you call. I am His servant. I am Her messenger. It sent me, Hiram. I fulfill Its

     American Queer

will. And I gotcha'! FOR I AM AN ANGEL OF THE LORD!"
A new thought struck the angel, followed by a new gale of
laughter. It pointed a wing toward the stars, zoomed its face into
Patrick's, and spit a stinging whisper: "And ain't it just like Him
to send you a Black one."

A thunderous whoop blasted Patrick's ears. The angel
flapped and leaped into the street, hopped, and skipped a jig,
bobbed and howled as though at some joke with a secret
punchline. "Home!" it squawked. "Going home at last! Home at
last, sweet Jesus! Home!"

To the cowering man in the corner, the apparition
appeared to ascend a spotlight of raining glitter. He heard
another far-off "home …" then stared at the phantom until it
vanished, the tempest sucked up with a loud, concluding slurp,
leaving instead of its fury, a silent night.

Quivering, fighting the urge to urinate, eyes agog and
mouth agape, Patrick fell asleep.

Patrick awoke with a start. He tried to move, but his
joints felt chilled to the bone, his body bruised all
over. Disoriented, he followed green-grid,
wrapping paper rolling down the stairway.

And remembered. Or tried. Every memory a muddle,
dubious, incredible. A fantastic dream co-starring himself and
who? Or what? He wondered if he had suffered a concussion,
been bewitched, crazy, or just too high? Or robbed! He checked
for his billfold, still in his hip pocket, for his watch, still on his
wrist, ticking and lingering at four a.m. He swore a church bell
had chimed that hour recently, yet snow dusted him and a few
feet away, a hat, garbage bag, coats, tennis shoes with
boomerangs. He cautiously kicked the pile and jumped back.
Nothing. He felt for the Rona. Gone. In its place: a wad of
money. Only one set of footprints led up the steps. His.

Patrick brushed the snow off himself. He did a double
take at the door's scribbled sign: *Beware of Dog*. He thought of

home, his warm bed and sleep, but before leaving the porch, he listened. In this city of ten million, he did not hear one sound.

As if by design, the temperature deliberately dropped, and the wind, blowing and abating at will, whipped up tiny tornadoes of sparkling flurries, much like the events swirling in Patrick's head. Bent against the blusters, he trudged through the white banks of snow and recalled feeling like a Mountie. As if on autopilot, he arrived at 99th Street and Riverside Drive, fumbled for the right key, and, at last, entered his castle in the sky on the second floor. He was surprised he did not feel hungover, nor the weight of the world on his shoulders.

"Honey," called Patrick, "I'm home!"

No one returned his greeting.

Scattered about the table lay fragments of a broken angel, a puzzle he thought could be glued back together.

He took a long, steamy shower, made hot tea, put on his red union suit, and wrapped himself in blankets, trying to thaw out, to bring back life to his numb body and brain.

Though aching and exhausted, he could not sleep, nor get the face of the mystifying figure out of his head. Rising out of his bed as the sun did out of the east, he put pencil to pad and rapidly drew a dozen sketches. Flipping through them, he did not know what he believed about his ghost, angel, dream?—except that his subject, angel or human, was either way, yes, beatific.

Walking back to bed, Patrick saw an envelope on the floor by the front door and wondered how he had missed it. His heart raced; his hands trembled. On the outside, a familiar script: *Paddy*; on the inside, a note: *Call me.*

After five rings: *"Hi, this is Daniel ..."*

Patrick waited patiently for the beep. "Merry Christmas. I—uh—just found your message. Surprised, to say the least, especially since I—um—. So much to say. Most of all, how sorry I—"

"Paddy?"

This voice was alive.

The two chatted for a while, and that while passed into decades, and after decades of love, the successful artist recognized and thanked the first face he saw after he took his last

    American Queer

breath. For now, it was good to know there's chocolate in heaven.

Night Rogue: New York, 1979

Part I. DOUCHE
Half-naked, working his
        muscles,
racing he sends corpuscles
to maintain the line
of his figure fine,
to enhance his fight
for a successful night.
Full of vigor and vim
the man at the gym
pays no heed to chatters.
To them, all that matters
is always *FABULOUS(!)*,
and like Narcissus
they gaze at shallow pools,
playing the hollow fools.
He pushes and he pumps
and he grunts and he humps
as his heart sends blood
in a torrent, a flood
to swell his arteries, veins.
He's healthy (in vain).
His glazed skin glistens,
        sweats.
To dance sweet duets,
to be one of a deuce,
a Ganymede to Zeus,
he feeds his body lithe,
makes it hurt and writhe
for athletic effects.
And all for sex?
What of his hungry heart?
Forget it, time to depart.
In full manly bloom
nude men in the locker room
emit their manly perfume,
maybe one his future groom.
He dresses, and in the streets
winces at the horde's bleats

in this concrete, asphalt trap,
this unlikely life map,
this growling, filthy
        Rome.
Vigilant, he walks home
in his magical city(?!).
A scraggly, starving kitty
slows his smug swag.
The hand of a hag,
grabbing and greasy,
he helps, feels queasy.
Peering in a shop window
at the end of this rainbow
where the fools' gold is,
he wonders where are his
lovely things he can't afford
(even though he'd soon be
        bored).
"Where's my mound of
        cash?"
He sidesteps a mound of trash
and buys a bouquet
to sweeten his buffet.
To begin the switching task
he removes his day mask,
unknots the hangman's silk
        noose
(he's used the tie to seduce
those wishing a tender whip),
and dances a silly strip.
'Neath a spraying cascade
he feels his day dissolve, fade
in the air hot and steamy.
Naked and dreamy,
blue-white skin without
        blemish
(with creamy envy others
        wish),
he can't scrub away secrets,

follows rolling rivulets
down to his bushy crotch,
hopes to score tonight's notch,
shudders a thankful breath
that the green-gray death
of the paper day
is baptized away.
Emerging from the shower
this tall and tempting tower,
pearled wet and dripping,
stands with scotch-rocks
    sipping,
in front of a fogged mirror,
wipes it to see clearer
an inquiring expression,
an attractive reflection
of bulging pecs
and biceps to flex.
Strategic spots of cologne
are applied during a drone
of a re-run Larry-Moe-Shemp,
then *Sacre du Printemps*.
Another stiff drink
helps him cope, helps him
    think.
To show off his chest, his
    rear,
the babe dons his gear
(his fashion to convert)
of a too tight t-shirt,
undesigned blue jeans—
a uniform, a means
in heeled, pointy-toed boots
to butterfly the drab suit's
chrysalis into Night Rogue:
vernal, cavalier, in vogue,
graceful and handsome,
Prince of Luck's Kingdom,
the Knight of Queer Noblesse,

rich with life's physical
    largesse.
Studs on his belt beam, burn
    bright
in the blazing bathroom light,
brilliantly ribboned
like dabs of diamond
on tanned bull hide hung.
He's his own hero unsung,
just a kid, a spiv,
using his wits to live.
He licks his lips, full and
    sexy,
thinks, "Nothing wrecks me.
OWW-OOO!" he howls,
his lupine call for wild
    prowls.
A longing last look—
yes, tonight he'll cook,
take his cache of chemicals.
"Debacle? No chance," he
    mulls.
So holding arm in arm
(thinking of no harm
in his rush affairs inane),
sultry Miss Mary Jane
and frantic Amy Nitrate,
each a delectable date,
with him strut-stride along,
and enter the clanging throng
with casual aplomb.
He quotes the 23rd psalm.

Part II. <u>CINEMA VERITÉ</u>
Like this summer night,
    August,
The Rogue, one of the hottest,
descends to a hellish sauna,

a zoo of grotesque fauna
with sweltering faces stupid
in the subway so humid.
Sunglasses cut the glare in the
          train,
an odd stage to entertain,
but through his darkened view
a potential rendezvous
among passengers he can spy.
A Spanish lullaby
to her niña a mama hums.
A cripple without thumbs
on make-shift wheels
          beseeches
while Reverend Stilts
          preaches,
"Look to Jesus! Edify
your empty faith! Sanctify
your unholy trysts!"
Gawking, wide-eyed tourists,
theater-goers converse.
Scripts in hand, actors
          rehearse.
Birds gang members flip.
Bridge 'n tunnel girls giggle,
          gossip.
In a corner lovers coo.
Fifties, 8th Avenue,
by hidden voices' great care,
he's instinctively drawn there
to his lodestar, *The Adonis*,
dedicated to the phallus,
a theater vast and dark.
An adventure from Denmark,
Gage Goes Groovey,
is about dad's odd adultery,
and though mute poster
          fictions
promise passionate frictions,

The Rogue hesitates,
and his ego debates
if a film risqué
will cede a protégé.
Doubtful of the movie,
but to escape the eve so sultry,
he'll cool in the sleazy palace.
Faces desperate yet dauntless
stand ogling in shadow
like a silent movie tableau.
Already he's pawed
by one he judges flawed.
The Rogue smiles with
          contempt
at an absurd attempt
(he's really not snobby)
to make love in the lobby,
moldy and shoddy,
to dare touch his body,
to make a smelly embrace,
blithely caress his face.
But what once was theirs
is now lost to naïve heirs:
"I was you and you'll be me!"
The Rogue cannot see
in the pseudo church
their faces full of search,
nor hear their subconscious
          urge,
the ageless, echoing dirge,
a noiseless, futile lament
of phony sins to repent,
of secret, silent screams
that rise from crushed dreams.
Eyeing a fellow rebel,
The Rogue follows faithful.
Off to the head they go,
the buck behind his beau
who's as darling as Beatty.

Amidst the graffiti—
*Edith Head gives great
            costume—*
they themselves entomb
in a plastic tiled shrine.
On a communion of gold wine
the beau needs to be nursed,
but the buck has no thirst.
Emotions terminate
as both only urinate.
The confessional toilet
            flushed,
lost is the lust
of these choosy players,
their unanswered prayers
failing to bless and anoint.
So The Rogue smokes a joint
off the velvet-curtained
            balcony,
floor made sticky from
            groaned glee.
Up on the colossal screen,
naked giants preen,
bend into thrusts carnal
with acrobatic marvel
for hugely hung arousers.
Hands rustling down trousers,
raspy voices who whisper
brush The Rogue's ears with
            soft slur.
He moves to the loge
and like some puerile doge
puts up his feet
on the back of a seat.
A man perfumed in Halston
murmurs, "God, you're a doll,
            son,"
then kneels inside him
to gurgle his hymn.

Bound by a two leg'd bridle,
licking, adoring his idol,
breathing heavy sighs
between hairy thighs,
the man from Des Moines
receives joy from a groin.
The Rogue giving him seven,
the man's in heaven.
Buried in cornsilk,
savoring thick, rich milk,
he begs to be kissed.
Seeing a gold ring, limp wrist,
"Stop," warns The Rogue,
who stands, breaks the yoke.
"Be fair to your wife,
or happy with half a life."
Abrupt, unfinished,
his excitement diminished,
he takes one last toke,
flees the temple baroque
away from the quagmire,
from the leeching vampire.
Into honking hacks
zooming the city's racetrack,
into canyons of skyscrapers—
cathedrals sanctifying
            papers—
into decaying Times Square,
into the neon glare
of bulbs that sizzle,
into the bells, smells, and
            whistles
of the devil's porn parish,
strident and garish,
he enters a noisy arcade
where pretty boys get paid
prices they negotiate.
(Older teens soon depreciate.)
Children fresh off the bus

learn to avoid pimps, acts
         discuss,
and what little they won't sell
for an hour in a seedy hotel
or minutes in a bookstore's
         booth.
Revisiting his youth,
The Rogue's all at sea.
He hops in a taxi
dirty and yellow
driven by a fellow
with a Van Dyke, vague and
         pallid.
The Rogue questions what
         was valid.

Part III. MASQUERADE

On Herr Issyvoo's Street
it's Boy's Town complete.
Quelle surprise!—a bay
         window
with palm tree and flamingo.
A bum wanders, blithers.
A druggist slithers,
rings a quiet ice cream bell,
"Joints, 'ludes, mesc to sell."
Comics shoot their pistols.
BopBachBowie blare
         minstrels.
A cassette-taped piano
accompanies a dear soprano.
Everyone's got their schtick.
Against rough, red brick
The Rogue stands on the side
and watches the manly tide.
Shouting la-di-das,
lads in Adidas
(bred on Farina)

hail Roller-Arena
who knights with her scepter
all those who accept her:
mechanics, brokers, waiters,
models wearing polos with
         'gators,
collegiates and cowboys
engaging private, sweet ploys.
From the dunes of Egypt
leans a Black man well-
         equipped,
muscles bulging steroidal
like a cathedral gargoyle.
Ready to yell "Yessirs!"
bogus khaki soldiers
salute curious flirts.
Kowalski t-shirts
cruise flanneled Paul
         Bunyans.
A suit n' tie from London
eyes the curves of Latinos
in shark-skin tight chinos.
Hair is buzzed, layered, weird,
pony-tailed, in 'staches,
         beards,
in colors to black as a raven.
Some are bald or clean
         shaven.
Barracks, office, gym,
a penthouse pool to swim,
ranch, campus, pub —
all reflect the Rogue's roving
         club.
Aided by keys knotted
in right or left pocket,
color-coded kerchiefs
denote favored mischiefs,
signaling in this Sodom
who's the top, who's the

bottom.
Down by the idle dock
he stands — barely one
        o'clock.
"Hey handsome sailor,
Uncle Sam your tailor?"
calls a parading sex seller
to a buyer near the dive
        Kellers.
Lady Girl's a clever minx,
promises thrilling hijinks.
She waves to a bald exec
who lives on mommy's blank
        check.
John's slightly avuncular
with a blobby jugular.
Built like Il Duce
and shoed by Gucci,
he smokes a blue Gitane.
Lady Girl vows feats profane,
positions precarious,
laughs at John, hilarious
from the proposed squeeze
she'll wield on him to please
with lips hot, sassy, and pink.
Her gig to lip sync
Lady Girl will skip;
for her gent she'll strip.
("This John gon' pay for a
        mink —
maybe even my shrink,
who swears my gay gene
turned me into this May
        queen.")
Womb-wrapped in his limo
climb and curl John and the
        bimbo
who pretends she's an heiress
on the Concorde to Paris

to replace her ruffled hot
        pants
with haute couture from
        France.
For now it rains pink
        champagne
and snows ivory cocaine.
John will try to need her,
but someday will beat her.
In a fleet of motor steeds,
a truck driver spies, then
        kneads
his groin with ears pricked,
        keen.
Lace panties of silky sheen
round his hips girly,
caress his body burly
put on in his bedroom fluffy.
But butch and scruffy,
he beckons to a redneck
from nearby Teaneck.
Both swear, "I ain't no
        queen."
Each was a former Marine.
The river along the pier
lures The Rogue, the mutineer
to cross the highway and roam
a bombed-like catacomb.
He crawls through mangled
        fences
with heightened senses,
by cement chunks, buckled
        girders
ripe for bloody-blade murders
in a warehouse where one
        quiver—
splash! down deep in the dark
        river.
The red dot from a cig's

cherry,
all that's seen, makes him
	wary.
The moon shines on planks
	rotten,
on souls misbegotten.
Each one's inner heart churns
to a soundtrack of nocturnes,
adagio and lusty.
In the air thick and fusty,
patrolling the warehouse
	derelict,
a man in chains, an addict
testy and sweaty
(missing a movie with Bette)
wants to get kissed
or back into a fist,
so wears only a jock.
Tick-tock, tick tock …
Time here seems not to exist.
A glitter of grist,
disturbed motes, drift like
	white
snow-sparkles in shafts of
	light.
To The Rogue, the scene's
	hypnotic.
But wait. An act quixotic
of a smile and slight bow
makes him raise an eyebrow.
The guy looks tense,
	exhausted.
Moon beams have frosted
his face argent. They don't
	speak
in this game of hide 'n seek,
each softly mumbling
in the ruins crumbling,
sure of what they look for:

to experience the lore
of thrills from dangers
excited by strangers,
a scene intoxicating
and only abating
when The Rogue unsteady
thinks he sees a machete.
He abandons the ruin,
romantic but an illusion.
Time to lift a veil.
He eats his MDA cocktail.
Sound shocks addictive
(never predictive),
a creeping current of waves—
just what The Rogue craves—
come carnivaling toward him,
nervously faint, mica slim,
pendulating in the breeze
like tingling chimes Chinese.
His spine no longer rigid,
unaware his feet fidget,
jerk to a rhythm
that becomes one with him,
pulls him, moves him to sway
back across the highway
to a bustling club,
The Cockring, a dancing hub.
He opens the door,
moist thrills fill every pore,
senses overload from the blast
into the pit he's been cast.
At home The Rogue beholds
this mindless myth that
	unfolds
in a glass encased cage
where a priestly gage
of peaks, ebbs, and harmony
celebrates this sacred
	ceremony,

taps urges primal
on spinning discs of vinyl.
As the master deejays
so the crowd obeys,
but as the crowd feeds
so the deejay heeds.
They gift reciprocal praise,
the dancers ablaze!
Elations phallic,
vibrations supersonic
engulf this group gone wild,
forgetting they've been
          exiled.
On the floor fired
this man-mass made tired
of boring, blank lives,
of dry, red-rimmed eyes
scans for perfect lovers
to take home to mothers:
a saucy Cinderella,
or hunky, horny fella,
a rich, charming Princeling,
anyone who'll slip on a gold
          ring.
These beings crowded,
all of them doubted
before they came to prance
they'd find true romance,
yet hope like a magnet
jerks all back to the man-net.
Laughter and talk strive
to be heard above the hive
with its deafening din.
In this den of imagined sin—
invented by bitter priests,
torturers more like beasts,
like ancient Pharisees
stoking heresies—
colors whiz, lightning sparks.

Flavored flares of quarks
spot and knife the cheering
          lair,
measle and slash the air.
Bolts blend blemishes unfair
and thicken the thinning hair
of those who aren't beautiful,
who once were so dutiful
to dear Dad and Mom,
and who numb from faraway
          'Nam,
blot hidden scars left unhealed
from buried frights revealed
during a rank time of war.
Home, many hearts sore
cry, rage, only stare.
Death some learned to defy,
          dare.
Litanies from speakers scream
and his acolytes cream
as *I Who Have Nothing*
by the 70s Bing
almost makes The Rogue
          swoon,
his ears honeyed by the croon.
Touched to his inner core
he beelines to the throbbing
          floor,
stakes out a territory,
dances his own story,
joins the hysteria,
dissolves in the mania
of this disco bacchanal.
A glittering ball
throws whirling lashes,
strobing glimpses it flashes
of physiques vaunted,
of styles flaunted.
Inducing extreme heat,

a thunderous beat
infects limbs that flail,
all primitive males
born to be alive!
Whistles, tambourines jive
with clicking castanets
like a thousand crickets,
and feathered fans blurred
wave like wings on a bizarre
    bird,
like a scarlet ibis
sacrificed to Isis.
Fuel inhaled from bottles
is raised to nostrils,
and suddenly on Mars,
upside down on monkey bars,
hearts send blood too swift,
brains begin to drift.
On strings of scorch, puppets
    speed
to match the rate of blood-
    feed
this potent potion
produced, this LOCO-motion.
A lovely queen in drag
sprays ethyl on a rag—
a miracle recipe
of modern chemistry—
shoves it down The Rogue's
    throat.
His mind zooms! His head
    afloat
soars in ecstatic ecstasy,
a fantastic fantasy!
With jerking spasms,
concurrent, crackling chasms
split apart this bit of earth!
It's an orgy of mirth!
Dancing, he undulates

with pelvic punches, and
    states,
"Beats my high-school prom.
My brain's a ticking time-
    bomb!"
Swearing it's a déjà vu,
he stares at the hairdo
of a muscled Rasta Medusa
in a tank top fuchsia.
Or is he a sexy alien?
An Episcopalian?
Could he be Venus
with a startling penis?
Yanked from his bliss
he falls into an abyss,
can't tell the spiritual
from a satanic ritual
where appearing angelic
people mutate, turn demonic.
He denies the mental knock
of a shape shifting warlock,
and when Buddha
becomes a hunk of gouda,
he breaks free of this hell
laughing and aborting the
    spell.
Bathed in splashes of sweat,
The Rogue spies someone to
    pet.
"Ah heartbreaker,
    heartbreaker,
bouncing like a shaker!
Come salt yourself next to me
and give yourself glee.
No need to hold my hand;
just press the right love
    gland."
Desires in the mind begin,
and like from a summoned

jinn,
appear miraculously
with joyful jubilee.
"My heart you've
        harpooned!"
Poof! Gone. "No! I am
        marooned."
With an invisible wound
(his heart again cocooned),
The Rogue flees the decadent,
stands under the firmament.
It was lust at first sight
for the twelfth time this night.

Part IV.
WALPURGISNACHT

Looking for a lay
on the West Side Highway,
various forms of street life
try to forget their strife,
and dressing the promenade,
        stroll
past the Spike and a gloryhole
on this posed Tuileries
void of a bush, a tree.
Adamant on protocol,
M's seek S's on the mall.
A "sergeant" hopes
his array of ropes
bind a man to a satin tether
to lap slime wax off leather.
A "cop" strokes his crotch,
law and order for this night
        watch.
Lured to be held captive
can be hot and attractive;
but those liking it rough
discover they're not so tough

when behaviors fun and frisky
cross the line, become risky,
illegal, without escape, lethal.
Outside the Eagle,
ears incessantly humming,
feet slightly drumming,
The Rogue enters the select
        coven
out of summer's al fresco
        oven.
All part of the night's scheme,
again, music reigns supreme,
a dynamic, aural skin,
a dome of loud heroin
infusing the air
without anyone could not
        bear.
To all the inverts,
the bar offers cool comforts.
They gather to practice rites,
to display the united might
of fairies, fruits, and cocks.
So he sips on scotch-rocks—
nude pix behind him in
        neon—
needs the bar to lean on,
hooks a boot heel on the foot
        rest
like he's a cowboy out West.
A man ambles by,
turns after massaging his
        thigh.
The object of The Rogue's
        cruise
aches for a kiss, not a bruise.
In flirty semaphore,
revealing what each looks for,
soundless arias—dittos
with identical librettos—

wing across the packed bar.
The two share a want, a scar,
to declare selves sane,
to heal their hurt, salve their
          pain.
But the imagined affair
doesn't stand a prayer
as The Rogue's eyes zoom
to the dark back room.
He halts. He's not quite ready.
Pool players study
the lay of the balls.
"Side pocket," one calls,
cue stick ejaculating,
eye calculating
the cause and effect
his bent pelvis will select.
He pauses, uses the chalk,
annoyed by a drunk peacock.
The Rogue leaves the green
          felt,
his urges can't be helped.
At night's picnic in Babel
fashionable rabble
lurk in a coiling haze of
          smoke,
a gray velvet cloak
draping this Fellini-fest.
In ironic drag, in jest
stalk rhinestone panthers,
pace Nazi jodhpurs
with dangling manacles,
'neath flags devoted to cycles,
by posters of American bars
and Hollywood macho stars,
living anachronisms
steeped in hedonism.
The Rogue walks with a
          swagger

laden with feigned languor
to the video set.
A bearded Nordic coquet
balls a nymph Boticelli,
far from being nelly,
and everyone gawks
like lemmings in a black box,
wishing they could defy space
and trade their bitty place,
ascend up to the mirage
as the third in a menage.
Hungers to nourish
and with a flourish,
deeper The Rogue veers,
into a serpentine maze steers
through lingering men
where every Hephaestion
chases his Alexander.
In this human knot like an
          Escher,
integral links mesh
this tide of hooked flesh.
His nonchalant nerve churns.
Zealous touches The Rogue
          yearns.
Eyes on him are glued
undressing him nude.
He's cool, waits for his
          chance.
He checks an old gelding's
          glance.
A dreg he corrects.
A beaut close by projects
the appropriate signs.
Again, The Rogue declines.
They vest his ego thrill.
Hard pressed in this anthill,
tentacles and pincers crush,
antennae softly brush,

bemoan, "Be mine, be mine.
Let me warm in your
        sunshine."
He ignores these pleas
from his vital sleaze
because now he's occupied
with a hot man he's spied,
who mouths, "Be my beau."
With The Rogue all aglow
the two solve life's puzzles
in tender neck nuzzles.
Their evolving vignette
outlines a silhouette:
smiles stretch gently,
passions mount intently,
fists rub a hard rocket
deep in the other's pocket,
and tongues fight a wet
        duel.
But jealous and cruel,
strangers' hands explore
uninvited. The two deplore
these parasites, worshippers
who drop their knickers,
beseeching salvation,
squirming in frustration.
Broken is the bond
of the boys so fond.
Destroyed is what was
        offered:
the bliss they each proffered.
Reluctantly, to get out,
The Rogue filled with doubt
through zombies' claws,
through shouts like crows'
        caws,
through a miasma of scents:
a raw and rugged incense
that syrups his lung

of poppers and dung,
of the gooey gum
from ecstasies shrieked dumb
as daggers end their duel,
ooze lotions, salty gruel
and jets shoot cropless seed.
Through all wafts the sweet
        weed
swirling and seducing,
clouding and reducing
its heady perfume
to a Byzantine harem abloom.
Gasping, escaping the snare
he gulps soggy night air.
Digested from the bowels,
sticky from the paws, the
        jowls,
the spit of this hungry beast,
he's sick of being its feast,
of being ripped and rammed.
The courtship of the damned,
simply children hand in hand,
may delay kismet's last stand,
but everything is not
at all what The Rogue
        thought.

Part V. <u>PROLOGUE</u>

Comfort me with apples,
for I am sick with love.
        Song of Solomon 2:5

"EAT, EAT" the Empire
        Diner
flashes boys smeared with
        eyeliner.
Hopeful, wide-eyed, and

                    American Queer

        wired,
not finding what he desired,
The Rogue, cruising for hours
street after street, scours
the magic of his city(!?),
elegant to gritty.
On sidewalks of yellow brick,
he dodges pools slick
from an ebbing drizzle.
Unlike tears artificial,
it gifts its cleanse
to his soul's lens,
to the city's soul:
a sky-fall to make all whole,
nature's intended duty.
A city sound of beauty —
tires roll with wet whine
over streets that shine …
The Rogue loves the shush
so soothing, so lush.
The bark of a stray dog
breaks the quiet in the fog.
Streetlamps enshroud
the block, reflect off low
        clouds
the curving arc of a golden
        dome
writing a mystical tome.
Weaving near the Hudson,
The Rogue thinks, "I am
        undone,"
knows he's fucked up,
needs to suck it up.
He's misplaced his purity,
his inner security,
and in a world that hates fags
his mind zig zags.
Reliving in flashback
his night with a laugh track,

he smiles at the dramatics
not knowing he's a phoenix.
Birth will begin anew,
and loyal to every cue,
The Rogue will claim his
        rights.
Out of life he'll take huge
        bites
and try to outwit
just for the fun of it.
Red blooms a wall festoon.
He sits still, enchanted, jejune
on a green wood bench,
yet with thirsts to quench.
In the morning mist
he tries to grasp the gist
of all these strange events,
why his energy he vents
on such a reality,
so much triviality.
For reasons most likely moot,
helpless 'gainst some piper's
        flute
with his heart full of life's
        fire,
he'd been a sleeping jaguar
in rioting forests West.
Here came Patroclus in quest
of his Achilles,
finding only his heart's
        unease.
Eyes wide with witchery,
        wile,
The Rogue can't help but
        smile
at diversity so vast,
at the size of tonight's cast
who answered the call of
        Wilde

with mating signs beguiled,
of knowing, naughty winks
divulging common kinks
draped by day for the public,
by night displayed for their
          clique.
"There's love, there's danger.
To this, I've been no stranger.
I'm a brother of my kind,
born with this state of mind.
My family, we're special;
others deny how crucial.
In the consequence
lies the sublime suspense."
Echoes declare another dog's
          bark.
There's time: the baths, Anvil,
          Central Park.
Divinely tranquil, he sours
on these open after hours
where all crave intimacy,
where all is fallacy.
He asks, "Am I blessed or
          bleak?"
The sun's ruddy peek
brightens the Parrish blue
          dark;
morning birds sing their lark.
Swaddled in the hush
of the day's first blush
as night begins its morrow,
he'll lick his wounds, his
          sorrow.
In this land of make believe
he'll learn soon enough to
          grieve,
that within his heart's fracture
can lie his rapture,
that everyone's history

is their deepest mystery,
that every cupid's caprice
their potential golden fleece,
that everyone's an apostle
writing their own gospel,
that there's no need to ration
spoonfuls of compassion.
"I have no use for fear,
sneers, jeers. I cheer I'm
          queer!
But myself only I can save."
Grinning and brave,
he declares "God, I had fun!"
And that's a battle won,
to avoid being jaded
before youth has faded,
to hang on to survival,
absorb every eyeful.
For this holy grail,
there is no heavenly fail,
and while on earth in his
          prime,
yes, there's always next time.
"But please," he asks,
          "where's the balm
to bless and anoint my calm?"
His thoughts get muddled,
and on the pavement puddled
the click of his boot heels
ring companion peels
of this night's destined lover:
The Night Rogue's twin
          brother.
A face peers through shutters.
A newspaper crawls, flutters;
"GACY" in big black letters
shows him in fetters,
tells tales of skeleton,
corpses just gelatin.

Ode To Jonny V.*

1981

** "V": 22nd letter of the alphabet; initial of J's last name; not to be confused with the Roman symbol's Arabic numerical counterpart "5"; which is a shame because if the "V" in the title was to be misconstrued, as in Jonny the Fifth, thereby, implying four (4) predecessors, the world would not be what we think we know it is today, and would be four times sweeter.*

Was there ever an egg so queer[1]
from Queens, a chap so dear,
as this Jonny Varvatsas
with his quips so levitous,[2]
his 'tude so hunky-dory,
his chocolate eyes just for me.
(Was there ever a tryst
where both parties had cysts?)
Stars aligned the night we met.
His 'stache, black as jet,
was soft as mink,
his long lashes would wink,
his kisses wet and wild,
offered delights as he smiled.
He loved the color and liqueur of chartreuse,
knew every bar that served pineapple juice,
his favorite cocktail, a pina colada.[3]
On them, he'd get blotto
and wash down tabs of acid, candies quaalude.[4]
He'd admit—trés gay, trés lewd.

---

[1] "queer egg," a favorite label of Jonny Varvatsas.

[2] his made-up word, a riff on levity

[3] JV loved umbrellas and pineapple juice, flamingos and palm trees

[4] the guy could never get enough

American Queer

After spending the night he'd awaken
hungry for an English muffin with cream cheese and bacon.
Not chickpeas, not soup of the street,
no, not even salmon would he eat.
Is it a wonder he got lost in a supermarket?[5]
A gentleman rarc, he'd light your cigarette,[6]
but he was an anarchistic agitator,
especially towards Izod alligators(!),[7]
for those who preened
in polos of pink or green
drove him mad,
so he played with rubber stamps to make himself glad.
He knew a good fag hag was hard to find.[8]
"But then, so is my mind.
I'm a garbage head."[9]
Could there be truth in what he had said?
For having a vision that was at times myopic,
he sure could be a mother with a dick.[10]
Oh well,
what the hell.
That's the breaks.
That's the breaks.
"Jonny V., Jonny V., Jonny V.," mocked friends of Rick,
sick of hearing about his Greek
with the tingling eyebrows,
always mocking Manhattan's highbrow.
Yet even though he'd never seen a gym,
everybody loved him.
So while he was around, I inked his pads indigo,[11]
stalked and caught him a flamingo,
but he was sad at the bird's locked flight,

---

[5] loved the song by The Clash

[6] how we met at Barbary Coast, 14th and 7th Avenue 1981

[7] JV hated Izod shirts, especially in pink or mint green

[8] He loved his girls; not such a pejorative label then

[9] self-deprecating, but brilliant

[10] favorite saying

[11] quite creative with colored ink pads and dozens of stamps

so I set the pink soaring like a kite.
True, he could be bitchy
cuz his skin was always so itchy.
I'd have loved to invent him a skin balm,
grow him a soothing green palm,
his favorite tree.
I know he loved me
cuz once he said, "I just wanna be wit'cha,[12]
so please be careful of things that can hit'cha.
And all through your life,
be it full of love, full of strife,
always be a good little fairy.
And don't be a Mary![13]
Of you, the only task
I'll ever ask,
is if you see a cycling dyke,
knock her off. I want a bike."[14]
I wonder where he is.
Life with him was always filled with fizz.
I pray the world never loses Jonny's sense of fun,
                but one never knows, do one?[15]

---

[12] proud of his Queens background

[13] another favorite label, but he was so sweet when he used it

[14] he didn't mean it, just thought it was funny to say

[15] ditto

Star Machine in celestial cathedral

Mr. X: *The Saint*, New York, 1981

Early afternoon in the candy store, I visit my travel agent who issues me a ticket for a surprise destination. I will be traveling very far. I will be dancing on the moon, then beyond its silvery glow.

When I leave I see a van parked across the street and a man in it staring at me. The van drives away. Who is this, this Mr. X?

I rest all day, prepare with great care, nap, and shower. Testicles-spectacles-wallet-watch-keys. Packing complete and ready to embark, my ticket has a blue flying saucer printed on it. I tuck my ticket to nirvana in a capsule half-filled with a dingy dust nestled round a quarter of a white 'lude. "Lewd" pops into my mind—I smile.

And quickly claim a taxi, always a good omen. The moist air reflects the city lights, fogging the night in a cloak of gold velvet. The driver keeps glancing in his rearview mirror, meeting my eyes with a quizzical gaze. I cannot see his face, but on the dashboard, I see a dim picture with a name full of consonants. I feel funny, like I should know who he is. Mr. X? Right now, it is impossible to tell.

Standing before a nondescript building—the perfect camouflage for a secret spaceship I and few others know and cherish—I open the brass and glass door hearing a pneumatic sigh as it slowly shuts. One in a line of eclectic tourists, I pay my fare, check through customs with pleasant stewards, and walk through a neon-lit tunnel into a massive salon.

Thrills stimulate my senses. A far off bunka-bunka like a massive heartbeat vibrates within the bowels of our vessel, absorbing the heartbeats within the chests of men who carpet the lounge in a varied pile. Amidst grating, pipes, ducts, purposely placed spots create shadowy nooks where groups chatter and giggle, lovers caress and converse, singles on the prowl flirt, muse, or peruse. Everyone observes the parade of men who pass by in pools of brilliant beams from light to dark, from awareness to denial, from radiance to gloom. Observed or observer, all gather to purge themselves of the depravity and corruption of the ungodly critics who blight our tense outside world, its sole aim to shame. But not here. Not in our ship. Not on this voyage.

At a drink station, blooms like primeval spears from fantastic planets stand tall and brutal. Protea like anemones of the ocean deep bleed unearthly colors. Standing next to delicate purple petals, lustrous in their pinpoint of light, I follow the motes of dust floating in every direction—makes me dizzy. My throat constricts. I ask a steward (Mr. X?) for a libation. I feel ceremonious. I feel sacrificial.

In a mirror I see the reflection of a man. He is backlit by a spotlight that surrounds him in a saintly glow but silhouettes his features. I think the black eclipse could be a kind man or a killer. I am about to speak when someone else catches his attention. He walks away. I drink my drink fast and follow him, but quickly lose him. Mr. X. Not to worry. The night is young, and so am I. For now.

I get another drink, sit on a box in a corner, gazing at our circular ship like I'm inside a blue flying saucer. I pop my passport-in-a-pill into my mouth, and now that blue flying saucer is inside me. Soon I regret swallowing it—or maybe it swallowed me—because it's zigzagging in my stomach like a dinging pinball. I think about sticking my finger down my throat to make the saucer fly back out, but I dislike disgorging. Too late now. I have passed the point of no return. I am anxious, expectant.

To help the hearts pump and power the ship, my fellow passengers have ingested their own passports like wafers for an extraordinary communion—eat, take this body; drink, take this blood—a bizarre but no less holy transubstantiation. We fuel our flights and systems; we build a camaraderie, a synergy; it's how we gain admission to the transport and leave *terra firma* behind. There is no place for it here, for if you are here you belong, as a member of an ancient fraternity.

Departure is imminent, anticipation palpable. A deep drone hums throughout, and the hive buzzes like thousands of insect jets revving up for a night of flight. And then a song … a thousand ears prick up, and heeding the call, I and others rush to

                                                      American Queer

ascend the grand staircase of this pleasure palace and enter the crowded theater of dance to claim our square foot of space. The trip begins. I tingle.

The inferno smacks me in the face like a sadistic seductress bewitching me, luring me in deeply, all stimuli so profoundly fierce. Arches soar high above this colossal spherical temple, this planetarium dedicated to delight. Smothering heat and smells, boggling lights, booming sound, jam-packed, interjacent bodies—all stun me, ravish me. I stagger to the periphery, step up onto a banquette, touch this humongous dome pulsating with gradients of dusk or dawn, with patterns of multi-colored lights splattered across its sky.

Yes, I touch the sky.

Unready, unsteady I feel my encapsulated passport melt into my bloodstream, its contents surfing blood waves with every heartbeat. The infusion washes throughout me, enraptures me, terrifies me, and like a junkie I embrace my addiction, afraid of its irresistible allure yet impatient to experience its path to the glory I know will come.

I hover near the bridge of our ship, the deejay booth where the co-pilots take charge of the music and lights for the evening: gracious, skillful, plotting our course with stunning surprise in mind. They man our mission control, indeed, control our mission with black disks and sliders and buttons and turntables and headsets. We nod to each other with a wink and a knowing smile. Either or both. Mr. X.

Music as pure as silken syrup thickens the atmosphere, stokes the sweltering furnace of celebration. Daring to test the waters, I step down into the round pool flooded with a pack of men. After all, dancing is the reason we're all here. (Isn't it?) Nameless melodies sound louder to me; waterfalls of light bathe and pelt me; dancers welcome and make room for me. I am nervous and doubtful, feel stiff, clumsy, foolish. My feet tread lightly, tentatively, my hips oscillate. I stop thinking; I tremble.

Our captains steer us with one song blending into the next for a prolonged, collective countdown, building upon our anticipation, playing with us who beg for the climax of sight and sound. At last, the long rumble crescendos and bursts. A dazzling round diamond ball descends from the center of the dome and glitters the setting in whirling prismatic patterns. The mass shouts and raises its arms in praise and adoration, dances its rite of spring, of any season, for here in the time machine the night is seasonless. The star machine speckles the sky, constellations rotating with such rapidity that a thousand years disappear. Has the priapic altar propelled us forward to dance under the generator of a space station or backward under a trilithon of Stonehenge? No one cares, for the moment simply is, and the isness of the moment is all that matters. This one and the next and the next and the next.

Pops strike the air—it crackles—and I snap my fingers and laugh at the breakfast cereal sounds, and with a collective cry of relief, the music sweeps us away, and I am swept away, swept far away. Blast off! Everyone and everything takes off— the ship, the guys, many shirts. Thousands of roaring, half-naked men throb, bob, gyrate and jump. A luscious dew of sweat coats us all. Choreography is chaotic, sensual, primitive, yet a childlike sense of fun pervades this playland as men hug, hump, are simply happy. Lift-off is complete. We break free of earth, and at the speed of light, we travel in space where we are the dance, we are the music, and we tremble.

The blue saucer still flies around my stomach. Everyone looks slightly odd. I blink my eyes. Red blotches blemish faces. I blink my eyes. Sharp horns grow from temples. I blink my eyes. Halos crown heads, and wings sprout from backs. I close my eyes. Vaginal lava folds into itself, churning, aglow, prehistoric. Too high, I am too fucking high! Let me down, bring me down! But higher I go and higher still. I retreat to the rim of the towering gumdrop and plop down on the edge of its radiance, hold my head to keep it from exploding or imploding. A song arrives with a thundering boom! My kaleidoscopic mind's eye freezes this mental molten mire—I surrender! and burst through it, jagged shards and shattered splinters falling away to reveal a void I fill. I am as vast as a galaxy of stars, as insignificant as a grain of sand. I am constant and unpredictable. From its centrifugal force I rocket in that baby-blue saucer flying in my stomach at the speed of lavender light, through mint green galaxies, passing soft pink planets, lemon-yellow comets. It is a trip through Lucky Charms in black milk. It is Easter time at the end of the Big Bang Rainbow, time to fasten the seatbelt on this atavistic voyage.

My eyes blur. My ears isolate certain percussive sounds. The place becomes a musical zoo, our pilots for the evening gamekeepers and conductors of the ark's orchestra. Performing for the enjoyment of all are a bull with tambourine, a giraffe with wood blocks, a chihuahua with mariachis, a firebird with finger cymbals, a panther with paddle-castanets. A school of rainbow fish wave fans like fins; one wears a turban of fruit. A peacock wears ribbons round his waist, and as he twirls, Sufi-like, the fluttering filaments blaze an electric trail of multi-colored arcs.

I think I see a friend, but that cannot be, for the boy died to avoid a man on a mountain road. He sailed down to the bottom of a canyon landing in a river. This twin is gone in a flash. Was he Mr. X? No, what am I thinking?

I'm thinking my jets need cooling. Like an explorer traversing unknown terrain, I set out for the bathroom. My legs feel as though they plod through quicksand, underwater, or on the moon. Finally, there, I view four legs from one stall and myself in the mirror, which I quickly quit. At last, I urinate, convulse. Mmmm … what a rush …

Seeking respite, I ascend an endless, circular stairwell, stepping up and up, round and round, climbing grated steps that checker my sight above and below. Breathlessly, I arrive atop this Babel, in a balcony of carpeted bleachers, providing the platform for spectators to lounge like Ottoman royalty or to wrestle like Greek athletes. A faint miasma of smoke and steam whitens the darkness. I look down on the dome and try to make sense of my view. The hemisphere is like an enormous egg half-buried in a ginormous incubator. Through its diaphanous membrane, a mass of tiny men practices antediluvian rites.

I hide in the highest corner and touch the heaven of a celestial netherworld. OK, it's a black wall, but my hands cup and hold twinkling stars, at least, that's what it looks like. In a loud volume vocalists from Valhalla sing love lyrics, and I know nearby Thor strikes his anvil to maintain the hammering tempo of these Northern Lights. His thunder makes the panorama glow and pulsate. Bolts ricochet across me, and I am ablaze with white-heat, I sizzle and drip a sweet sweat.

　　　　　　　　　　　　　　　　　　American Queer

Shadows lose their shape, run into each other, make a Rorschach watercolor of ebony ink washed with a wide brush. The black hole takes on a whale-like, gibbous form that sprays its splats many times from many hot little spouts accompanied by shouts. Some shadows escape. Others arrive, lose themselves within the black shape and keep the animal active, feed and gorge it unendingly so that it becomes one many-tongued, many-holed, many-backed, slimy, salivating, fucking animal, and it fucks itself again and again and again. Heaven or hell, it is most surely a humpback or sperm whale-like shadow form.

I need to calm down and force myself to look away from the beast. Snaked in the corner, a coiled fire hose melts and drips down to the ground, slithers and hisses on the ground. It spies me, hypnotically eyes me, moves up the steps toward me. It hooks round my feet, spirals my legs then my thighs, circles my waist, uses my spine as a ladder to creep up my back. It curls round my neck, plants a delicate, flicking kiss upon my lips, parts my teeth, crawls down my throat, feels its way with its slick and thin forked tongue, zigzags through my intestines and colon and rectum and shits itself out my sphincter. Yowza! I quiver.

And somehow on my knees I revel in this most unusual rimming, but gradually the tongue is no longer split. It's thicker and rougher and belongs to a man who kneels behind me, preparing me, then bites me and slurps the nape of my neck. He turns me around, presses me back, lifts my legs. He's wearing a black eye mask, but I see eyes that convey knowledge. His delicate brushes of my flesh and his forceful grabs of my appendages electrify the body that his lingua licks and his digits probe. He knows this body will meld with his own and give him delectable gratification, give him all he desires. Give him all, period.

In a deep voice, the man whispers his orders, his sweet nasties, his name (rhymes with checks?). His face is scruffy and scratches my face as he kisses me voluptuously. I taste myself in his mouth. His sword seeks its sheath, finds it, and I surrender to his pounding that matches a metronome gone haywire. With eyes shut tight, I see atoms of light, star points against the dark, blinding flashes of brilliance streaking and strobing my sparkling horizon, and when he cries out, I open my eyes to see his face of joy, hear him cry out with rapture, and with a final thrust, he shoots my heart with his soul bullets and strokes me with his velvet palm, and I arch my back as it is my turn to cry out, and I erupt, and we writhe and buck for an eternity slowing, slowing, slowing, until stillness descends and envelopes us in a pod of quiet and peace and privacy. The man withdraws, I inhale—tsssssss!—and he holds my head to kiss me, tongues duel—I shudder—then he shakes my hand and leaves me. The deal has been consummated, and I have been consumed. Inertia sets in; I slip into a boundless abyss of bliss, and I am the lowly archangel who must fly away from this whale of shadows that fucks itself and spurts from hundreds of hot, little spouts.

Who was that masked man? The Lone Ranger? The Caped Crusader, Zorro, Romeo? The Red Death? Remove your veil, Mr. X.

In a sink, I splash water on my face and baptize myself in the name of the body and the blood. The wet rinses off the sweat, the dried drool and gruel of love (?), cools my fever, my flush face. Opalescent pearls cling to my skin, lips, brows, lashes. Like threads of dazzling diamonds, rivulets roll down my cheeks, dribble down my neck and chest, leaving chilly trails as they fall into the sink. I dry my face … then shake like a chihuahua!

Whoooooooshshsh swishshshsh shoooommmm!

I want more, and I zoom to the dance floor. Like a cauldron it boils, and I adore being bumped and pressed by all the slick and sweaty bodies. The men fly by, as do the hours to alien worlds taking vacations (void of other tourists) where no one would believe the picture postcards. We are all individual spaceships, sister ships, hurtling capsules released by time. The heart of the spaceship and the hearts of men radiate a united rhythm with awesome vitality. I pant and thirst and hunger. I am ravenous and must catch my breath.

At a steward's station I drink and drink and drink and peel a waxy yellow tube and put the long piece of fruit in my mouth. Under a soaring proscenium arch I lean against the bar on a huge stage, watching the parade of my fellow travelers, our roles reversed: I am the audience, they are the actors. I look up and on the catwalk a man leans over and stares at me.

I think any one of them could be Mr. X, and I think this is all too much, too goddamn much, and the music crescendos to a tempestuous speed and roaring volume and propulsive beat, and on the last beat of the song's cold ending, our captains slap us with silence and still light. The passengers roar their approval, the applause then fades, but far from quiet, a pulsating energy permeates the air, alive and anticipatory. This is the moment we who have lasted have waited for all night, all week, all month.

Maintaining the helm with happy mischief, our pilots slyly shift gears and steer us toward sleaze. A musical lust, oh yes, tunes with a slow tempo, enchanting instrumentals, or songs with nonsensical lyrics, and hearing the siren call, I quickly rise, levitate, and float back to the dance floor.

The night's exhaust of ethyls, piss, perspiration, puke, dung has created a heated perfume that sugars the air like rotted icing. It hits me with a fetid atomic fusion. The crowd has thinned, but not the intensity. No, the power of the night surges.

With room to move, we dance our own dances for ourselves, for the pleasure of anyone who wants to watch. Again, I am hot and wet with sweat. I rejoice, exultant with jubilation, rejuvenation. Every pore of my being brims with rapturous delight beyond reason and sanity and judgment. I stand, eyes closed, simply sway like a tropical tree. My serenity is a meditative hush. Or I whir, whiz, hop, step high, spin till I am dizzy, lurch and leap. My frenzy is an orgasm of ecstasy. I am as graceful as a gazelle. I am as clumsy as a colt. I am happy. Hell, I am fucked up!

The fleet of men before me take me, bear me away as I take them and bear them away. I know each and every one of them, but still, I sigh, they are strangers. They could all be Mr. X.

I gladly drown in the melodic ambrosia of our singing divas and dudes, our celestial voices who sing our special songs. Those of us who can dance on impulse power, coast on a communal high, a gleeful common energy, a divine connection with the music and light masters who propel everyone to the same wavelength. This simultaneous agreement by this

brotherhood of pleasure, of mind and body, electrifies the air
with an energized stillness that passes through each of us, that
needs no communication. The air about us cooks, simmers, spits
a steady steam in this pregnant quiet, delicious and luscious. And
I ache from birthing a heavenly rapture.

Individual energies permeate the air within and without
us with no beginning and without end. Atomic by nature, I
become a charged particle pulled into a personal orbit rotating
round the nucleus of the star machine, and my orbit changes the
very substance of this massive molecule, but I am only one of
many.

And one of those many finds me. I feel his arms go
round me. My arms go round him. His warm body is wonderful
to hold and to be held by. A galvanic current flows between our
glistening skins. We grind and undulate. We are nasty and
naughty. We are wide-eyed and unsullied. We are piquant
bacchants. We play. We are boys at a sock hop in a stinky gym
or a prom in a cotton candy paradise dancing beneath the
splendor of the stars. We cling joyfully to each other, to the
belief that the night has no end, to the secrets we and few
fathom. We feel love and crave more of the stardust filtering
down upon us, our shimmering manna from heaven.

For this stop of the voyage, we have worked our bodies
hard, vigorously, unrelentingly, and shed them for the other body
and blood of thee and me. Sore muscles and aching feet affirm
the testament of our pilgrimage. We are deliriously drunk on the
ambrosia of music and dance, my tribe's supernatural mythos,
our reward, our aphrodisiac of life, our songs of Apollo, given to
us on Earth as it shall be in some future Elysian heaven.

(At times, the beauty, the joy take my breath away.)

And I wish the man I am with is Mr. X. But even he
drifts away.

The co-pilots land the saucer—if only I would stop
spinning. The music fades, silence explodes, white lights blind,
perpetual motion ends. We who remain, who have returned from
the stars nod to each other, wink with a knowing smile. About
the coliseum of dance, surviving gladiators litter the arena. Some
roam in a stupor, some bounce or skip, some prop up others,

some flop, some giggle, some chat, some discover continued company, some wonder what is next, some merely wander.

Wearing black sunglasses, a flat top, and no expression or shirt, a vampire guy guards an exit. Maybe he seeks his next victim. Maybe he fears facing the day. Maybe he is Mr. X. Maybe the vampire bit me earlier because as I exit the brass and glass door and before I don my tinted goggles, my contacts melt onto my eyes, and I am ablaze in the fire of sun rays, a purifying immolation, an absolution to sanctify my voyage, the gift, to bless and guard my safe return.

Parts of my clothing are dirty or damp or salt-stained or stiff. The world bustles by me on its way to nowhere.

A man sleeps in a doorway. His wrinkled face maps the evidence of a thousand sorrowful roads he has traveled. I imagine if only I would touch him, the youthful oil of my hands would provide the magical elixir that would smooth his skin, make strong the sinew of his joints, unclog the veins of his heart. And he would smile, and I would claim my Mr. X.

For my next excursion to Never-Neverland, I must remember to make a reservation with my travel agent at the candy store. Funny, if he is Mr. X.

My mind still buzzes; my body begs to be put to bed. Time has passed so unbelievably fast. I short-circuit. Like grits in grease my brain fries so I tilt my head to let the gray tar ooze out my ear. I am exhausted. I feel dreamy. Avalon appears to be just over the horizon. I may someday reach my purpose if only the target would stop moving—this glory forever and ever. Amen.

And I wonder if I exchange one masquerade for another, but I scan the sky and know I have traveled beyond the blue with my brothers true. We have danced on the moon and beyond its silvery glow. With all my heart I thank the pilots for their joyful journey of music and light and celebration and sheer fun—also for their safe landing. If this is temptation, never deliver me from its goodness only we lucky know and that the outer evil would destroy, but instead, lead me into its temptation.

I walk languorously with a blithe spirit. I pass a blind man with a cane. I wave, but I don't think he notices me. I ask

  American Queer

him the time. He turns to me and starts whistling. I've a funny feeling I know him.

AllahBuddhaJCKrishnaAllahBuddhaJCKrishnaZeus!

And I think, perhaps, that I am Mr. X.

The Vanished

1984

Sitting on his front porch, Ray Bates watched the orange sky igniting the sawtooth peaks of the Rockies gradually turn navy blue, twilight ending the summer solstice of 1984. He pulled the tab on a can of Coors and thought the snap—pisht!—was the best sound of summer, that and the chirrups of the cicadas' evening love songs. But the snap seemed to have flipped a switch. The insects hushed, and the air crepitated. Smeared by heavenly hands, crackling bright lights spread across Ray's horizon, undulating like shimmering opals.

Few in the town of Lipton, Colorado (population 3,019) saw the ephemeral aurora. Ray did not know what to do but gape.

Absorbing so much light became unbearable. Though he marveled at the beauty and grandeur of the sight, he instinctively went inside his tri-level home, not forgetting his beer, preferring to marvel through the presumed safety of the big picture window. The light show lasted only minutes—then nothing. Ray heard a siren's blare a few blocks away and noticed not a star twinkled in the blackest cosmos.

He rushed into the kitchen, exclaiming, "Did you see that, that—the sky? The sky, the colors, flaring to the ground!"

His wife was talking on the wall-mounted phone. "Ray, please," said Claire, twirling the long, coiled cord. "Nan, are you there? Hello?" She had been talking with her sister who lived in the town north. Yes, she saw the bright light and thought it was a car's headlights. She wondered if her sister had hung up on her. "I redialed," said Claire, "but now the connection is all clicky."

"Honey," said Ray, "ask your sis if she saw anything weird just before your call dropped."

"I can't. The line is dead."

Ray flew downstairs, but instead of bursting into his teenage son's bedroom, he knocked on the door, a grudgingly agreed upon parental compromise. With no response, he pounded on the door and yelled his son's name.

Colton emerged wearing a Duran hoodie and earphones synced to a video game exploding behind him. Ray noticed his 9th grade son was almost tall enough to look him in his eye.

Colton unplugged and said, "Dude, my tee."

"Dude, my dollars." Ray did not like his son's familiarity, but though it was tight, did like wearing his Daffy Duck t-shirt.

"What do you want?" asked Colton. He was impatient to end a space invasion, and his room looked like the aftermath of a losing one.

Ray chose to pick that battle another day.

"Seriously," said Colton, pointing behind him, "the aliens are winning."

Ray asked if anything strange had occurred in the last few minutes. Colton said his Atari console had crashed and he had to reboot, but the drive was just spinning. Father told son not to stay up too late—son gave father a roll of eyes—and to remember to take out the trash for collection.

Ray turned on the TV, catching the news anchor in mid-sentence, his lips moving without sound sporadically. "—massive solar flare pushed solar winds—force of a billion hurric—Earth's star, penetrating its weakened atmosphere. Opponents say this is not proof of climate ch—ing satellite send—dramatic pictures." An astral film depicted a massive solar flare exploding off the sun's surface, licking the dark space around it like a tongue of fire. The anchor sequed to a grinning sportscaster, appearing for a minute before he could be heard. "—kies insurmountable deficit in the ninth inning—fifth loss in a row. Desperate to hang on—winning secret of the team is—" The screen went black, the secret unrevealed. The floor lamp flickered but remained lit.

Later in bed next to Claire, Ray felt her warmth and the air, charged and quiet. After lying awake for hours, he kicked off the covers, heard another siren, faint and far away, then fell asleep.

The next morning Ray prepared his son's lunch. Before leaving for her beauty salon, Claire's Hair Affair, his wife gave her husband a peck on the cheek.

"Is that all, Mrs. Bates?"

"For now, Mr. Bates." She smiled, smoothed a strand of blond hair, grabbed her purple bag, and entered the garage.

Ray walked to the living room and gazed out the big picture window at the bluest sky. The leaves of Claire's aspens flickered like green coins. The marigolds, mailbox, fence, pothole: His world was still there. He waved to his wife driving away. Neighbor Marty Miller was wheeling his trash can to the street, the Bates's was invisible, and Colton was not up yet. A perfectly normal day. Except for a van a couple houses down crooked to the curb. He opened the front door and called to his neighbor, "Good morning."

"Not if you saw the game." Nodding toward the badly parked vehicle, Marty said, "Coop's Dodge. His bowling championship was last night."

"Hard telling if he won or lost," said Ray.

"Coop's got a problem all right," said Marty. "Remember the Memorial Day picnic?"

"Hard to forget," said Ray. "Say Marty, did you happen to see that big light show last night? About 8:30, big splash of rainbow across the sky."

"Unlike you, I, the dedicated fan, was watching the massacre." Gazing at the trash can, Marty scratched his deep red beard and adjusted his ballcap. "Should toss this hat."

"Blasphemy, neighbor." Ray knelt and yanked a weed.

"They were getting creamed like corn," said Marty. "Outside got really bright. On TV, too, blacked out for a few minutes. Commentators said something about a power surge. Sound was awful. Showed nothing but stupid commercials. Game never came back on, and no paper today, but maybe—"

"They lost."

"Hmmm. Well, thanks, Ray." Marty tossed his hat in the trash. "Thanks for the update."

"Well, that's what the news said last night. Last thing I heard."

A teenage girl in tight jeans and a top with puffy sleeves came out of the Miller's garage. "I need to get to school."

"OK," said Marty. "Get in the truck."

"What?"

"Get in the truck."

"Daddy, I'm right here, you don't have to yell."

"I did not—Say hello to Mr. Bates."

Wendy grinned and rolled her eyes. "Hello." She returned to the garage and got into the Ford pick-up, Marty staring after the mystery that was his daughter.

Ray smiled. "She'll grow out of it."

"She gives me a headache," said Marty, rubbing his temple. "She wants braces and bras."

"My boy wants a skateboard and a Mac."

"Like a Big Mac?"

"I don't think he means a hamburger."

"Then what's a Mac?"

"Hell if I know," said Ray. "I better see if my headache is out of bed. Leave without him if you need to."

"Yeah," said Marty, "we must not bow to the royals." He picked out his hat from the trash, brushed it off, and put it back on.

"Colton," Ray called downstairs, "time to go. And take out the trash. You forgot."

He returned to the kitchen, spread mayo on white bread, and added cheddar cheese. He put the plastic wrapped sandwich, a bag of Cheetos, and a tangerine into a *Mr. T* lunch box, wondering if his boy was into some weird orange food phase. I pity the fool, thought Ray, chuckling, who tries to know what goes on in the mind of a teenager. "Colton! Mr. Miller is waiting." No answer. "You'll have to walk, and don't forget your lunch." Ray checked upstairs—"Colton?"—then heard the pick-up drive off. *Mr. T* still sat on the kitchen counter. That kid, he thought. Not a big deal, I guess. Mother Nature's extravaganza, now that was a big deal. Odd, on the longest day of the year. He listened, didn't move. He heard the wail of a far-off siren fade away. And the hallway clock ticking. So quiet. That was odd, too.

The phone rang, and he jumped a little. It was Claire asking him to bring her billfold. "It's on the kitchen table. I forgot it."

"Will do," said Ray. "So … anything odd going on?"

"Like what?"

"I don't know, anything."

"Town seems deader than usual, if that's possible. Barb didn't show, but neither did her first appointment."

"And that's odd?"

"Not exactly. Barb's chronically late, but Mrs. Valdéz has never no-showed. Why, what's going on?"

"Nothing. I need to stop off at Colton's school."

"What's wrong with Colton? Is he OK?"

"Relax, he forgot his lunch, then I'll bring your—" Ray heard static and a click like a hang-up, then a dial-tone. "Hello? Honey?"

He dialed his wife's work number, and after six rings, voice-mail answered, but he hung up. He thought Mrs. Valdéz probably arrived. He grabbed Claire's billfold, *Mr. T*, and got in his Corolla.

Passing his neighbor's white van, Ray slowed down, then pulled into Coop's driveway. Trash from a knocked over bin littered the sidewalk and gutter. The front door was open; a small dog wiggled and wagged its tail like a frenzied metronome.

"Hey Moxie, where's your daddy?" Ray rang the doorbell and called loudly, "Coop!" Not wanting to alarm his neighbor's wife, he announced himself. "Marilyn, it's Ray! Anyone home?"

Upset about something, the mutt whined and bounced off the screen door. As soon as Ray opened it, Moxie sniffed his feet and jumped on his legs. "What's the matter, girl?" The dog ran, and with the car door open, hopped into the front seat, yawning, licking her lips, and panting. "OK, then."

Ray headed to Colton's junior high school. Traffic was light. He stopped at a truck half in the right lane and half on the sidewalk. It was Marty's Ford pick-up. The engine was running, but no one was around. He got out and shut off its ignition.

"Colton! Marty!" Within seconds of hearing a screeching siren, he sprung back when a cop car roared past him. "Jesus!" He called for his neighbor's daughter, for anyone, receiving no response.

Ray ran stop signs and red lights getting to his son's school. A few bikes were chained to the stand; several lay on the grass or sidewalk, one in the middle of the street. He parked in the student drop off lane, against the rules but a rule he felt like breaking, and rushed to the front office with Colton's lunch box.

Miss Kinney greeted him in her clipped and feminine formality. "Good morning, Raymond."

Twenty years seemed to evaporate, and he was embarrassed he wore a juvenile's t-shirt. "Good morning, Miss Kinney," said Ray. He thought the school secretary wore the same blue, ruffled blouse buttoned to her neck as she did when he was a student. Today, she looked ancient and weary. "Have you seen Colton?"

"Why, no," said Miss Kinney, "I'm sorry."

"He left with Marty Miller," said Ray, "but I saw his truck and it was, uh, never mind. I brought Colton's lunch. Would you please let him know?"

"Of course, dear," said Miss Kinney.

"Thank you," said Ray.

She looked at the lunch box distractedly. "Quite a few absentees today, not to mention teachers. And the phones … unreliable, crackling noise if anything."

Ray was about to ask to use the phone to call the police about his missing son, but maybe there was a simple explanation. "Did Wendy Miller come to school?"

"Who?"

"Wendy Miller, my neighbor's daughter."

"I've not seen her either." Miss Kinney shook her head. "I don't know what the world is coming to, Raymond. And those lights last night."

"You saw the sky?"

Miss Kinney leaned into her former student and looked over her glasses. "Oh, yes, about 8:30. I was making popcorn on the stove—I always do when I watch movies on TV—and suddenly the popping stopped, and so did Carole Lombard."

                                        American Queer

"Your TV stopped?"

"Hmm? … oh, yes. Such a talented lady, so beautiful," sighed Miss Kinney with a smile. "And tragic. From a different world," she said softly. "I saw bright light so I stepped outside. Astonishing, like I was witnessing a spectacular event that was also inexplicably distressing. I'm tired, Raymond, very tired. This world … yes, she and I … "

"Who, Miss Kinney?" asked Ray. "This Carole person?"

"Oh … oh, um, no … Elinor, um Miss Glenn, my, my companion …" The old woman took off her glasses, frowned, and shut her eyes, whispering with incredulity. "So sudden … mere seconds … and she just wasn't there … but that's lunacy … so confused, so tired. Sweet Elinor. And I keep seeing flashes of light, and hearing static like an old radio, and I don't want to!" she shouted.

Ray had never known Miss Kinney to raise her voice.

She looked through the office window, puzzled and upset, then, through tearful eyes, said, "She'll return; she must." Miss Kinney pulled out a lace handkerchief, daubed her eyes, and replaced her glasses. "Heavens to betsy, I probably just need bi-focals and hearing aids." She began writing names on small, pink papers. "Lots of absentee slips to fill out."

Squished by the steering wheel, Moxie nestled in Ray's lap, whimpering and shaking. Ray started his car and turned on the radio, hearing *Time After Time* wane to nothing. He tuned into another station, but the sound kept cutting out. "—creating auroras all ov—at the poles, but close to the equator, as near as Hawaii and Singa—ding to General Ohrman, NASA spokesman, sa—est in space, witnessing a geomagnetic storm of unprecedented size and destru—sing interruption of worldwide satellite commun—til scien—spheric activation of a viral disease of instantaneous disintegra—" And then silence. He tuned the dial along its band, receiving only static a couple times.

Ray shut off the car, stared out the windshield, and didn't move. He ached for his son, his wife, himself, everyone. He scratched the dog's ears for mutual assurance. "Sweet Moxie." In the eerie quiet, the sound of his own voice creeped him out.

 American Queer

He went back inside the school, searched for Miss Kinney in the office, but found no sign of her. He stepped behind the counter and called 911, getting sounds like the crinkling of a sheet of cellophane and a recording. "What the hell?" He called Claire again and got her recording again.

Ray walked down the hallway. A few students passed him slowly or stood immobile at lockers, staring at him. Some classrooms had a teacher and several desks occupied by students; others were empty of anyone. In Room 13, a teacher noticed him, turned her head, wide-eyed with mouth open, and seemed about to speak, but he had already rushed by the door.

Colton played the trumpet in the school band; so had Ray. He hoped his son might be in the rehearsal room. Sheet music and black stands littered the floor. Halfway up staggered risers, he recognized Kyle Bings, a tall, skinny student with acne and a crew cut. He sat next to a tuba, gaping at his weirdly distorted reflection in the curving brass.

"Kyle?"

"Ah!" Startled, the kid said, "Oh, hi, Mr.—" He seemed to know Ray's face.

"Bates."

"I didn't see you." The kid chuckled.

"Kyle, have you seen Colton?"

"Who?"

"My son."

"I thought I saw—" the kid began, returning to stare at his distorted face in the brass mirror, "Mr. Wolfe."

"The band director?"

"But ... sooo freaky."

"What is?" asked Ray.

"He was here—I was waiting for—and then he wasn't. The invisible man." Kyle let out a goofy scoff, again hypnotized by his own grotesque reflection. "I heard snaps like that cereal with the elves, then I think I saw ... freaky, man, and I haven't smoked a thing, I swear, and then he—" His voice stuck and he swallowed hard, incapable of finishing his thought. He picked a pimple on his cheek, and it started to bleed, but he kept picking.

"Let's get you to the nurse," said Ray, "then Miss Kinney. She'll know—"

Kyle lurched up, kicking back his chair and knocking over the instrument and music stand with a loud clatter. He ran out of the room, Ray after him. He thought he saw a flash, looked left, right, but didn't see the kid in either direction of the hall. "Where the hell did he go?" He called for Miss Kinney, but got no response. He thought he'd talk with the teacher in the room he had passed, but when he looked through its window, no one was there.

Ray trotted to his car and heard the school's front door open, then his name and brief noises like bubble wrap reports. He turned around and saw a rainbow streak for seconds. Small pink papers fluttered to the sidewalk. As soon as Ray opened the car door, Moxie growled, barked, ricocheted off the back seat, and bolted.

He sped to Claire's salon, but driving by the Shamrock station, he saw a gas nozzle laying on the cement, pulled in, and re-hooked the hose. Owner Bart didn't greet him, and wife Sandy wasn't minding the register, open with cash spilling out. Behind the counter, Ray put the phone receiver to his ear and pumped the hook switch to clear the landline and connect. He needed to find his son. "C'mon, goddammit!" Dial tone— "Jackpot!"—the loveliest droning note he'd ever heard. Ray dialed 911 … ringing … recording. He dialed again. Continuous ringing. "Somebody answer!" And again, busy signal. Ray thought maybe he had dialed wrong, but how can you misdial 911? He redialed. This time, nothing.

Ray called Claire. Same results: connected, voicemail, redialed, ringing over and over, then busy signal, no dial-tone, dead. "I don't believe this."

Ray slammed the receiver down on its cradle and ran to his car. He laid rubber pulling away from the gas pump, but braked hard when he heard the fast approaching crescendo of a howling ambulance, a blur of red and blue lights rushing by on its way to save someone somewhere, he hoped.

On Jackson Avenue, more derelict vehicles splayed across the lanes and onto the sidewalk. Pedestrians meandered drunkenly or ran crazily as though fleeing something. Ray opened his car window and called to them, but either they fled or stared mutely, and he knew some of them. County Clerk Molly

Semple screamed. He screeched up to his wife's salon just off Lipton's main drag, not bothering to parallel park. Like Coop, he thought. The front door was wide open.

"Claire!" No answer.

The portable TV was on with jumbled pictures and scrambled sound: Witness accounts and weird happenings, the president's and world governments' responses, stocking up on food and water and guns, fires and wrecks and riots, the military running amok. But in some areas, not a movement, not a sound, not a person. Then the screen changed to the emergency broadcasting test with its annoying, grating alarm, then to noisy, fuzzy gray dots. And then to black.

The world had collapsed.

As Ray backed away, he turned to the full length mirror by the shampoo station. Scruffy, eyes bloodshot, he looked like a crazy man in a Daffy Duck t-shirt and sweatpants.

"Ray?"

He'd recognize that beautiful alto voice anywhere. Claire smiled at him in the mirror. He saw himself smile and then a flash of colorful light. He heard static and pops, and … she disappeared. She was there. Then not there. He blinked, turned around, and saw no one. He ran to where his wife had stood. No clothes, no blood, flesh, bone. No wedding band. Nothing. No Claire. No love of his life. She was gone.

Ray dropped to his knees. "GOD!"

The salon's phone rang loud as a cathedral's bell— "Jesus!"—scaring him so hard he jerked, shook his head in disbelief the phone was working, and lunged for it. "Hello!"

"Dad!"

"Colton, thank God, are you OK?"

"Yeah."

"Where are you?"

"Home," said Colton, panting, his voice terrified. "Dad, we were on our way to school, and then Mr. Morris and then Wendy, they, they—I'm going crazy."

"You're not."

"Why is this happening!"

"I don't know, son."

"Have you seen Mom?"

   American Queer

"Yes, yes, I saw your Mom." Ray didn't know what else to say. "Stay put, you hear me?"

"Yes! Hurry, Dad, please, I'm so scared and I don't want to—"

Click.

"No, no, NO!" Silence. So quiet, his ears rang. "Colton? Colton!"

Ray ran out of the salon, shouting into the bluest sky, "I'm on my way, I love you, and—"

The last thing he heard was the roar of sharp crackling before he crossed a warm and dazzling shaft of rainbow light.

And then, he too, vanished.

American Queer

HIDING NO MORE

1995-1999

El Baño del Olvido
(The Bath of Forgetfulness)

1995

*The light of the body is the eye; if therefore
thine eye be single, thy whole body shall be
full of light.*
  Matthew 6:22, Sermon on the Mount

Within a cloud, I lie naked in a white porcelain pool filled with hot and oily water that smells of grapefruit. Out of one eye I see the most beautiful Mexican man with ears like valentine halves and a black mustache that for some reason I know is soft as mink. On his knees, he smiles at me. He caresses my body with a velvety, tan sponge while his other hand cradles my head. I glimpse the shiny belt buckle of a pouncing jungle cat and a gummy red thread that cuts his cheek. A large patch covers my own, and it twinges. My skin stings; my body throbs; a foot like a club. And my other eye? I hope it's not blind. I hope the beautiful Mexican man is not an angel because I don't like them. Angels are God's tattletales.

Odd nurses attend me. Pulling back a brightly colored sheet, a little brown blossom enters and whispers soft Spanish words to the man. She touches the patched smear of raspberry jam branded below my bottom lip that travels up the side of my face—for good luck?—then leaves. A toothless mummy tenderly places a cool rag on my forehead with her fried and splotchy fingers. On one finger burns a veined boil of blue fire.

Candles flicker on the sink, the toilet, a small table on which sits a vase of dried yellow roses. The tick-tock of an old camel clock, the face in its hump, and the plops of water drops from a rusty faucet break the stillness. I strive to penetrate time, the dim veil of my vision, a shroud of death or the caul of rebirth, I cannot discern. Effort exhausts me.

Between a small window and a mirror on the wall before me, a votive illumines a cracked and chipped Holy Mother, serene, rosy-cheeked, and milky white. She spreads her arms downward, palms forward. Her face tilts slightly to the side, and she eyes me curiously. Flickering shadows play upon her pale blue robes as though ruffled by a breeze. Yet how can her gaze be so *un*ruffled? How can she not know what's going on?

Because above the Virgin hangs her Son. His arms spread too, but straight across, palms punctured and bloody. A freakish crucifix, this dark skinned, goateed Christ is also branded. A crimson heart burns in the middle of his chest like a torched wound. He looks frightened, surprised, and with gaping big brown eyes and parted lips, appears about to implore heaven and cry out, "What the hell is going on here?" My own heart flames; tears roll down my cheeks from my one blue eye, and I implore heaven with the same question. Behind my other eye, the tears are dammed. Am I? Damned, that is. *If thine eye be single*—true words, but something hides within them.

Dressed in black, a short, plump beetle with a hairy mole and bosom big as a sofa cushion waddles in with a bottle and pours amber liquid into a green glass. Is that a worm in the bottom of the bottle? The beautiful Mexican man sends her away, takes the glass, puts it to my lips, and tips it, splitting my cracked and caked lips. "Drink," he says. The amber liquid is fire to my parched throat. I cough, and my chest feels bound by a clamp of spikes.

My mind's a mist like the moist and foggy air here, yet I recall another steamy room with this beautiful Mexican man and quiver, savoring the vision. He smiles at me and caresses my body with the velvety, tan sponge. It moves to my groin, is replaced by a tight grasp, and in seconds, I am erect. At least that is not damaged. Between passion and pain, I shudder again. Angry red threads like the one on the beautiful Mexican man and patches of red sandpaper stripe and splotch my body, and the hot water stings, the plum-colored stains pain me, and by a flash of lightning, I see the gaping gullet of a laughing mouth with a golden spark, and fists rain blow after blow upon me. I throw up my hands to block the pounding, but two strong hands restrain my thrashing about; a voice soothes me and causes me to lie back enfeebled and babe-like. Cast adrift in this oily ocean, I am in heaven; I am in hell. Someone save me.

And someone does. Holding me like he'll never let me go, the beautiful Mexican man tenderly blinks his *beso de la mariposa,* kiss of the butterfly, on my forehead. I calm down, try to smile, but my thick lips cannot curve, so like a cyclops, I send my smile through my working eye. *If thine eye be single—*

I know this beautiful Mexican man with eyes like two chocolate candy kisses. I have taught him English. He has taught me a language I had forgotten. He has loved me, fought for me, killed for—or did I? For him …

Why do I think I sit on a lion's clawed paws hooked round balls of the earth?

The worm has done its job, my blood turned to warm liquid amber, and I'm asea in oblivion. A necklace of Christmas candy glass beads rests on my chest. I hold one up to my good eye with a jeweler's squint, and in the candlelight, the kaleidoscopic bead depicts a dioramic design. Stare long enough at anything, you can see anything. And I see my ever-present guardian look to a large pad resting on his knee, then move a pencil. Is he sketching me? I should comb my hair, but die a little, luscious death …

***

… I sit alone in a vast theater. The curtain parts. Dionisio de las Flores stands center stage emanating the essence of wine and flowers. He is tall, lithe, with a mustache, wavy blue-black hair, lips the color of burgundy. I watch myself rise up from below the stage and play my part. Dionisio smiles at me with lovely white teeth. And his eyes, his eyes … I do not deserve such a gaze, and look away.

It's my 32nd birthday. I am the human resources director for a large hotel, but lately, lack my own personal supply. In my office I resurrect a photograph … of whom? Oh yes, Brian. Brian, sweet and funny, dead and dust. A commotion interrupts my reverie. I bury Brian again—will I ever cry over him?—with his smile and his white tennis togs, in the dark drawer of my desk, and walk into a common area.

   American Queer

Three speak in Spanish to Juan, short and pudgy, a security officer with a sparkling golden tooth and unctuous, gaping laugh. He translates to my assistant, who twirls her hair round a finger and asks questions of Juan, who translates back to the immigrants, who laugh amidst the clatter of two languages, so happy to be in my America.

Buenos Días, I say, and all go silent. Juan introduces his brother, hoping I will give him a job. *Señor Victor Gottisaul, mi hermano, Dionisio de las Flores*. And I am drunk from the spirit and scent of his name alone.

A beautiful Mexican man steps forward. He is Cortez, Moctezuma, *Americano*. He wears a Yankees ballcap, which he removes, jeans, a plaid shirt with pearled buttons, and green lizard cowboy boots with pointed toes and angled heels.

Usually, my raspberry birthmark guides people's eyes like a beacon to my cheek, then ensnares them with fascination or disgust. But not Dionisio de las Flores. He bows slightly, shakes my hand, looks only in my eyes, stripping away my suit, discovering long-buried treasure. So red-faced, I wonder if my birthmark is visible.

The beautiful Mexican man says, *Usted es way cool*, then repeats my first name, *Beektrrr*. I am not *way cool*. Definitely not.

He teasingly tugs the braid of his baby sister Fabiola, Fobby, crisply dressed and missing a front tooth with tiny crosses stapled to her delicate ears. His other arm drapes across his mamá, Señora Sofía, shawled in black, wearing a gold crucifix round her thick neck.

I smile and greet them, kneel before Fobby, and offer my hand. She touches my purple-red smudge, and I jerk, startling her, the mother pulling her back. I place Fobby's little palm over my cheek, and bashfully, she lets it rest there, then hides behind her mother's skirts.

Separated from this sentimental scene, a thin, chalky woman with wild, jet-black hair like charred scrub-brush stands to the side clutching a red purse strapped around her neck and shoulder. She wears red spiked heels, a short skirt, no hose, no crosses of any kind. Juan struts to where she stands and introduces her, his eyes undressing his brother's betrothed. She says nothing through her scarlet lips. She is a watcher. Her sharp black eyes survey the group with languid contempt, but track every move of her Dionisio, her groom-to-be, like a jungle bird of prey. Inez, the Intended.

Juan announces her impending motherhood. With possessive conceit, he cups the pouch of the Intended's stomach, evidence of the birth to be (and more I think), his leer changing his jowls to two jelly rolls. I watch Dionisio struggle, then, in spite of his brother's insolence, smile with fatherly pride. Señora Sofía mutters and crosses herself. Inez glares at Juan and removes his hand from her pouch. *What? I will be tío to mi sobrino.* He smiles and winks. Fobby misses nothing.

Juan volunteers me to teach Dionisio English, says this in Spanish to his brother, who says *Way cool* again. Through Juan, he tells me he looks forward to learning from *Señor Beektrrr*. I look away, and my eyes stop at Inez, who nods with a barely perceptible grin on her bloody lips. I should have died that instant. I return to my office, shut the door, and shake.

Not a minute goes by when my boss enters—Becker, Benjamin Becker, Becker the Pecker; I think of him as Benny Ann. He takes off his glasses, rubs his eyes, and wishes me happy birthday. I thank him. He stares at my cheek. *You'd think I'd be used to it by now*, he says with an uncomfortable chuckle. *Yeah, me too*, I reply.

Becker stands aside to let a policeman stroll in with hips jutting forward and eyes shaded. The brothers de las Flores appear nervous until the cop puts a portable player on my desk, handcuffs my wrists, and pushes me down onto my chair. He flips a switch and begins to dance to *Macho Man*. With a single flourish, he whips off his uniform, revealing tiny underwear. He shakes his ass and bulge in my face, sits on my lap, secretly squeezes my crotch. He removes his sunglasses, hesitates at my blot, ablaze even brighter, but plants a big wet kiss on my lips anyway. The stripper whispers to me, *let it happen though you don't understand it.* His dark eyes and goatee leave as quickly as they arrived.

Quite a show. Peers, staff, and visitors laugh and cheer; even Señora Sofía cannot hide her smile, but she shields Fobby behind her. Dionisio wishes me *Feliz Cumpleaños*. My purple-

     American Queer

red scorch flares fluorescent, and though a dozen company policies have been broken, I am the good sport thanking all for their birthday wishes.

Like a firecracker above the din, I hear Juan say with disgust, *Marrecón*. In a flash, his brother bolts for his throat and backs him up against the nearest wall, the mamá trying to break her sons' throttling. Becker ducks, I'm out of my seat; my assistant calls security. And the Intended? She watches and smiles.

In my office after the fight ends, I argue with Becker, first to unlock my wrists with the key he dangles in my face, and then that we cannot allow the hotel to become the brothers' battleground for some internecine family feud. Becker argues that we need workers; my job is to fill openings, and if I don't, I'm fired. I tell him my job is to protect this hotel from legal fiascoes; why would he fire me for doing my job? Becker removes his glasses and rubs his eyes again, leans on my desk, and spits, *Because you're a faggot.* Well. That answers that question. *No witnesses,* Benny Ann says, *so don't bother reporting me.*

I go back out and ask Mr. Flores for his *tarjeta verde*. This time, he looks away but hands it to me. I rub my thumb over his photograph, renaissance-like in its beauty. Slightly raised, it's fake, and Dion knows I know. I hire Dionisio de las Flores on the spot—I'll find some position for him to fill—who cannot contain his jubilance …

***

… Who naps in a chair next to the white porcelain pool filled with hot and oily water that smells of … *toronja*. How do I know this word? Tiny raindrops bead his brow as the sultry air glosses his handsome face, so peaceful in repose. But I can recall the savage turbulence of its passion, its reproach, its defense. I stare in disbelief that he's here beside me.

The big black beetle dozes on a round padded stool, and with her hands folded in her lap, appears bowed in prayer. She's probably just sleeping, but this much I know. Along with Holy Mary and her man-child on the candlelit wall before me, two mothers, two sons watch over me.

     American Queer

One eye is still forcibly closed; my other I cannot keep open and gladly let the lid fall …

***

… Another curtain in my mind rises. Spanish and English words float across the stage. Teaching each other our native languages, we shorten each other's first name. My eager student calls me Vic, *Beek*, but prefers *Señor Beektrrr*. Eager too, I rename him, and he's pleased; no one has ever called him *Dion* before.

Dion brings me little presents. I explain as best I can that giving me gifts is inappropriate, unprofessional. He doesn't understand—not the words, the idea. He tells me to consider them birthday presents, and his gift-giving goes on: a yo-yo, a string of glass beads, a plushy chihuahua from a fast-food promotion that amuses him. He's become American so quickly. I don't return the favors, and Dion doesn't seem to mind, which isn't very American.

We conduct our lessons after working hours in my office with the door always open. No one ever filled the drab navy uniform like Dion does, as though the petroleum in the polyester cloth melts from the heat of his body, molds to his shape baiting me to strip him, to feel the softness and smoothness of his clear mocha skin, to kiss his full lips, to taste his mustache, to feel the hardness between his legs and of his hips. And I wonder why I continue down this trail of temptation.

One early evening, I have to force my focus. I ask Dion what he likes about America. Pop-Tarts are his favorite food, *way cool*, and he's amazed at the row upon row of jeans in K-Mart, in my America, in this land of riches beyond belief.

I ask Dion what he likes to do, and he looks down and tells me he likes to draw. I request a showing of his sketches, but he grins and shakes his head in embarrassment. I ask about his father. The grin fades. His papá died before he could live his dream of living in America. On his 16th birthday, his papá gave him a belt of finely tooled leather and a silver buckle of a lunging jaguar, the only possession he brought across the border to his new home. He stops, realizes his admission, but decides to

American Queer

trust me. Dion pets the ferocious feline, his papá's presence gladdens him. Looking lower, I can tell so does mine.

Inez's does not. I ask about her. Dion frowns, calls her *la hechicera* and chuckles, but there is unease in his laugh. Even a witch commands respect. His papá arranged their match many years ago with another family in his village. Inez arrived here with his grandmother; they live with Juan in his apartment. Naively, Dion explains that it would be sinful for his *prometida* to live under the same roof as he. I imagine other sins performed under the other roof despite a chaperone. Dion looks forward to being a father, though he sheepishly hangs his head and confesses the Intended got him drunk and sat on him.

It is not me, he says. *Entiendes, Señor Beektrrr?*

Yes, I understand.

Dion invites me to his home for a *Cinco de Mayo* celebration. I decline, he insists. His mamá wants to thank me for giving her family a chance to stay in this country they love so dearly. Fobby wants me because I paid her attention. *Sentimientos de una niñita*, Dion says to me with a shrug. I have no wish to trifle with the feelings of a little girl.

I close my eyes, and Brian appears with his smile and his white tennis togs. He's happy and mutely mouths, *If thine eye be single* to remind me of something. Dion pleads again for me to come to his barbecue. I open my eyes and accept.

Dion stands up, grabs my face, and kisses me on the cheek. His whole face is alive. He speedily talks in Spanish, the little I understand indicating his mamá will be excited, and Fobby will wet her pants when he tells her, words to that effect. He rushes out of my office, and I shake my head. He gives himself so freely, so easily to me. He unnerves me.

But I touch my cheek where the beautiful Mexican man grazed my blemish with his mustache. Like being swiped by a paintbrush made of fine fur, I still feel his kiss …

***

… And feel something draining out of me, like I'm running on a collapsing suspension bridge above a jungle gorge, each slat plunging behind me as I race to the other side, as though each memory I remember for the last time.

I keep waiting for the sun to rise, for the eclipse to end, but my friend, the camel, shows me it's far from arriving. Funny, do its hands run backward? Thank heavens there are such pretty rainbows in limbo land. I finger the beads round my neck like a rosary and lose myself in their refraction.

My club foot is numb. The beautiful Mexican man sketches. Something hums in my ears.

The heat in this void, so equatorial and unrelenting. And I lie baffled and languorous in hot and oily water that smells of grapefruit …

***

… The wrong side of the tracks is a real place. Ugly trains snake the landscape and slither through weeds and trash as I drive toward the address of Dion and Fobby and Señora Sofía. In heat, through a chemical stink, an electric hum drones in the air. A power tower soars above the horizon like a giant erector-set skeleton, and I pass abandoned vehicles baked to ruin and rust. I'm lost until I hear faint music, see a field of clunkers, low-riders, and shiny new trucks. I recognize Dion's '50's DeSoto with fins and tail lights like two red gladiolas. Next to it, I park my shiny new S.U.V.

In full swing, everyone stops partying, and the music stops playing. An intruder, I cannot bring myself to get out, yet cannot refuse this face that approaches me. The crowd parts as Señora Sofía waddles up to my window, waving her hands joyfully, greeting me with more Spanish than I can decipher. Her eyes disappear in squints of happiness, and I wonder how she can see. Still smooth, hers is a face slightly sorrowed by life, yet grateful to make a new one in a new country.

And Fobby! She comes bounding across the grassless front yard like a brown-eyed fawn, brakes, and hides behind her mamá's black skirt, takes a fold, and puts it in her mouth. Señora Sofía lays her arm around her child and chuckles at her embarrassed delight.

I give the mother *un ramo de rosas amarillas*. From the look on her face, she has never held such a bouquet of gold. To Fobby, *perfúme para una niñita muey bonita*, because she is a pretty little girl I tell her, *y para tu el baño, aciete de fresa,*

        American Queer

manzana, toronja, bath oils of strawberry, apple, grapefruit. Pop-eyed with gladness, Fobby takes my hand and pulls me toward the party. I bring nothing for Dion, nothing that's visible.

Following the matriarch, I hold tightly to Fobby. We look at each other, silently declare a secret pact, and I know my little angel will never tattle like those other angels. She lets go of my hand, skips ahead to hopscotch chunks of sidewalk that cleave the barren yard and lie askew, then holds it again.

I must be on my best behavior because I recognize some of the guests as employees from the hotel. I say *Buenos Días* many times, and they greet me because I am *El Jefe, Patrón*. With Fobby on one side, the matriarch takes my other hand. It's a speechless action no one dares contradict. The party resumes.

We walk underneath three huge trees, all laden with the new green leaves of spring. Tables filled with food and chairs with people rest beneath their shade, and the volume of sibilant and clicking Spanish increases. Spicy aromas from grilling meats sizzle in my nose, and mariachi music blaring from a ghetto blaster swirls in my ears. Young couples dance suggestively, the older gently bounce. Children scream and run up and down the porch. There is much life here: love, tradition, passion. The scene is as foreign to me as I am to it.

A thousand cats seem to have scratched the tiny shack of my hosts in preparation for a paint job that's late in coming. All of it sags with exhausted ugliness. A rickety railing and stairs rise to a rickety porch where glass chimes sway and tinkle.

Munching on a Pop-Tart, Dionisio de las Flores pushes open the torn mesh of a screen door, sees me, and smiles. He exits, and the screen door slaps shut. He tosses his pastry gobbled by a stray dog, jumps down the steps, takes one of my hands in both of his, and shakes it until I laugh and stop him. I am red like Fobby before me but have no skirts to hide behind.

Following Dion, Inez slinks onto the porch like a sly puss sleepy and satisfied, her red lipstick like a smear of fresh bird blood on her lips. She wears her red purse, red spiked heels, an apron over her pouch, and though his back is to her, she senses Dion's delight, glares at me, and returns to the shade of the shack. Light is not her natural element.

   American Queer

From around a corner of the porch, Juan emerges from a gang of *cholos* I'm sure he doesn't want me to know he knows—belongs to, bullies? He wears a straw cowboy hat and eyes me, Dion, the departure of the Intended. His cocked head and scowl accentuate his jelly jowls, but Juan turns on his hospitality with a fawning laugh and struts down the steps to offer me *tequila y cerveza.* I decline the worm.

My escorts pull me up the steps into the shack. Señora Sofía barks a command to Juan, who obeys, and invites me into her palace. Dion says, *Mi casa es su casa.* I stifle my urge to laugh at the cliché because I know he means it. Their home is immaculate, the few pieces of furniture old and frayed. A blue parakeet flits in a wire cage and nibbles Fobby's finger. Blankets of Aztec patterns keep out the brilliant sun, and despite having electricity, an oil lamp with an orange shade casts a sunset about the room. Statues of the Virgin and a saint for every affliction people the room in mute attendance. Like a gallery, icons tell tales of the Christ: with Lazarus, the whore, the Baptist and dove; the marriage at Canaan; bound and beaten by Roman centurions; hung and splayed with the two thieves; the mystery of the tomb; the bliss of Ascension.

Near the kitchen, the Intended stands idle but not for long because she moves reluctantly to the click of the matriarch's orders.

Señora Sofía introduces me to the grandmother she cares for, wiping drool from the toothless, mummified face. La Doña sits enthroned on a well-worn wingback chair, her crinkly hands resting regally on a falcon-headed cane. Like a royal dowager she offers one to me. Am I to kiss the ring of fiery blue turquoise on her taloned finger? I only shake her gnarly claw that's clammy but grips strongly. She chews her gums and cackles her assessment of me, *Muey guapo scandinavia.* Though blond and blue-eyed, I'm not a handsome Scandinavian, but don't argue. Through watery hazel eyes, La Doña squints at the stigma on my cheek, leans forward, chews out, *Y la marca del corazón Cristi.* At least she didn't call it the mark of Cain. The crone nods, then crosses herself. Sensing the Intended staring at her—surely a blur to her milky vision—La Doña crosses herself again and

  American Queer

sputters *La hechicera*. The Intended merely smirks as though saying *Your time will come, old woman.*

Señora Sofía clicks another order to her future daughter-in-law, then continues the tour. A sergeant could bounce a quarter off her twin bed and Fobby's cot. One crucifix and one statue of Mary with a burning candle stand guard on a beat-up bureau.

Dionisio's room is almost identical without the cot. Cowboys gallop across his bedspread, lasso livestock, or snooze around a campfire. An open sketchpad and pencils crowd his dresser. I move to look at it, but he says, *Más tarde*, and closes the pad. He blushes, and I imagine him as a little boy hiding behind his mamá's skirt.

Señora Sofía beams when she pulls back a brightly colored sheet to reveal her indoor bathroom. An old-fashioned, white porcelain tub, its feet the clawed paws of a lion hooked round balls of the earth, takes up most of the space, but there's room enough for Mary and Jesus. I notice the crimson beacon in the middle of the Savior's chest, his Sacred Heart, La Doña's *corazón Cristi*.

I play baseball and tag Juan out at home plate, knocking off his cowboy hat, my bloody knee a proud trophy. He curses and spits but oozes a greasy grin.

Dion steals three bases and a kiss from me when he takes me for a walk, backs me up to a boxcar, wraps his arms around me and pulls out my shirt. *Eres way cool*, he says of me. The heat of his hands vibrates my back, or is it the hum of the power station? I turn my raspberry flaw from him, but he touches it and guides my lips to his, wetly sucking the breath of life out of me, wetly resuscitating me with every exhalation.

The boxcar door is ajar. Dion strains to slide it open, jumps up into the darkness, hoists me up. The sun shining through slats stripes us and glitters the dancing motes of floating dust. It smells musty from airless enclosure and, with my nose buried in Dion's neck, musky from the sweat of the hot day.

I look into his face, and one of the golden ribbons of sun illumines his eyes, glowing from within like pools of dark honey. He cups my buttocks; his hands move underneath my shorts, and pressed against me, I feel his lurching cat buckle mauling my zipper to claw its way inside, feel his rigid desire. I know he feels mine, for a hand kneads my groin like it needs my groin, and we crash onto a crate, Dion kissing me all over, falling to his knees, kissing my scabby knee, then up my shorts to my crotch, tickling me. My hands run through his thick, wavy blue-black hair, but behind my closed eyes, I sense the light blinking. I open them and see a shadow move.

I break away, jump down, see no one, run away! When Dion catches up to me, he wheels me around and with his eyes speaks a wordless language that I—that I am afraid to understand. Though I do. Perfectly. He takes my hand, and we walk among the tracks and ruts, weeds and trash.

Evening approaches. We return to the celebration during the children's hour, that indecisive delay from day to night when the sky is electric blue, the air infused with grace. Crickets chirp, and a cool breeze brushes our backs. Yard lights illuminate areas in pools of white.

From the rear kitchen door, Inez sees us. She does not betray herself, but I feel her eyes. Dion smiles and waves; the Intended nods.

In his bedroom, he hesitates, then shows me his sketches. I flip through the pages, and the delicacy and force of his charcoal strokes amaze me. He captures the core of his subjects: the innocence of his sister, the beatitude of his mamá, the bravado of his brother, the carnality of his Intended. La Doña could be an antediluvian priestess. I compliment him, encourage him to take classes, offer to help him find a good school. He turns red-faced. I find drawings of me: kneeling, holding a small hand to my cheek; handcuffed in suit and tie, nude. I close the book and leave his bedroom. He follows immediately, afraid I am offended. I assure him I am not.

We rejoin the picnic. We eat melon, and he wipes a dribble from my chin. I'm nervous someone sees us, but everyone is preoccupied with cheering innocent violence.

Children pass a blindfold and a broom handle and take turns batting a piñata, a pink crepe donkey. Hit after hit, no shrieking child fractures its frilly hide. Materializing out of nowhere, Inez grabs the stick and whacks once, breaking the

     American Queer

donkey's back, the children falling upon its sweet guts like a swarm of starved bees. The Intended disappears.

I leave with tamales and flan from the mother, a bouquet of dandelions from Fobby, many *muchas gracias* from me. Dion gives me another belated birthday present, a charcoal drawing of his new home in America, transforming this wasteland of cable and concrete and steelwork into a cool Eden …

***

… Unlike this stifling sauna where I soak and ache. The beautiful Mexican man props his green-booted feet on the edge of the tub and pops the last bite of a piece of frosted pastry into his mouth. He reads a superhero comic, and without taking his eyes off the blast of colors, pulls out a yo-yo from his pocket, throws it down, snaps it up, repeats. Who is this man-child who notices I am awake, who removes a patch and daubs salve on the gash on my cheek?

Why is everything so thick? My eye, my lips and tongue and throat and every bone in my body seem to have doubled in size. Like green-violet plums, odd tattoos color my arms and grow larger, rather pretty but painful. I would lament, but am voiceless. If I could drink the mist—Is that a ticking hump? The hands on the camel clock have barely moved, yet the void seems to spin such a myriad of scenes …

***

… I'm in my office, and Becker talks to me about a heads up he's received from Mr. Charlie, officer of the Immigration and Naturalization Service. He takes off his glasses, rubs his eyes, says that it seems good ol' Charlie is going to bust our hotel for illegal aliens, and unless we cooperate, he'll close us down. I ask Becker if he hasn't been giving good ol' Charlie enough comp rooms to our sister resorts. He rubs his eyes again, tells me to do my job; he'll do his. *Charlie just wants a couple names,* says Becker, *so he can tell his bosses that he's doing his job, and so are we. We wouldn't want to break any laws, now would we? And you don't want us all, including your little spic families, to lose our jobs, do you? I didn't think so. Heard you had a good time at some picnic, a very good time.*

American Queer

I say nothing.

Look Gottisaul, do your damn audit—bound to be plenty invaders to choose from—then give Charlie three names, and everyone's happy.

Except those three, I say. And the ones who love them.

During this exchange, my office door is open. Juan gripes about an insurance problem to my assistant, who wraps a curl around her finger, so he hears Becker and me and leaves quickly. Following Becker out of my office, I tell him he just guaranteed that word will get out fast, and absenteeism will skyrocket until this INS travesty blows over. Becker the Pecker grunts, and I do my job.

I call the INS and give them 30 ID numbers. To my surprise, only four employees work illegally. Two housekeepers, Juan, and his brother. I leave my report with only three names in Benny Ann's office, then search for Dion to warn him. He's working the graveyard shift. I'd call his home, but he doesn't have a phone.

The security man on duty says Juan left in a hurry, *una emergencia*, so Dion stayed to finish his brother's shift. I must find Dion. I walk the cavernous bowels of the hotel—at night a dark and quiet, creepy maze. I stop and listen for the echo of footsteps I imagine behind me.

Gratefully, I find Dion closing down the swimming pool. Only the underwater lights remain lit, quivering reflections licking everything. Seeing me, Dion grins. He's not talked to Juan. I tell him I have something important to discuss, but he starts talking about the barbecue and how his mamá and Fobby love me, and he won't let me get a word in edgewise. He grabs my arms, wants me, doesn't care about Inez or anybody. I tell him to stop, to listen to me, try to break free, trip over myself, and fall into a silent green and chlorine sea …

***

… A hot cascade roars from the faucet roiling the water in the white porcelain pool, its turbid haze swirling upward, agitating the sediment in my mind. I panic. The beautiful Mexican man is gone. The mummy sits in his place, points her birded cane, and chews, "Agua caliente para tu el baño del

　　　　　　　　　　　　　American Queer

olvido." In my bath of forgetfulness, the camel hump reminds
me the hour remains little changed. How can this be? Oblivion
means feeling nothing, but I feel keenly.

I whisper. "Dónde está Dionisio?"

"En la cocina, Señor," says another voice, the beetle
with her hand on the faucet, "la cocina." I try to look back at the
kitchen, but it's impossible. The plump, black beetle looks at me
intently, asks me a question. I barely nod, "Si, Señora, estoy
enamorado de tu hijo." That I love her son does not betray the
mother's face. She says, "Entonces Dios debe encontrar una
manera. Yo no puedo."

"And if God cannot find a way," I vow, "We will find
our own."

With a toothless cackle and "Si, si, si!" the mummy
thumps her cane, the blue boil on her finger shimmering afire.
Somehow, she understands my blasphemous defiance and raises
her leathery fist to heaven. "Tu es el hombre con corazón Cristi!"
And I wonder who has the sharper beak, the falcon-headed cane
or this wizened woman who strokes her daughter's arm.

Chilled and trembling, I slide underwater into a hot
world …

***

… The bubble of silence bursts as Dion jumps in after
me. Four arms flail as we grapple in the pool, Dion grabbing me
about the neck, tugging us both to safety. I gasp for breath, break
his grip. We stand up coughing and sputtering in four feet of
water, stop for a second, burst out laughing, then embrace each
other forehead to forehead. I wonder, *What the hell am I doing*?
and labor toward the edge of the pool. Dion lunges, turns me
around, and kisses me, cutting short my protests and kissing me
again. He coils his arms and legs around me. I push him away,
and he falls back splashing in the water, thinking I'm playing. I
struggle to drag my soggy body out of the pool, and from the
side, shout, *What's the matter with you? Someone might see us.
Do you want us to lose our jobs!?* But Dion doesn't care. He
slaps the water, scoops and sprays me, throws up his arms and
yells ecstatically *Te amo mi Señor Beektrrr! Te amo!* I bark at
him, *Never say that to me again. Ever!*

                                           American Queer

Dion winces, the punch of my words knocking the breath out of him. I stand in a puddle and wish never to see that crestfallen expression again, wish neither of us had to keep our wits about us. Dion swims to the edge, says he has another uniform in his locker—he'll wear his street clothes—and shrugs off my touch. After we get dry clothes, we sneak into the steam room. It's locked for the night and Dion has the key. Someone might see us in the men's locker room.

The red light of fake coals casts a glow over our dripping, steaming bodies. I take off my shoes, socks, and pants. My soaked polo shirt gets stuck on my head, and I ask Dion for help, but instead feel a tongue lapping my chest and teeth nibbling my nipple. I squirm and tell him to stop, but tongue and teeth travel the bridge across my sternum to my other nipple. I back away, but Dion holds me around my waist, and I bat him with my bound arms. The tongue finds an armpit, and through muffled dark, I moan and curse as teeth return and pull the tiny hairs on my chest. I retreat, sit down hard on a hot redwood bench that bites my butt. I am pressed down firmly on fluffy white towels that cushion my back. I kick and buck, but Dion forces one of my legs over the bench, my arms over my head, and I lie splayed before this beautiful Mexican man I cannot see. Eucalyptus, sweat, boiling air singe my nostrils. He slides my underwear down my legs, off my body. I feel trapped, and I can't help but surge, and I don't care how this man knows what to do so expertly, only that he does it to me, and I surrender.

My shirt comes up over my head, leaving my arms bound. Standing naked and glowing from the red cast of the fake coals, a smiling, lovely devil looks down upon me, straddles the bench, leans low like he's about to ride a motorbike fast in a high wind. I beg him to let me up, barely hear *Shhhh*, then he stifles my protests with his lips and tongue, his eyelashes delicately brushing my tainted cheek. *Butterfly kisses*, I whisper. Dion looks at me quizzically. I translate, *Los besos de la mariposa.* He caresses my face, my raspberry sear, and into my ear murmurs, *Beso de Cristos*, kisses my sear and murmurs, *Beso de Dionisio. Ahhh, eres way cool. Te amo Señor Beektrrr, te amo tu.* I strain my neck up to kiss him like a butterfly, a butterfly straining to emerge from its binding, hot, and humid cocoon, and I whisper to his eyes, *Te amo también, Dionisio de las Flores, te amo tu.*

Dion looks to heaven, back to me, and we kiss deeply. He wraps my legs around his waist, pushes my thighs back, aims and enters me, and I hiss and tightly shut my eyes, and deeper and deeper, the beautiful Mexican man begins his rhythm, holds on to my hard horn like on a saddle, rides me with an easy gait, mounting to a gallop, and before long, we are bucking; he's pumping me; I beg him to let go, afraid to let go until it's too late and our animal groans of peaking ecstasy become one voice howled into the dark red void. Though burned to my marrow, to the essence of my being, I shiver. I open my eyes to see the man in and above me in the throes of rapture.

It is quite a carnal sight to behold.

Dion pulls my polo off my arms, and my hands grab his hips and pull him in deeper. His smile conveys contentment, an understanding of giving and receiving, his steady, sweet breath reminding me of what I had forgotten. He kisses me softly and lies on me with his full weight. Peculiar, how in his arms after our passion, I feel blessed by Brian. There is no time but this time, no place but this place. We are in a cloudy heaven, a sweltering hell. It is all we desire and all we need.

Until the outside world violates us.

Someone follows a trail of watery footprints from a locker room to this steamy, pungent room. I see a grinning hole and a glint of gold peek through a small square window. What the face cannot see clearly, it imagines, and disappears.

I freeze and incite Dion, tell him that we've got to go now, that he must get back to work before he's missed! But he's lethargic, playful, and I squirm beneath his heaviness to get dressed, get out. And getting dressed, Dion mentions that his brother is meeting him at his break; he didn't say why, only that it's urgent. Dion pulls me back down—He's aroused again already—asks me what I wanted to talk about, and I know I should answer, but I ignore the question because all I can think of is sneaking out of this stifling hothouse as quickly as possible.

As I get in my S.U.V. The sky booms and trembles in the distance, dazzled by lightning hiding in massive pillows of cloud …

                                   American Queer

***

… I twitch awake, wrench from the pain, sink back. The crackle of paper has startled me; the artist has turned a page of his pad, but he drops it and attends to my needs.

Will the air never cool? Such heat, I expect a tropical cloudburst any moment, and remember my beautiful demolished S.U.V. I am in it; it's a piñata and hangs from the tallest of three trees. I want to cry out, but my throat hurts, and it's difficult to swallow, to keep my eyes open, as another curtain rises, revealing another reality. From behind the brightly colored sheet, I hear a little girl sob …

***

… When I pull into my driveway and exit my S.U.V., the rainstorm soaks me before I reach my house. A small blue bird is nailed to the front door.

I sit in the dark and listen to the river falling from the sky. Wrapping my arms around myself, I wrap Dion around me, for I still swim in his clothes that are too big for me. I smell his cleanness and freshness but feel dirty and contaminated from my cowardice.

The phone rings; I jolt—Becker calling from the hotel. I hear him take off his glasses and rub his eyes. He's looked at my report with the three names. He tells me, *Good job, but you listed the wrong Flores. It's Dionisio, not Juan, who's the illegal parasite in our country. An understandable mistake given the video of the pool I've just seen, but a grave mistake given the liability for the hotel. Luckily, we have a conscientious security officer, an eyewitness to a lot more. Don't worry about the hotel and good ol' Charlie. I'll take care of him. By the way,* Benny Ann sneers, *You're fired.* I don't replace the receiver until an incessant beeping startles me.

Headlights lurch through my living room window as a car bounces to a halt on my front lawn. To the beating on the front door, I let in a burst of storm and a drenched and furious Dionisio.

He pushes me back onto my couch shouting, *Traidor! Traidor!* I can't understand every word of his rapid tirade but the gist is clear. After I fled the hotel, Juan found his brother and

          American Queer

told him I had given Immigration Dion's name, but Dion denied I would do such a thing, defending the honor of the one he loves. The one he loves! Juan called him *marrecón!*, rushed and punched Dion yelling that the baby Inez carries is not Dion's but his—How could a *marrecón* ever make a baby!—that she hates Dion and loves him, Juan, *Un macho hombre!* They are to be married because now Dion must leave America and go back to the poverty of his village in Mexico. If their papá was alive, he would die of shame!

Dionisio de las Flores agrees, hates me, pounds his head, hates himself. He raises his fist, and I cringe. He throws a tennis trophy, shattering mementoes, then rushes out the front door. I catch my breath, then pick up the torn paper of a framed verse in calligraphy—

> *The light of the body is the eye; if*
> *therefore thine eye be single, thy*
> *whole body shall be full of light.*
>   *Love, Brian*

His portrait is shattered, and I think the dead should not smile so happily, but putrefy like the corpses they portray. *If thine eye be single* … Enough. No time for this; I must retrieve my honor—funny, I never knew I had any to lose—and run outside.

Dion is trying to start his car, and through the loud rain and his open window, I swear I'm not a traitor, beg him to stay, to talk, to listen, but the ignition catches fire, and he grinds the gears and guns the engine of his old DeSoto, screeching away, its taillights like red rockets, swerving down the road and disappearing.

I tear off in my S.U.V., the stuffed chihuahua and dead dandelions chiding me as they roll off the dashboard. I lose Dion and my way to his home, but the dark deluge does not deter me, and when I finally find the shack and park next to a truck, the lightning makes the humble house look like the one from Kansas that fell on a witch.

A faint light shines in the front door window. I run up the stairs—*DION!*— and through a white lace curtain, I see shadows move. I knock but no one answers. *DION!* I pound the screen door frantically. This is madness! *What am I doing*, I say, but I know exactly what I'm doing for the first time in a long time.

A face appears, obscured by the curtain, and cautiously, a long, thin hand with long, red nails pulls it aside. The Intended stares at me, and I see Juan disappear into the kitchen, but no sign of La Doña, the mamá or niñita, and no Dionisio de las Flores.

Dion, por favor! I shout.

The Intended takes her time to reply. *Dionisio is not home*, she says with a trace of victory through the window.

I am surprised she speaks English, as if expecting only indigenous incantations to leave those thin red lips. *Where is he?* I demand.

Up to the challenge, the witch opens the door, folds her arms, leans against the framed screen. And smiles. *He leaves, back to Mexico.*

No! When? I must see him. I try to open the screen door, but it's latched, and catlike the Intended quickly steps back.

He does not want to see you. You betray his brother. You betray him. He hates your America. He hates you!

No!

Yes! But he will come back to me. Only I can give him what you can never give him.

A child?

Yes.

It's not his.

Liar.

Juan told him.

He lies.

He knows.

The Intended stares, quickly explodes, screaming a torrent of ancient sounds, her black hair flying madly, her arms whipping wildly. Then, as quickly, she freezes. Pressing her face against the screen, her eyes slits of black, she snarls, *You betray me. And now I have no husband, only this fatness that I hate.* The Intended strikes her stomach. *And you, you that I hate most. You*

                                        American Queer

possess my husband. Marrecón. Marrecón, marrecón, go to hell!
May the devil take your soul and God never give it back to you!

Yes, very good English. The front door slams shut, the white lace curtain swishing from the impact.

The rain dwindles to a soft pelting. I slide down and clasp my knees. *Dion. Where are you? Where is everybody?* I look up across the barren yard; a shadow stands beneath the shortest tree. *Dion? DION!*

I jump up and leap down the steps but stumble as headlights blind me. Silhouettes appear in front of me, and I dash to my S.U.V., but the black ghosts are upon me. I flail and kick, but they grab me, rip off my shirt, hoist my legs up, pull off my shoes, easily yank off Dion's oversized pants. I am naked before them as they hold my arms.

One of the shadows, short and pudgy, jelly jowled, struts up to leer in my face, in a flash of lightning, gold sparks flash from its ghastly grin. With the heel of a boot, it stomps my foot and grinds, and I lurch back, but a punch to my stomach knocks the wind out of me, and I fall forward, jerk my knee up hard and swift into the groin of the witch's minion who grunts, but it's not long until my head is wrenched back by my hair, and a fist smashes my face again and again and again.

Hands hold my head in a vice. The honcho stands on his toes to lick and kiss my cheek sloppily. He whispers something I don't understand, but the *cholos* nearest him chuckle, and he struts back to show off to his gang, laughs, fields comments from his audience. After the sniggering ceases, he leaps upon me and whoosh! Out comes a blade, crescent and serrated, run by my eye to make sure I see it. He grabs my groin and squeezes until I cry out, and in a single swipe, flays the flesh of my purple-red mark. I scream; someone gets a heavy stick, calls me *piñata marrecón*, and they throw me to the ground, take turns beating the candy out of me, kicking and stomping me with their pointy-toed shit-kickers.

They stop. I hear a few giggles, many *marrecóns*, the clicks and slithers of vulgarities like the rubbings of night insects. Globs of spit land upon me. Attentions shift as stick to metal, rock to glass, I hear my S.U.V. destroyed. The pudgy shadow swaggers away; the crackle of boots on gravel recedes; a roaring truck spews dirt in my face. And in the absence of headlights, unfathomable black surrounds me.

It's quiet, the thunder a distant, low rumbling. My chest hurts, and I can't breathe through my nose; it feels thick and sticky. My mouth seems to have shrunk though my lips bulge. I am covered in mud and blood. Leadenly, I turn over, and my hand feels a piece of wet meat. I brush it off, get up, and take the slice of my cheek thinking maybe someone can sew it back onto my face. I limp a few feet, collapse, and crawl up the steps.

A drape of burnt orange light covers me. The screen door squeaks open, slaps shut, footfalls come nearer, and red spiked heels step on the rotted wood. Flee, run, fly! I roll on my back but can move no further. With my single eye, I see a taloned hand reach into a purse hanging by a hip and take out a knife. The figure advances, holds on to the wobbly railing, places one foot on a lower step, and raises its other spiked heel to hover above my open eye. The witch bends down, cocks her head, curious, taking aim. When I breathe, a clamp of nails punctures my heart. I surrender and wait for the blinding stab.

But there is a scuffle above me. I hear grunts and groans, a masculine cry, cracks of splintered wood, a feminine cry, a thud. The disturbed glass chimes clang loudly, subsiding to a gentle tinkle. My teeth hurt, and I taste a salty syrup as a hand goes under my neck.

She said you'd gone. She said—She said you hate me. The voice attached to the hand hushes me. *She wanted to hurt me. You—You should have let her. What am I saying? I do hurt.*

Silencio, silencio. I could not let her hurt the one I love.

I maneuver just enough to clutch his knees. *Por favor, perdóname, perdóname.*

No, no, it is for you to forgive me.

I can't stop shaking.

The beautiful Mexican man covers my nakedness, wrapping me in a soft, warm blanket and his big, strong arms. He holds me tighter, strokes my head in his lap, and though it hurts me, I endure. *Come inside,* he says to me, *come into my fire.*

I've been in his home before, and once, his fire has come in me. I weigh the difference between house and home, between

    American Queer

the consummation of a physical act and being consumed, between lost alone and lost within another, and I am frightened of this fire I feel so keenly. *¿Su fuego es mi fuego?*

Si, si, Señor Beektrrr. Somos uno.

In this moment, the fire of our unity burns blue bright, and I do not question its speed.

The old floorboards creak from quick, light steps. A handkerchief gently wipes the blood from my mouth and chin, and a small tender hand touches my stain that can never be wiped away. I squeal and scare her, for she and the beautiful Mexican man discover it's no longer there. I had it a moment ago, in my hand. Can it be sewn back on? Or maybe grow back? Silly to wonder, but I do …

***

… And I wonder if, finally, I am here, if I have caught up with the camel clock, that we tick together. The last act ends, the curtain descends, the stage in my mind disassembles and disappears, and my performance melts into the now.

The mud and blood have been washed away. The beautiful Mexican man kisses my forehead, his mustache soft as mink. He wipes my brow with a velvety, tan sponge and places a cool cloth on my forehead. When he helps me sip cool water, I notice a gummy red thread on his cheek.

"You're hurt."

"Nada."

"The Intended?"

"I hit her. With her knife she cuts me. I push and she falls, then runs."

"The baby?"

"It is not mine."

"She might lose it. Or kill it."

"Mañana, Senior Beektrrr, mañana."

"Su hermano?"

"No sé. Policía —"

"You must run."

"I cannot. When my mamá and my sister and me, we cross the river, I lose them. I hear cries; I run. A man holds them; they kick and scream. I do not think; I hit him. He does not get up. Tonight, I take us to the cathedral, and to a priest I tell my sin."

It is my turn to soothe. "Shhhh." Yesterday, I would have said much more, but I cannot judge. We all have our own private closets.

"I run no more. I must pay for my sin."

"With what coin? How, when? I shall go with you."

The beautiful Mexican man protests, but I drag an arm from the bottom of this sea of grapefruit, of *toronja*, and place fingers on his lips. He lightly holds my hand, and with my other one, I grab the ripped collar of a plaid shirt with pearled buttons, gaze into the essence of wine and flowers, pull it close to me, forehead to forehead. "Nothing, no one, can ever come between us. Never. Somos uno."

Uneven stepping precedes the punch of a cane and a voice chewy and adamant. "El hombre necesita médico."

"Thirsty," I rasp, and my love helps me sip more of the blue ice.

The two talk and leave the room.

Alone.

I pull the artist's tablet toward me and turn the pages, viewing various angles and poses of a face mangled and grotesque. I pull the pad into the tub and drown the charcoal monster until its gray contoured lines and black blended streaks blur and float off the page.

With the skin of a prune, like a man on a moon in a hot Sea of Torpidity, I dissolve in a solution of *agua caliente y aciete de toronja* for a bizarre absolution. Too late to toss a message in a bottle. Or perhaps, I have drunk from one picked up on the moon's airless beach and swallowed a worm.

From one eye, I finally cry for the dead young man in tennis togs who smiles so whitely in a picture buried in a drawer somewhere. And from the small window before me, the sun begins to highlight the camel's hump, signaling the end of something. Or its beginning.

Deconstructed, I begin to build a new foundation. Between the plops of water drops from the faucet, eternity passes. Yellow roses bloom with fresh petals. The candlelight flickers, swaying and reaching up, yearning to escape—to what?

　　　　　　　　　　　　　　American Queer

And in this ceiling-less room, through the vapor, the Virgin aglow—Was she always clutching her breast?—melds her chip and crack. Together with the Man on the crucifix—was he always so untroubled looking down upon me?—they rise up and dissolve in the swirling white.

I close the eye I can close—*if thine eye be single*—and for the life of me, I cannot remember my dead lover's name. I cannot remember the people whose presence I know is nearby. I cannot remember my mother, my father. I cannot remember my livelihood, my home, my heritage, my country. I cannot remember my name. And fearlessly, pacifically, I cannot remember my face nor my body.

I am all lovers, all creation, all names, faces, and bodies. I am the seed and the completion. I am everchangingly changeless, seamless, specific, and boundless. I am the center. I am the circumference. Sublimely null inside, I smile the smile of the All. If this is oblivion, I welcome it, as I, too, rise up and dissolve in the swirling white of this hot and oily ocean that smells of grapefruit …

Lady in the Hatbox

John Preston Erotic Writing Award,
Preston Memorial Conference,
Brown University, Providence, RI, 1995
originally published
Labonté, Richard, ed. *Best Gay Erotica 1997*. Cleis Press,
Pittsburgh. 1997.

FLESH AND THE WORD

WINNERS OF THE JOHN PRESTON EROTIC WRITING PRIZE

Rick Kitzman
Denver, Colorado
"The Lady in the Hat Box"

The John Preston Erotic Writing Prize was sponsored by: icbb, On Our Backs and Masquerade Books. The judges for the prize were: Bayla Travis, Michael Lassell, Pat Califia and Steven Saylor.

Lady in the Hatbox

1995

So you're hot and tired and bored and alone, and you climb out of your bedroom window onto the steel fire escape in the alley. Crouching, you can see into your neighbor's apartment. Red neon from the street flashes *Terminal Bar* and bathes the two occupants pink and the shadows maroon and the blue lava lamp purple.

Despite the heat, the one named Bear wears unbuttoned dress pants, a trench coat—its belt hanging on the sides of his waist like two limp snakes—no shirt, no socks, no shoes. You can see his furry chest, and his left nipple winks like a little pink twinkle light because it's pierced with a gold ring. His feet are large with long toes and clean clipped nails. Bear's head, capped with thick black hair, tops a thick neck. His glasses slide halfway down his flat sweaty nose and perch over lips thin as two threads. His unshaven cheeks look like he's smeared coffee grinds, espresso, on his face. He's butch and beefy and you squirm a little, but quietly.

The other occupant, Hubert, wears sweatpants and baggy white socks and a tank tee printed with *Psst, JESUS IS COMING, look busy* in bold, gothic letters. A tiny cross dangles from his right ear. He is slight of build and covered with pale, unblemished skin. His straight, long and light-brown hair—even in this heat—wafts when he moves, and you see finer hair yet hanging from his armpits when his lithe limbs reach for things. He's a bit of a femme fatale, pretty as a Botticelli, and you ache not a little at such a sight of beauty.

Hubert irons a cowboy shirt with teal piping and pearl buttons by the light of a yellow pole lamp. It illuminates a poster of a death child dressed all in black with a studded and tattooed face who looks over Hubert's shoulder and proclaims: *No-Time! After Generation X, Generation Why?* She stares down at Bear, who slouches at a small table, works a crossword puzzle—and coughs. A hatbox sits in front of him. Hubert can look down on it and frequently does. It's frilly and lacy and light blue, then lavender, then light blue again, over and over except for the bottom, which seems to be stained. That part … well that part—when the outside red neon flashes—turns redder.

You can see the two men clear as the living day, but it's the dead of night, and oddly, they can't see you. Except for occasional traffic, the alley is quiet, and with their window open you can hear them perfectly. It's an acoustic and visual miracle. Thank heaven something is. You know it would have to be a miracle if you can see clean clipped toenails.

Bear coughs again: dry, deep, raw. Hubert tells him he's sick. Bear chuckles and comments how he, Hubert, doesn't know how sick, but he, Bear, doesn't call him Hubert. He calls him Hubbie. And Hubert, or Hubbie, corrects him and says his name is Hubert, not Hubbie.

"For the love of Mike, shut up" says Bear.

"No you shut up."

"No you shut up."

"No you shut up!" yells Hubert, and then he exclaims "Infinity!" in triumph, short lived, because Bear barks back "No, you shut up, Infinity *PLUS* one!" He adds a "ha!" And that's that.

Bear sucks on a pencil, green, and without looking up asks Hubert for an eight-letter word meaning sudden grasp of reality, simple and striking.

Hubert looks up slowly from the cowboy shirt he irons, stares long and hard at Bear, scrunches his face, and replies with a sigh "hmm, epiphany."

"Epiphany. E-p-i-f-u-n-n-y" spells Bear. "Right?"

"Riiiight."

"Just fits" Bear adds, to which Hubert, again staring long and hard at Bear, asks "How did a guy like you get to be a guy like you?" to which Bear replies "Just the luck of the DNA draw I guess."

Hubert shuts off the iron, hangs up the cowboy shirt, and turns toward the sink, strands of his hair brushed by the move. He picks a pomegranate from a silver bowl and a nearby knife, slicing and folding back its flesh like red leather, sucking out the

    American Queer

hard red seeds like little rubies. He puts the knife back in the sink, red drops dribbling down his chin. You see him do this, and you wonder how you can see red drops dribbling down his chin, but then you remember this is an acoustic and visual miracle, thank you very much.

Hubert points to the pale blue/lavender hatbox and says "It's leaking" to which Bear grumbles "Oh for the love of Mike." Hubert says how beef-brained Bear is and that he should have used more plastic so the blood wouldn't leak. At least that's what you think he said, you're not sure, but it would explain why the bottom of the light blue hatbox turns redder when the outside red neon flashes.

Hubert walks over to the table where Bear is concentrating on his crossword puzzle and asks Bear "Who's Mike?"

Bear responds "Mike who?"

"The Mike you always want the love of" says Hubert.

Bear looks up at Hubert and calls him "A pip, pal, you're a real pip, you know that?"

But what Hubert still wants to know is "Who's Mike?"

Bear claims that "It's nobody, just an expression."

Hubert tears the pomegranate's red flesh and sucks out more hard red seeds and asks "Wasn't that your daddy's name?" to which Bear stands up fast, throws down the pencil, green, leans forward, points at Hubert, and growls through clenched teeth—you know, like he's practicing ventriloquism—"Don't push it."

Hubert smiles and goes back to the sink. He washes his hands and dries them on paper towel. He walks back to the table—Bear still stands— lifts off the lid of the pale blue/lavender hatbox and lifts a tiara, but it's stuck in some hair, so he disentangles it, then pulls it out. In the weird light, the tiara sparkles and turns from dazzling diamonds to radiant rubies, diamonds to rubies, diamonds to rubies, you know, like pomegranate seeds. Hubert puts the tiara on top of his long and light-brown hair and tells Bear to "Look at me, I'm a Gabor sister." And with his clear complexion and full lips, he wouldn't need much rouge or lipstick to look like someone's sister.

Bear says "Don't do that."

Hubert says "Relax, she doesn't need it anymore."

Bear says "What's the matter with you? Show the lady a little respect."

Hubert says "You're right, you're absolutely right. I lost my head."

And then Bear says "Are you trying to be funny? Although, truth be told, you do look like she did."

And Hubert comes back with "Yes, it takes balls to be a drag queen."

Bear furrows his face and says "Dr. Godit is waiting for both pieces of merchandise, delivered on time and in prime condition. If we don't, we're lion's meat, not to mention we don't get paid, and I for one want to get paid so I can get out of this rat hole"—which you take offense to because you live here too, right next door as a matter of fact, and choose not to think of your hole as a rat hole, a mouse hole maybe—"So put the damn thing back in the box" and this Bear screams: "*AND PUT THE LID ON!*"

Hubert doesn't flinch. Hubert doesn't blink. Hubert merely sighs "Put *ON* the lid" and Bear shakes his head and says "What?" Hubert replies that "You should never end a sentence with a preposition; say put *ON* the lid, not put the lid *ON*." Bear is clearly looking at Hubert like he's speaking Portuguese and spits out "What are you talking about Hubbie" to which Hubert/Hubbie spits back "My name is Hubert, not Hubbie." But Bear only grins and sings "Riiiight." Hubert says it's guys like Bear with his ungrammatical sentence structure and trigger-happy temper who give thugs a bad name.

"Like this?" asks Bear, grinning and whipping out a gun from his trench coat.

This time, Hubert flinches. He blinks too. And he sighs "Yeah, something like that."

Bear's gun is big, thick, a dull gun-metal gray with a rounded and grooved blunt-nosed barrel. His hand that holds it trembles.

"You should lay off the espresso," says Hubert. "It'll kill you, Sugar Bear."

"Don't call me that" says Bear, motioning with the gun. "I've gone over to decaf; what more do you want—*Hubbie*?"

    American Queer

"For you to put that gun down" answers Hubert.

Bear continues grinning—he really does have the most extraordinarily white and beautiful teeth, teeth that blink pink—and asks "Don't you mean put *DOWN* that gun?"

So Hubert repeats his request for Bear to put *DOWN* the gun, but Bear, through his Cheshire smile, whispers something which is the first time during this acoustic and visual miracle you have not been able to hear what was said. But you're not the only one because Hubert asks in a tone of incredulity "What?" so maybe he did hear Bear but couldn't believe what he had heard. Bear repeats himself for Hubert. And this time you hear it too.

"Strip."

This situation is rollercoastering to an out of hand land, but you can't get off, can't move because you'd be discovered, and Bear has a gun, and he probably knows how to use it, and you prefer your life, such as it is, even in your meager mouse hole. And also you can't move because, well, because you don't want to move, so you stay crouched and quiet.

"Strip" repeats Bear.

Hubert asks him if he's crazy, and Bear replies that he is "crazy, yeah man crazy, so … *strip*." The command zips out of Bear's mouth like he's blowing a poison dart through a tiny pole of bamboo. Then he adds "as in" and then he sings "77" and then he snaps his fingers twice—*snap! snap!*—and sings "Sunset *STRIP!*" Hubert asks him if this is his imitation of Kookie, and Bear hisses "Yessss, yes it is, wanna borrow my comb?" Hubert says "If I have to strip, combing my hair would be an effort in futility because it will muss." Bear blurts "Ha! Poor baby's hair gets mussed, but it won't matter; nothing will matter in the end." And as a clever afterthought, he adds "Except your sweet end, soooooooo sssstrip."

"No" says Hubert quietly, calmly, blandly "and stop waving that gun like John Wayne; what will the neighbors think?" But you, being a neighbor, think Bear's waving that gun more like Travis Bickle than John Wayne. Bear shouts "Stop telling me what to do and *STRIP!* Or so help me I'll hold real still and shoot you between your eyes!" And he is holding out his arm real still, almost touching Hubert's forehead. And you stiffen with the hope that Bear doesn't fire and blast a Hindu-like blood spot between those lovely eyes. Oh yes, even from where you crouch, you can see Hubert has lovely eyes.

Whose slender, delicate hands rise slowly and grasp the diamond/ruby tiara, and he removes it as though he's passing on the crown, which he is because he sets it on the lady in the hatbox. A few stones of the top of the tiara peek out of the pale blue/lavender hatbox. And you can see Hubert's hands carefully take the bottom of his tank tee—*Psst, JESUS IS COMING, look busy*—slowly bringing it up over his screwhead navel and his flat, satiny stomach, and then up a little further exposing his rosy puce nipple buds—the left one pierced with a gold ring just like Bear, which makes you wonder if they exchanged vows, which makes you chortle inside—and then finally lifting it up over his head revealing the light brown soft down of his armpits. He completes pulling the tank tee over his head, and his long and light-brown hair is mussed for a second, but Hubert shakes his head and it all falls back into place.

And then you sneeze—and freeze.

In the same second, Bear whips round and whispers "What was that?" You can see the sweat beaded on his forehead and glittering his hairy heaving chest and you pray you blend into the maroon gloom and he doesn't see you.

But no worry, as Bear is distracted when Hubert takes his chance and knocks away Bear's hand and Hubert flies away—but the gun doesn't—away to the tiny kitchenette (it's not far) to reach the sink. Bear curses Hubert, lunges after him, his glasses falling from his face. Trying to get round the table, he knocks it, spills the silver bowl of fruit, rocks the pale blue/lavender hatbox with the red/redder stain and the crossword and the green pencil and the ironing table, and the iron it props up drops with a thud and the lamp cord rips from its socket and all is plunged into blinking red *Terminal Bar* shade.

Like watching a flickering silent film with strobe lights, you see just before Hubert reaches the sink Bear grabs him by his long and light-brown hair and pulls him back from the sink. Hubert cries out, and his head snaps back, and Bear wheels him around, and face to face they dance a *danse macabre* like some spastic Charleston, trampling the cowboy shirt with teal piping and pearl buttons.

          American Queer

The red neon light stops flashing. It must be very, very late.

In the tumble, the refrigerator door swings open and slams against the stove, and its bright and white light electrifies the scrambling scene full of grunts and groans and trench coat shadows and flashes of flesh. And you wish you had a spotlight to see better (the acoustic and visual miracle does have its limitations). But you don't, so you unfreeze and climb in through the window and kneel close to a wall; you're so close you could be another layer of paint. You can see the back of Bear's trench coat and his thick neck and black locks and the dull glint of gun metal gray again pressed against Hubert's temple. In the fridge's bare bulb glare, you can see Hubert's terrified face and his strained eyes from trying to see the gun and from gazing into the face of Bear only inches away. You can feel the cool air of the open fridge float your way, and as it hits the hot air, a steamy mist softens the arctic-white light.

"Now what?" asks Bear, breathing heavily.

"You—had pizza for lunch" says Hubert.

But Bear is not amused and yanks on the long and light-brown hair he squeezes, and Hubert yelps as his head snaps back again. Bear binds Hubert with one arm and with the other, never loses his grasp of the gun (nor of the situation) and leans on him hard against the kitchen counter.

"Sweet Baby Bear, don't" pleads Hubert.

"Stop calling me that" says Bear, and Bear is a raging bear and calls Hubert names and says how he's "gonna teach *Hubbie* a lesson."

"What are you going to do?"

"You should know what I'm going to do."

"I don't know Bear, I don't know, I've, I've got an idea" —Hubert winces—"it's just an idea, mind you but still, you'd have to be crazy." Bear says "Crazy—you think I'm crazy" and he jerks, and Hubert cries out "Ah!" and Bear starts chanting "crazy crazy crazy" and making soft, weird noises, ape noises and grunts, but he's so soft and yet so menacing as he rubs the gun on Hubert's temple, in Hubert's ear, parting Hubert's beautiful lips, tapping Hubert's teeth. Then Bear whispers for Hubert to "be very quiet, be *vewy* quiet, it's *wabbit* season." He snorts a laugh and then yanks at Hubert's sweatpants, which makes Hubert emit another scared "Ah!"

"Baby don't, you're hurting Hubbie."

But again Bear tugs hard, and again Hubert cries "Ah!" and Bear sneers "I thought your name was Hubert."

"Yes, yes" agrees Hubert, "lost my head again."

"Metaphorically speaking" says Bear.

"Well, yes" says Hubert "not, you know—"

"Shut up" says Bear.

"There you go again, ending your sentence with a prep—"

"And I'm going to end something else right now." Bear demands Hubert turn around, but he can't turn around, so Bear eases up leaning on him, then Hubert can turn around, and he does turn around, dropping his arms in the sink—the sink, where a sharp and silvery opportunity awaits—and after Hubert sighs relief, Bear says "Ain't it amazing how everything is so … so relative?" and asks "Is Hubbie comfortable?"

Hubert begs Bear not to do it like this, says "Let's go lay down." Bear snaps "lay *DOWN*?" and Hubert tries to grab back his grammatical *faux pas* and says "Or is it lie down, never can remember." Bear tells him to "Watch your prepositions, buster." Hubert shouts "*GOD!* Get it over with, get it over *WITH!*" and Bear pauses and chuckles and sings "Oooohhhhkaaaayyyy."

With the gun in one hand, Bear's other hand gropes the mid-section of his body, and all you can hear is the rustle of his trench coat, and all you can see is the maneuvering of his arm as Hubert's sweatpants disappear ever further down his smooth and hairless hips and thighs, and Bear's pants fall about his lovely, long-toed feet. Hubert cries out again because with his free hand Bear has found something of his own and has thrust his pelvis forward.

"Wait" stops Hubert, and Bear wonders out loud "What now" and Hubert implores him to use some lubricant, and Bear rephrases "lubri*CUNT?*" Again he jabs Hubert who again beseeches Bear for "anything anything." Bear says "for the love of—" and breaks off and adds "such a delicate thing." And Hubert agrees "Yes yes, delicate delicate." Bear threatens Hubert not to think about going anywhere, not to think period, and

   American Queer

Hubert agrees with "No thinking no thinking, do just do." And he droops his head.

Bear turns and leans back and rummages through the refrigerator, knocking over ketchup and pickles and blue cheese dressing—the gun still dents Hubert's cheek. And while Bear rummages, Hubert fumbles in the sink and holds up the knife that you see flash in the fridge light. He grasps it tightly, lowering it and his hands back into the sink.

Bear pulls out a banana and declares "Don't need that" and he pulls out a sausage and says "Don't need that" then a tube of biscuits and declares "We have got to go grocery shopping. Aha!" discovers Bear. It sounds and looks like he's opening a jar. Then he pulls out a glob of something and puts it up to Hubert's mouth and whispers in Hubert's ear to "Taste it … go on … llllick it."

Hubert does. He says "Raspberry."

"Razz for your azz baby" says Bear who hoots a couple of ha-has and echoes, "Razz for your azz. Pretty funny huh, pretty baby."

Hubert agrees with the "hysterically humorous quality" of Bear's wisecrack about his crack and urges Bear to "just get on with it."

Bear yells "Don't tell me what to do; don't you *EVER* tell me what to do!" And while he repeats this so very loudly in Hubert's ear, Hubert is crying. "Sorry sorry so sorry" but Bear misses the soft sobbing apology. He thrusts his hips forward and reminds Hubert to "Remember it's *cocked. Cocked*, get it?"

"Yeah Bear" says Hubert "I get it" and Bear nudges Hubert's cheek with the gun, adding "cocked and ready to go off any minute." Bear reaches into the refrigerator again and scoops out another glob of razz for Hubert's azz and applies it under his trench coat.

And then Bear moves to mount his Hubbie, and with one splitting plunge, he rams into Hubert, and Hubert screams "*STOP* Bear, you're killing me!" and he bucks and he tries to get away, but Bear shouts louder "*SHUT UP*" then whispers "shut up, shut up, you'll wake the neighbors, and we wouldn't want that now, would we?" (And of course being a neighbor, you're already awake, very awake, but appreciate the consideration.)

Hubert grimaces, tries to relax, ekes out "No no, we wouldn't want that" and Bear says "But you like this Hubbie, huh, you like this" and he pokes his hips forward and then back and forth, back and forth, back and forth, and asks again "Huh, Hubbie?" All Hubert says is—and this in rhythmic stutters through gritted teeth—all Hubert says is "my—name—is—Hu—bert." Bear goes on "Riiiight, but you like this eh? (*pound*) you like your Baby Bear like this? (*pound*) huh? (*pound*) *HUH? (POUND)!*"

And with his free hand—yucky and sticky, you think—Bear grasps the straight, long and light-brown hair of Hubert and turns his head, and he plants his thin lips hard on those full and rosy lips of Hubert's and sticks in his wet tongue far, and you can see Bear's cheeks making chewing motions, swallowing whatever he can suck from his crude and carnal thirst. Hubert breaks away from the lip-lock—you see some silvery strands of hair stay within Bear's paw—and laments, "I hate this."

"Oh really" says Bear. "We'll see about that" and his paw disappears under the trench coat, and you can see his arm move forward and around Hubert's waist, and he bends a little further over Hubert, and once again he puts his mouth close to Hubert's ear and coos "Oooooooo baby, I think what I have in my hand answers my question." And he pulls out his hand and puts it up to Hubert's mouth and says "lick it." Again "lick it." Again "*LICK IT!*"

Hubert's tongue comes out slowly. He licks it.

"Salty, huh?" says Bear.

Hubert says "a little bit, all this raspberry shit, everything sticky."

"Shut up" says Bear, and back goes his hand round Hubert's waist, and as he moves his hips, so he moves that arm.

Hubert prays "No god no" and calls Bear a sick bastard, and Bear twists his statement to "Yes god yes" and calls Hubert a sick liar, and they go back and forth:

"Bastard!"

"Liar!"

"Bastard!"

"Liar!"

Bastardliarbastardliar*BASTARD!*

   American Queer

"*LIAR INFINITY!*" roars Bear, and he slams into Hubert one last deep thrust, one final assaulting inner caress (ha!), freezes, shivers, and he gushes deep into his Hubbie, who with every hammer bangs the sink and bucks back, gulps and gasps "No god don't make me don't make me Bear stop *DON'T MAKE ME!*—" but the inferno burning below his belly boils over and pukes into the pistoning hand, both panting and writhing, incoherent and mute.

At least, that's what your acoustic and visual miracle tells you.

And then the two-backed beast collapses. Hell, you collapse.

But oddly—a thought, given all you've witnessed, that almost makes you laugh out loud—oddly, only you hear Hubert whisper "infinity plus one"—you know, the miracle thing—because Bear is quietly recuperating from his little death. And you hear Hubert begin to chant "I'll kill you I'll kill you I'll kill you killyoukillyoukillyoukillkillkill" each with a faster, more adamant conviction.

And then Bear starts coughing. Bear coughs again and then again and the cough grows, it's dry and deep and raw, and Hubert sees his chance, and with a bawl he throws off Bear, and Bear goes flying back, and he whacks his head on the fridge, and lays there on the kitchen floor moaning but not moving.

The gun takes winged flight—and lands by your hand.

Hubert slumps forward and hangs on the counter, heaving, trying to catch his breath, his senses. Starting with his back you see it blotched red and button-dented from the force of Bear's press, and you see sore looking red stripes between the shoulder blades and taut muscles. Some of his long and light-brown hair is matted. Red smears shade the two moonlike globes of his azz, and you're captivated by the black crevice of his quivering crack as he rocks back and forth and shakes from snotty sobs. He pushes his sweatpants further down the dark side of his moons and steps out of the legs. The shadow of the concave curve of his waist draws you down to the curve of a buttock with a fridge-lit rose tattoo you haven't noticed before. He feels himself, and he brings up a goo that glistens. From the sink he raises the knife like a holy icon offered to the gods, to glint in the blazing sun from the fridge.

Hubert turns around—again, you hold your breath and pray you're invisible—and you see bruises forming on his chest from the edge of the sink, on his face from the pokes of the pistol, on his neck from the maw of his Sweet Baby Bear. Where Bear sprawls, he straddles his chest and sits on it. With astonishing clarity—still weird and amazing—you can see the name *Mike* surrounded by a heart scripted on Hubert's chest, but then your attention is jerked back to the knife in Hubert's hand, pointing and resting shakily under the neck of his Bear.

Hubert slaps Bear. "Oh Beeeeaaaarrrr" he sings. He slaps Bear again. "Bear. Wake up Sugar Bear. Come on, wake *UP*" and Hubert mumbles something about prepositions, but even though this is an acoustic and visual miracle, you don't hear all of it. (It's selective, you notice, this miracle thing.)

Bear stirs. "What … what … what the—"

"Don't move" says Hubert tightly. "Be *vewy vewy* quiet. It's *wabbit* season." But on second thought adds "but wait. It's not a *wabbit* in my *twap*. It's a *beaw* in my *twap*. A Sugar Sweet (*jab with knife*) Baby (*jab*) *Beaw twap* (*JAB*)."

"Ow." Bear focuses. "Hubbie … Hubbie put that knife down."

"*HUBERT!*" screams Hubert, looking up to the heavens—in this case blocked by a grimy, paint-peeling ceiling—and he shakes his head and looks down at Bear and asks, "Don't you mean put *DOWN* that knife?"

"Uh, for the love of Mike. I, uh … lost my head—"

"Really, Bear? What happened to show the lady a little respect?"

"Oh, right right, OK, put *DOWN* that—"

"Oh, shut up" interrupts Hubert. "I'm going to cut it off."

"What?" asks Bear.

"*It*. I'm going to cut" and he reaches back and rustles into the trench coat and grasps what he seeks and continues "*it* off. *It* being a different kind of head than the one in the box."

"What?"

"You heard me."

     American Queer

"What are you crazy?" says Bear and Hubert agrees
"Yeah crazy man crazy" and now it's Bear's turn to swear "No
man no, I swear" and Hubert butts in with "Yes man yes, I
swear" and then they both go no, yes, noyesno*YES!* And Hubert
adds triumphantly "*YESSSS!*, infinity" and with a concluding
cackle tosses in "plus one." And that's that.

"Now" he continues, "I'm going to cut it off, place it
strategically with Lady, and send the box to Dr. Godit. He's an
art collector—among so many other things. He'll get a little
extra for his money. Call it Fellatio, Still Life number 37."

Bear begs "no nononofortheloveofMike *NOOOOO!*"
and Hubert over yells "*YESSSSSSSS!*" and Bear's head tosses
with fright—is he sobbing now?—and after a spell, so softly you
barely hear, Hubert says "unless … "

"What" whines Bear, and when he gets no answer,
whines again "Unless what?" His voice cracks, and Hubert tells
him to "Shush, I'm contemplating." Bear begs again "C'mon
man, what what what, I'll do anything, *WHAT?*"

After a teasing time lapse, Hubert answers "I'll make
you manless unless … "—another teasing time with Bear
whispering "yes yes?" and you straining ever so bravely closer—
and finally, Hubert continues with a grin. "I'll make you
manless, unless … unless you do it again."

"Again?" asks Bear.

"Again." answers Hubert. "And this time, put some
oomph into it."

Hubert pokes his bear, who jerks and cries "*OW!* What's
the matter with you?" He touches red wetness on his neck. "You
cut me; you cut me, you son of a—" but Hubert stifles this tirade
with another poke and a "Shush, it's just a scratch, you big sweet
baby bear. Now get it on—bang-a-gong! *Now!*"

Bear can tell Hubert means business and whines "I
can't" but Hubert says "Think, think that you can." With mucus
on his nose and lip, Bear's voice, high and cracking again, emits
a saliva filled choke of "But I can't, not with that—that thing
pointing at me."

Hubert's face belies no reaction. He looks Bear in the
eye. He turns slightly, reaches back, grasps the object of his
desire, points the knife at it, and pointedly says, "Tryyyyy."

　　　　　　　　　　　　　　　　　　American Queer

"OK" says Bear. "OK OK. I think I can I think I can IthinkIcan." Hubert nestles close to Bear's ear and sings "That's it. Like the train sings, baby, choo-choo, choo-chooooo Sweet Baby Sugar Bear."

They shift their weight; adjustments are made. Hubert sits up, throws back his head, and emits a long "ahhhhhhhh." They pause for an eternal moment. Their nipple rings twinkle.

"Hubert" says Bear.

"What" says Hubert.

"Can we shut this door?"

"Why?"

"It's blinding me."

"Sure, Sugar Bear, sure" says Hubert. He shuts the refrigerator door, and all is blue lava lamp shadow. "God" he whispers "what a sticky mess."

"Sweet razz for your azz." Bear grins, then frowns. "Have you seen my glasses?" Hubert sees them on the floor, hands them to him, and Bear says "I want to see you. Lucky they didn't break" and Hubert says "Yeah, ain't we lucky." Bear fingers the gold cross earring dangling from Hubert's ear. Hubert finds the cowboy shirt with teal piping and pearl buttons on the floor, wads it up, and puts it under Bear's head.

Bear coughs.

Hubert puts down the knife. He spits on a finger and dabs the cut on Bear's thick neck, sticks the finger in his mouth and sucks on it, pulling it out with a pop.

"Bear?"

"Yes."

"Do you have it?"

"Yes."

"Do I have it now?"

"Probably."

"Will it hurt?"

"No."

"We're so sticky."

"Yes."

"Did you know the Lady?"

"No. Did you?"

"No. Kiss me?"

   American Queer

"Yes." Bear caresses Hubert's straight, long—and sticky—light-brown hair.

A couple cats hiss and yowl. A car drives through the alley.

And in the time of No-Time, in the shadow of this acoustic and visual miracle—is that moon glow or the lava lamp?—you can see Hubert bend forward, see their mouths part, lips press, teeth and tongues devour and slurp and smack as Bear grasps Hubert's hips and pumps his own, all witnessed by the death child in the poster offering her benediction.

You will bid adieu to the lady in the hatbox, and you will back out of the apartment window onto the steel fire escape—red neon from the street starts flashing *Terminal Bar* again—and you will leave before they finish any more of this scene because you can't stand to see this scene, and because in this moment you can leave, so you do leave, as quietly as you came, like a ghost mouse back to its ghost hole.

You take the gun with you.

Love Sea, Eternal

1995

Though you do not know my name,
we have the same name.
And though you do not hear my cries, you do;
the cry, we share the same.
Beguiled, my Beloved, by the blue in your eyes
and the red flesh and hot white flash of your smiles—
I am beguiled—alas, unblessed.

Heart mystically pin-pricked, scarred and scared
like the river I must be,
like the river flawless, always flowing,
meandering from the fountainhead,
never pushed, never pulled,
never again awash and splashing this rock or that,
forever ending in the never-ending,
in the love sea, eternal.

So when you feel the soft brush of a breeze,
or a rolling drop of rain,
know that I kiss your cheek,
caress your brow,
and whisper in your ear:
"Beloved, touch your heart.
Its flutter I charge,
its current like the river,
rushing, rushing, rushing,
savvy within its dashing swirl.
Beloved, touch your heart, touch your heart!
For there, there!
In two rivers merging,
in two rivers surging
with dispassionate passion,

our cool, elemental confluence continues.
Where? Where not?
Beloved, touch my heart, touch my heart!
Healed and whole,
yours the same,
we dip from our banks
into each other's soul,
falling and floating in the love sea, eternal."

You know my name.
We have the same name,
where we two become the one,
conjoin the One.
Oh, Gentle Grace—
For now, for an eon, we afloat,
eddy about the boundless and bankless,
carried away
in the muddy tidewater of the delta mouth,
flow into the ocean
forever,
on and on into the love sea, eternal.

Lunch At Café Euphoria

1996

Troy and Thena looked forward to one of the few things they enjoyed together: Saturdays at the high-end mall with its hangars of expensive things and a cinema. After Thena shopped and Troy saw a film, they would meet for lunch at Café Euphoria.

The couple wasn't particularly happy, but neither were they unhappy. They'd been married 15 years. Thena needed nothing material, and Troy lived vicariously through the adventures he saw in movies. Husband and wife had become used to each other, and the weekly time spent to purchase things and view film pleasant.

The husband thought his wife was still beautiful. He admired much about her, but she used to be softer. Recently, she seemed to wear an expression of sadness tinged with boredom. He tried to please her. True, his neck was thicker, his black hair thinner and more salt than pepper. He knew Thena loved his mustache, his blue eyes, his tallness, and when he wore shirts that exposed his chest hair. Sometimes he felt like her escort. The money helps, he thought. When doesn't it?

On today's sunny Saturday, Troy was driving his small, red convertible with its comfy bucket seats. He loved experiencing the art of the clutch and stick shift while humming a classic rock song. Since the top was down, Thena wore a gold paisley scarf to wrap her long, wavy auburn hair. "Darling," was all Thena had to say. He shut off the radio and asked her to stop flicking her fingernail.

Going from the glaring sun into the dark parking lot, the car's headlights turned on.

Troy noticed Thena taking off her sunglasses, then squinting to read signs. "Are you ever going to the optometrist?"

American Queer

"Please stop nagging," said Thena, flicking her fingernail.

"But you miss out on seeing the world."

"I see that man, Troy, stop!"

"Oh, my God!"

As his arm flew out to block Thena from hitting the dashboard, Troy slammed on the brakes, Thena jerked forward, and a young man flapped his arms like a startled bird.

He was tall and lanky, wore a black leather jacket with fringed sleeves and a black t-shirt. Heavy gauge earrings and eyebrow studs punctured his hard face. He had a bleached crew-cut, black mustache, and goatee. Looking like a blond capped crow, the man raised one of his fringed wings, pointed at Troy through a fingerless glove, and flipped him off. Then he mouthed, "You are mine," each word exaggerated and clear.

"What?" Troy pressed the clutch and opened the door, putting his foot on the ground. "Hey, wait! I'm sorry! Hey!" The car began to roll, and by the time Troy braked and looked up, the man had disappeared.

"Did you see that?" asked Troy, breathing hard and white-knuckling the steering wheel.

"Oh, these hooligans," said Thena.

"He walked right in front of me," said Troy. "I might have killed him."

"And I might as well get out here," said Thena, putting her purse over her shoulder. She popped open the visor's lighted mirror, pulled the paisley scarf down around her neck, and smoothed her hair.

"Could you tell what he said to me?"

"I didn't hear a thing."

"He mouthed something. Really Thena, glasses or contacts or surgery. I insist."

"We'll see."

"That's the point. You don't."

"What did he say?"

"That I am—oh, never mind."

"Meet me at Fortunato's makeup counter," said Thena. She got out of the car and looked in both directions.

Troy leaned over to the passenger side and said, "Go left."

"Thank you, darling," sighed Thena. "I'll just feel my way along the wall." She blew a kiss and went in search of things to buy.

Troy chuckled and shook his head. Honking horns howled high hopes that he would soon move his car. He drove on in search of that sacred patch of shopping real estate: a parking space. The mall's valet service was available, but Troy looked forward to his hunt, his quest. Round and round the ramps, finally a vacancy appeared. He backed into it, a skill he proudly employed. These actions, like driving a stick shift, got him in the mood for today's action film starring an Austrian bodybuilder.

When he entered the stairs' foyer, the blond crow stood against a wall. Troy froze. The man's black cargo pants ended mid-calf and exaggerated his menacing black boots, more military weapon than footwear. He stood on one leg, the other bent backward, its foot braced against the cement wall. One hand hooked a pants pocket, the other held a cigarette. He pointed that hand at Troy and—out loud this time—said, "You are mine."

"How did you—Look, I said I was sorry." Troy scanned the area for signs of security. "Are you following me? I can get the police, you know. I didn't even touch you."

Walking backwards into the lot, Troy almost ran into a purple Cadillac, driven by an old woman barely visible over the steering wheel. Her honk made him jump just in time. The powdered face with blueish gray hair and smeared pink lipstick coasted by and croaked, "Moron." When Troy turned around, the man had vanished.

Panting and upset, he entered the crowded mall a bit muddle-headed. He found Fortunato's and saw in the distance Thena at its makeup counter. Not wanting to interrupt, Troy stood to the side. She was talking to a sales associate, a beautiful Black woman dressed in a leopard print blouse with furry cuffs. Her fingernails were painted white, and she held Thena's hand. The associate rubbed a cream on her cheek, then caressed it with the back of her hand. Troy thought the tenderness had nothing to do with cosmetics. He could barely hear her, but his wife was

American Queer

giggling. He couldn't remember the last time he had heard Thena's girlish, carefree laugh, instead of the phony one she used for her philanthropic parties or his feeble witticisms. The associate held his wife's hand in both of hers. They chatted a bit more, Thena nodding, as though agreeing to something. Troy walked toward her. She left the counter, saw her husband, and headed in his direction.

"Troy," called Thena, "excellent timing."

"There you are," said Troy.

"So King Arthur, get a good parking spot?" she asked. "I know how the holy grail thrills you."

"No need to poke fun," he said.

"Perhaps a little."

"But you'll never guess."

"Hmm? Guess what?"

Troy decided not to tell her about his stalker. "Some biddy driving a Caddy nearly hit me."

"Darling," said Thena, "how awful for you."

"Do you know her?" asked Troy.

"The biddy in the Caddy? How could I?"

"No, the saleswoman in leopard who's staring at you, over there, behind the counter."

"I hardly think I know a shopgirl."

Troy looked back; the woman was gone.

They entered a glass elevator and rose above the crowd of consumers. One caught his eye. Riding a descending escalator, the blond crow again pointed at Troy and mouthed what he guessed was his overly enunciated declaration of ownership.

"There he is again."

"Who, darling?"

"That kid from the garage."

"I can't see him."

"You couldn't see King Kong if he was down there."

Troy didn't understand why he was having a hard time breathing. He jerked around, knocking into a little girl who screamed and buried her head in Mommy's thick, plaid thigh. Mommy chastised Troy for his carelessness, urging him to, "Remember the little people."

　　　　　　　　　　　　　　　　　American Queer

"I'm so sorry," said Troy.

When the elevator door opened, Thena grabbed Troy's arm, brusquely moved Mommy aside, and said, "Can't stand other people's little people."

Troy pulled away and looked over the railing at the escalator. Once again, the bird had flown.

"Who are you looking for?" asked Thena. She thought she'd seen a blurry likeness of the man Troy had almost run over. She wasn't as blind as she pretended.

"No one," answered Troy. "That underwear store. I've got time before the movie starts."

"You mean Next-2-Skins. Please get something besides white briefs."

"But I like white briefs."

"Troy, you're so predictable," lamented Thena. "I'm off to Bacchus. See you at Café Euphoria, two-ish. I'm famished for their crab cakes."

Troy found Next-2-Skins and browsed among the hundreds of choices offered: bikinis and thongs, animal prints, burgundies and yellows, silk to flannel, but no white cotton briefs.

"May I help you?" asked a clerk in a chartreuse shirt and turquoise tie.

"All these choices," said Troy. "All I want is someone to hold my … "

"Hold your … ?"

"What?"

"What?"

"Something." Troy did a double-take and corrected himself. "I need something to hold my—you know, support. God, I need support."

"Of course, sir."

Troy cleared his throat and said, "Simple, white cotton briefs."

"Right this way," replied the clerk.

Wiping his brow, Troy said, "I'm so hot in here."

"You certainly are," said the clerk.

"Pardon?"

The clerk whispered, "You're sweating." He walked to a nearby section, and said, "Here you are, sir, white cotton briefs," then added, "I'm available should you need help." He grinned and attended to another customer.

Troy flipped through the familiar plastic marshmallow packages and found his size. The model pictured was lit so every muscle of his flat abdomen rippled like beach sand lapped by ocean waves. The wide v-shape of his hips began at the waist, narrowed to a bulging point at the crotch, and ended where two muscled thighs came together. No head, arms, knees. A modern, classical torso of mystery and desire, courtesy of Madison Avenue.

Someone squeezed by him in the narrow aisle, but didn't walk on.

"Excuse me," said Troy.

Then the person rubbed his backside and pressed harder, forcing Troy to bend over the counter.

"Now wait just a—"

"Drop that," said a man, thrusting a tube into his hand, "and buy this."

Troy shut his eyes tightly. He recognized the voice, and the store got hotter.

"Put it on. Meet me in five minutes at E-6. Look for a black van in a corner. And don't be late. I've got your license number."

When Troy opened his eyes, he looked at the tube in his hand and thought the pocket square of a suit was made of more cloth. He wheeled around and saw the back of his blond crow exiting the store. He rushed to the sales counter, cutting in front of an irritated old man with handlebar mustaches, and tossed a twenty-dollar bill. "Sir," called the clerk, "that's not enough!"

"Seriously?" Troy threw another bill onto the counter and trotted to the exit.

In the noisy artery of the mall, he looked down at purple paisley showing through the clear tube, wondering where he could change. "Wait," he said, stopping still. Am I going to change? The guy's creepy, not to be trusted, threatening. And what about Thena? I'll find his van and get his license plate to be safe. Now, where in hell is that lot?

     American Queer

And he was off, running through the crowd, blurting hurried sorry's and excuse me's, bumping into human obstacles. Passing the concierge desk, Troy slid to a stop. "Excuse me, where's parking lot E-6?"

A woman with orange hair and penciled eyebrows said, "That's employee parking," and gave him directions.

The secluded lot on the top floor was quiet and almost empty of vehicles. A few neon tubes cast an icy light. Smelling heat and exhaust, Troy walked the marked columns: E-4, E-5, E-6. E-6 … Where is he, where is he? he wondered. E-7, E-8. Then a dead-end. No black van, no blond capped crow.

Embarrassed, out of breath, sticky from sweating in the hot garage, Troy leaned over and braced himself on his knees. He was angry at himself for succumbing to what he wasn't quite sure of. An absurd assumption? Underwear? He was anxious, terrified. All of which belied his disappointment and the tears gathering behind his eyes. I must be crazy, he thought. The guy demanded, and I obeyed. Who does that? OK, if I run into him again, I'll tell him to forget it, and that if he bothers me or puts Thena in danger, I'll go to the police. That's it. Your demands of me were highly presumptuous, you've got the wrong guy, buddy, end of story.

Troy turned to go, but out of the corner of his eye, he spotted a flash of flame. He looked in its direction, and there, leaning against a black van tucked into a dimly lit corner, was the blond crow blowing out a match and smoke from a cigarette. He made a cocky nod with his head, motioning Troy toward him.

Troy's heart leapt, hit a brick wall, then sunk like a bucket of rocks. He walked to the man who had taken off his leather coat. As Troy got closer, he discerned lean, taut muscles and tattoos on his arms and legs. He could read his sleeveless t-shirt—The Monkey Spankers, a punk band he guessed—and in his mind tomorrow's headline: Murder at the Mall. On the side window of the van was a sticker: After Gen X? Gen Why? That's what I'd like to know, he thought. Why?

The young man opened the sliding door to his van. Troy smelled old smoke, stained with a hint of something sweet. He hesitated.

"Now or never, man."

                                                     American Queer

"How do I know—"

"You don't. I told you to change."

"I didn't have—"

The man snatched the tube out of Troy's hand and ripped it open, thrusting its paisley snippet onto his chest. "I'll watch." He ruffled Troy's chest hair. Troy gasped. "I like furry." He motioned towards the back of his van. Troy stepped up, looked behind him, and entered. The man followed, and with a loud clatter, slid the door shut, locked it, and pulled a curtain.

***

"Sir? Sir? Hey," came a clicking voice, "what's the matter?"

Troy looked up from the green marble sink with brass fixtures into a mirror. He was startled to see an ancient face staring back. It was pasty and creased, topped by a thin crest of gray hair, its neck bulging over a white shirt with bowtie askew. Troy shifted his stare to see his own face beaded with the cold water he had splashed on himself. Relieved, he said, "Scared the piss out of me."

"Urinal's behind you," said the restroom attendant, clicking through ill-fitting dentures. He handed his guest a towel. "Tip jar's to your left."

Troy dried his hands and face, then saw the time on a wall clock. "Shit! I need help."

"Like I haven't heard that one before."

"What, no, what, no, no," stammered Troy. "I'm turned around. Which direction is Café Euphoria from here?"

"Exit, turn right," answered the attendant. "Tip jar's to your left."

"For what?" asked Troy in a dissatisfied voice.

"Gave you a towel, didn't I? Directions twice. I'm 69 years old and work in a bathroom."

Troy put a large bill in his hand.

In the mirror Troy saw a red mark on his neck. "And I'm too old for a hickey," he said. The attendant rolled his eyes. Troy thought he could use some of Thena's makeup when he got home. He adjusted his shirt collar, used balm on his chapped lips, and combed his hair.

                                     American Queer

Racing to Café Euphoria, Troy worried about what to tell Thena. Since he'd known her, his lies to her had been few, little, and white, or so he told himself. He watched people pass him and wondered if their lives were this complicated. Or deceptive. How do they manage? How does Thena? How do I?

Planning a speech, Troy saw Thena down a narrow hall backing out of a brass door with a large sign: Fortunato's Employee Entrance. He stood near a column. She was talking to someone inside. She reached in with one hand and pulled out someone else's hand, smooth and brown with white fingernails, its wrist ringed with a furry cuff ending a sleeve of leopard print. The hand caressed her face, then gently bopped her nose. Another hand gave Thena a little lavender box with a tiny bow which Thena put in her purse. She kissed the hands; the hands withdrew; the door shut; Thena stood still. She pulled a tube of lipstick from her purse, and in her reflection on the brass door, opened her mouth to an "ah" shape, swiped once, licked, and used a finger to blend the edges of her lips. She touched up her hair, then entered an artery of the mall.

Troy pretended to be walking unaware of her. She saw him; he thought she looked surprised. There was a glow to her skin and a sparkle in her eye that Troy knew he had not put there in quite a while.

"Thena," he called.

"There you are," she said. "I waited for you at Café Euphoria."

"I'm sorry," said Troy. "I looked for you but didn't see you. I waited a bit, then left, walked around."

"I was tucked into that back corner."

"I know the one. Sorry. How were the crab cakes?"

"Hmm?"

"You were looking forward to them."

"Oh, yes, crab cakes," said Thena, "delicious."

"I asked the maître d'," said Troy, "said he hadn't seated anyone of your description."

After saying in unison, "The fool," they laughed, both looking amazed at each other.

"So," asked Thena, "did you enjoy it?"

Troy took a deep breath. "Enjoy what?"

　　　　　　　　　　　　　　　　　American Queer

"The movie."

Relieved and knowing Thena could not care less, he replied with his stock answer, "Great, fine. It was fine."

"What was it about?"

"Hmm?" Troy tried to remain calm. "About?"

"Yes, the movie."

"Oh, you know, good guy beats up bad guys." Troy notched a mental reminder to see the film soon. "In Europe or Africa, they all look the same."

Thena looked at her husband as if for the first time in a long time. "You don't."

"Are you hot? I am so hot. Don't what?"

"Look the same. You look brighter, if a bit untidy."

"Well, jeez, I could say the same about you, your hair, a bit untidy. Suits you though." Troy was surprised. His wife glowed.

"I got a makeover."

"Beautiful job."

"Yes, she did. Thank you."

"But beautiful to begin with."

"You're sweet, darling," said Thena. "Troy, what's the matter?

"Nothing."

"You're acting so queer."

"What?" Troy coughed and cleared his throat. "Can't I compliment my wife?"

"Sorry darling, forget it," said Thena. She looked about the bazaar of store fronts, all of them promising joy and fulfillment but for a time unguaranteed.

"No packages or bags today?" asked Troy. "Don't remember the last time that happened."

"And I had a lovely time," said Thena. "Troy, do you remember when we met?"

How could he forget? It was a lovely memory. In college a friend had introduced them. Thena was the most wonderful woman he'd ever met. She was Greek. Her first name was Athena, but thought it overdone, so she dropped the 'A'. The friend knew Troy and Thena were destined for each other. Eventually, they agreed.

"Of course I remember." He looked at Thena. "What brings this on?"

"Don't know," said Thena. "We had nothing but each other."

"Ready to go home?" asked Troy.

"Yes, home," answered Thena, "but would you mind bringing the car here? These wretched heels."

"Not at all," said Troy, kissing her cheek. "I'll pick you up by the entrance down this hall." He noticed something missing from Thena's ensemble. "Your scarf."

"My scarf?" Thena felt around her neck.

"It's gone."

"Must have fallen off."

"I'll check lost and found."

"No, don't. I've hundreds. Someone else will enjoy it."

Troy settled Thena in a cushy chair and headed to his convertible. He recognized the hall and a store front under construction. Draped by enormous plastic sheets, scaffolds framed the site flanked by two walls of decorative panels. There was no sign of activity. He read a large, elegant sign on an easel announcing in a fancy font: Please excuse our appearance. Café Euphoria is closed for renovation. Our Grand Re-Opening will be announced soon!

It seemed to him that he had spent all afternoon fighting for breath, running out of it, and gasping for it. He needed a deep breath again because just then, the beautiful woman in a leopard print blouse and furry cuffs walked by—a gold paisley scarf decorously flowing about her neck and shoulders. He was about to stop her, then stopped himself instead. His wife hadn't looked so soft in a long time. He reached into his pants pocket for his car keys and felt his own paisley souvenir. Troy smiled and breathed deeply. He wasn't worried and kept walking. He supposed they should talk. About what, he wasn't sure.

Thena felt restless, fidgeting with her blouse collar and flicking her fingernail. She strolled down the hall to meet Troy, walked by a storefront under construction, then stopped. She recognized the location of Café Euphoria and walked back, bending closely to read a blurry sign on an easel. She read it again to make sure. Just then, the young man with wings of black fringe swaggered by her.

Waiting on the curb, she heard the faint echoes of guitars and drums approach. A smile reposed sweetly on Thena's face, as did the little lavender box in her purse. She was glad her husband looked brighter. But she wondered if there was a wooden horse in their future, and what they would do next Saturday, if they'd ever again have lunch at Café Euphoria.

Testaments

Bush, Russell. 1998. Affectionate Men.
New York: St. Martin's Press, p. 57.

Testaments

1997

<u>Ash Wednesday</u>

Late for his doctor's appointment, Nathan Waters checked in with the receptionist who stared at the smudged cross on his forehead. She thought the symbol of grief was like a strange third eye and said to it, "Please have a seat."

Nathan had attended a service at the cathedral, his first in the new millennium, finding comfort in the bells and smells. His discomfort lay in his car: a packet of pictures six years old he finally had developed. Ben. Locating a business that dealt with film had been difficult. He didn't like digital photographs; he couldn't hold them.

Just as the nurse called his name, Nathan thought he saw a shadow move outside an office window, but it had disappeared.

Glad to give good tidings, the doctor said, "I'm afraid you're going to live a long and normal life."

Not half afraid as I am, the doomed patient thought.

When he failed to respond with the expected gratitude, she tapped the desk with her pen. "Aren't you pleased?"

To the ceiling, Nathan said, "I thought I'd be done by now."

"We're almost finished," said the doctor.

Nathan didn't correct her. Maybe I'll give up the ghost for Lent, he thought. From a plastic box with flowers, he pulled a tissue, spit on it, and wiped the holy mark off his forehead.

<u>Six Weeks Later</u>

In front of his house, Nathan sat in his car listening to the rainstorm beat the metal roof in sporadic waves of intensity and pitch. Mesmerized in his steel cocoon, he absorbed the soothing thuds, the gray outside, the waterfall on glass before him. His breath faintly fogged the windshield where, in a corner printed on a sticker, was a long overdue date for maintenance at Ben's Garage. Nathan thought he saw someone in his house and blinked. A rain trick.

Chunks of cement gouged the driveway and prevented use of the garage—evidence of a project abandoned. The neighbors complained. Let them, he thought. It's only been six years, the same length of time since the photos in the packet on the car seat had been taken. Clutching the packet to his breast, he decided to make a dash to the front door, but his umbrella failed to lock and drooped over him like a black shroud. Huddled over, head down, he trotted toward the front door.

Which is why they collided. Nathan didn't see the rollerblader in a green slicker and baggy khakis wearing a baseball cap backwards and headphones. Deaf to the outside world, the young man careened around the corner, speedily pawing the ground with his feet, and checking their angle. When he raised his head, he yelled, "Duuuude!" and crashed into Nathan, both in that violent moment attracted and repelled, flapping apart, the briefcase airborne, papers and pictures exploding like a piñata, Nathan bouncing onto the curb with a crack and crying out. The blader spun around, arms and legs flailing, rolled back on his heels, and hit the hard wet lawn, his backpack flying off his shoulders, his sneakers laced together and thrown over his shoulders. smacking him in the face.

"What the hell!" The young man shook his head, stood, and unsteadily propelled himself to the moaning man. "Dude, are you all right?"

Nathan lay on his stomach and watched twigs and leaves flow by in the murky gutter. He turned over and tried to focus, but the pelting rain speckled his cockeyed glasses. He moved, grimaced, and wailed as pain shot through his foot.

"Don't move, man," said the blader. "I'll call an ambulance."

"No!" said Nathan, grabbing a green sleeve. "Help me up." From behind and under his arms, the young man lifted him. He tried to stand but buckled back into the arms of his perpetrator. "Lean on me," said his rescuer, draping Nathan's

    American Queer

arm around his shoulders. On wheels and one foot, together they rolled and hopped to the porch and up the steps. Nathan saw photos littering the front lawn. "Ben."

Once inside they maneuvered towards the sofa, Nathan plunking down on it, the young man quickly bracing himself on the back of the sofa astride Nathan's head. Nathan moaned, leaned back, and took off his glasses. The young man's close face fixed upon his. He was pretty and scruffy. Raindrops like clear pearls clung to the long lashes skirting his eyes and dripped from his ponytail. One drop hung from the end of his nose. Nathan watched it fall to his crotch and jerked. He smelled wet hair, rain fresh.

The blader cleared his throat and said, "I'd better get our stuff." Walking on wheels, he sheepishly giggled, "Like, these blades don't work so well on carpet, know what I mean?"

Nathan thought, No, I don't, and I don't want this.

Minutes later, the young man reentered with his arms and hands clutching pictures and papers, a briefcase, backpack, a bent umbrella tucked under a pit, and sneakers around his neck. "Sorry for the rockin' crash," he said.

Nathan wondered why his hands hurt. "Wet *Aspern Papers*."

"Ass burn?" asked the blader, grinning. "I might want to take your class."

"*As-pern*," articulated Nathan. "Book reports."

"Yeah, Henry James," said the blader. "Tell your students to print them again."

"I had just finished grading them." Nathan noticed red marks on the papers, then his scraped and bleeding fingertips and palms.

"Let me see your hands," said the blader, reaching for them.

"They're fine," said Nathan.

"All right," said the blader, backing away.

Ignoring his wounds, Nathan picked out the photos. They reminded him of Ben toward the end, limp and dappled. He untucked his shirt and tried to dry and smooth them out, leaving red smears on the tail. "Ruined."

"Sorry about the pics," the blader apologized again.

                                                American Queer

"You should be!" yelled Nathan, yelling again when throwing the pictures fired agony from his injury.

"Dude, chill," said the blader. "It was an accident."

The young man yanked his slicker over his head, exposing for a moment the feathery hair of armpits, and dropped to the floor to take off his inline skates. A big toe, painted pink, poked through a hole in his white sock. Catching Nathan staring, he said, "Pink's the new black. Suave, don't you think?"

Nathan tried not to look.

The young man rose tall and lithe. A sleeveless, red t-shirt re-tucked inside two inches of exposed plaid underwear revealed a lightning bolt tattoo on a bicep. Inexplicably hanging on no hips and a concave waist, his khakis, each leg as baggy as a gunny sack, flouted gravity.

Nathan wondered how easily his pants fell down.

"Let's get that shoe off," ordered the blader. He helped Nathan remove his suit jacket, inhaling his manly smell and wet wool. He moved a large bowl of multi-colored marble eggs, sat on the large ottoman, and grabbed a pillow. He placed it, then Nathan's foot on his lap, unlaced the wingtip, and pulled. Nathan braced himself and objected to the removal of his sock, but the young man delicately slid it down Nathan's calf, over the heel and the arching curves of his sole and instep, gently urging it with each pull.

"Sweet feet," said the blader.

"I beg your pardon."

"Foot actually. I'm studying to be a podiatrist," said the blader. "Your lucky day."

"Not really," said Nathan. "How old are you?"

"Old enough to be studying podiatry." Frowning with concentration, the blader asked, "Can you move your foot?"

"Barely," replied Nathan, wincing as he tried. He felt warm hands deftly examine the ridges and indents of skin and muscle and bone. When the future foot doctor neared his ankle, he flinched.

"Sorry," said the blader. "Could be the talus, or fibula, or tibia, or malleolus, this knuckle part. Take off your pants."

"I beg your pardon."

   American Queer

"There's like ultra swelling going on, so unless you don't mind your fancy pants getting cut off … "

Nathan unbuttoned, unzipped, and scooted down his pants, the young man tugging the legs and surveying the pale territory of Nathan's exposed stomach. He followed a thin, yum-yum trail of hair that led up to his belly button and beyond the folds of a blood stained, white button-down shirt. Nathan yanked his shirt down. The blader cracked up.

"What's so funny?" asked Nathan.

"Dude, yellow banana boxers?"

"If I'd known you were coming over, I'd have worn silk, now—"

"No, no, they're cool, way cool."

"—please leave."

"We'll save the silk ones for later," said the blader, wiggling his eyebrows. "Look, man, we've got to get you to emergency and your foot x-rayed. Know what I mean?"

Nathan did and refused. Hospitals. Ben.

"Dude, a fourth of the bones in your body are in this area. You might have fractured one, or torn a ligament: the calcaneal-fibular, posterior talofibular, syndesmotic, or deltoid. By your movement and my feel, I'd say it's the anterior talo-fibular ligament. ATFL for short."

"Are you always such a showoff?"

"Only when I'm pissed off."

Nathan declared himself capable of driving.

"Pops, it's your right foot," said the blader.

"I'll call a taxi or a friend," said Nathan, "so if you'll please leave?"

"You're weird." The young man became aware of the living room. It was in chaotic disarray. On a worktable of sawhorses, a wide black brush, seam roller and other tools crowded several rolls of dusty wallpaper lying next to a long, dry tray. Stacked furniture filled a corner. A ladder leaned against the wall that was partially stripped of its covering, pock-marked, and scabbed with huge black leeches. "This place is a way rare mess."

"I beg your pardon."

"Man, stop begging."

    American Queer

"A project interrupted by—" said Nathan, recalling the reason "—an interruption."

"Looks like you've been working on it for a while."

"Six years."

"How long?"

"Six years, six years, six."

"OK." The young man recognized charred splotches and asked if there had been a fire, but no, not since Nathan had lived here. On a desk, white plastic bottles surrounded a portrait of two men in a pale gold frame. The blader picked it up and asked, "Daddy or boyfriend or both?"

"Put that down," said Nathan.

"Jeez, relax, dude."

"And stop calling me that."

"Ok, *Mr.* Dude." The blader winked and said, "I mean like, you know, it's totally cool if he's your lover."

"I don't need you to tell me that," said Nathan.

"He's way older than you, Pops."

"*Was*," said Nathan. "He *was* older than me. What do you think all those pills are—were for?"

"His?"

"Not all of them. Now I'm sure you'll wish to scurry away."

"I'm not a rat."

And he did not wish to scurry away. Nathan did not wish to call a taxi or a friend. When the young man offered to drive him to the emergency room, Nathan declined based on the way he skated.

"Buck up, little camper," said the blader. "Take a chance, and let's get cracking. Sorry, dude, bad choice of words."

"My name is Nathan," he said, tired of dealing with this puppy, "not *dude*, or *camper*, or *Pops*. Please go."

"Whatever, Nate—"

"Nathan, not Nate!"

"Man, you are some wingnut. I'm out of here." The blader removed Nathan's pillow and foot from his lap a little rougher than intended causing Nathan to wince. He put on his slicker, and picked up his pack and blades. "My name's Kory. With a *K* and no freaking *e*."

A faint rustle came from the wall behind Nathan. Kory's eyes followed the sound, and Nathan craned his neck to follow them. A long piece of old wallpaper with brown stripes curled down like a chocolate shaving, stopping when a corner hit a rung of the ladder. Partially revealed under the strip was a brown square secured by brown tape.

"Check it out." Kory dropped his belongings and walked over to the wall.

"What is it?"

"How should I know? Should I take it out?"

"Yes, but be careful."

"Have to. Left my jackhammer at home." Kory peeled down more of the strip, picked off old tape, and tried to pull the contents from the wall. "Some sort of niche," he said, glancing over his shoulder at Nathan, "and yeah, I know what a niche is. I'm young, not a tool." A rectangle had been carved out of the plaster allowing an inserted box to stay flush within the wall. "It's stuck. Got a crowbar?"

"No!"

"Jeez, kidding."

"Use that screwdriver," said Nathan.

After cautiously chipping and prying, Kory extracted a thin package wrapped in an old paper bag. He blew off decades of dust and offered it to Nathan.

"Wait, my hands," he said. "Bring me that utility knife and those gloves."

"What's the magic word?" prompted Kory.

Nathan scowled. "Please."

Kory smiled. "That's better."

Nathan put on the gloves, inspected the box for markings, saw none, and brushed off more aged grit. "Odd."

"Major odd-age." Kory leaned over the back of the sofa and scanned the back of Nathan's head. Soft-looking, wet brown hair with barely perceptible gray strands ended in a V-shaped point near a freckle on his nape. A pale down grew on the top curve of his ears.

Gingerly slitting stiff, dry paper, Nathan unwrapped the box. Inside was a maroon velvet case with a gold clasp, and inside of it, a black-and-white photograph of two men.

In the background a two-story brick building lined the street. An apartment with brick arches above its windows, one half-open and dark, occupied the second floor. The sloping roof of a wood porch in need of paint sheltered wash hung out to dry. An unidentifiable business occupied the street level. Tree limbs with leaves gave the illusion they hung from a telephone pole next to the rear end of an old car. A clear sky completed the backdrop of a warm, sunny day.

The two beaming subjects faced each other, profiled almost nose to nose. The man on the left appeared slightly shorter and thicker. He had rugged skin, hair slicked-back and short-cropped, and a big ear like half a valentine. He wore a light gray shirt, and beltless, dark jeans. Wrinkles around his eye suggested much grinning, not age, but he seemed the older of the two. The man on the right had a fair complexion, light hair and a fine nose and ear, another valentine half. He wore dark slacks and a sweater vest over a white shirt with cufflinks. A gap separated their torsos of flat stomachs and the curve of slim hips. The man on the left clasped his hands around the other's neck, his locked fingers drawing the other's face towards his. In the middle of a wide and dimpled smile, as though moving into a hug, the hand of the man on the right partially blocked his partner's face, not from resistance, but with the blurred reach of reciprocation. On this hand, on his wedding finger, a broad band shined brightly. There they stood, frozen forever young and handsome, almost embracing, almost dancing, almost kissing.

Joy is what first came to Nathan's mind. Then he wondered who held the camera. "Why would anyone immure a photograph?"

"My turn. Beg your pardon?"

"Bury in a wall."

"Rad, for sure a couple of hotties," said Kory. He noticed a slip of paper had fallen to the floor and picked it up. "Pops, check this out:

  "For M,
   By the man who dreams patiently

Nathan took the note from Kory. The handwriting was neat and assertive in the black ink of a fountain pen. Specks of mold spotted the yellowed paper of heavy stock. He read, "*Love always*, exclamation point. Always."

"It's sweet. Maybe they're still alive. Wouldn't it be awesome to find them? And, like, find out why they buried their pic? L and M. They had to be—"

"Stop it," demanded Nathan.

"Yes, sir, Sergeant Dude." Kory saluted and laughed. "Sorry, it's hard to take orders from someone in a tie and banana boxers."

Nathan was ashen and wiped away the sweat on his brow.

"You don't look so good, Nate."

"My name is Nathan. Can't you get that through your adolescent brain?"

"Harsh."

Nathan tried to stand, bumped his foot on the ottoman, and collapsed in agony. Resigned to needing someone, he inquired about Kory possessing a driver's license.

Kory rolled his eyes. "Do you have any sweatpants?"

"I wouldn't be caught dead in sweatpants," replied Nathan.

"Lingerie, buck naked. I wouldn't mind either."

"Bedroom on the left, bottom drawer."

Kory returned with flannel pajama bottoms and a snicker. "Upsy-daisy, little camper. Let's get your cowboy jammies on."

"Not those," said Nathan. "They were—"

"No time for a fashion show. I'll help you."

"I can manage."

Hours later, they returned from the emergency ward. Like handling a rag doll, Kory helped Nathan flop onto the sofa, his patient falling forward onto his shoulder.

American Queer

"You shmell so—" slurred Nathan "—young."

"Nate, sit up," said Kory.

"Name's Nathan, 'member? How am I supposed to get into beddy-bye?"

"You can manage."

"Tuck me in?" giggled Nathan. "Kiss me goodnight?"

"Not tonight," said Kory, ensuring the stabilizing sock fit properly. "You'd screech at me like you did the doctor."

"I had reasons." Nathan watched Kory's large hands delicately touching his foot. "And I don't screech."

"You don't handle injuries very well."

"You don't handle sick people very well."

"You're not sick."

Nathan shoved Kory's hands off him. "What do you know about being sick? Slapping hands with the doctor in macho self-congratulations."

"I'll get some ice," said Kory, going to the kitchen. He returned and applied the pack to Nathan's foot. "It was a high-five."

"In your vernacular," called Nathan, "whatever."

"Not to brag, but my diagnosis was right. Sprained ATFL. I am Super Podiatrist!" He began squeezing Nathan's toes. "This little piggy went to market."

"Stop it," said Nathan.

"Usually a crowd pleaser."

"Hand me that wine."

"You're already loopy on painkillers."

"Is that your diagnosis, Dr. Cocky?"

"Observation."

Nathan lowered his eyes. "You don't understand."

"So, your name is on some of the pill bottles." Kory wrapped a towel around the ice and foot. "Don't walk on your ankle. I've nuked the heating pad. Alternate that with ice until you go to sleep. Be sure to prop your foot so it's above your heart."

Kory promised to call and gave Nathan his number in case he needed it. Nathan assured him he would not, saw his reflection in a mirror, and strained to retrieve a comb from his discarded suit pants.

"What's with the '80's hairdo, man?" asked Kory.

"I beg your pardon," said Nathan.

"I know you do," said Kory. "You're a hottie, that's all."

"No," said Nathan, "I'm chilly."

Kory threw him a comforter. "Sleep here," he said. "And stay away from the wine."

"Yes sir, Kory doc, sir," smiled Nathan.

Kory stared, was about to say something, then walked out the door.

"But first … " Nathan stretched for the red wine and poured himself a glass.

The old photo and note lay on the ottoman. They seemed to demand solving, as though secreted away for so long, they refused to remain a riddle. Nathan recognized the view from his front yard. Across the street, the storefront was a neighborhood coffee house now. The second-story apartment had been renovated. The brick arches encased modern, double-paned windows, and a perpendicular roof sheltered a balcony bound by an iron railing with curlicues. The telephone pole was still there, and the tree and now his car. He wondered if the two men were anywhere on this planet at all, if they had been brothers or buddies or lovers, if they had kissed. He read the note again. "He's wrong. It's not sweet. It's passionate."

Nathan slept fitfully—his foot higher than his heart—and dreamed of the two men as though he had been the cameraman. They were laughing and horse playing. He told them to keep still, which they could not, and snapped their profiles just as the fair-haired man moved. At the click of the camera, he woke up, but even with his eyes open he heard giggles, "Love always," and his own voice complaining, "You guys moved." He witnessed their consummated kiss and heard more faint laughter that diminished to silence.

He sat up and had to pee. Nathan grabbed his crutches and cringed, having forgotten his scraped palms, and hobbled to the bathroom. In the mirror he moved his face side to side. "A hottie, eh? And what's wrong with my hair?" He thought he saw a shadow move behind him and turned around. Painkillers, he thought, and wine. The fresh smell of wet hair lingered.

Maundy Thursday

Nathan woke up with a headache and sat in the kitchen nook drinking coffee, staring at spoiled snapshots, their edges curled and brittle like dead leaves. He switched his focus to the exhumed photo, a captured second of love, or so he wanted to believe. Under an eave on the back porch, a red-breasted finch fluttered like a yo-yo, rebuilding a nest that the wind always blew apart. "Stupid bird," said Nathan. "Where's *your* mate?" He swept the reflections of his dead lover into a bag and limped out to the alley. He saw his neighbor timidly step around puddles of rain to dig in her garden, hoping she wouldn't see him. He discarded the bag in the trash barrel and felt nauseated.

"Land's sake, Mr. Waters!" exclaimed Mrs. Grady. "What happened to you?" She wore an old man's shabby sweater and an apron flowered with faded daisies; strands of white hair had escaped her barrette and flew about her rosy face.

Nathan recapped his accident. The old lady *oohed* and *ahed* and segued into a litany of her own aches and pains. Nathan figured he might as well do some digging of his own. Mrs. Grady had lived in her home all her long and married life. After her recital ended, Nathan inquired if she remembered who lived in his house during the 30s and 40s.

"Oh my, that's long before you and Mr. McLean, rest his sweet soul." Mrs. Grady sniffled and wrinkled up her already wrinkled face. "Land's sake, there's been so many renters. I think I met the owner once, before you nice boys moved in. Stuffy woman. Complained that Mephistopheles, rest his furry soul, used her lawn for—" she paused to whisper "—his kitty box. Never bothered me. But let's see … Just before the war a nice man lived there with a boarder or roommate, I think. They seemed like close friends. Both very handsome, but land's sake, that was decades ago. One of them came back after the war and bought the place, then gave it to that woman. No other bells ringing, Mr. Waters. Most of mine lost their ding-a-ling long ago. If the Judge was alive, rest his cantankerous soul, he'd know. Mind like a filing cabinet the size of a zeppelin."

                                                  American Queer

Mrs. Grady's beaming pride quickly clouded. She started to sob and pulled the old sweater closer about her. "I'm sorry, Mr. Waters. I tear up ten times a day thinking about the Judge. Sort of comforting really. That, and my flower garden. You be sure and pick all you want. I wish the Lord would pick me, but I guess He doesn't want me yet. Besides," she sniffled again, taking out a crumpled handkerchief and wiping her nose, "the daffodils are beginning to bloom. But I sure do miss that old puss."

Nathan didn't know if the old woman referred to Mephistopheles or the Judge, but felt his chest tighten. As fast as possible, he stomped and swung on his crutches back inside the house. He was light-headed, and his foot throbbed. Panting and leaning against a wall, he put his hands on his knees and squeezed himself internally. My God, thought Nathan, I've become an old woman. Gradually, his breath returned, and gratefully, his feelings flattened.

Inhaling deeply, Nathan wobbled to a closet, dug around, and found the purchase contract for the house. Sitting again at the kitchen table, he steeled himself before unfastening the thick packet. Buyers: Ben McLean and Nathan Waters. Seller: Hannah Pick. Three signatures followed a black and white blur of legalese: Ben's bold and broad, his florid and precise, Mrs. Pick's tight and simple. She hadn't attended the closing. Her attorney had presented signed papers verified by a notary public, her realtor the keys. Nathan relived how they had tinkled; how he and Ben had immediately driven to their new house to envision their new home, how they had toasted each other with a bottle of champagne and made love that afternoon on blankets and pillows, how their friends had helped in the frantic move, and later on, how some had remained through Ben's illness, how some had disappeared. They had been happy in this old house for almost five years. Hard to believe he'd been living here for over a decade. Renovating the old gem had been a joy. Replacing the driveway and re-papering the living room would complete a phase of their plans. Then, to relax and relish their home. But Ben got sick, the work stopped, and in a shockingly short two months, he was gone. Six years ago. A blessing Ben didn't linger, someone had said. Which friend

Nathan couldn't remember—gone like most of them—but he did remember his reply: "A blessing for whom?"

Awareness of a nearby phone book interrupted his memories; he grabbed it and searched for *Pick*. Four listings but no *Hannah* or *H. Pick*. He wrote down the numbers, clenched the sheet in his mouth, moved to the living room, and dialed each number. A child named Mitzi had to go potty and screamed *MoOOOm*, but Mom was no help. Next, he woke up a grumpy man who cursed and threatened him with an unpleasant sex act if he called back. Another was disconnected; he left messages at the remaining two.

The phone rang, and Nathan picked it up, thinking it a quick reply.

"What's up, Pops?"

"Who's this?"

"Dude, are you still high? It's Kory."

"Oh, yes."

"How's your foot?"

"I'll live."

"You're weird. And your hands?"

"Tender."

"You'll live. I'll bring some salve. Tonight, we dine on Chinese food."

"I beg your pardon."

"Like, man, don't start that again," implored Kory.

He wanted to check Nathan's bandage, but Nathan said it was fine, invented a friend coming over and bid goodbye. No, tomorrow he had plans.

"Nate, if you don't want to see me, you don't have to lie."

"I beg—"

"Beg all you want." Click.

Nathan said "leave me alone" to a dial tone.

At dusk he awoke on the sofa to a loud ring, swearing he'd bring charges against that kid. Ben's recorded message— still achingly soothing—led to the voice of a Jim Pick. Quickly and clumsily grabbing the phone, Nathan answered, "Sorry, hello?" Hannah Pick was his distant cousin, recently back from a vacation in Switzerland. Her number was unlisted. Would Jim

    American Queer

Pick be so kind as to call and let her know that Nathan Waters wanted to talk about the property he had bought from her. He'd found something, and Mrs. Pick might want the items. No, no problems. The house must have quite a history.

Nathan surveyed the disaster of black blotches and peeling paper, exposed plaster, and gobs of dried, old glue. He could almost see Ben soaking and scraping and sanding the wall, while he himself cooked dinner and flipped through a sample book of new patterns. The doorbell ended his delight. Nathan ignored it.

"I know you're in there," came a muffled voice.

Nathan wished him gone, but the chime continued its needling announcement, so he hobbled to unlock the front door.

"Hungry?" invited Kory. Balancing himself on his blades, he held the screen door ajar and a big, white bag. "Fried dumplings and sesame seed chicken, no m.s.g., I swear, man. I brought enough for three."

"Three?"

"Yeah, your friend, you and me."

"Friend? Oh right, look, Kirk—"

"Kory."

"Kory. Not counting running into me and breaking my foot—"

"Your foot's not broken," interrupted Kory.

"—Thank you for all you did yesterday," continued Nathan, "but your role as good Samaritan has ended. I release you from any debt you may think you owe me."

"Are you on crack? I don't owe you a damn thing," said Kory. "The accident was just as much your fault as mine. If anybody owes anything, Mr. Dude, you owe me for busting my phone."

"I was minding my own business," argued Nathan, "when you recklessly came speeding around the corner on your roller-skates—"

"Bombin' blades, man," protested Kory, "not some girly toy."

"Fine," said Nathan. "I'll pay for your phone, anything, as long as you leave me alone. Do you want money for taking me to the hospital, too?"

    American Queer

"Man, I don't need your money," said Kory, jabbing his finger. "For your information, *Nathan*, I'm on a full scholarship. I thought we could have some victuals together, you know, hang out. You've got a major 'tude, dude. Later, much later. Enjoy dinner." With a push off the door frame, he dropped the white bag, jumped the steps and zoomed down the sidewalk, leaning into a swift turn, his body bent gracefully, his arms and legs swaying and gliding with skillful precision. On a dime, he braked and pivoted. Returning to Nathan, Kory rummaged through his backpack and flung an envelope at his feet. "I stole your negatives. There's a new set of pics."

"I don't want them."

"Whatever. You know, I was going to say I'm sorry I hung up on you, but I ain't the sorry one here."

"Well, you're the—the—annoying one here!" shouted Nathan. "Yes! That's what you are. Ha! Annoying—!" He tried to slam the door shut, but the bottom corner caught a crutch, knocked it out from under his arm, and he collapsed with a loud crash and cry.

Kory stood over Nathan, shaking his head, saying "What the hell, Pops," and helping him to the sofa. "If you still hurt in the morning, go back to the clinic."

"And how do you propose I get there?"

"Ask your friend. I'm rolling."

Before Kory leaped out the front door again, Nathan blurted, "The pictures."

Kory stopped.

"What do I owe you?"

Kory turned and gaped. "Man, you really don't get it. Later."

"Sorry," said Nathan. "I'm sorry. Thank you."

"Welcome." Kory picked up the envelope of prints and handed them to Nathan. "I used the same place you did. They're like antiques."

"So did you snoop?" asked Nathan.

"No," replied Kory. Nathan looked doubtful. "OK, I confess, yes. Very sweet. But you have got to get a different hair-do, dude."

                                    American Queer

"What is wrong with my hair? You have a strange obsession, young man." Nathan felt himself smiling.

"The man smiles. Another confession."

"Am I your priest now?"

"Yes, Holy Father. After the accident, when we got you on the sofa, remember?"

"No," Nathan lied.

"I almost kissed you."

Nathan said nothing.

"But I didn't think you were in the mood … So, when's your friend coming over?" asked Kory.

Nathan fidgeted. "No one is coming."

"No shit. Hungry?"

"Chinese." Nathan hated Chinese food. "I'm starving."

"Awesome," said Kory. "I hate to eat alone." He opened the white bag, dished up two plates, and ate cross-legged on the ottoman. Encouraging Nathan to try something new, he fed him a dumpling clamped between chopsticks.

"It's Maundy Thursday," said Nathan.

"And?"

"Maundy Thursday. The Last Supper."

"Our first. You're weird."

"Catholic."

"Like I said." Kory accepted a piece of chicken dropped from Nathan's sticks. "But," he said through a mouthful, "this is groovy."

"At last," said Nathan, "a word I comprehend."

"*Groovy*'s making a comeback."

Kory drank beer and smoked cigarettes. Nathan didn't mind the smell of tobacco; Ben had smoked. Kory talked of all his grand plans, the unbridled kind that youth declare with the exuberance of a puppy, with no fear of failure or the future. As a child, Kory's foot had been crushed in a car wreck. Told he would never walk properly, Kory vowed he would and much more, sports included. After he chose his profession, he also vowed he'd never give up on his patients.

Uncovered and unbound, Kory's shiny hair fell loosely about his shoulders. Nathan listened and sipped wine. Kory realized he'd been doing all the talking and questioned Nathan

        American Queer

about himself. Nathan taught English at the college, starting about when he met Ben, owner of a small garage where he took his car for service. Ben was tall and beefy. They dated, loved; Ben got sick, died. End of story.

"Tell me about him," said Kory. Nathan didn't say anything. "Sucks." Kory clipped him gently on the chin. "Buck up, little camper." He fondled a red marble egg from the bowl on the ottoman. "This is the coolest one. I could play the Easter Bunny and hide them." Kory smiled.

Nathan smiled. And thought Kory was so young, how his language made him cringe, that he probably liked to go comatose with video games or bang his head in dance clubs to music that sounded like hyenas in traps. And then he remembered using variations of these same excuses to Ben, 10 years older, not college educated, a fan of country western music. He had talked of engines, metric tire treads, lubricants not used in the bedroom, and not Dickens, syntax, or Mahler. But Ben was kind and intelligent, creative and funny, brimming with common sense. Still, Nathan doubted. "Where will we ever find common ground?" he had asked him. All their differences made no difference to Ben, who had responded to Nathan's question by taking his hand, placing it on his heart, and answering simply, "Here."

"Take it," said Nathan.

"For serious?"

"Take it."

"Sweet, thanks," said Kory, holding the red egg. "Pops, have you thought about what we found?"

"No," lied Nathan.

"I have," said Kory. "Imagine loving someone so much you'd *immure* their picture." He grinned.

Nathan grinned, too. "You don't know what you're asking for."

"Inform me."

"Don't play coy."

"So, talk about it. Teach me."

"OK," said Nathan. "Cocktail time."

     American Queer

One by one, Nathan opened five bottles, and looking Kory in the eye, took pills from each and swallowed them. "Wine chaser," said Nathan.

Kory flipped his red egg from hand to hand like a hot potato. "You don't scare me."

"I damn well should," said Nathan.

"You're weird," said Kory.

"Isn't everybody?" Nathan watched Kory clean up the dishes and prepare to leave. "Last year … " he began.

Kory stood still.

"Last year, Christmas cards came addressed to one name or two. I don't know which was worse. Before, when Ben was sick, the whole time was so macabre and cruel and pathetic and grisly and revolting—Shall I go on?"

"If you want."

"I don't want. And terrifying. And sad. And it all happened so fast."

"I know he's not forgotten," said Kory, motioning to the photo in the gold frame, "but is he unassailable?"

"What kind of quest—" began Nathan. "Don't answer, and don't give yourself away so easily. And I *am* old enough to be your *pops*."

Cutting off Kory's attempt to argue, the phone rang. Kory answered; it was a Mrs. Pick. After taking the receiver and a few animated minutes, Nathan held the print of L and M, and said, "Meet Mr. Merlin Smythe."

"You dog," said Kory. "Which bro is Merlin?"

"We'll find out tomorrow," said Nathan.

That night, he slept alone in his own Gethsemane. He confessed he remembered when the young stranger almost kissed him, and ached. Not again, he thought. I can't do this again. Something within wanted to argue.

Good Friday

After a drive the next morning beneath gray Good Friday clouds, Nathan and Kory sat in vinyl chairs next to a plastic rubber tree in the lobby of the Alpine Chateaux for Living. The rest home was neither mountain cabin nor castle-like

　　　　　　　　　　　　　　　　　American Queer

in design, but boxy and colorless. Disinfectant masked old smells, infusing the air with lemon scented decay.

"Why do you keep staring at me?" asked Kory. Clean-shaven, he wore a blue, button-down shirt, slacks, dress shoes, his long hair brushed and neatly bound.

"I'm not," said Nathan.

"I clean up nice, huh, Pops?"

"Behave."

The two men had checked in with the receptionist and were waiting for Mrs. Pick. Wearing a cantaloupe-colored suit with matching high heels, a large, mature woman entered the lobby. Her hair was dyed rust and streaked blond, teased and shellacked, whipped into a swirl about her head like a frosted cinnamon roll.

"Mrs. Pick?" inquired Nathan, rising on his crutches and with a glance that stirred Kory to do likewise.

"Yes," replied the woman warily.

"I'm Nathan Waters, and this is my—friend, Kory … "

"Addison," filled in Kory.

"Addison," repeated Nathan.

"You don't know your friend's last name?" asked Mrs. Pick.

"Brief memory lapse in the excitement of our meeting, ma'am," replied Nathan.

"Hmm." Mrs. Pick looked doubtful. "My father is not a well man, Mr. Waters. Any excitement may bring about his … "

"Understood, Mrs. Pick," said Nathan, "however, I think he may want to see what we have."

"May I?" she asked.

"It's of a personal nature, ma'am." said Nathan. "I hope you understand."

"I don't," said Mrs. Pick. "Never did. Whatever you've found, it must concern Levi."

"Levi?" asked Nathan.

Eyeing one man, then the next, Mrs. Pick said, "I don't pretend to be a modern woman, Mr. Waters. It was a relationship from long ago I knew very little about. I preferred it that way, and so did Father."

     American Queer

"Shall we, ma'am?" said Nathan, motioning for Mrs. Pick to lead the way.

Somewhat mollified by Nathan's manners, Mrs. Pick preceded the two men down a glossy corridor. They passed the cheery receptionist and aides and nurses and janitors, all greeting them with cheery nods and hellos. A TV set blared *One Life to Live*. A cheery volunteer announced Bingo numbers to residents, concentrating, confused, or quiescent. A few defiant souls performed chair-isthenics to movements called by a cheery woman in stretch pants accompanied by Glen Miller.

Entering a private room, Mrs. Pick sang her greeting, "Father, your visitors are here!"

A cuckoo clock with pine cones dangling from chains hung above a hospital bed. French windows opened onto a patio and framed a green and violet mountain view. Merlin Smythe lay in the bed with metal railings raised high. His mouth gaped, drool glistened on his unshaven chin, and his thick, white hair burst like a tumbleweed. His left hand, blue-veined and liver spotted, stuck out of the covers and twitched. A ring encircled its wedding finger.

Mrs. Pick turned red from embarrassment and exasperation. "Father?" No movement. "Father?" she called again more urgently and bent close to his face. "Father!" He snorted loudly; she shrieked short and high.

"Daughter?" inquired the old man in a gravelly English accent.

"Oh my, yes, it's Hannah," twittered Mrs. Pick with relief. "I was afraid—"

"Not yet, Daughter," he rasped. "Keep you on your twinkle toes." Kory covered up a chuckle. Detecting the presence of two other people, Mr. Smythe squinted and said, "Bring the morticians, did you?"

"Apparently for nothing," said Mrs. Pick, joining her father's joke. "We're all terribly disappointed."

"Not by half as much as me."

"Why aren't you up? I called earlier for the staff to have you clean and dressed. Have you had breakfast?"

"I don't know."

"You don't know?"

     American Queer

"If I knew, I'd know, wouldn't I?" retorted Mr. Smythe. "Yes, if you call cold mush breakfast. Threw it at the damn nurse and told her I wanted kippers and French toast, then a nap. I like naps. Now Daughter, who in Hades are these lovely lads?"

"The visitors I told you about," answered Mrs. Pick. "Don't you remember?"

"Mr. Addison and Mr. Waters," said Mr. Smythe. "I'm old, not senile."

Mrs. Pick helped her father sit up and placed pillows behind his back. Nathan stepped forward and introduced himself and Kory.

"Crutches?" asked Mr. Smythe. "You should be more attentive, young man."

"Yes, sir," said Nathan, noticing Kory's smile. He detailed the reason behind their visit and said, "We found something that might interest you."

"I'm a living mummy living in a tomb," said Mr. Smythe. "Medieval this place is—I'm allowed to mix my metaphors—and nothing interests me anymore except leaving it. I shall miss that TV show, what's it called, oh yes, *Friends*. So young and cutesy. They'll be that way forever, unlike the rest of us who have not been burned onto film."

"But you are on film," said Nathan.

"Me?" asked Mr. Smythe. Receiving the velvet case, he ran his dry and gnarled fingers over the soft material a bit anxiously. Lingering on the gold clasp, he unfastened it and looked at the photo. "Hand me my specs, Daughter. Let's see, what have we here?" At the moment of recognition, Mr. Smythe's eyes opened wide as big, blue buttons magnified by thick lenses. His mouth dropped open, and he stared out the French windows as though trying to focus on something he saw. Mr. Smythe turned away and let the case fall onto his lap as big tears flowed down his cheeks and little moans escaped from his chest. The cuckoo clock squawked its hour.

"Father, Father," said Mrs. Pick, patting his shoulder. "I warned you, Mr. Waters. Please leave."

Before Kory unlocked the car, he hopped a jig. "That was freak-alicious, know what I mean?"

     American Queer

"Unfortunately, yes," said Nathan, "but this was painful for Mr. Smythe."

"Yeah, you're right. We'll come back."

"Maybe we made a mistake."

"No way. Mr. Smythe is one cool dude, and you found your man." Under his breath Kory added, "and not just him."

Nathan thought about how he would feel if, 50 years from now, a stranger presented a portrait of him and Ben. He imagined the sorrow, once thought erased, rising and surprising from unknown depths.

"We forgot our pic," said Kory.

"It's not ours," said Nathan.

Holy Saturday

"But why?" asked Kory, listening to Nathan retell his conversation with Mrs. Pick as he drove them back to the Alpine Chateaux.

After their visit yesterday, a frantic and somewhat jealous Mrs. Pick had called from the nursing home. "He insists on seeing you now," she had said. "Both of you." Father had hounded Daughter to bring back the lads and the staff to bugger off, the head nurse informing her that she either calm her father or consider moving him. She had relented to her father's demand and hoped Mr. Waters and Mr. Addison would comply.

"Apparently, Mr. Smythe kept repeating," said Nathan, answering Kory's question, "*Someone must know. Someone must know.*"

"Like, know what?" asked Kory.

In a fuchsia frock outside her father's room, Mrs. Pick paced like a sentry guarding its golden goose. Without greeting, she said, "They're threatening to expel my father, or at the very least, drug or restrain him. I won't stand for that. I hope you accept your responsibility."

"Mrs. Pick, I understand how difficult this must be, and thank you for making the arrangement, but we are here at your father's request," said Nathan. "The last thing we want to do is upset him."

　　　　　　　　　　　　　　　　American Queer

"It's a bit late for that," said Mrs. Pick, "but he's calm now." And, as though she alone cared, added, "You don't know how hard I've tried to—" She looked away for a moment. "It doesn't matter."

"Yes, it does, Mrs. Pick," said Nathan. "Love always matters. A great deal."

Mrs. Pick looked surprised.

In a striped robe, Merlin Smythe, shaved and his hair combed, sat in a high-backed wheelchair and dozed. He hugged the velvet case close to his heart. Hearing noise, he scowled and peered over his specs. "Thought you were the bloody nurse come to wake me to give me my sleeping pill."

Kory stifled a snicker.

Mrs. Pick clucked and puffed her father's pillow. "Now Father, the nice staff is here to take care of you," she said. "If you don't behave, they'll make you leave."

"You leave," said Mr. Smythe.

"But Daddy!"

"Leave us, Daughter," commanded Father.

Mrs. Pick reluctantly departed with a warning eye to Nathan.

Once the door shut, Mr. Smythe opened the velvet case and beheld its reflection. He looked out the French window, a slight breeze blowing in and fluttering the curtain. "I can almost see him before me," said Mr. Smythe. "Bette Davis was right. Old age isn't for sissies, and I'm the biggest sissy bugger in the world." He sniffled and rubbed his eyes. "Anybody still smoke in this bloody world?"

Kory wheeled out Mr. Smythe, wearing a shawl and lap rug, onto a patio where they sat around a table. The late afternoon ceiling of clouds moved east, and breaking through a stripe of clear sky on the horizon, the setting sun dazzled the three men with its gold-white blaze. The air was unusually warm, and fragrant air promised spring. Nathan saw traces of the handsome, happy youth in the photograph, but today, he thought Mr. Smythe looked more like a fragile skeleton with cellophane skin than a man. For now, he lived. Kory lit cigarettes for them both, and Mr. Smythe inhaled deeply.

"Ahhh," he exhaled, "the breath of life."

　　　　　　　　　　　　　　　　American Queer

"Getting buzzed, Mr. Smythe?" asked Kory.

"Oh my, yes," Merlin cackled. "Call me Merlin. I say, dear boy, you wouldn't happen to have any brandy on you?"

"Sorry, dude, sir dude—Merlin, no."

"Adorable." Merlin smiled and prompted, "Don't you think he's adorable, Mr. Waters? Or am I being presumptuous?"

"Nate here thinks I'm a juvenile delinquent," said Kory. His subject frowned.

"Youth must have its day, for night comes soon enough. So," said Merlin, tapping the velvet case in his lap. "You want a story. What once was lost, now is found."

"Only what you care to share," said Nathan.

"Yes, well, so much flying around up here," said Merlin, pointing to his head, "let's see what lands." He returned his gaze to the photograph, and sighed, "My God, he was a handsome bloke. Not that you can tell from this."

"You were a hottie, too," said Kory.

"Beg pardon?"

"A handsome bloke."

"Bless you, dear boy," said Merlin. "Handy around the house, too, he was. I was chief cook and bottle washer. Lovely Levi." The old man drifted off.

"When was the picture taken?" asked Nathan.

Merlin returned from his reverie. "Beg pardon?"

"When was it taken?" repeated Nathan.

"What?"

"The photograph."

"Oh. Haven't the foggiest," said Merlin. "No, let's see … sometime in the late 30s? That's when we met at the newspaper. Levi was a reporter. Hmm, let's see … then I was promoted to photographer, and to celebrate, I bought a … a tripod. Oh my, well done, Merlin. Suddenly, like yesterday. We were trying it out in the front yard, and Levi caught me off guard because he … He presented me with a wedding band. He'd just bought us rings, platinum bands, a bit outrageous, but lovely. So lovely. It's a wonder we weren't tarred and feathered and ran out of town because a neighbor saw us, wife of a judge, if memory serves me. But she must have liked poufs. She married one, an ugly old bugger."

"Who took the picture?" asked Nathan.

Merlin sucked on his cigarette as though he drew his last breath. "I did."

"You?" Nathan looked confused. "How?"

"With my other hand. That's me on the right. I held a hidden press-button attached to a cord running to the camera." Merlin cackled and said, "Silly shenanigans, especially for Levi, who was a bit of a snob, from the Spenser-Sutton clan. He was 10 years older than me, loved Sinatra. Mind you, I couldn't abide that skinny gangster, had a voice like stepping on a cat's tail. Levi graduated from university; me, from the school of hard knocks. I've the bruises to prove it. Pluck and luck got me that newspaper job. But Levi and I—We were happy. Then war came, bunch of malarkey, that. Bloody Hitler and Stalin, the bastards, just wait till I see them. Mad as hatters in a cake-tin. Levi and I were eventually drafted; I was an American citizen by then. We were both stationed in London. Pluck and luck that. Levi became an officer, and I was assigned a benign duty— that's what the upstairs said—to record for history our glorious victories. If what I saw was benign or glorious … my God, the carnage. Levi was part of the Normandy Invasion, died on some blood-soaked beach. There's a white cross in France with his name on it. Visited him once. That was enough. Our few years together, however, were not. All spilled milk now."

Merlin dragged deeply off his cigarette and looked into the distance, lost in his past and not returning to his present. Nathan and Kory looked at each other, wondering if they should call someone, until falling ashes brought the old man back to the Alpine Chateaux.

"Good Lord," said Merlin, brushing his lap. The two strangers startled him, and he panicked. "Who in Hades are you? Where's Daughter? I want Daughter!"

"Sir, we're Kory and Nathan," said Nathan. "You've been telling us about Levi."

"Levi?" Merlin twisted his ring and peered through his thick specs painfully perplexed.

"The photograph," said Kory. "Levi, your lover."

"He's dead!" cried Merlin, but recognizing the velvet case snapped him back to reality. His breathing returned to

     American Queer

normal, and he sighed heavily. "Oh … oh, yes. Spilled milk …
all spilled … "

Nathan said, "We should come back another time."

"No," insisted Merlin. "Forgive my lunacy. There is
little time. Where did I leave off babbling?"

"The Normandy Invasion," said Kory.

"That was eons ago, dear boy," said Merlin.

"Yes, sir," said Kory.

"Ah, yes … carnage … hatters in a cake-tin," mumbled
Merlin. "After Levi died … a—how shall I say—sympathetic
superior considered me a war widow and transferred me to the
states to settle Levi's affairs. He'd left me a life insurance policy,
quite a large one. Pluck and luck that. So like him to keep it
secret. We had to keep so much secret then, not like now, bugger
boys on the telly everywhere, delicious, if frustrating. After the
war, the house we had rented together was for sale, so I bought
it. Ever hear of anything so morbidly sentimental? There was a
small fire, and not from my clumsy smoking habits. Every
snapshot burned but this one. Hated seeing it. But destroying this
last bit of our history—your history, sweet boys—was out of the
question. So, being a silly nit, I buried it in the wall when I was
cleaning up the fire mess. Plum forgot about it. Don't know what
I expected. Wet and soppy, I was. Decades later, I retired and put
the house in Daughter's name, the least I could do. I vowed
never to love again. I haven't." Merlin wiped his nose on his
sleeve and stubbed out his cigarette. "A mistake that. My 2-year-
old mind races, and this ancient body sags. Bloody horror. But
it's only a body." Clearing his throat, he inquired, "So, are you
two lovers?"

Nathan stammered a nonsensical denial; Kory remained
silent.

"A simple question, sir, you can relax your knickers,"
said Merlin, "and take advice from an old sod. Life isn't just, but
love evens the odds a smidge." He focused on the captured
second of his past again and said, "What a lovely testament.
Turned not a few heads in our day we did. Levi loved me. I made
him happy. It's the only decent thing I ever did."

The breeze blew the curtain again.

"Father?" came a voice from inside.

                              American Queer

Merlin cringed at the sound of his daughter's voice. "Including siring her, same year I met Levi. I wasn't myself, and then thanks to him, I was. She and I, we tolerate and torment each other. I wish she traveled more. Did you see that bloody cuckoo she brought me?"

"Very rad," said Kory.

"Beg pardon?" asked Merlin.

"I like it."

"I'd like to wring its neck."

Kory laughed but stopped when tears trickled down the old man's cheek.

With a shaking hand, Merlin gave the velvet case to him. "Take it. I'm done. And chilly, take me in." Gathering the shawl around him, he composed himself and appealed to Kory, "I say, dear boy, could I trouble you for another fag? And matches. Bloody nurse keeps stealing them, and what good's a fag without fire?"

During the drive back, Kory said, "Old people sure beg pardon a lot," but neither had much else to say.

Upon entering his house, Nathan picked up the ringing phone, Mrs. Pick calling to say Father wanted to talk to him. His breath was shallow, his voice weak, and Nathan strained to hear him.

"By any chance, Mr. Waters," asked Merlin, "did you find a note in the velvet case?"

"The note, yes, oh no, we forgot it," said Nathan. "I am so sorry, Mr. Smythe, we forgot to bring it, but hold on please."

Kory scrambled through papers, found the slip of yellowed paper, and handed it to Nathan.

"Mr. Smythe, I've got it."

"A trifle of piffle really, but would you mind terribly reading it to me?"

"I'd be happy to.

> *"For M,*
>
> *By the man who dreams patiently*
> *near the lagoon on the Isle of Irony*
> *in the violent, violet Sea of Uncertainty*
> *is hooked in a net splashing with ecstasy.*
>
> *Love always!*

Merlin repeated, "*Love always! L.* Soon, I shall be sailing that sea. Hope it's not too violent. Oceans make me queasy. Ah well, pluck and—" He was quiet for a moment, then said he had gifts for the lads for all their trouble, and, if convenient, Daughter would deliver them. He asked about the house, and Nathan invited him to come see for himself. Merlin thought that a delightful idea; they could drink brandy and smoke cigarettes and watch bugger boys on the telly. He cackled, which started a coughing fit, and when it subsided, said, "Thank you for indulging Methuselah's whims. Remember us, Mr. Waters. Beautiful Levi and me. Remember."

Hours later, Mrs. Pick arrived carrying an old camera and a Swiss box. "I am to give you this," she said, and handed Kory the cuckoo clock.

"Awesome," said Kory. "Nate, check it out."

Mrs. Pick was miffed. "I thought Father would like it."

"Tell Sir Dude—Mr. Smythe—thanks," said Kory.

From her purse Mrs. Pick pulled out a tarnished ring. "You may keep the photo; I certainly don't want it back. The ring," she said, "is to be placed on the wedding finger of one of you, and—"

Above "What!" and "Impossible!" and "Ridiculous!"— all coming from Nathan—Mrs. Pick's voice rose. "Please! And I am to witness the act and take two pictures."

"With that Polaroid?" asked Kory. "Love the retro."

"Your father is obviously not himself," said Nathan. "I don't mean to sound insensitive—"

"But you are," interrupted Kory. "Why two?"

"*In case of fire,*" said Mrs. Pick, "was Father's reply."

"Why are you doing this?" asked Nathan.

"Because if I don't," answered Mrs. Pick, "Father said he'd disinherit me— and return."

"Like, to haunt you?" asked Kory. "That's jacked."

Mrs. Pick glared at Kory. "I am not a superstitious woman, Mr. Addison. You can do what you want after I leave, but Father's instructions were explicit."

"And what if Nate refuses?" asked Kory.

To him Nathan asked, "And you're not?"

"It's a dying man's last request, and if I can't deny it—" Mrs. Pick stopped, then pushed on, "—how can you? He's my father, Mr. Waters … my father."

Kory took Nathan's hand and the ring from Mrs. Pick, sliding it on his wedding finger. Nathan, bracing himself on his crutches, tipped slightly; Kory caught him and looked into his eyes. They sparkled. After clicks and flashes, grinding gears and the chops of an old camera disgorging its record, two pictures lay drying on a table.

Mrs. Pick slipped her purse over her elbow. "I'd best be getting back to Father. He wants a full report."

Kory saw the daughter to the door. "How is Mr. Smythe?"

"Tonight," said Mrs. Pick, "Father smiled at me."

Nathan sat on the sofa. He took off the band and placed it on the velvet case. "I can't," he said.

"No surprise," said Kory. "You can't even say my name." He sat next to Nathan. "Come on. Like Sir Dude said, to even the odds a titch."

"Smidge. You should go."

"Nathan—"

"Don't. Please, Kory?"

"At least you said my name." The young man walked out the front door, locking it as he did.

In the middle of the night, Nathan woke up thinking he heard Ben's voice.

Glowing in moonlight, a tall, blurry silhouette stood by his bed.

"Who are you?"

"The Easter Bunny."

"How'd you get in?"

"Hopped … forgot to leave your keys."

"What do you want?"

"Show me how to love you." The lambent figure stripped, peeled back the covers, and depressed the big, big bed of love, straddling Nathan, sitting on his thighs.

"You're heavy."

"So harsh. I'll leave."

"Someday. Or me you."

"Someday."

The shadow put a ring on his finger, and one by one, it kissed his injured fingertips and palms.

"Stop."

"Shhh. If you want to fall in love," the shadow whispered in his ear, "you'll fall in love."

Nathan caressed a lightning bolt tattoo on a bicep. "I must be mad."

"As a hatter in a cake-tin."

<u>Easter</u>

Early Sunday morning, Nathan rose to bright light and a cuckoo squawk. He found something hard and cold under the sheets and removed a red marble egg. Been a long time since anything got laid in this bed, he thought. Resurrecting himself and careful of his wrapped foot, he waddled to the living room and witnessed a new man placing three photographs and a note in plastic wrap, then in a velvet box, then in a plastic bag, then inside a niche in a damaged wall. The gold frame held the same picture of him and Ben, but another of them had been replaced by a new picture of him almost kissing this new man. The pill bottles had been neatly arranged. Only his remained next to a packet of photos and a jar of salve.

The new man walked to Nathan. "Morning, camper," he said, and wrapped his arms around his waist. "Silk boxers. Sweet. Man, you've got some serious '80's bed-head going on. Nice face. Why hide it?"

"Lose the hat, and pull up your pants."

"Deal."

In the bathroom, Nathan washed his nice face, combed his '80's hair, and decided to get a haircut. But why the kid was obsessed with his hair, he never understood.

"Can you hear me?" hollered the new voice.

"Yes!" Nathan caught snippets of his plans: finishing the living room, fixing the driveway, setting up a blade course, something about grabbing 180s and edge riding and doing a gap to bank off the roof—all expressed with the happiness of a puppy. The neighbors will complain. Let them.

"Are you listening to me?" hollered the new voice again.

"Yes!" Yes, thought Nathan, talk forever. I understand little you're saying, but you make lovely sounds.

He shuffled to the alley to pick a small bouquet from Mrs. Grady's garden. This morning, two finches attempted to rebuild their nest, defying gravity with their yo-yo act like the new man in his home planning similar feats on boots with wheels. He liked the feel of the ring on his finger. Then, he coughed, and thought he saw a ghost among the daffodils.

WOLF!

1997

A Family History Dedicated to:

Focus on the Family, Anita Bryant,
Pat Buchanan, Jerry Falwell,
Jesse Helms, Rush Limbaugh,
Fred Phelps and his brood,
the Pope, Ronald Reagan, Oral Roberts,
Pat Robertson, Phyllis Schlafly—

and the Forever-Changing American Family

Strange, how I almost killed him that early, foggy morning. Nearly run him over. Been sheriff these past 15 years and ain't never run no one over. Didn't feel like starting then. Hell, I thought, damn drunk hippie. Braked so hard my tires smoked, almost swerved into the bar ditch. Damn pup.

He had come stumbling down the steep slope of the mountainside, running onto the road, waving his arms like a crazy man, almost buck naked. Not that I ever seen a naked buck, but he wasn't wearing even a smile from the waist down. Talk about rode hard and put away wet. His shirt was in shreds, bloody stripes of scratches everywhere—face, chest, arms, legs, buttocks—long, girly hair quilled with twigs and leaves. His eyes—ain't never gonna forget 'em. Bug-eyed, bloodshot, wide with—with horror. Blue they was. I reckon they still is.

Stranger still, his story. At least, to hear him tell it.

Anyway, fit to spit and nail his cute ass behind bars or somewhere, I was getting out of my truck, and the kid damn near tore the driver door off. I was about to punch him a good one when he pulled me out and grabbed me by the arms—small, but strong he was—when I noticed a silver band on his ring finger. I swear it burned me or cut me, and I yanked away. He looked right into me, mouth open like he wanted to scream, say something, but couldn't. His terrified eyes rolled back into his head like two pearl marbles, and dead limp he went like a wet sock falling into my arms. We sunk to the ground. He was shaking, so I fetched a blanket out of the back and covered him up, but not before I got a good look at him. Pretty young man, blond. Hung mighty fine, I'll say that for the kid. Of course, I looked. Any man would, and those who say contrary are liars. I could tell he was a looker even though his sweet face appeared like he'd shaved with a cheese grater. Them scratches, some of them deep, and tooth marks on the neck and shoulders? Wolf. I should know. Seen a few dead dogs and deer these past years, a steer or two. Rare for a wolf to attack a human, ain't never heard of it, but it's possible. Anything is possible. There was that once, quite a while ago. Yep, lucky to be alive. I should know.

I had a thermos of hot coffee in the truck. Got it out, knelt, sat him up, and we leaned against the truck. Held him in my arms. Soft skin he had but scraped god-awful like he'd been dragged over rough ground. And his wrists were covered in big red puncture-like marks. I held the cup to his lips, poured a little down his mouth but he choked, then sipped on his own, dribbling coffee down his chin. He moved to take my hands, but I told him I'd guide the cup. I didn't want another burn from that silver band. He looked up at me, pitiful. Oh God, was all he said. I thought, good, he can talk.

I said, Son, what happened to you? He looked at me, eyes wide open again, mouth ready to make a sound, but no sound coming out. I'm going to radio for an ambulance, I said.

Please don't, he said. Please.

He huddled in my arms, couldn't get close enough, kind of whimpering-like. Now son, I said, you need a doctor.

No! he blurted out.

I told him, I'm the sheriff, and I've got to report this. Tell me what happened.

He said, I've been—but he couldn't go on.

Attacked? He nodded yes and squeezed his eyes shut, but I knew he couldn't shut out what he was seeing in his mind. Who did this? I asked. I was checking to see if he'd name someone, but he didn't bite.

   American Queer

Who? he asked.

What then, what did this to you? The kid shook his head side to side, tears streaming out of his eyes like tiny waterfalls. Now look, I said, a little more forcefully, I've got to radio in.

No! he shouted.

Sonny boy, I started, but before I could finish, he agreed. OK, I'll tell you, he said, but don't leave me, he begged. Please don't leave me.

I declare I ain't going nowhere, son. You are worn slap out, so just relax, and tell me real slow what happened. Take your time. I'm here for you.

So, there we sat on the road. Me leaning back against my truck, him in my arms, his head on my chest, the fog swirling around us painting everything like a black and white TV set on the fritz. His story was a real doozy. You ain't gonna believe it. This is what he told me.

***

I was hiking up Ghost Ridge Trail. It's the week before finals, and I like to come up here to study and relax. I'm supposed to graduate next month, become a zoologist. Now, all I want to do is die.

Anyway, I came to a beautiful meadow and decided to make camp for the night along its forest edge. I built a fire, made a little dinner, and watched the sun set over the mountains. I laid against a log for hours, thinking about the future, but now, nothing matters. Anyway, I laid there so long a full moon rose. And even though the beacon was bright, beautiful stars speckled the blackness. Like God had thrown a fist full of diamonds up into the night, and there they sparkled. But there is no God.

I rolled a joint, took a few tokes. I shouldn't be telling this to an officer of the law, but I want you to know everything. Everything. I stared at the last few flames of the fire, imagining all sorts of things—Pompeii and Thor, dragons, beating hearts. Dreamy and fantastic what you see in the coals and the embers and the fire. I was stoned and tired, so I doused the fire, rolled out my sleeping bag, took off my jeans, and climbed in. I left my shirt and long johns on because the air was chilly, but the bag was nice and cozy. I was asleep before my head hit the pillow.

American Queer

I was awakened by a loud, sharp snap. I thought a log on the fire might have flamed up. I heard a couple more, looked up, saw the bushes move. Good pot, I said out loud, and started to whistle, but it didn't help. Another snap.

Who's there? I called. No one answered. In my backpack I found my knife.

The bushes rustled and a growl, low and deep, came from them, then circled until it was behind me. It's a bear, I thought. Or a cougar. Ha! I should have been so lucky. Soon, a howl followed, and I knew. Wolf.

God, I can hear it now, and it won't get out of my head, this howl, shrill, high, and loud and long it was. I tried to stop breathing, didn't dare turn around. Stay still, I said to myself, don't panic and it'll go away. Wolves are afraid of humans, but this one was not. This—this dog-beast growled again, and I could hear it crawling toward me, feel it crouching and slinking and scraping along the ground. I've got to run for it; it's my only chance, I thought. So, I clutched my knife tighter and prepared to bolt, to run for my life, get away from it, fly away fast.

I was shaking and sweating, my heart pounding painfully, the presence, whatever it was, sneaking closer. So, I lurched out of the bag and crawled as fast as I could, making it to my knees with one leg up, about to stand and run when—when with a horrible roar it was upon me. I screamed and it grabbed my legs, pulling me back, dragging my face on the ground, my knife flying beyond my reach. In those long seconds I waited for the ripping and biting and slashing. Instead, a huge weight dropped itself on my back and sat very still. It started snorting and breathing hard. This was no ordinary wolf. Because— because it was smelling me, it's playing with me, no, no, no, it's playing with me. It's going to cripple me and later, feed me to the wolves. Ha! That's a good one, feed me to the wolves. Ha-ha-ha!

The creature growled again and then howled again. I was so scared, I was crying, everything was blurry, and snot was choking me, and I could hardly breathe with this weight upon me. Suddenly, the mauling started again, and I screamed and screamed. I could feel claws like razor blades slicing my skin. I was so terrified and tried to get away and clawed the ground, but

  American Queer

it would just yank me back. The beast wasn't slashing me to
shreds like I kept waiting for, no. It was tearing off my long-
johns, shredding them until—until I was naked under the stars.

Its weight shifted again. And I felt coarse fur—like steel
wool—moving over my buttocks and thighs as it lay on my legs.
I heard more sniffing, and a cold, wet nudge worked its way
between my—my cheeks, and I thought, God, it's going to
gobble my ass off in one chunk. But it didn't. I only felt
drippings, and hot, heavy breath. I could smell it, rotten and
bloody, a dead smell.

And then, this wet, rough thing stuck itself—between
me. And—and it started licking me—licking me. I'm not lying, I
swear to you, please believe me! It licked me like it was lapping
at water. I could hear that clicking sound, and a deep purring
noise—the beast was purring!—and its big, raspy tongue dug
deep and stayed there, for what? In god's name, for what?

The creature stretched itself on top of my body. For
chrissakes, what the hell is this? I still couldn't see it, and I
waited—waited for the killing bite. Oh, I got bites all right, but
the killing bite never came. One quick bite, one hard shake, one
snap of the neck, and I wouldn't have known what was to come.
The monster had other plans.

Next—the next thing—a hand, more like a paw, purple-
veined and hairy with long claws, came round and seized my
wrist, and its other paw came up and seized my other wrist. What
kind of animal would grip a man's wrists like that? No animal
I've ever studied. It breathed in my ear and dripped on my
neck—God, the stench—and its drool rolled down my face. And
then—then it spread my legs with its scratchy knees and I—and I
felt—

Don't look at me, don't look at me. But I've got to tell
someone, yes, got to get it out. Yeah, get it out all right. Maybe
this is a nightmare and I'll wake up and you'll tell me so, won't
you? Won't you? No, I guess you won't. You can't.

Then, I felt something—something hot and hard. And—
and it poked me between my cheeks, and I shrieked and tried to
get away, to buck off this freak, and I didn't care if it ripped out
my heart, but not that, jesuschrist, not that! I tried, but I couldn't.
You've got to believe me; I couldn't get away! It dug its claws

into my wrists, and I cried out and it roared so loud in my ear I thought my head would split in two and it kept jabbing and grinding its hips trying to get in—to get in me. I clenched tight, as tight as I could, but this stinging thing kept punching me and it was so stiff and strong and forceful, and it kept at me and at me until I couldn't keep it out any longer. I tried to keep it out. I tried, but this satyr of the forest was aroused with a raw hunger I knew I couldn't resist. So, I let go, and laid there, whimpering like a—like a baby.

Once I surrendered, it ripped inside me! Oh god, the pain! The blood-engorged bulge swelling bigger and bigger, thrusting deeper and deeper, gouging me until it could go no further.

I want to die, let me die please, oh Lord, let me die!

But a funny thing happened. Yeah, real funny. The beast stopped moving. Everything went so still, so quiet. All I could sense was this bulge throbbing to the beating of my heart until they seemed to become one. My heart and this hardness, both sharing one internal, synchronized pulse. For a moment, I and the beast were one.

I wanted to die, but I didn't.

No, I didn't die. I could feel myself against the dirt and I—and I—I was aroused. And I—I don't know. Its paws released my wrists, and then its claws hooked my hips and jerked me to my knees. It moaned and grunted, reached around my chest, and wrapped its arms around me pulling me to itself, slamming me onto itself, squeezing me, suffocating me until I felt faint. I could feel its steely fur scratching my skin. It bit my neck and I thought the killing bite had come. I expected my head to jerk and my neck to snap and for all to go dark. How I wished that, how I wished to feel nothing. But its sharp teeth didn't sink deeper, more like, clamped onto me to keep me still, to finish its ferocious rutting. And there, there I was—the beast thrusting into me and my god, rock hard, jutting straight out, bouncing up and down. I've never been so erect.

I repulse you, don't I? I make you sick. I'm making myself sick, but I have to go on. And—and I can feel you, feel that you want me to go on.

I didn't think I could take it much longer, but longer it went on. One of its paws gripped me by my— No! I shrieked. No, it's going to rip it off, no! I didn't dare push the paw away and the claws of its other paw raked my chest over and over as though the demon wanted to dig out my heart. But—but it didn't hurt me—not down there. The pads of its palm were soft, leathery, and caressing me, and now I—I was dripping, and I could feel myself hard as a tube of iron. I thought, this is it, this is it, I'm going to die, but hell, at least I'm going to die in ecstasy.

I must have done a poor job dousing the fire because the hairy hulk kicked the ashes, reviving sparks, then crackling flames, and all I could see was a glowing shadow, the shadow of a big black beast with two backs. I was terrified the beast would burst through my belly. It slobbered all over me and growled and roared and still it stabbed me over and over. In the shadow I saw the beast throw its head back and with a furious burst of booming sound and a bellow of steamy, stinking breath, I knew it was shooting its savage slime as I felt its molten seed scalding my insides, and this blazing feeling outside me as I—as I blasted, and I was dying, all the life rushing, bursting, splatting out of me, and it went on and on and on, I didn't think I'd ever stop. And all the while, this demon behind me held me tightly and jerked and convulsed and snarled until finally, it yowled a long, wailing cry offering its lusty, shrill bay up, up to the full moon.

And all of me was alight inside from the carnal fire of the fiend.

***

Like I said, a real doozy.

I cleared my throat and moved a little. I don't mind telling you I had to adjust myself. I've seen and heard just about everything there is to see and hear, but this was one hell of a yarn. I said to the kid, You're safe now.

I don't think so, he said.

From where I looked down upon him, I could see his pretty eyes looking out at the gray mist of nothing, and I could see the curl of his long lashes, the fullness of his parted lips like

                                    American Queer

a puckered flower bud. In a daze he was, disoriented obviously, crazy possibly.

I've lost my mind, the kid said.

All I wanted to do was hold the poor little guy and protect him. Shush now, son, I told him. All you've lost is your way. You're tired and beat up, and we've got to get a wiggle on and get you to a doctor.

Not yet, he whispered, pleaded.

Son, you're in mighty rough shape.

The kid grabbed my hand and kissed it. Please don't turn me in.

I yanked my hand away, and said, Careful, that ring has a sharp edge, it cut me. You should take it off.

No, said the kid. It's all that's keeping me sane.

OK, OK. You don't want to see a doctor? Why?

Because—because—because that's not all.

What do you mean, that's not all?

What's today? the kid asked.

Tuesday, I replied, the seventeenth.

Nine days.

The boy continued his story.

***

Nine days. Nine days ago, I started this hike. After the beast had—had used me, I passed out, I guess. I kept waking up, but the dream—the nightmare kept going, on and on. I must have wandered from my campsite. I found a cave—maybe a cabin in ruins—and remember laying on leaves and moss and waking up shivering from the night cold. I was so sore, God it burned, the blood flowing out of me. I was afraid I'd bleed to death. I found some rags—and plugged the heavy flow.

And I swear I remember someone lying next to me and keeping me warm with the comforting heat of its body. I say someone because I think I saw arms around me, normal with normal hands. Thought I saw a tattoo, a star or something. Once in a while, I would feel a nuzzle close to my ear and hear a purring hum, soft and gentle. And I was terrified the beast had returned. I must have been dreaming. I never saw it—or that sick man, if it was a man, never saw the brute that kept me captive.

    American Queer

I remember eating berries and some green leaves, and I drank cool water from a little pool. I'd dunk my head in it. The cold felt good. And then a bag of food appeared. I didn't care how; I wasn't hungry. I remember passing out and waking to hands stroking my chest and my hair. Like you're doing now.

And every time I'd wake up, I burned more and more until I—I felt so nauseated, so full, and not from eating. I don't know how else to describe it—this fullness in my gut. I'd wake up to cramps, and I'd heave and still I burned more, and my stomach felt fuller.

And then—oh God help me—it moved. I felt something move in my stomach. I swear I'm telling you the truth. I'm not making this up. I felt something move in my stomach. And then I'd pass out again and wake up feeling even fuller than before.

I guess the days went by. They had to, didn't they? Nine of them at any rate. I woke up—this morning I guess, must be—and there was a violent kick in my stomach. I thought I was going to puke my guts out, or something was going to burst inside me. And this movement seemed to be going down, you know, to get out. I was terrified, I didn't know what was happening. I got on my knees. That was the only way I could bear the pain. Something inside was stretching and shifting, but I wasn't. Yes, I was forcing it out, so I pulled the sopping bloody rags out of me. Get out of me, I screamed, get out! My contractions kept moving it along, and I didn't know if this was going to kill me, but even if it did, I wanted it out. Whatever it was. And it wanted out, was trying to get out. I screamed and grunted and heaved. I was losing my mind and losing this—this thing inside me. Out! Get out of me! With one huge force I pushed, and I thought I'd shit my guts out, thought I'd die!

And then, I heard this—this wet plop. On the ground behind me. I slumped forward. I was exhausted and sweating and crying and groaning, and I was on fire again. I felt my blood gushing out of me. I heard this little cry, this little yelp. I knew right then I'd gone over the edge—over the edge of my soul.

I didn't want to know what had come out of me, and I don't know how, but I crawled out of the cave or cabin, whatever it was. I didn't know where the demon was, didn't care. Let it find me and rip my throat out. I hoped it would. I got up. I was so stiff and bruised; every part of me hurt.

And so, I walked. I just walked. I headed downhill, probably because it was easier. And I kept walking, walking through this fog like I was walking through my mind—what was left of it—until the hill got steeper, and I couldn't stop myself, and I thought I'd fall but I didn't. And then I found this road and—and you came along.

Why didn't you run me over? Why? Why didn't you kill me? Because—because don't you see? Don't you understand? I liked it. Not this cramping and—but the other, the before. God help me, but I liked it. As much as I felt like dying, and still do, I've never felt more alive, such pure ecstasy. During this primal mating, the fiend consumed me as sure as if he'd eaten me. It devoured my soul, and with all my soul, I loved this unnatural act with this unnatural beast. And now, I am no more.

***

The kid's last words echoed in the silence of the foggy morning.

God help me, I loved it, said the kid again.

Shush, my young man, I said. Quiet, quiet now.

You believe me, don't you? the kid asked me. Say you believe me.

I believe, I said, that you've been out in the woods too long. Exposure, shock. Might be there was more in that marijuana you smoked than you think. Something happened, some varmint got you. I can see that. But son, that tale stretches from one horse to another. Let's keep it between you and me.

You think I made it up? asked the kid.

He looked up at me with a look I'll never forget. It doesn't matter what I think, I said. The kid closed his eyes and leaned back into me. I told him, Now, before they send the posse out looking for me, I've got to call the station and get you to a doctor.

No! the kid yelled. Leave me, leave me, let me die.

Son, you're tore up mighty bad, and I can't let you die. I—I don't want you to die.

Right then, from the embankment came the sound of rustling and a small rockslide and movement down the steep mountainside. We heard a sound, soft at first, then louder as it came closer. Sort of a whimpering. We were still sitting on the ground with our backs to the truck, and we could hear whatever it was moving by the truck's front grill. The kid looked terrified. Slowly, I released my gun from its holster and unlocked it. The sun was shining through the fog. What came around was all black shadow, and I aimed to fire when I realized sudden-like what it was: a crawling, bawling baby. A baby. Naked and dirty. But instead of being on its hands and knees, it crawled on its hands and—and feet. Its thighs were more like the back legs or haunches of a dog, its cute little butt sticking straight up in the air. It looked at me so wide-eyed and innocent, scared, lost.

I knew it wouldn't hurt me, so I put my gun down, gently shifted the kid, stood up, walked over to the pup, and knelt down. I said, What you doing out here all by yourself? My, you're a cute little feller, but for a baby, you sure could use a shave.

When I turned around, the kid was pointing and fixing to shoot the pup. Son, now hold your horses, I said real calm-like.

How do I shoot this thing? he asked.

Pretty simple, I answered. Pull the trigger.

The kid screamed at me, It's got to die!

The way he was shaking and waving that piece, I was afraid he'd shoot me and I'd die—not that a plain, little old bullet could ever kill me. I said, Put the gun down, son. You don't want to hurt nobody, least of all this baby, and I will pitch a hissy fit if you shoot me. Hurts like hell.

The kid started to cry and shake his head from side to side saying, This can't be happening, this can't be real, can't be. And he turned the gun on himself pointing it at his heart.

I started walking and talking real soft-like to him, almost purring. Son, you don't want to hurt yourself. You don't want to hurt nobody. Come on now, give me the gun, that's it. I knelt down, took hold of his hands and eased the gun out of his grip, relocking and slipping it back into my holster.

With his big blue eyes staring at me, the kid said, You. I should've shot you.

                                   American Queer

What? Why?

On the back of your hand. A star tattoo.

So?

It's you. You're the beast.

Now, c'mon. That dog ain't never gonna hunt.

Oh, you're more than a dog, much more. I should have shot you.

Naw, I said. You know you don't really want to do that. Besides, getting shot hurts, and I don't like to hurt. Wouldn't hurt forever, but silver now is deadly. I put on a leather glove, took his hand with the silver ring, and began tugging it off.

He jerked back, trying to hold onto the ring and yelled, What are you doing?

The kid struggled, but he was weak as a limp bean and easy to overpower.

No sense anyone getting burned, I said, getting the ring off. I'll keep it real safe. I tossed the band into the back of the truck. We'll get you a gold ring.

I don't want a gold ring! sobbed the kid.

The pup began to whimper. I figured it was hungry. I picked it up and it reached for the kid. I said, It wants you.

The kid stared at me and the baby. Hold it, I said. Go on, just hold it. He started to scoot back saying, No, get it away. I set the baby down on the kid's chest anyway. It went right for the kid's tit. He screamed and tore the baby away. His tit was all bloody. I looked in the baby's mouth. Alrighty, nice set of canines, tiny and sharp.

Go on, I said. Try it again.

The kid couldn't whip a gnat. He passed out, his head thumping against the truck. The hungry baby attacked him again.

I looked down and said to the young man with the amazing blue eyes, though I knew he couldn't hear me, Glad to hear you liked it, loved it, because I sure as the dickens always have a hankering. We'll go at it again. When the time is right. Glad to finally have a family. I get mighty lonesome up here.

I could hear low rumblings, almost a purring, the slurping clicks of sucking, kind of sweet-like.

Never did call the station. Nor get him to the doctor. I took care of the kid, and of course, he's no longer a kid.

*** *

The sheriff was sitting on his son's soft bed. His son, reclining under warm covers, his hands under his head resting on fluffy pillows, stared at the ceiling.

"And that's how I met your mother, or rather, your other father," said the sheriff.

"Sure not like the families of the kids at school," said the son.

"There's all kinds of families all over the world," said the sheriff. "We're different."

"I see that in the locker room," said the son. "I'm so much hairier, and, um … "

"What?"

"You know, bigger… down there."

"Runs in the family, son."

"What happened to him?" asked the son. "I need to know."

"Yep, I reckon you do," sighed the sheriff. "He's been well taken care of all these years. In a nice place not too far from here, Ghost Ridge Trail. Sort of a cabin built into an old Indian cave. I fixed it up real nice, visit him often."

"Can I see him?"

"We'll see about that someday."

"Is he OK?"

"Don't you worry," said the sheriff. "He's quiet and peaceful-like, doesn't talk much. But when I visit, I sure do bring a smile to his face, and his pretty blue eyes, well, they twinkle like Christmas lights. And that's a fact, even if I do say so myself. Now, no more jibber-jabber; it's time you was in bed."

"Dad," said the son with a grin, "I am in bed."

"Oh, think you're funny, you young pup?" said the sheriff, wrestling and tickling his son. He sighed. "Last time I'll be calling you that. Tomorrow you're 18. You'll be a man. And so much more."

"For old time's sake," said the son, "read me a bedtime story, one of the old ones." He pulled out *The Three Little Pigs* and *Little Red Riding Hood* from his nightstand.

"Son, it's high time you put away childish things." The sheriff took the children's books.

                          American Queer

"Then maybe I could get a tattoo like you?"

"We'll see."

"Thanks, Dad, for telling me." The son looked confused. "Quite a story."

"Quite a history," agreed the sheriff. "You're old enough to know about your family. Be proud and preserve it. It's all you ever have."

The sheriff rose from the bed, patted his son on the head, rubbed his nose, scratched his ears and said, "Nighty-night. Don't let the bedbugs bite you."

"Goodnight, Dad," said the son, purring.

Before he turned out the light, the sheriff added, "Remind me next week. We got to get you to the dentist real soon."

"OK. Can I have a bunny before I go to sleep?" asked the son.

"Enough already," said the sheriff, tussling his son's hairy head. "Well, I guess one more won't hurt. But don't forget to floss, and don't stay up too late. We're going to need all the rest we can get. Tomorrow night's a full moon. Maybe we'll visit your other father, make it a real family fun time. A midnight picnic. I think he'd like that, like it a lot. We'll make sure he does."

May this family be welcomed by:

Focus on the Family, Anita Bryant,
Pat Buchanan, Jerry Falwell,
Jesse Helms, Rush Limbaugh,
Fred Phelps and his brood,
the Pope, Ronald Reagan, Oral Roberts,
Pat Robertson, Phyllis Schlafly—

as another addition to the
Forever Changing American Family!

At Brown's Hotel

1997

The present is when the past changes your future. Soon, all I will have is the past.

To: Ronald Dowl, Morris Frost, T.J. O'Hara:

By the time you receive this letter, I shall be dead. Pain, tumors, 23 pills a day, bronchoscopies—enough. But I did give Deep Throat a whole new meaning.

Which is why I'm writing you, so you can decide if you want to seek help or advice, medical, spiritual, whatever. I was very ill when I "enjoyed" each of you:

Ronald, my business advisor, because you robbed me;

T.J., my competition, because you stole my lover;

Morris, my brother-in-law, because you crushed my sister's heart;

With friends like you, etc.

Don't bother suing my estate. Thanks to Ronald, there's not much left. There is, however, enough for the three of you at Brown's Hotel, Thursday, 8 p.m. I invite you as my guests for a last supper, maybe a surprise or two.

Your dear friend and MOST sincerely,

Robert Edward Masters

P.S. In the future—whatever's left—consider using protection. We're all living proof you can't trust anyone, but never let it be said I lost my sense of humor. Plus, I get the last laugh. Bon appetit!

***

Morris re-read the letter. *Future, dead, heart, supper, trust.* He became light-headed, nauseated. *Enjoyed?* Oh yes, he remembered enjoying Bobby—every sensuous moment. But about five weeks later, the marble-sized lump under his arm had terrified him, so he made a doctor's appointment for tomorrow.

Dinner? "But that's tonight."

Morris broke speed limits to get to the hotel by eight. The city skyline loomed ahead, black clouds promising a wet rupture. He pulled up to the torn brown awning and Tuscan pillars of the hotel, handing his keys to a cute valet wearing unraveling epaulets.

Entering the atrium lobby, he remembered how he and Berta had always marveled at the chandelier that burst like an art deco supernova in the main lobby. On the tarnished brass and pitted granite front desk, Morris read a list of the day's events. *Robert Masters, Last Supper, Ambassadors Room, 4th floor.*

The old elevator was a cage of iron grillwork, missing some curlicues, and traveled the atrium like a slow yo-yo. Wrapping around the interior, each floor's hallway was a balcony overlooking it. Morris poked the up button over and over which did nothing to speed its descent. He gazed at his reflection in a mirror. A frown exaggerated wrinkles round his eyes and mouth. His short hair seemed grayer since this morning. He brushed lint off his tweed jacket with suede elbow patches and adjusted the collar of his pale yellow shirt.

When the door opened, he almost ran into a couple. "Excuse me," said Morris, letting the miffed passengers exit.

Wary of the creaking ascent, Morris scanned the lobby: frayed carpet, wilting anthuriums, worn red circle sofa, burned out bulbs in the chandelier, few people.

The century-old hotel seemed like a dowager whose gilded age had declined to shabby-genteel. The Ambassadors Room displayed more evidence. Standing in its doorway, Morris saw everything was in need of repair or replacement: peeling, flocked wallpaper, chairs in faded brocades, broken bronzes of cowboys. Crooked, burgundy curtains and stained, green carpet devoured the rose-colored light spread by cracked nightclub lanterns. A flame licked the charred marble fireplace bracketed by winged lions in chipped and jagged stone.

"Damn you, Bobby." Morris hit the door.

"Frosty!" said a red-haired man, blowing smoke from a cigarette and startling Morris. T.J. O'Hara had draped himself on a sagging, leather couch. One long leg dangled over the torn armrest patched with tape; the other added another scuff to the

　　　　　　　　　　　　　American Queer

coffee table and threatened a fractured, porcelain shepherdess. "You're late."

"You came," said a short, soft man rushing up to Morris. Ronald Dowl pushed up his glasses, brushed his limp blond hair off his forehead, and greeted Morris with an awkward hug.

"I only got my mail an hour ago," said Morris.

"Long time no see," said T.J.

"So good to see you," said Ronald.

"What's going on?" asked Morris.

"I don't have any idea," said Ronald, adding with a nervous chuckle, "Why would I?"

"A reunion of those who done him wrong," said T.J. "Clear enough in the letter, Ronnie."

"Please call me Ronald."

"Sorry. Have a drink, Ronald; they're free. I checked."

A tall waiter in a tux with a large mole the size of a brown dime on his chin entered the Ambassadors Room.

"Coxy, just in time," said T.J.

"It's Cox, sir," said the waiter, "and I'm sorry, sir, smoking is not allowed inside. However, you may indulge yourself on the outer patio behind you."

T.J. stubbed out his cigarette in the basket of the shepherdess and handed the waiter his glass. "Another martini, three olives."

Cox asked Morris his pleasure. My pleasure? thought Morris. Not to be here. "Manhattan, rocks."

"And for you, sir?" said Cox to Ronald.

"Nothing."

"Have a drink," said T.J. "You look as if you could use a stiff one."

"I don't want a drink," said Ronald. "But I do want to know—wait." He motioned toward the waiter, who, after distributing cocktails, left the room. "Why just us? We can't be the only ones Robert thought wronged him."

"The letter's pretty clear," said Morris. "I agree with O'Hara."

"Oh my, Frosty," cooed T.J. "That cost you dearly."

"Hard to believe Bobby is dead," said Morris.

"The last time I saw him he was his usual handsome self." Ronald swayed.

"You'd better sit down," said T.J.

Ronald sat in a throne-like chair and brushed the hair off his forehead. "And so energetic."

"When was that?" asked T.J.

"A few months ago."

"I saw him shortly after you," said T.J. "Didn't look sick then."

"I was wondering—" Ronald cleared his throat "—what he was sick with."

"The plague," said T.J.

"Don't say that."

"Then don't be stupid."

"Maybe he became deluded," said Morris, "and I don't know, made up this madness?"

"Yes, it has to be that," said Ronald. "Whatever his illness, it drove him crazy—some diseases eat the brain—because Robert would never do this otherwise. He was always so—so sane."

"Masters, sane?" said T.J. "Bob always knew what he was doing. We're here, aren't we?"

"I only came because I thought you two would make sense of it for me," said Ronald.

"My conscience is clear," said T.J. "He was a cruel bastard, and you both know it."

No one said a word, each reflecting on his own inferred demise and the man they thought a friend who had reduced their odds of a lengthy life.

"Why Brown's?" asked Morris.

"So like Bob," said T.J., "cheap, disintegrating, and dying."

"It's certainly theatrical," said Morris. "Reminds me of a set for one of his Chekhov productions."

"Exactly, Frosty," said T.J. "Bob always was a whacko. Working for him was maddening."

"I wonder who brought the pictures," said Ronald, moving to the dining table.

American Queer

On a discolored white tablecloth, it had four place settings and five chairs. At the fifth place, instead of dinnerware, cutlery, and glasses, a hinged frame displayed two photographs of their absent host. In one he lounged on his boat the *Hesperus*, tanned, wearing stripes and khaki, thick hair wind-tossed, eyes and smile sparkling. The other photo showed him in a theatrical production with the burning eyes of revenge, a blurred, Black military man in the background.

"One looks like an ad for toothpaste," said T.J. "The other, he's definitely whacko."

"He was acting," said Ronald. "That photo had to be taken years ago. When I was his accountant."

"And I was his trainer," said T.J. "About five years ago. Morris had just married Berta."

Morris looked out a window and asked, "When did Bobby die?"

"I believe I can answer that question."

The sudden voice startled the three men. When Morris turned around, a large man with a white Van Dyke and thick, white hair, wearing a black suit, grasped the chair behind the photos. He grinned with stubby gray teeth and exposed pink gums. "I'm guessing you are Mr. Frost."

"Good guess," said Morris.

"Adrian Karniva, Esquire." The point of his beard bounced when he talked.

"Bobby's lawyer?" asked Morris.

"I represent Robert Edward Masters, yes," said the lawyer, motioning to the pictures in front of him.

"Karniva," said T.J. "What kind of name is that?"

"Mine," said the lawyer, pointing to him. "Reddish hair, forgive my presumption, you must be Mr. O'Hara. Leaving you to be Mr. Dowd. Gentlemen, sit."

The three men gathered around the table. The waiter entered with a bottle of wine.

"Ah, Cox," said Karniva. "I chose an excellent vintage. Something about wine enriches the soul, wouldn't you agree?" Cox pulled out a chair for the lawyer. He uncorked the bottle and poured a small amount in a goblet. Karniva tasted, approved, and allowed Cox to pour more. "Anyone else?" The three men declined. "Suit yourself. Thank you, Cox." The waiter nodded, but did not move. "I said thank you. You may serve dinner in 15 minutes." The waiter closed the French doors with difficulty; one was warped. "I'm so glad you all made it, especially given the deplorable state of the mail. To answer your question, Mr. Frost, your friend expired one week ago this night. Per his instructions, there was no notification, no funeral."

"What about his sister, Berta?" asked Morris.

"She is away—"

"At a looney camp," said T.J, "right Morris?"

Morris looked away.

Karniva said, "She is away presently, and knows of her brother's unfortunate passing. I shall be meeting with her soon, as she is the prime beneficiary"—Karniva paused and looked at Ronald—"of what's left." He sipped his wine, and after a moment's discernment, sighed his pleasure. He snapped his napkin folded like a limp swan and dabbed each corner of his mouth. "Mr. Masters contacted me the morning before he died to dictate the letter you all received and make final arrangements."

T.J. lit a cigarette. "The prick couldn't have been of sound mind."

"I assure you Mr. Masters was coherent and adamant," said Karniva, "quite enjoying himself, laughing often." He drank more wine and licked his lips. "Please take your cigarette outside," said the lawyer. "Mr. Masters planned to be here—"

T.J. chuckled, blew smoke, then put out his cigarette on a butter plate.

"—but his condition worsened," continued Karniva, "requiring, shall we say, changes."

Morris asked, "Do you know what Bobby died of, Mr. Karniva?"

"Yes, yes," said Ronald, "what did Robert die of exactly?"

"We know what the prick died from," said T.J. "We'll all know firsthand."

"Really, T.J.," said Ronald, "stop interrupting."

"Gentlemen, please. I do not know. Cause is immaterial to the accurate delivery of my duties. I am his legal counsel, not his medical advisor."

     American Queer

"Don't you mean, you *were* his shyster?" asked T.J., slouching in a chair.

Karniva stared at T.J. before answering. T.J. sat up.

"Mr. O'Hara, my client may be dead," said the lawyer, "but until my final duties are disposed of, Mr. Masters lives."

Ronald pushed up his glasses and brushed the hair off his brow. Smiling, he turned to T.J. "I wonder about Alan?"

"What about him?" asked T.J.

"I'd have thought Robert's lover would be here," said Ronald. "He left you, right T.J.?

"That was years ago."

"Moved in again with Robert."

"And moved out again," said T.J., "so shut up, Ronnie Ron-Ron."

"It's Ronald! All these years—my name is—"

"All right, all right. Touchy, touchy."

"If you're referring to Alan Waters," said Karniva, "he was not invited. Mr. Masters was quite clear about that. His legacy is separate from this arrangement. Now let us begin." The lawyer placed his briefcase on his client's empty seat, opened it, and took out a folder. "Although you obviously received the letter, my command per our host is to read it aloud."

"What a crock," said T.J.

"Is that necessary?" asked Ronald.

"Yes, Mr. Dowl. My duty is to execute my client's wishes exactly as he dictated to the best of my ability. And I am quite able." The lawyer pulled out a spectacle case from an inner jacket pocket, put on half-glasses, and read aloud.

Morris stirred his drink with his cherry, T.J. tossed up an olive and caught it in his mouth, Ronald sat with his elbows on the table almost covering his ears with his hands.

When Karniva concluded the letter, he said, "Fully aware of the irony, Mr. Masters would now like us all to toast his health—"

T.J. barked a short, loud laugh. "You can't be serious."

"Allow me to finish, Mr. O'Hara." The lawyer looked down through his glasses and read, *"In remembrance of your last encounter with me, a memorable occasion for us all. 'Me,'* of course, referring to Mr. Masters. Did any of you see him after your last visit to the boat?"

No one had.

"He told you about us?" asked Ronald.

"Only to the extent required in the letter you received." The lawyer made a sour face. "I needed no details. There's more." Karniva continued reading. "*If you want to survive the wreck of the Hesperus, you will stay until midnight tonight in this room. My lawyer is instructed to give those who meet that criteria $25,000. The portion of those who do not will be divided by those who do.*"

"That's impossible," whispered Ronald.

"So, potentially, 75k to one of us," said T.J.

"Potentially, yes," said Karniva, "or nothing to anyone."

"How do we know there's enough money for this scam?" asked T.J.

"I never represent fraud, Mr. O'Hara," said Karniva. "As three potential beneficiaries, I told you the bulk of his estate is left in trust for his sister. After I liquidate his assets, should you fulfill the requirements of his bequest, the money will be available."

"Mr. Karniva," said Morris, "why wouldn't Bobby leave all his money to his sister? Why give us any, since as the letter states, we all hurt him? And if there's not much in his estate?"

"Excellent questions," said Karniva. "I can tell you his sister will be well taken care of for the remainder of her life."

"So, 75 plus Berta's—?" said Ronald. "But I thought there wasn't any more mon—" Ronald cut himself off and flushed.

"Any more what, Mr. Dowl?" asked Karniva, peering over his glasses.

Ronald grabbed a glass of ice water, almost knocking it over, and raised it. "To Robert."

Morris lifted his tumbler. "To Bobby."

T.J. looked at the three. "Drink to that son of a—"

"Mr. O'Hara," said Karniva, "if you please."

T.J. raised his glass and said, "Up yours, Masters."

Everyone drank. T.J. downed his martini and threw the glass in the fireplace that hissed and spit.

"He is paying for this last supper, isn't he?" asked T.J.

"Up to a point," said Karniva.

T.J. leaned forward and cocked his head. "What's to prevent us from suing Master's estate? Maybe he lied in his letter, hid some assets. Maybe Ronnie didn't steal all of his money."

Ronald stood and hit the table. "I did not steal any of his money."

"Whatever," said T.J. "What he did to us, isn't that against some law?"

"Such as?"

"Thou shall not infect thy fellow human being with a deadly disease?"

"Did he?"

"By his own admission, he infected us. We should sue."

"Has anyone been tested? Does anyone have symptoms? Anyone have any proof of any kind?" When no one answered, Karniva continued, "Mr. O'Hara, you, all of you, may do whatever you wish. Representation would be expensive, medical records confidential, and exhumation impossible as Mr. Masters was cremated, his ashes scattered. You would have to argue against your own responsibility for protection. But do not let me dissuade you. This is not a court of law. I do not sit here and judge my client's culpability," said Karniva, his eyes meeting T.J.'s gaze. "Nor yours."

"Lawyers." T.J. sat back and faked a smile. "Always got it worked out."

"It's my client who worked it out," said Karniva. "He didn't have to tell you anything, nor offer you any remuneration, and yet, he did."

"Maybe he felt guilty," said Ronald.

T.J. laughed. "Oh, please. He might as well have shot or stabbed us. Which, come to think of it, boys, he did in a manner of speaking. Except Saint Ron-Ron, of course."

"Would you shut up!" shouted Ronald.

A loud noise from the French doors sounded like something trying to open them. After a squeaky lurch, the waiter wheeled in a cart with food.

"Ah, Cox," said the lawyer, "perfect timing." He stood, gathered his documents, then finished his glass of wine. "Pity to waste. Please see to our guests' needs, Cox." The waiter nodded with a slight bow. The lawyer removed his half-glasses and placed them in their case. "Cox here will also verify your presence through midnight. And now, gentlemen," he said with the final bounces of his pointy beard, "good night and bon appetit." Adrian Karniva, Esquire backed out of the room and shut the French doors, one at a time, as tight as the warp allowed, leaving behind a smear of gray teeth and pink gums.

Ronald dropped into his chair, catching the tablecloth and jingling the silverware and crystal.

"Garçon," said T.J., "another martini."

The waiter set up the buffet dinner on a sideboard, then made the cocktail. T.J. drank, Morris picked, and Ronald refilled his water glass from a cloudy crystal carafe.

"Don't know why I'm so thirsty," said Ronald. "I can't stand looking at those photos." He rose and moved to the window.

T.J. asked, "What's the one with the Black guy behind him?"

"Robert played Iago in *Othello*," said Ronald. "There's a story."

After he did not continue, T.J. asked, "Are you going to tell us?"

"It's a story of vengeance."

"We all know that."

"Like this one." Ronald continued gazing out the window. He took off his glasses. The reflections of the fire, meager lamps, and office buildings outside confused him. Dimensions disappeared. So pretty, he thought. A gust of wind slammed the window like a malicious force trying to get him, and he stepped back. The fire crackled with an occasional, loud pop.

"He was on the boat," said Morris, "about 6 weeks ago. Now he's gone."

"What?" said T.J.

"The picture on the left," said Morris, staring at a fork of broccoli. "That was when Bobby and I were … together. The

    American Queer

only time. On his boat, the *Hesperus*. He looked handsome and healthy."

"I thought so, too when I saw him." T.J. paused mid-sip, "What about you Ronald?"

Both of you, thought Ronald, within weeks of me? I'm such a fool. "It's supposed to pour tonight. I think I need new tires." He turned around and stared at T.J. and Morris, then said, "Robert lied about everything in the letter. Well, about me. I was never with him on the *Hesperus*."

"You've never been on Bob's boat?" asked T.J. "Never saw him recently?"

"I'm tired," said Ronald, "and I've got an important meeting tomorrow morning."

"What are you going to do?" asked Morris.

"Do?"

"Are you going to see a doctor?"

"Why should I?"

"You forget, Frosty," said T.J. "Ronnie never consummated his relations with our host—"

"You're disgusting," said Ronald.

"So he's got nothing to worry about," continued T.J. "Ain't that right, Ronnie—oops, Ronald?"

"Shut up!"

"Everyone knows your heart has pined away for Bob for decades."

"Robert and I were friends," said Ronald. "I'd say I'm sorry for the two of you, but I'm not." Pushing up his glasses and brushing back his hair, Ronald tried to exit as dramatically as his statement, but the door briefly stuck.

"More bucks for you and me, Morris. I need a cig," said T.J., putting on his jacket. "He was naked. On the boat, a month before me. Bob showed me a picture he'd taken." T.J. opened the balcony door, bracing for the wet wind. "Hung like a horse."

"Who?" asked Morris.

"Ronald" answered T.J. "What a waste." Finding shelter, he smoked his cigarette in the growing storm.

***

By the time Ronald drove along the river boulevard, his windshield wipers could barely keep up with the deluge nor his mind with the upsetting evening. He shuddered over the consequences of his friend's invitation months ago to his boat—and his bankruptcy meeting the next day. Even if he had stayed at Brown's Hotel, those thousands would not have come close to what he needed.

In spite of everything, Robert had desired him, had said, *For old times' sake*, like when he had first seduced him during their college days. On the *Hesperus* Robert had smiled in that boyish way of his, then simply crawled into his bunk.

And now I'm going to die? I thought he had forgiven me. It's been years since his stocks dived. And it's not my fault.

The highway dipped, and Ronald drove through a trough of water, his car hydroplaning, the engine revving until it made contact with the road. Damn, I really do need new tires. And to see a doctor. Ronald clasped a hand over his mouth, sobbed and choked.

If only I'd known you had all that money stashed away. What does Berta need it for anyway? She's crazy. And Morris, T.J.? Screw them. Which you did. Serves them right.

Driving through the torrent and back spray was like going through a car wash. The reflections from headlights and streetlamps multiplied like a constantly swirling kaleidoscope. Ronald brushed back his hair, then removed his glasses, rubbed his eyes, looked up—A concrete 'v' loomed ahead. He swerved, his car lifted off the road, the engine revving again, and then he was floating, spinning round and round in dizzying colors. He heard loud crushing metal and the snap of his neck.

***

T.J. snorted and twitched on the couch.

It's so cold. Surrounded by assholes. Karniva, the creep, Dowl, the simp, Frosty the wimp. Three Stooges. And one sly devil. A few months ago, you sure didn't look sick, didn't have any problem performing, and sure as hell ignored my pleas about pain, seemed to spur you on, to rise to the occasion. Often.

T.J. groaned, remembering the fun time, his night on the *Hesperus* with Bob now worth over 37k. That made him grin.

He remembered telling Bob he was glad they'd put all the crap about Alan behind them. Maybe Bob had forgiven him; he didn't really care. And it was Alan's idea to leave Masters.

                                    American Queer

Well, mostly. Alan had shown up at his place with a black eye
and bruises on his back. Bob had begged him to come back.
"And blamed me," he cried out. Always knew he was whacko.
That damn letter and this last supper prove it.

Protection—that word in Bob's letter. Either you get it,
thought T.J., or you don't. We're all adults, and since I've
already got it, Alan too probably … I'm glad you're dead, you
prick. Glad! But Jesus, I don't want to die like you, not from
that! The payoff doesn't seem adequate, considering the horrors
to come. But if I could get Morris to leave … 75,000 dollars …
maybe I could even get Alan back.

T.J.'s body shook in a series of mild fits, and he emitted
a slight yip.

***

Drawn by a small cry, Morris looked at T.J. on the
couch, whimpering like a sleeping dog chasing a squirrel. Sitting
at the dinner table, he resumed staring at his plate of picked over
veal drowned in coagulated gravy. When the marble in his
armpit expressed its tenderness, he thought, What if this is a sign
of—no, Bobby wouldn't …

He thought about Berta, Bobby's twin sister, his ex-wife.
This'll really put her over the edge. Morris discovered she'd
always been near that edge, but not until after they had married.
Then he met Bobby, and his world collapsed in confusion. Even
Berta had said, *I think you'd rather have Bobby.* The divorce was
awful, her mental collapse excruciating. Maybe it was my fault.
Bobby certainly thought so.

Which was why Morris had been surprised at Bobby's
invitation to the *Hesperus*, but thought maybe Bobby had
forgiven him. *Too bad*, Bobby had said, *you didn't realize you
preferred men before you married Roberta. So, let's explore.
We're not blood related.* He had laughed, then said, *And I've
never popped a virgin. Who better to trust than me?* Anyone
else, apparently.

Morris had secretly agreed with Berta's declaration. And
before he died, he did have Bobby, and Bobby had him. On that
night he was in heaven. Now he's in hell.

***

                                             American Queer

Bong! The large ormolu clock hammered its first of 12 strikes, and as if on cue, the lights went out. Morris knocked over his coffee cup and yelled, sure that clock hadn't chimed once all evening. T.J. cried out and stirred, but didn't wake up. **Bong**! Flat, blunt, loud. The fire gave little light; Morris threw a log on it, hoping the waiter would arrive soon and bring candles. **Bong**! In the fading echo, Morris heard the clock's straining gears, grinding a century of grease and grime until the next … **Bong**! It grated on his nerves. The hinged frame of Robert fell over. Morris jerked. "Jesus!" **Bong**! The rain pounded against the windows—**Bong**!—and a furious wind pushed against the glass trying to get inside. **Bong**! Why doesn't O'Hara wake up, how can that bastard sleep— **Bong**!—through this? A windy noise from the hearth made the fire flare, its blaze taking a chomp out of the darkness—**Bong**!—and as quickly, leaving only a yellow glow. **Bong**! Morris heard another cry from T.J. and the squeaky rubs of cloth on the leather couch. "T.J." called Morris. "T.J.!" **Bong**! A large, tall shadow approached Morris from the direction where Robert's fallen pictures had sat. It lowered its head and leaned toward him, reaching for him like a big, black ball of void. **Bong**!

"BOO!"

Morris shouted and fell backwards into a dining chair.

"Christ, Frosty," the shadow laughed, "you are a chump!"

"Damn you, O'Hara!"

"What happened to the lights?"

"How the hell should I know?"

T.J. tried the switch. No luck. He went to the window. "There are lights in other buildings. Try the phone."

Morris did; it was dead.

"Frosty, it's after midnight," said T.J. "We made it! 37,000 buckaroos and don't forget the 500."

They heard a noise outside the hallway, then a loud BAM! on the French doors, becoming a sustained, creaking push for some force to get in, the warped doors bending inward, until they flew open with a loud smack and clatter. Again, a tall shadow stood in the door frame barely lit by the dying coals. With growing dread, T.J. wailed, "Masters? No, God, NO!" The figure advanced, T.J. backed away and crashed over the coffee table, hitting his head on a winged lion with a surprised cry and skull crack. He did not move.

"Oh, dear," said the tall man with a mole, carrying a candelabra. Lighting its candles, Cox said with the rise of an eyebrow, "Gentlemen, we've had a power failure." He stirred the fire, surging once more, illuminating a bloody spray and a spreading red puddle.

***

The next morning, Morris sat in his doctor's office, afraid to ask for the test. He consoled himself by picturing a check for 75,000 dollars. And to think, he had almost missed the strange night at Brown's Hotel.

A man, all skin and bones, gray and blotched, walked in, and stopped at the receptionist's desk. He was hooked up to an oxygen tank and accompanied by a caregiver. God, thought Morris, please don't let me die like that. But what's better? Like T.J.? Or like he had heard on the radio about Ronald dying in a car accident. It's all too freaky, like Bobby is pulling strings from beyond—Don't be ridiculous. But he was still scared.

"Mr. Frost!" Morris jumped. "Sorry, deary," said the receptionist, scratching her pile of beige hair with a pen. "The doctor will see you now."

In the examining room a man, not his usual doctor, entered abruptly and noisily, startling Morris. He wore a black hairpiece, his back was hunched, and he limped. Sitting on a stool, he rolled to his patient, offering a clammy, weak hand and shaking Morris's.

"Dr. Kert, infectious diseases like your Haddock. He was called away, emergency. We fill in for each other. So, what's the problem?"

"I've got a lump under my armpit, but—" Morris blurted out what he wanted.

"Serious test," said the doctor. "Reason?"

"Only one."

"One is all it takes. Any other symptoms … "

As Dr. Kert listed more signs of infection, his voice faded to a buzz in Morris's ears. Bobby, Bobby, Bobby, he thought, getting dizzy, losing his bearing and control, shouting,

American Queer

"Damn you Robert Edward Masters, damn you!" He sobbed and after a minute, apologized.

The doctor offered a tissue. "Couldn't help hearing a name."

"My ex-brother-in-law," sniffed Morris.

"Extraordinary," said Dr. Kert. "I was his attending physician, with him when he died."

"What?"

The doctor folded his arms, and because his hunch was more pronounced sitting on the stool, talked to the floor. Morris noticed his simulated scalp in the part of his toupee. "Lucid to the end. Laughed a lot, not that he had much to laugh about." The doctor looked up with a furrowed brow.

"He was the one," said Morris.

"One what?"

"The one I was with," said Morris, "over a month and a half ago, the reason for this … this test." Morris did not think it necessary to mention the man he'd been with since Bobby.

"Mister—" the doctor referred to a folder, "Frost. If Robert Masters is the reason you're having this test, you don't need it."

Morris asked, "What do you mean?"

"He didn't die of it; he wasn't even infected with the disease."

"What?" said Morris, dumbfounded. "But the tumors, the bronchi whatever, all his pills?"

"That's all I'm saying, and that was too much," said Dr. Kert. "We'll draw blood to make sure. Haddock will review the results." He stood up, placed his hands on his hunched back and stretched with a groan. "Now let's check that lump."

When Morris got home, he made a stiff drink. His armpit was sore from the biopsy, the lump probably nothing. He would have lab results in a few days. Nothing to worry about. They had done nothing unsafe, he and the man from the bar. Well, almost nothing.

Afternoon of a Mastodon: Denver, 1999

Camus, Albert. *The Plague*. Translated from the French by
Stuart Gilbert.   Harmondsworth, Middlesex, Great Britain:
Penguin Books Ltd., 1960, pp. 236-237.

Cher, et al. *Believe*. Warner Brothers. 1998.

Eliot, T.S. *The Waste Land, Section III: "The Fire Sermon."*
World Masterpieces Since the Renaissance. Ed. Maynard Mack.
W.W. Norton & Co., Inc., New York, 1973, lines 175 & 179, p.
1707.

Reed, Lou. *Walk on the Wild Side*. David Bowie and Mick
Ronson producers. London, Trident, RCA Records, August,
1972.

Siouxsie & the Banshees. *Peek-a-boo*. Dreamhouse/Chappell
Music Co. ASCAP, 1988. Geffen Records, 9130 Sunset Blvd.,
Los Angeles, CA, 90069.

Map of the Viaduct

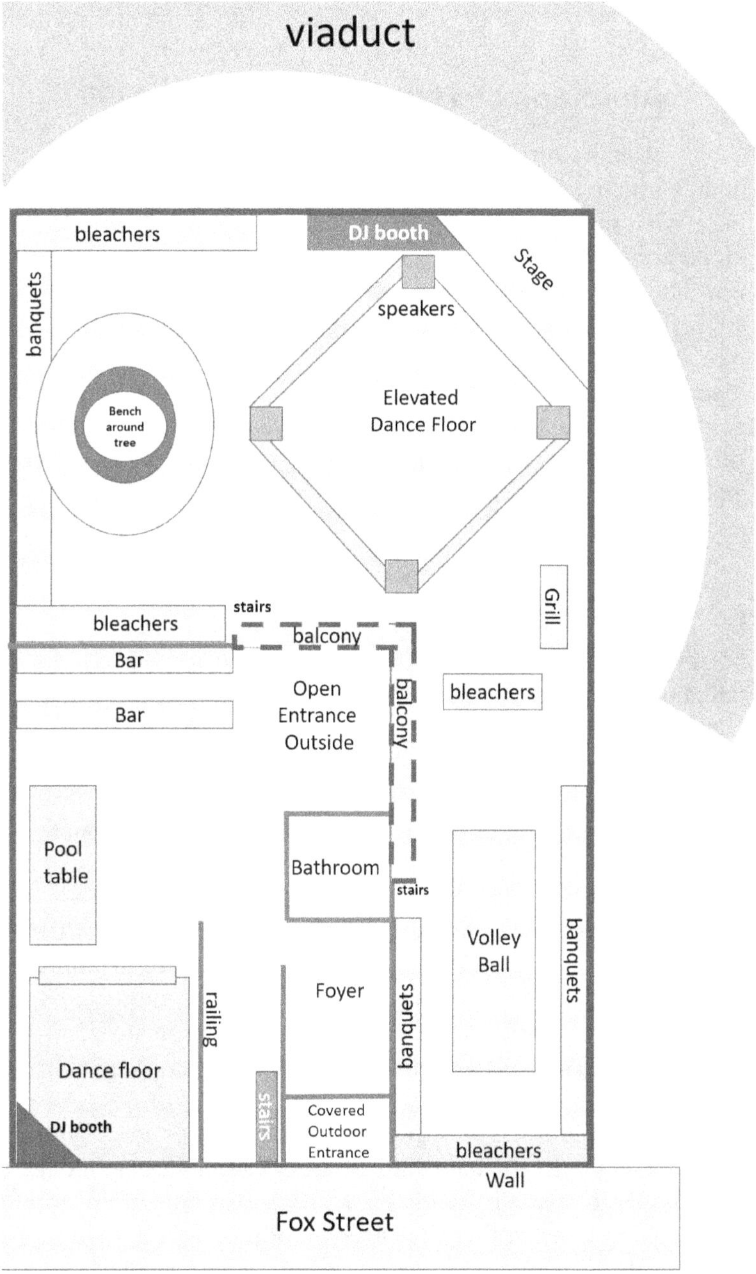

American Queer

Afternoon of a Mastodon: Denver, 1999

Linus Cottage, though biologically alive, was a dead man. Unseen parts of him had rotted—yes, very Dorian Gray-like. What remained of his remains had aged little: flourishing blond curls, straight white teeth, unblemished skin, full burgundy lips that unconsciously urged warm kisses. He, however, was cold. He had always been desired, still was, until people met him. Then, these accidental necrophiliacs thought him conceited, themselves better, and kept their distance, which never contracted. He nourished the gap; it grew, and that suited him fine. Beauty was wasted on him, a god-given joke, a gene-driven embarrassment because in the eyes of most others, he was always naked.

—1—

On a summer Saturday evening, Linus arrived from a business trip at the airport in the city where he grew up. Hours late, he missed his connecting flight home, every departure sold out until Monday. After all the angry travelers, the perky ticket agent, whose perkiness was waning, mistook his jet lag for polite sympathy and booked him first class. "Have a lovely lip—I mean trip, Mr. Cottage," she said, turning red as her kerchief. Linus was used to these gaffes. He said, "Thank you," smiled apologetically, then left in search of a pay phone.

He hesitated before calling his friend Mark, one of the few left alive in his hometown, or anywhere else, for that matter. They shared a history, that part of youth and exploration.

I could use the hotel voucher to catch up on sleep, thought Linus, and Mark would never be the wiser. A quick hello, no harm in that.

"Paging Mr. Linus Cottage, Mr. Linus Cottage," said Mark. "Please pick up the white courtesy telephone ringing up your ass. You're staying with me. I'm in the middle of my spring '97 cleaning whether the place needs it or not, but I'll have a fresh bottle of maraschino cherries awaiting your arrival." Some people eat gumdrops; Linus ate sweet red mothballs. Mark asked, "Where were you?"

"Dublin."

"And how was your flight on Air Cunnilingus?"

Linus wasn't in the mood for his old jokes. "I'll just use my vouchers."

"No! It's been 10 eons—"

"How many?"

"Ten—shut up—it's been a long time. Besides, hotels are so impersonal."

Which was the reason Linus preferred hotels: One has meager expectations, and they expect nothing of you except to spend money, pay the bill, and be quiet.

Why did I call, Linus wondered in the taxi to Mark's place. And why did I agree to stay with him?

Passing sites he hadn't seen in decades, Linus felt vague familiarity and regret. He had left home long ago; no family remained here or elsewhere. His ride ended at a small duplex, its porch bathed in soft blue light. He thought his host was the last person in America to hold vigil for a cure of their personal plague.

Mark was happy to see his friend. He had a nice little body, a big nose with ears to match, and bright eyes. After what the two had witnessed, Linus was amazed anyone's eyes could still look bright. They hugged, Linus avoiding a kiss on the lips.

"I don't go any more, but I'd hit the bars if you want to."

"No, I'm jet lagged."

"Are you sure?"

"Positive," said Linus, "I mean, yes."

"Don't be so sensitive," said Mark.

"I didn't want you to think—"

"I can think for myself. More wine?"

"God, yes. So," said Linus, gobbling a cherry as Mark filled their glasses, "what's new?"

"I'm going to a fabulous new church."

"Found God again?"

"What an odd question. Can one lose Her? Now if I could just find my watch," said Mark. He told his guest about plans for tomorrow's beer bust, but Linus declined. "Five

      American Queer

hundred penises, and you don't care!" Linus squinted and wrinkled his nose. "One of these days," his host warned, "they'll revoke your pink card."

Since college, Mark had joked that "they" were the self-appointed arbiters of penises, the Pottery Barn, Puccini, and exclusive distributors of an imaginary gay membership card. Linus had never cared to fulfill these imagined standards; he was not a size queen, hated shopping, and opera bored him. He declined Mark's invitation to go to church.

"You should," said his host. "It keeps me from bar hopping Saturday nights. My new church is so happy, and your soul could use some food."

"Allergies," said Linus.

Mark made up a bed on his couch, and, lying amidst cleaning products, rags, and displaced furniture, Linus couldn't stop thinking. All this religion crap. He remembered Mark telling him that when he had heard the tale of the crucifixion at the age of 6 on the playground, he decided he could never remain Jewish for life, nor convert to Christianity. "With so much violence, everyone's a victim." Mark had said, then laughed and added, "Such a pity party. You'd have fit right in."

From the living room Linus saw the glow of a night-light, reminding him of how as Mark's college roommate, he had unplugged an annoying Mickey Mouse plug-in. Mark had awakened upset in the middle of the night. Linus pretended the bulb had burned out, climbed into his bed, cradling him like a big spoon to a little spoon until his shakes ended. Weird, thought Linus. That was the only time we ever made … had sex. In the bathroom, Mickey Angelo's *David* replaced the mouse.

Monday's so far away, thought Linus. And he could not sleep. The room smelled of pine and bleach. He checked out Mark's refrigerator: grape juice, maraschino cherries, Reese's Pieces, potato chips, pickles, mayonnaise, white bread, orange cheese, and mini-marshmallows. "Since when was Mark a vegetarian? And no more wine." He poured a glass of juice, grabbed the marshmallows, and turned on the TV. Bored, he bombed Boris, an enemy agent of *Rocky and Bullwinkle* in mute play with the spongy puffs.

—2—

    American Queer

Sunday morning, Linus awakened to a mumbling, scratching mouse that turned out to be his host meditating and scribbling in his journal. Mark apologized for waking him, but church services started early. When he came home a few hours later, he said, "God can be so exhausting," and took a nap. Linus returned to his book.

Emerging an hour later, squinting and sweaty, Mark plopped into his barco-lounger, his hair sticking up like the short brown comb of an odd bird. Noticing the bulge in his underwear was more fully awake than the rest of him, he covered it, grinned, and closed his eyes.

Linus thought how Mark was not quite ready to return to this world, how nappers rarely are. They awaken, gape about stupidly, if not pissed off. Some vague familiarity with their environment surfaces. Slowly identity, location, and life zoom into consciousness, the body trap shutting with a loud mental clang. Oh yes, now I remember, admits the napper, so much better where I was, wondering how in hell they got here of all places and not quite sure what to do next. Linus didn't need a nap to feel that way.

The twitch of a muscle or the flicker of an eyelid indicated Mark was somewhere else other than here, and Linus wished he, too, was somewhere else other than here. He watched his dozing host breathe, cozily curled into the shape of an *s*. His relaxed face seemed as innocent as it had during their college days in this city. Even I was innocent, thought Linus, back then. For Mark over the following decade, the party had never ended until his discovery of God. For Linus, the party ended when the number of funerals hit double digits. And Mark insisted on intruding in his life. He called often—Linus never called—to update him on their circle of friends, shrunken to a dot in the last 15 years, people Linus had ceased caring about long ago, or so he told himself. It was a safer state of mind. Their friendship had been synthesized to perform a favor, making sure the other was alive. Both were unaware the thin thread of their connection was for each a rope of survival.

Linus returned to his book, Camus's *The Plague:*

*But he knew, too, that to love someone
means relatively little; or, rather, that love is
never strong enough to find the words befitting
it.*[16]

A snort and a yawn distracted him and dilated Mark's
face into a black hole with teeth, a momentary, epileptic stretch
of paralyzing contentment.

"Why are you reading *that*?" asked his host. "You're
living one, or haven't you noticed?"

Such bland questions out of Mark's mouth were often
filled with accusation or anger or resentment because Linus did
not live his life the way Mark thought he should. Linus cracked
his toes and smiled. "Call it my reference manual."

"Call it whatever you like," said Mark. "Why are their
marshmallows on the floor?"

"Sorry," said Linus, picking them up. "I'll take care of
it."

"Do that," said Mark, leaving to shower. "And I don't
want to know."

Linus hoped the water washed him nicer. He flipped
open his laptop and checked his email, one from Toy4U. After a
month of chatting online, Toy4U wanted to meet. Linus deleted
the message and, without hesitating, the cyber-guy's profile.

"Hey, Goldy," Mark called out, "come here and pluck
my ear hair." Since college, he had always called his guest
Goldy, an abbreviation of Goldilocks, when he wanted to make
up for being a bitch. "Christ, long enough to braid. God has an
evil sense of humor. He replaces a hairy head with ears hairier
than a marmoset."

"You're so weird," said Linus, tweezing, "and not bald.
Stand still." Finished, he watched his host apply moisturizer to
his face, spray to his hair, a corrosive paste to his teeth.

"Sure you won't go?" asked Mark.

"I'm just passing through."

---

[16] Albert Camus, *The Plague*, (Great Britain: Penguin Books Ltd. 1960), p. 236.

                                          American Queer

"You're always just passing through. Would you rather I stay, and we play Yahtzee, listen to Mantovani records, knit? Come on, for me? Please!"

"Oh my god, all right."

"Yes!"

Linus thought, it'll be my farewell appearance.

"You never could resist my charm," said Mark. "Bathroom's all yours."

Linus ran a hand through his hair and gargled mouthwash. "Ready."

Mark eyed his guest in the mirror. "I hate you." Linus shrugged and smiled; Mark looked himself over. He wore black jeans, All-Stars, and a tight t-shirt cut above the waist with the musical *Rent* logo.

"I'm wearing my lucky underwear."

"I'll bite."

"The kind if anybody sees them, I'm lucky. Besides my doctor. It's been three years since someone else has. Ugh." Mark grimaced and tried to press down a cowlick. "No wonder I'm nutty. Thank God for God."

"Stop fussing," said Linus. "Do we have to go?"

"Stop whining," said Mark. "We're supporting a good cause?" In the mirror, he looked his guest in the eyes. "I'm so goddamn sick of good fucking causes."

"Do I detect a note of cynicism?"

"Try a whole symphony."

Linus looked away and left the bathroom.

—3—

Linus treated Mark to a late lunch at the Dead Slobster, Mark's favorite. They then headed to The Glorious Rainbow Benefit for AIDS holding its annual fundraiser at The Viaduct, a dance club nestled near an interstate highway and derelict train tracks. Looking for parking in congested traffic, they drove by three young men who laughed loudly as they taunted the slowly passing cars. "You're alone, loser! Alone! Loser! A couple, winners!"

     American Queer

"Ah, youth," said Mark, searching for a space, Linus for familiarity. "May they spend an eternity listening to Anita Bryant records."

"They won't know who she is," said Linus.

Once on the seedier side of town, The Viaduct had been their denizens' private fraternity before gay life became—as Mark would scream—so PUBLIC! But now, paved streets replaced weedy roads, million-dollar lofts derelict warehouses, chic restaurants and swank apartments the dives and hotels of the down-and-out.

Parking blocks away, the two walked to the bar. Underneath the overpass—today, a six-lane artery swooping into downtown—Linus stared at saplings, joggers, and baby strollers. "Is that a bike trail?" he asked as though tasting cough syrup. His host confirmed that the city had turned their haunt into a park for environmentalists, families, and the health-conscious.

Twenty years ago, men had entered The Viaduct to find, then lose themselves, in the revelation and safety of music, sex, and men. Outside, rain or shine, intrigue had lurked under the rickety, two-lane overpass, also music, sex, men, and, occasionally, a surprised vagrant. Crumbling asphalt, rusted iron girders, chain-link fence, and discarded chunks of concrete had provided the perfect stage to hide and seek for the poetic and the depraved. Linus knew then that was a fine line. Blanketing their moans of ecstasy and the passing traffic above, the music from the patio would wing through the dark, the backdrop of stars and skyscrapers twinkling a lovely light show. It was all so trashy, but so, so romantic. Linus had stopped trying to understand why. It just was. And though the plague had decimated his community, he was not about to forfeit the magic of its time.

Some things remained constant. Near the dance club's entrance, motorcycles formed a queue like a chorus line with their front wheels precisely cocked. The purple and pink neon sign still sputtered like sun-fried grease, and the music's beat still boomed, sending a coded call through a brick jungle to tease urban nerves.

The backs of heads and shoulders bobbed above a solid, wood fence as people watched a volleyball game from bleachers. One head faced the street. Linus saw a man in a blue shirt staring at him and jerked away. Mark noticed the man at the same time, asking, "Wasn't that—" but Linus cut him off and told him no, it was not. Mark insisted, and so did Linus.

"Remember how stupid and goofy you'd get around him," Mark said. "Didn't he have a sickeningly sweet nickname for you?"

"He died." That'll shut you up, thought Linus, and it did.

Linus couldn't believe they had to wait in a long line to get into The Viaduct. Security guards patrolled the area in neon lime shirts with headsets and walkie-talkies. A shiny, new car pulled up, and a candidate for political office in a suit and tie began to shake hands with anyone willing. Pill programs, pained concern, and promises oozed from his unctuous smiles.

"Where were you 15 years ago?" shouted Mark, ready for battle.

"In junior high," replied the candidate.

"Yeah, well," said Mark, "fuck you."

Approaching the entrance, they were sprayed by a soft cool mist. Linus stood under the spritzer for several moments, then stepped into the dark foyer. The same biker club flags hung from the ceiling, and the same erotic posters lined black walls like a gallery, spotlit and promising forbidden pleasures. They were forbidden now, thought Linus, but for different reasons. Even the bartenders and barbacks looked the same, hairless and cute, or hairy and butch. A few new trophies crammed the glass case, and a blue strip of neon circled a mirrored ball transforming it into a Saturn. The dance floor was empty, the dancers outside under the sun. Linus recalled memories when the small square inside had been packed with sweaty, shirtless guys, spilling onto the sidelines. We danced like there was no tomorrow, remembered Linus. For many, there wasn't.

Mark paid their cover charges and wrote a check as a donation. Seeing the figure, the cashier whistled and wheezed, "Thanks for the generous donation, Mark." Hanging onto him, he stood up with difficulty and kissed him on the lips. Mark took his cup of beer from the keg; Linus opted for a coke. "Party animal," said his host. Linus could get his drink at the bar where he quickly wanted to go, but the crowd prevented him. "Linus?"

     American Queer

asked the cashier. "I know," said Mark, beaming. "Can you believe it?"

Linus stopped and turned around to face Henry Pullman. An avuncular legend, he had built The Viaduct decades ago, providing one of the first havens for men in this city. Known as Uncle Hank, he loved the boys—Linus knew he could charm the pants off you—and some of the boys loved him back. Not hard to do with his porn star good looks. If they were 21, he gave them a job; if not, he got them help with organizations he had vetted and supported. He was generous to a fault, and some of his boys stole more than his heart, but he never banned them from the bar. "Bad boys need a place to come back to" was his rationale because Uncle Hank was really a mother, The Viaduct his den. He would swear off love until the next sad, cute case walked through the door, and never give up that he was "the one." Linus doubted Hank, now in his 60s, would see his 70s. A thin layer of gray skin covered his skull. Linus had deejayed for him.

"My god, I haven't seen you in years," said Hank, his eyes tearing up, "which have been kinder to you than me. I'd recognize you anywhere." After he searched Linus's face, something dawned within him. "Come here; I want to show you something."

"What?" asked Linus.

"A memory," said Hank.

He turned over door duties to a young man with dyed red hair and a studded chin, his latest "one." Hank clutched his walker, and like an advancing staple remover, pulled himself through the throng that parted respectfully, his pace slow and deliberate. "Excuse me ladies," he said to two pool players, to Linus, "Remember this?" On a corner pocket was scratched a date. Mark peered over Linus's shoulder.

"Yeah, Hank," said Linus. "I remember." The dance floor and deejay booth were nearby.

"And remember how you spun us all into heaven with your music? Rare and precious times, like jewels of the mind. But so are these times, my boy, so are these. You in love?" Before Linus could make up an answer, the studded redhead called from the foyer to Hank, who hollered back that he would be right there. "Sweet kid, but thinks two plus two equals 22. When Stevie was six, his parents pulled down his pants and told him bad men would whack his pee-pee with a steel pipe. I'm proving them wrong." He smiled. "By the way, there's somebody here who I know would love to see you."

"Me?" Linus fidgeted. "Can't imagine."

"Oh," grinned Hank, "I think you can."

Mark looked at Linus, was about to say something, but when Linus glared, changed his mind.

Hank let go of his walker, embraced Linus, and tried to kiss him on the lips, but Linus turned his cheek. Hank raised an eyebrow. "There was a time—Good to see you, Linus."

"And you," Linus lied.

Mark told Hank about the punks outside his bar. He said he would talk to them, and motioned to Mimi, his six-foot-three, two-forty head of security. "If they're of age Mimi, invite them in as my guest. If not, I'll drag my sorry ass out there. Somebody's got to teach them manners. Thanks again, Mark, for the donation." Hank's hands returned to the walker and pulled the rest of his bent, bony body to the foyer.

Linus noticed a skull and crossbones flyer taped to the entrance of a basement. Where passions and disease had passed from man to man, he thought. Seeing the thick, steel padlock, he caught his breath. A barback ripped off the paper and barked, "Who keeps doing this? Oh hi, Mark." Mark said hi, told Linus that was Billy, who used to work for him at the clothing store, and bragged about not using protection. "I must chat with this barebacking barback. Say that 10 times."

Linus said, "He looks healthy."

Mark said, "It's only a matter of time."

A bearded man sat at the bar fingering rosary beads, and Linus thought, Well, it is Sunday. The Catholic interrupted his reverie long enough to halt a hairy man wearing bunny ears and a petticoat pouring beer from pitchers. He then chugged his refilled cup and resumed his holy mumblings.

The din of the beer bust had increased, Linus waiting in line again, then leaning closely to the bartender to order. He wore a nametag and looked like he should be cleaning pools in Southern California. "Basil," said Linus, "a coke please."

"It's pronounced *Bahzl*," he corrected, ignoring Linus's apology.

"Add some embalmed cherries to that coke," said Mark. "And by the way, sweetie-pie-snookums *Bahzl*," Mark whispered, "you've got a little something … your nose." The bartender rubbed this way and that. "Almost got it. Got it."

Mark and Linus left the bar, Mark saying "Oh my god, you're smiling."

"I was about to offer him my hanky."

"You carry a hanky?"

"What's wrong with that?"

"What color is it?"

"It's not that kind of hanky."

—4—

Mark and Linus squeezed their way through people watching a big screen TV, playing video games, talking, cruising. They walked onto the enormous outdoor patio, the late afternoon sun blinding them, the summer heat enveloping them, a huge crowd yelling and dancing to loud music and a seismic beat overwhelming them. A game was underway on the sandy volleyball court next to a red and white awning where meat sizzled on a large grill, free to be gobbled up by the long line of the hungry.

Different birds of a feather flocked together at this benefit. Men and women and those in between from butch to femme to young to old danced or watched with a camaraderie of uniqueness and freedom. Both sets of S and Ms— sado/masochists, stand and models—stomped with cowboys and cowgirls. Bodies built moved with bodies so-so. Those wearing khaki cargo shorts and polo shirts bumped with tattooed, studded Goths all in black. Smoke, grease, faces, faces, sun, noise, music, music, the music …

Linus's mind whirled as he took in the enormous dance floor, two steps up and cornered by monolithic speakers, busy as a hive of bees. The deejay booth, where he had spent many happy hours, was off to the side of the roofed stage like a raised pulpit that had been perfect for surveying his acolytes.

He and Mark moved to a banquette near a tree of Swiss Family Robinson size spreading its stately green branches and shade over them and a slatted bench that encircled its large trunk. Linus's mind whirled again as he remembered the last time he had been here. He imagined he heard the man in the blue shirt call his name.

Mark pointed out a friend of his as though Linus could discern one person out of this mob. "The one with all the moles on his face?" Linus asked. "No, and those aren't moles," his host said.

Before Mark could redirect his guest's gaze, a large, heavy-set man with a graying goat-tee grabbed and hugged him, and said something about what the cat dragged in. The man, Murray, also recognized Linus. "Jesus H, you haven't changed a bit." He leaned his head back and laughed revealing several missing teeth, then nudged his thick glasses up his nose. Linus stiffened when he hugged him and turned to avoid a kiss.

Murray put his arm around a short, muscled man wearing a white tank top and leather sash with studs and initials on it. Murray introduced him as Shawn, back from Chicago, winner of the Mr. Universal Leather King something-or-other title. After Linus shook hands and congratulated him, Shawn edged Murray out of the way. Mark was delighted with Shawn and asked him questions about the competition. Shawn replied that 30 contestants competed from all over the world, that four thousand packed the city's convention center, that he had to answer "intellectual questions" and autograph his picture for a line of hundreds of fans. "I got writer's cramp," Shawn giggled.

Murray was negotiating with a studio for a triple X video. Shawn said he was worried he'd have problems memorizing his lines. "But if you were in it," Shawn said to Linus, "I would have no problem at all. My apartment's not far." Linus laughed and told him he would be very disappointed, and besides, he was with his host.

"If heaven wants love to blossom," said Mark, "who am I to stand in its way?"

"Linus," laughed Shawn, "you're blushing."

Like a good PR manager, Murray saw someone important and maneuvered his ticket to a future porn career in

     American Queer

that direction. Shawn's eyes lit up. Murray nudged up his glasses, saying his good-byes and "let's do dinner."

From afar, a kid with a bandage around his wrist and an adult behind him in tow waved at them. Mark warned Linus this was Binky Terra who monthly fell in love and hyphenated his name. "He tried it with mine, but decided Terra-Fleschman didn't flow right. He's one of my sales associates, awful, but I don't have the heart to get rid of him. A true innocent. Or truly stupid. Hard to tell."

Binky hobbled up to Linus. "Hi, I'm Binky Terra-Misoni."

"Sounds like the Italian dessert," said Linus.

Binky did a double take.

"Don't even try, Binky," said Mark.

"I'm Linus."

Binky was short, had a high-pitched voice and thin, frosted hair, bald by 30, Linus bet, but he was cute.

He said, "Before I forget Marky, I need to change my tax form."

"Don't call me Marky, and you are not changing your name for the 37th time."

"But this is Mario," said Binky, introducing his accompanying adult, "and today, I am *sun*sational!"

"And your wrist?" asked Mark.

"Sprained, my foot too." Binky also wore a blue boot.

"Those darn ceiling fans can do a lot of damage," said Mark.

Binky blanked, then a light went on, and he laughed. "Cripes no, Marky."

"Stop calling me Marky. I suppose you need time off?"

"Gosh, yes."

"Yet you came to a beer bust."

"I insisted," said Mario.

The tall Mediterranean was thick all over: hair, thighs, lips, biceps, crotch. Binky looked up and down Linus, causing his knight errant to step between the two and eagerly offer to fetch more beer. The look on his face as he left, realizing he would be leaving his Binky alone with the competition, was the opposite of the look on Binky's face.

                                   American Queer

"So how did you hurt yourself?" asked Mark.

"Mario took me swing dancing at The Church. Did you know it really used to be a church? Made me nervous. Anyway, we were getting all the fancy moves down. Mario throws me out, reels me back in, throws me out, reels me back in, throws me out, forgets to reel me back in. Mario was so sweet. I fell into a really cute cocktail waiter. When he helped me up, I pretended to black out and fell back into his arms." Binky fanned himself and said in a conspiratorial whisper, "But don't tell Mario."

Mark zipped his lips, locked them with an invisible key, tossing it away.

"The waiter's name is Hoyt Wright; it makes me melt. What do you think of Terra-Wright?"

"I think it's Terra-Terra-Wrong. With a new boyfriend every month, I hope you're being careful."

"I don't—you know—sleep with any of them. I'll be a virgin until I get the ring. No ring, no rosebud."

"No what?"

"Cripes," said Binky, shaking his head, "you know."

"Oh, *that* rosebud," said Mark. "I thought you were referring to *Citizen Kane*."

"Does he call it a rosebud too?"

"If I explained," said Mark, "it would hurt. You're not serious about holding out, are you?"

"Cripes Marky, just because you don't. That's so 80s."

Mark closed his eyes tightly, letting the bite subside. "Remind me to fire you on Monday—you have no sick days left—and stop calling me Marky." Linus sensed Binky making a mental note about his impending termination.

"So, Linus, where's your blanket?" giggled Binky.

"He's never heard that one before," said Mark.

Unconcerned with his lack of originality, Binky said he adored bashful men, and asked Linus what his last name was. Before he could answer, Mark jumped in. "Cotta."

"Terra-Cotta, Terra-Cotta," mused Binky.

So only Linus could hear, Mark whispered, "Could not resist."

"I like it," said Binky.

Mario returned from his quest for beer, the paladin pleased and relieved to find his damsel in distress where he left him and who gifted him a homecoming kiss. Mario grinned; chivalry lived on; the damsel needed to sit. As they left, Binky hooked a finger into a belt loop above Mario's thick ass, Mario pulling him through the crowd, Binky glancing back and mouthing the words "call me" to Linus. That poor hyphen-of-the-month, he thought, begging for a bone he'll never get to chomp. Can you feel sorry for someone and envy them at the same time?

A shriek annoyed Linus, followed by, "Mark Fleschman, back from the dead." A burly, bearded man carried a pitcher of beer in each fist and air-kissed Mark. Karl wore angel wings, bunny ears, and a yellow petticoat with a matching tank top that didn't cover his hairy belly. Linus had seen men similarly dressed in different colors pouring beer. They were members of a club for the heavy and happy.

"You'll see Anastasia Azure, Charlene Chartreuse, Phoenicia Fuchsia, Scarlet Fiddle-de-dee. We're the Rainbow Girls," said Karl, tossing make-believe tresses from his bald head. "I'm Saffron Sally. Mabel Mauve's around here somewhere, but she drinks more than she pours. Probably sucking someone off in her camper, lucky bitch. Shit, there's Nagahyde Norma, I better get busy. When she's pissed, it's like she eats little penises for breakfast." With a call to Norma, he twirled away, his ruffled netting revealing no underwear.

"Gross," said Linus.

"They do a lot of good, and have fun doing it," said Mark. "Better pull your head out of your ass, Linus, before it's too late."

Like his comment about the book he was reading, Mark had lobbed another grenade, and though Linus had welded his armor of apathy for years, Mark possessed a power to pierce it with snide cruelty. Never a patient man, Mark's impatience had grown raw, as though people's failures to see clearly were wastes of precious time. "Got a problem, solve it, move on" was his credo. Zip, bing, bang. And anyone who did not believe his truth, Mark blessed but phased out of his life. Which made Linus wonder why his host kept in contact with him. He was not a model friend. It was not that Mark used his power over him with calculation nor knew he possessed it—Linus certainly wasn't going to tell him—and it was not that Linus cried or was crying now, but a familiar wet sting welled up behind his eyes as though his tear ducts produced onion juice. Linus would have left that moment, but he had no key to his host's duplex to get his things and that would entail too much talk. Linus squeezed the sting behind his eyes and swore this was the last time he would have anything to do with his host, that if anyone was going to bless and phase out, it was going to be him doing the phasing out, forget the blessing part. When he returned home and never answered his host's calls, Mark would figure it out. He's a bright man.

"Come on, Goldy," said Mark, putting his arm through Linus's. "Let's get you another coke."

And then like always, there was his friend, concerned about him and in this case, his simple thirst.

—5—

Before they could head back inside, so many friends greeted Mark that he practically held court under the tree. He met Barry, who recently earned a masters in food technology and is now employed by a meat packer. Joining him were Deb and her lover Deb, nurses at a local hospital.

Barry voraciously ate a hamburger, his first in years, saying "If you knew what I've found in meat, believe me, you'd be vegetarian, too."

"We know and are," Deb and Deb agreed.

Barry said through a mouthful, "I must be craving some enzyme."

The trio went to the same church as Mark, who had attended the Debs' commitment ceremony last month. They encouraged voting against an anti-abortion initiative sponsored by a Christian right-wing organization for an upcoming election.

"Girls, girls, girls," said Mark. "You balk at grilling a cow, but sucking a fetus out of its womb is okay?"

"It's not that simple," grumbled Deb.

As the trio walked away, Barry declared, "I need another burger."

                    American Queer

"What's wrong with you?" asked the other Deb.

Mark chatted with Kevin, whose lover, Percy, was dying by inches in their 4,000-square-foot home in a gated community. The house that drugs built, Mark had told Linus. Kevin and his pal Joe, who was happily married to an understanding wife with wonderful kids, were searching for fisting partners. "I don't believe we've met," said Joe to Linus. They had years ago, but Linus didn't bring it up. "Forget it, Joe," whispered Mark, "he has anal warts." Linus's mouth popped open; Kevin and Joe left them; Linus hit his host on the shoulder, and Mark said, "What? I'm trying to include you."

"Don't." Linus commented about all the red hankies, the only color that endured the hip-pocket code from their past. "It's just so … "

"Intimate?" His host was not surprised some survivors chose this extreme passion. "Hand next to heart, you've got to admit it's deeply intimate," said Mark. "But the closest I prefer that connection is when saying *The Pledge of Allegiance*. And I get so many opportunities to do that."

Then Del, a handsome Black man with a last name like a Dutch cheese, greeted them. He dragged a whip and led Leo, a cute white boy wearing work boots and a dirty jockstrap, by a long chain. They, too, attended Mark's church. What kind of a place is this? Linus wondered. Del and Mark chatted about an upcoming charity event, yet another good cause; they were both members of the board.

Leo stared at Linus. "Would you like to pee on me?" Del snapped the chain, and Leo buckled to his knees. Linus felt nauseated; Mark's eyes bugged out. He said, "The line to the bathroom can get pretty long."

Linus jumped and sloshed his coke. "Dammit!"

"Now what?"

"Someone pinched my ass," said Linus, looking for the culprit.

"Stop complaining."

Todd and Rod, Ned and Ted squealed like sorority sisters when they came upon Linus and Mark. Hug, hug, kiss, kiss. They had all partied together long ago. One of the four—Linus couldn't remember who—had left his lover Bartley when he became positive with the plague, a month later hooking up with his current lover. "I thought life partner meant for life," Mark had said to Linus at the time, "silly me." But since that change of plan, the inseparable foursome vacationed together, celebrated anniversaries, and had season tickets to the baseball team. Having arrived from a game, they described it excitedly.

"Rah," said Mark. "Until a teacher makes a million bucks a year, that's all the cheer I can muster."

The four fans chuckled and pretended to care. Ned and Ted segued to their posting of an IPO for their Internet business. They were now worth millions, but grumbled about how The Viaduct's benefit was not worth their combined 20 bucks, forget a donation. Todd and Rod recently adopted their second Chinese baby and showed them a picture of two little girls in kimonos. Mark asked them for the Chinese word for kimono. They condescended to find out, then shared—to them—a funny story.

"Remember how we used to say—"

"It's party time?' Now we say—"

"It's Potty Time!" Laugh, laugh. "That's a—"

"New video we play for Jade—"

"Because we're potty training her—"

"Isn't that—"

"A hoot!" Laugh, laugh. "Isn't that funny!"

"So funny," said Mark, "actual tears in my eyes. Hey, remember the Solstice Party here?"

"God, ages ago," said Rod. "Linus, you never played better."

"Isn't that when Bartley got sick," asked Mark, "and you moved in with Todd?"

"Not exactly," said Todd.

"But at the time," said Linus, "we had a good time."

The two couples forced the new times by asking Mark and Linus about their "little jobs" and boyfriends. When that didn't take long, a quiet descended on the six. Like saying "Whew!" with the wipe of a sweaty brow, the two couples left, Todd and Rod to relieve their mother-in-law's baby-sitting duties, Ned and Ted, because they were bored.

Linus heard one of them say, " … still gorgeous—"

"And still stuck up."

 American Queer

Laugh, laugh.

"There are times," said Mark, "when I understand why you're quiet."

"You weren't about Bartley," said Linus.

"Someone has to remember." Mark had bitten his lip so hard it was bleeding. He was about to blot it with a bar-nap, when a scrawny kid with a bush of unruly, blue streaked hair tried to kiss him. "Don't!" cried Mark, turning his head, incoming lips landing on his cheek.

"Hey, Mr. F.," said the kid.

"Johnny, don't do that to me. Ever."

"Ok, ok." His enthusiasm deflated, the kid's body sank, which dangerously lowered his baggy shorts and miraculously defied gravity. "Nice outfit, but I prefer you in that striped suit, very sexy." The young man moved in front of Linus and looked up at him with the eyes of a guileless child. "Call me Johnny. Are you Mr. F's lover?" Johnny asked, his tongue stud tapping against his teeth.

Linus stuttered his denial. Mark patted his shoulder and said, "Relax and repeat after me: When they ask, don't tell. This is my best friend, Linus. He has syphilis of the brain, and he doesn't live here."

"Way too bad," said Johnny, frowning. "Mr. F. needs a boyfriend. He thinks I'm too young for him."

"You work for me," said Mark, "and I don't dip my pen in the company ink."

"Whatever that means. Maybe I'll quit."

"Don't you dare. I need a stock-boy more than I need a lover."

"No, you don't," Johnny clicked.

"I wish you'd get rid of that barbell in your tongue." Mark winced at the noise. "Why?"

"Care to find out?" Johnny stuck out his tongue and licked the air.

"No, and stop that," said Mark. "I'm your boss."

"Sorry," said Johnny. "Linus. Like Linus Pauling?"

Linus rarely had his name connected to the scientist. "Yes," he said.

   American Queer

"Cool." Johnny explained he was studying to be a pharmacist. "You don't say much, do you?"

"No."

"Lighten up, dude," said Johnny, but his sweet smile made it hard for Linus to feel insulted.

"Behave," said Mark.

"Yes, Daddy," said Johnny.

"I am not your daddy," said Mark. "You just missed Binky."

"No, I saw him. He was nagging me for my last name, so I told him it was *bite*. He said Terra-Bite, Terra-Bite over and over. And didn't get it. What an idiot." Johnny inquired about the song playing. Mark told him to ask Linus, the expert on dance music, because he had once played for Uncle Hank.

"Only if it's old," said Linus. "This is *Love Pains* by Yvonne Elliman."

"Wow, your pretty lips moved," Johnny said. "Do you wear lipstick?"

"No," said Linus.

"You're so kissable," said Johnny.

Mark laughed, told him to behave again.

"Daddy gonna spank me?" asked Johnny.

Mark ignored him and then described how Linus was everyone's favorite deejay, giving them some of the best times of their lives. "The trick is to have survived the tricks," said Mark.

Linus no longer cared whether the memories of those fun times, unwillingly forfeited when the plague came, were worth having. Like licking a sweet sucker that gets yanked away, was it better to have tasted it or not? "I would never call survival a trick," said Linus. "More a cruel, disgusting, miserable, arrogant, humorless, two-timing twist of fate."

His host stared at him; the two burst into laughter.

"Ah good times, good times," said Mark.

"You old guys are weird," said Johnny.

"Did you hear that?" asked Mark.

Linus cupped his ear. "What?"

"He said we're old."

"Cold? In this heat?"

     American Queer

"Very funny," said Johnny, "but seriously, I wished I'd lived during those days. No rubbers, but I don't use them anyway."

Mark took a deep breath. "My dear Jonathan … "

Linus knew the commencing lecture by heart, how the posters depicting nude, pretty men with their grinning partners should be replaced by splotchy, emaciated figures with their grieving lovers, family, and friends. Johnny listened to Mark, much like Mark listened to his grandfather talk about World War II concentration camps, letting the geezer have his say about something he thought would never affect him. Mark wasn't so sure now. Linus had no use for rubbers, or any kind of precaution, but not for reasons of safety or sensation.

" … and next week," concluded Mark, "I shall take you somewhere special. Buchenwald has nothing over St. John's Hospice."

"Mr. F., you are way stressed," said Johnny. "I'm not a bug chaser, and I look out for gift givers."

"Decode for the grampas please," said Mark.

"Bug chasers want to get the virus," said Johnny.

"You're joking."

"Gift givers have it and give it away."

"Without disclosing?"

"The gift can be requested or a surprise."

"What is the matter with those guys?"

"That's why I have a group of buds; we get tested regularly and promise not to play outside the group," said Johnny. "Every Saturday night we meet at The Viaduct, dance, and then go to someone's apartment. Do you like this tune?" Johnny asked Linus, who nodded yes. "The Vengaboys, very tsssss." Linus assumed Johnny's noise meant good.

The deejay segued into *Coming Out of Hiding*, and Johnny said, "God, I love the classics."

"Like us," Mark said, "right, Linus?"

Linus nodded and felt a hundred years old.

Johnny's hips had never ceased gyrating. Linus declined his invitation to dance, so Johnny grabbed Mr. F., who said he would follow in a second.

"Boyfriend material?" asked Linus.

   American Queer

"You know I don't qualify for his club." Mark watched Johnny bounce into the throng of dancers. "They have no idea." Defiantly raising his plastic cup to the sky, he said, "Let us dance today, for tomorrow may never come. And unless my underwear works, neither will I."

"You go ahead."

Mark moved beyond the shade of the giant tree, into the hot and bright heat under a cloudless, blue sky. "Poor Linus, you don't get it."

And Linus thought, Poor booby, neither do you.

"You can't watch from the sidelines all your life," yelled Mark.

The hell you can't.

"Meet me here later."

"Somewhere else," Linus yelled back, but Mark had already melted into the moving mass.

—6—

To escape the crowd, Linus climbed steps to a balcony and observed the party below him. A pimply boy in an orange plaid kilt with combat boots and a spread-eagle tattoo on his skinny, hairless chest danced next to a cowboy. A gray-haired man wearing a rainbow umbrella hat shading his head shuffled along with the music, bumping a Goth girl in black eyeshadow and bat wings. Two Latino military men with buzz cuts— legitimate or costumed, it was impossible to tell—held each other, grinding their groins. A circle of boys in ecstasy, sucking pacifiers, writhed languorously and passed water bottles. A man wearing goggles and a fisherman's hat with a huge cock ring dangling in front of his yellow-lensed eyes wobbled drunkenly. Linus couldn't decide if the guy was advertising what he desired to catch or what he could deliver. A lesbian with auburn dreadlocks flying like a Medusa danced next to a Black woman with a shaved head smooth as an eight-ball.

Do you believe in life after love, sang Cher. No, Ms. No-Last-Name, answered Linus, I do not. The deejay mixed into *Born to Be Alive* by Patrick Hernandez. Linus always thought that song depended on your point of view. Madonna's latest followed, but the song that brought the dancers to a crescendo was *We Are Family* by Sister Sledge, a 1979 one-hit wonder. It never failed to jump start the wallflowers or peak the druggies, always leveling the dancers to a camaraderie that defied age, looks, or status. Linus couldn't even tap his foot.

Then he remembered standing in the deejay booth, playing that song long ago. "God, you played so hot tonight." That's what he had said. He wore a blue shirt that night, too. He had also said, "Come with me and be happy." The music … you played so … "Stop it," Linus had demanded. Instead, I ran away, and wasn't that the same day Mark told me he'd just been diagnosed?

But Linus wasn't standing in the deejay booth. That lifestyle would've killed me, he thought. Maybe I should've stayed in it.

A voice dripping with high-pitched, southern femininity interrupted his reverie. "Hey good lookin', what's cookin'?" A voluptuous drag queen in a mini-skirt and Tina Turner wig stood on five-inch heels that supported her six foot frame.

Linus looked up to nod hello.

"Care to dance?" she asked.

"No, thank you."

"Baby, you are one tasty little cracker. I'm Maisey."

"Linus."

"Like the cartoon? Oh, I love *Peanuts*, he's so cute, just like you. Can I buy you a drink?"

"It's coke."

"Staying sober, I like that in a man, especially for later, if you know what I mean. You new in town, Linus?"

"Sort of."

"You look lonesome, stranger."

"Not really."

"Sugar, how 'bout you take Maisey somewheres quiet like, take a rest on that blanket of yours?"

"No thank you, ma'am."

"Ma'am?" She tossed her head, flipped her wrist palm-up, and with her voice dropping octaves said, "Shit, Maisey, this ain't goin' nowhere." Her bowlegs stomped off, leaving Linus alone.

Every now and then he would see the top of her mop flopping above the heads of the dance pack, thrown back in pleasure, her long fingernails scratching the sky. Linus heard a Lou Reed song in his mind.

Linus saw the man in the blue shirt staring at him again. Thinking Linus gazed at him, the man smiled and waved. Linus moved away. He spotted his host dancing as agile as Johnny, who raised his legs in tai chi posturings and signed a mysterious language with his hands. Linus ran down the stairs by twos, and stepped onto the bench that encircled the tree.

Coming off the dance floor in a wet radiance, Mark said out of breath, "Look who I found."

Phil, part of their former dancing circle, greeted Linus with a handshake. He had a photographic memory and had settled for a federal job as a minor land management bureaucrat.

Linus listened to them talk on and on about their good old days like a duet of old codgers. Of course Linus remembered the disco naps, the pre-party drinks, the mass of men, capsules filled with acid, MDA, quaaludes—that was their cocktail back then, not the 13 pills taken by the ill today. He remembered how they would fly to New York or San Francisco for a night of dancing when rates were cheap and their discretionary income was used for flights of fancy, not IRA's or 401k's. Listening to their prattle, Linus felt prehistoric and nauseated again. Talking about old times led to talking about old friends.

"God, please, please stop reminding me," said Linus.

"Sorry," said Phil.

"Are you?" asked Linus. "No, Phil, I'm sorry. It's just the world didn't exist except for where we danced. Quite a legacy. Remember that time … or back then, we'd … like, before electricity? Before Christ? When mastodons and T-rexes and saber tooth tigers roamed the earth? The old days, the old gang, the old music. We're old, get it?" Linus plunked down on the bench around the tree.

"We're not extinct," said Mark. "And I am not old."

"And not everyone got old," said Phil.

"I am not old," said Mark again, "but I gotta sit down."

Linus laughed.

"Now he laughs," said Mark, "Our numbers do dwindle."

Saul was dead, Eddie, Freddie, Pete, and Louie, all gone, Martin just last year, names ticked off from a literal book of the dead, like musty mementos raked up from his past. Linus didn't know about Martin, who couldn't handle the rising death toll, drank four bottles of booze, and died in a gin-soaked coma. Phil told them about Barnaby Ford. This latest casualty upset Mark, who hadn't heard. Linus thought he'd be used to it by now. Mark seized one of the bunny-eared fairies who walked by, saying he'd take good care of the pitcher. "Go on, Phil."

Who told the story of poor Barnaby. Even he had not escaped the plague, if only indirectly, but Linus guessed that if you've been shot six times around the heart, that's splitting hairs, or ventricles and auricles. Phil found out from Gene Edmonton from D.C., who had talked to Andy Farrel from Ft. Lauderdale, more buddies of theirs, at a circuit party in Atlanta, "who had talked to Dick, what was his last name," questioned Phil, "Dick, Dick, Dick—"

"God, he's off again," said Mark.

"Dick Gaines."

"Glory Hole Gaines?" said Mark. "I'd have thought for sure he'd be dead by now."

But no, just Barnaby. A trust fund baby, short and plump with a pencil mustache, he talked incessantly and always had a bent for Latinos. He would love them like a philanthropist loves his latest charity, generously and enthusiastically until the thrills dwindled followed by fewer gifts. His Cuban lover for the summer season thought Barnaby had given him the plague though Barnaby was negative. An Iowa tourist found his bullet-riddled body on a beach near Miami.

"Do you think he was surprised?" asked Linus.

"The tourist?" Mark asked. Phil stared.

"When the bullets hit him," said Linus. "Was Barnaby surprised?"

"I hope he didn't know," said Phil.

"I can't get a picture out of my mind," said Linus, "of Barnaby being switched off for good on a lovely beach beneath a cloudless sky with the ocean gently lapping his bloody body. Of

                                     American Queer

course, I know nothing about the weather the day he was shot or how close his body was to the ocean, but still … Poor Barnaby."

"Poor tourist from bum-fuck Iowa," sighed Mark, filling his cup again.

"Which is why I'm taking early retirement," said Phil. "Not because of Barnaby, just all the more reason—"

"You don't have to explain," said Linus. "Congratulations."

Mark and Phil continued reminiscing about others and their fates or dissecting the latest gossip regarding the circuit. All this past sentimentality did nothing to quell Linus's queasy stomach, and their voices clicked like machine guns, each word a bullet strafing his mind, giving him a headache. And while Linus was a member of this party clique and knew these names and cities and clubs and good times, fantastic times, some ghost did those things.

Shit, I'm under the tree, he thought. He stood up quickly, and memory overwhelmed him: the man in the blue shirt, a hot summer night about 3 a.m., how he had spun his acolytes to ecstasy, how the two had sat under the giant tree and watched the cars and stars, how he had been—loved. "Come with me and be happy." And Linus remembered their brief story of courtship and intentions and joy, and he was lost in the embrace of wonderful arms and sweet breath and soft hair. And then he remembered how friends started catching colds, then getting sicker and growing hideous spots, then DYING! and nobody knew anything and nobody did anything except cry or walk around numb, angry, or confused, and he remembered how the government did nothing for the ill, and doctors and nurses were loath to treat the ill, and priests and clerics were fanatic to damn the ill, and he remembered how the numbers rose and rose with no end in sight, and how everyone held their breath for the other shoe to drop, and how for some, it did with barely a whimper, and most of all, he remembered the FEAR!, and how he left the man in the blue shirt and disappeared. Without saying a word. Everything blurred and cotton muffled his ears and sour sand grated his tongue. He was lost in a look of pain, a look he caused, on a handsome face that cried out his name from a long distance as though underwater that became louder and louder …

     American Queer

"Linus … Linus … LINUS!" shouted Mark.

"Nuh-what?" He felt seasick with a salty muck in his mouth.

"Did you just fucking faint?"

Linus realized he sat crookedly.

"I'm taking you home."

"I need a coke."

"We need to leave."

"No."

—7—

The sun was setting, a lemon wash gradating into a navy oblivion. Beyond the dancers bathed in a light show, vehicles like toy cars drove across the overpass, the city's skyline completing the backdrop, rising above the sweeping arc of the bridge, etching the children's hour in angles and curves. The two yapping friends grew quiet. Linus thanked some god; Mark pondered the sky; Phil walked away.

"I'll get your coke," said Mark.

Linus rose to follow, but a tall, fat man who spilled beer on him and almost burned him with his cigarette grabbed him and said, "Not so fast, gorgeous." To Mark, he asked, "What's the going rate for blond whores? More than you can afford, I'm sure."

"Raymond!" Mark pulled Linus away.

"Mark, darling!"

"Drunk already and barely eight o'clock," gushed Mark. "Linus Cottage, old college chum, meet Raymond Morales, old, very old, spawn of the Antichrist."

"Pleased to meet me, I'm sure. I can see why you've kept him a secret all these years," said Raymond.

"He's just passing through," said Mark.

"Lucky guy," said Raymond. His gel-packed hair, swept back from the low line over his brow delineating a widow's peak, shined like a helmet of black feathers framing a sallow face. His yellow teeth complemented his bloodshot eyes. A dribble of dried ketchup in the corner of his mouth suggested a vampire, recently fed.

"Last week, I called and got your answering machine blessing this and that, wishing everyone a-super-miracle-day," said Raymond. "Ick-shit."

"Funny. Ten years ago, I called Dial-a-Dick and got you."

"And you've had super miracle days ever since."

"And you've had," said Mark, "well, we all know what you've had."

"Jealous?"

"Curious, Raymond. Why didn't you leave a message?"

"Last week? Heart surgery."

"Didn't know you had one," said Mark.

"Not any longer," said Raymond, "safer that way."

Mark had known Raymond for years, and Linus had heard stories about him. He was a psychologist, partner in a large clinic. Mark told him Linus was a computer expert. Raymond immediately challenged him by asking obscure questions about software and hardware, but Linus held his own. Raymond said, "My, my, brains, body, and blond." This attack thwarted, he switched targets. "You look 20 years too young to have gone to school with our debauched bachelor here. Mark, you little tart," said Raymond, blowing smoke.

"Tartlet," corrected Mark. "Mother still lives." His civility strained, he mentioned meeting Mr. Universe Leather whatever.

"That harlot? The only thing he ever got at a gym was crabs," said Raymond, slopping his beer and waving his cigarette, "or the phone number of another *client*."

"He told us you gave him yours," said Mark.

"He wishes. Did you see his one-man show at Club B-way? The cast should have been cut in half." Raymond searched about him and said quietly, "I don't know why I come to these things. They make me so sad." Mark and Linus said nothing, and Raymond recovered. "Must be the free hotdogs, the only thing long and lean between buns I've licked in years." He laughed loudly, Mark politely, Linus managed a smile. "You're awfully quiet," he said to Linus, "but if I looked like you, I'd be arrogant, too."

                    American Queer

Before Mark could jump in, a man in a wheelchair rolled over Raymond's foot. He screamed at him, "Watch where you're rolling, bitch!"

"Then move your fat ass," said the man as he rolled over Raymond's foot again.

"OW!" screamed Raymond. "How'd you like to be a quadriplegic, you little—"

Pivoting quickly and at crotch level, the man said, "How'd you like to sing an octave higher?"

"Girls, girls!" said Mark.

"But 'cha are Blanche!" Raymond hollered. "'Ya are in that wheelchair!"

"Gee, never heard that one before," said the man rolling away.

"Raymond!" Mark grabbed the arm of his friend who yanked it away.

"All right!" He turned to give his profile and patted his ample gut, saying like a Southern Belle, "What do you think? Triplets? My doctor thinks I'm putting too much expectation on my heart, but what does he know of the homo's expectations of the heart?"

Raymond flicked his ashes into Linus's cup, then said to him, "Enjoying the show? Like that man campaigning in front of the bar? A liberal idiot, and I told him so. These people don't know how to deal with me."

"Who would want to?" said Mark. "You're a gay Republican, an oxymoron, emphasis on the moron."

Raymond threw his beer in Mark's face, Linus lurched, but Mark held him back. "Linus, don't! Raymond, go home."

Disgusted with the scene, others nearby moved back and grumbled. Raymond tottered, his lips slack, his eyes half closed, staring curiously at his empty cup. "Oh dear," he said, "out of this swill." He put his arms around Mark and hiccupped. "Why do you have to be—"

"Yes, I'm damaged goods," said Mark, struggling to support Raymond's weight. "Now, good-bye. Get in a taxi and go home."

"Call me?"

"I'll call you."

   American Queer

Raymond rudely bumped into bystanders and staggered away, then disappeared in the wake of parting people.

"I need a drink," said Mark.

They moved inside to the bar, where a couple stools down, the Catholic still fingered his beads and moved his lips silently. Mark asked *Bahzl* for a wet rag and a double bourbon, another coke with cherries for Linus. Mark took a big swig and let the burn settle. "Having fun?"

"Why do you put up with that creep?"

"He does have that annoying habit of breathing," said Mark, wiping his face and arms. "Because he's pissed at the world."

"Who isn't?" said Linus. "I feel sorry for him."

"Do you? Feel sorry for him?"

"Except for him treating you like a slut."

"I know, odd, huh? I've always wanted to be a slut. Sluts get such a bad rap." Mark took another drink and shuddered. "Alec, his ex he adored, left him for a richer man. Apparently, I'm the doppelgänger. Raymond will call *me* and buy me off with an expensive dinner along with his guilt. I enjoy watching him eat his liver."

"With onions?"

"Why Linus, you made a funny," laughed Mark.

While Mark continued wiping beer off himself, Linus observed the gathering outside, to him a bizarre cotillion. The crowd, restocked by the night birds, had not thinned. Despite looks or situation or age, no singular fates here, only a collective decree. "'The nymphs are departed,'" said Linus.[17]

"What?" asked Mark.

"From an Eliot poem."

"Linus, with all my heart, shut the fuck up." Mark downed his bourbon and said, "Let's make like fags and blow this joint."

Heading to the exit they met Phil. "Why are all the good ones taken?" he asked no one in particular.

"We're not," answered Mark.

"You know what I mean."

---

[17] T.S. Eliot, *The Waste Land*, (New York: W.W. Norton & Co., Inc., 1973), lines 175 & 179, p. 1707.

American Queer

"Yes, I do." Mark stared at him, then asked, "Why have we never gotten together?"

Phil shuffled and looked down. When he looked back at Mark, terrified embarrassment filled his eyes. Mark placed an arm around his friend's waist. Hesitating, Phil put his arm over Mark's shoulder and sighed as though releasing a long-held breath. Both tightened their grasp and rested their heads on each other.

Linus wondered how long it had been since either man had given and received an embrace of electrified desire. The potential breeze of physical release tempted the parting of a fluttering veil, not like their dead friends who had relinquished their bodies and swept aside the veil *of* their bodies, but a living release *for* the body, as a stripping of clothes, a touch of lips and limbs, a surrender to nakedness and hardness and slickness. Since both partings bring closeness and closure and new openings, Linus was attracted to neither, so deeply had his ennui sunk to his marrow. To him, Phil and Mark reflected an allure to a drive that was natural and denied and missed within, their subtle caresses agitating the same drive that Linus had discarded without resistance years ago, convincing himself the urge was unessential and most of all, forgotten. Despite his friends' similar heavy history, the two did not appear surprised to be in each other's arms, but rather, surprised they had found anyone's arms at all after such a long time in a desert of physical and emotional solitude.

Looking up to Phil, Mark said, "We can play safe, you know." Phil stood frozen.

Linus faded into the bathroom. It was the same ersatz prison from years ago: rusty pipes, gray walls, metal bars between the urinals emitting the same sweet sauerkraut stink from pink cakes. Probably the same ones, thought Linus. He wondered how many "inmates" had pissed here in the passing years, what value he or any of them had gleaned from the waste flowing from an organ that for him, was performing its only current function. I mean, thanks to Siouxie and the Banshees, thought Linus, what did you guys think of when you held your "flaccid ego in your hand?"[18]

Linus tucked in, zipped up, and standing before the sink, stared at the reflection in the cracked mirror. His face was sun-red and his bloodshot eyes burned. Another fractured image appeared. When he turned around the man in the blue shirt stood watching him.

"Hi!" said the man, grinning.

Linus didn't move. Neither did the man.

"I recognized you from behind." His grin widened. "And in the mirror. I kept seeing you from a distance, hoping I'd run into you."

"I'm afraid I … "

"It has been a lifetime." The man shook his head. "But you're the same gorgeous guy you always were. Keep an ugly painting of yourself in a closet somewhere?" he asked, chuckling, then sighing.

"You have me mixed up with smumnum—someone else." Linus moved to exit, but the man in the blue shirt touched his arm, Linus flinched and backed away.

Like being robbed, the man held up his hands. "Sorry, I didn't mean to—it's just that, you remind me of someone I knew from … from another time."

"Lucky guy," said Linus.

"Me, too. He disappeared, and I—" The man quieted his memory, shrugged his shoulders, and smiled sheepishly. "Forgive the rambling." He pulled out a slip of paper from a pocket and offered it to Linus. "I wrote down my number in case … maybe you could take it."

"There'd be no point," said Linus.

"Yeah, you're right," he said. "You're absolutely right." The man in the blue shirt did not leave for a long moment.

Linus ran cold water over his face. He hung his head, bracing himself on the sides of the sink. He cranked the dispenser and dried himself with rough, brown paper. Having ignored itches that demand scratching, he could no longer pretend he didn't have a rash.

---

[18] Siouxie and the Banshees, *Peek-A-Boo*, (Los Angeles: Geffen Records, 1988).

     American Queer

"You look like you've seen a ghost," said Mark. "Maybe we should get you a hotdog."

"I'd rather get out of here," said Linus. "Where's Phil?"

"Getting his car," said Mark, handing keys to his guest. "He says good-bye, and I say good-night. I got lucky."

"What? I might have to sit down. Who's the lucky guy?"

"Phil. He doesn't know how lucky, but he will. I'll be home in time to take you to the airport on my way to work."

Linus trembled. The ground seemed to shift. He was all at sea, adrift, unanchored.

"Well," said his host, "God didn't have much fun in you today, did He?"

"Don't you mean *she*?" said Linus.

"Sweet of you to remember."

"I'm trying to forget."

"And so proud of it." Mark took his guest's arm and moved him to the side for privacy. "Forgetting won't work."

"You won't let me," said Linus, shaking off his host's arm.

"Goldy, do you know why I call you?" Mark asked. "*You* remind *me*. I don't want to forget. But it's getting harder. Sometimes, I forget faces"—he squinted as though trying to remember one—"and that frightens me. Linus, if your … your lapses measure your sadness, imagine your love."

"I can't."

"Can't? Or afraid to?"

"Jesus, Mark," said Linus. "Look, you have fun with Phil."

He turned to leave, but Uncle Hank caught him before he could exit. "You look like shit."

"Thanks."

"Tom's here somewhere."

"Who?"

"Wait, he gave me—"

Linus rushed into the night, Mark following and calling after him, but he walked faster and faster. "Linus!" said Mark. "Linus, please stop!"

"What do you want from me?

"It's nobody's fault. You're not a computer, and they aren't a file you can delete or a disk you can erase with the stroke of a key."

"What are you talking about?"

"The dead," Mark said.

Linus stopped and spun around. "They hound me."

"You haven't given them a proper burial, and they will never comfort you until you do." Linus noticed the brightness in his friend's eyes turning wet. "You can't replace them. Don't even try," Mark said with a knowing chuckle.

Linus took a deep breath. "If I start crying, I'll never stop. I will never stop."

"But the longer you wait—"

"You know when you call, do I answer?"

"Yes."

"Do I hang up?"

"No."

"So, for right now … "

"OK," said Mark, "I get it. I'm sorry." He tousled his guest's golden curls. "Well, you won't forget this weekend soon. Thanks for sobering me up," he said.

He raised his arms to hug his guest, but Linus backed away. The disappointment on his host's face made him reconsider, but the distance was too great.

"I'm glad you stayed," said Mark. "Let's do it again. It's your home. Please?"

Linus nodded yes, and Mark nodded yes, both acknowledging their mutual mendacity.

Phil pulled up to the curb.

"Good to see you Phil," said Linus. "Enjoy retirement. Enjoy Mark. Now who's blushing."

"I am not—oh, hell," said Mark. "Phil, wait a minute, I forgot something." He headed back to the entrance.

Linus said good-bye to The Viaduct, the music, the tall, green tree, its limbs waving back in the gentle, summer breeze. The politician—sunburned, tieless with rolled up sleeves, and linked arm in arm with Maisy the drag queen—shoved a flier in his hand. *Jackson, He'll Show You Energy and Compassion.* Maisy blew a kiss to Linus and smiled as he passed her.

  American Queer

Cruising on autopilot, Linus arrived at his host's duplex, the porch glowing from its constant blue vigil. He searched in the medicine cabinet for something to soothe his rumbling stomach, swallowed the fizzy, pink frappé, barely keeping it down. He was exhausted but wired: jet lag, the sun and heat, the sweet syrup of too much nostalgia and cola, no food in hours, an overload of memories.

And they would not cease. Plopping down in the barco-lounger, Linus relived what his host had said to him over the phone two weeks ago. Mark had told him of yet another date gone awry.

"I don't know why you bother," Linus had said.

"And I don't know why you don't."

"Because it's tiring and useless and boring."

Mark had grunted. "You make a lousy homosexual, Linus, a great whiner, but a lousy homo."

"Thanks a lot. Dating is depressing."

"Of course it is. You're attracted to depression."

"Attracted?" Linus had asked .

"As though it's a jacket off a rack in my store, something comfortable you put on and take off at will."

"Why would I do that?"

"Because you don't have the guts to try and feel differently."

"Getting through the day," Linus said, "that's my goal. You're the one asking for love."

"Damn right I am. And so are you, Linus, so are you. Maybe not out loud, but oh yes, Linus, you are asking for love. And not for a love nameless, secretive, and quick. We're all boys and girls begging to be loved, whether we admit it or not. Love me, we all say, love me first, and maaaaybe I'll love you back. Nobody wants to be a cipher when they grow up. Except for you, so smug and self-contained and indifferent. Is that how you want to 'get through the day?'"

"Stop it."

"Loving someone, that's the hard part. And not many are up to it. You never tried," Mark had stressed. "You never once tried."

Linus covered his ears. His slitted eyes felt like they had been injected with a syringe of onion juice. "You're a shit, Mark!" he screamed in the empty home. "You all left me, and you're all shits! ShitshitSHIT!" Breathe. He couldn't breathe. Squash, compress, control, control! Where's that goddamn Janet Jackson song when you need it? He sensed more onion juice building behind his eyes, thought he was going to throw up, but only belched, shuddered, then said, "God, I'm hungry." The Dead Slobster had been a long time ago.

Linus wobbled to the kitchen, saw Mark's watch on the counter near spring cleaning rags, and opened the refrigerator. In the glare of the white light, he squeezed his eyes tightly. "Mark's funeral." Just thinking about it brought a fresh wave of onion juice. "I did try. Didn't I?"

He drank a tall glass of water, ate a cheese sandwich, and again took the bag of marshmallows to his bed on the couch. He blew his nose—must be the pine and bleach, he thought—cracked his toes, and picked up his book. Read, he thought, yes, read.

> *So, all a man could win in*
> *the conflict between plague and life*
> *was knowledge and memories. But*
> *Tarrou, perhaps, would have called*
> *that winning the match.*[19]

Memories are all I have left, cobwebbed memorabilia. Quite unlike Uncle Hank's glittering jewels. And I know more than I care to know. Some victory. "Hey, world, I'm a winner." Linus threw the book across the room. "No help, no fucking help at all!" Everything was as foreign as Dublin, and he felt lost in the narrow alleyways of his upper maze where no one, including himself, spoke a language he understood. He turned off the lamp, tucked his legs up to his stomach, and shivering, clutched tightly to the blanket. Binky was right, thought Linus, we are out of fashion. He brushed his cheek with his shield of soft cotton and thought of the man in the blue shirt, that maybe now he could satisfy himself. Nope, not even a twitch. Everything else was in

---

[19] Camus, *The Plague*, p. 237.

 American Queer

tip-top condition, healthy as a gelding, but even the man in the blue shirt was not enough to arouse him. Of course, Linus remembered him, remembered Tom whispering his nickname in his ear. I will always remember him. And Uncle Hank, Bloody Barnaby on a beach, all the others.

Linus thought about retrieving the file of Toy4U. I could, you know; after all, I'm the expert.

He turned on the TV, hummed the wacky theme song to *Rocky and Bullwinkle*, and again threw marshmallows at their evil foes. Funny, thought Linus, how they get blown up, but never die. Kind of like me, every death a bomb. He shut off the TV and stared in the liquid dark for a long time.

—9—

See, there's more than one way God skins a cat, and from what Mark told me, courtesy of his new religion, is that I have more than nine lives—and gosh darn it, I'm so looking forward to each and every one of them—and how there are a hundred, a thousand more planes of existence. Terrific. All I'm trying to do is salvage this one. Even a zombie has to breathe. Doesn't it?

I did try. I tried, but—

Hours later, a mumbling mouse scratches again, but it's only my host coming home. So many words from so many people reverberate in my head and keep me company for a lifetime—or ten. I don't know, I don't know, I don't know—

"Yes, you do," the voice of Tom says to me softly. "You need no words. You did not fail me, that summer long ago."

"Oh, didn't I?" I say to this ghost. "Maybe not then, maybe now. Maybe not you."

"You fail no one, ever. Rest, then arise. We shall all meet again."

A party plays in my mind. I miss everyone, those gone, those still here, those I never knew … and I ache. Replenishing those friends and lovers seems impossible, insulting, but keeping beat with my music, I dig graves in a green and grassy Elysian dance floor.

I turn over, pull the blanket more tightly around me, and in the inky darkness? What if all we have is this life? Because

　　　　　　　　　　　　　　　American Queer

I've read that when you die, you relive your entire life, so when you relive your death, do you relive your life all over again? Imagine, an eternity of the same life, an infinity of identical instants. An exact, orderly, fixed, repeating loop. In each replica, having this thought always at this moment. Never a surprise. Forever. And forever followed by the ceaseless repetition of dull death. How will I ever get it right? But … it's not over yet. Is it?

Am I awake, asleep, alive? I suppose mental masturbation is a natural substitute since I can't—but wait. Hmmm … what have we here?

The floor is cold on my bare feet. My host jerks. "What's the matter, what's wrong?"

"I—" I am erect.

An eyebrow cocks. "Put that away."

He pulls back the sheet. I crawl in. This time, he's the big spoon. He cradles my naked body next to his until my shakes stop.

"You can never leave me. Promise."

"If you do. To call him. I got his number."

"Whose?"

"You know whose, *my big, big bowl of yummy*. Enough to wretch. And I will pull your pink card."

After an eon passes, I drift, the gold of the night-light glowing around the corner like a sunrise. I swallow a cloud, my nymphs wing home, and I again relive a tale about a man I once knew who was dead …

BOOMER VOICE ACTIVE 2000-2024

WHATSHISNAME

2000

Pierre, Pierre
of face so fair,
I do declare
so beautiful when bare.

Pierre, Pierre
in your heart's lair
me you ensnare.
I must beware.

Pierre, Pierre
with dazzling glare
our souls a pair
made One. Trumpets blare!

Pierre, Pierre,
gazing elsewhere,
do I with courage so rare,
with flash and flair
care?

Shared Sleep

2000

My eyes lit up the first time I met Rudolfo Jones. Half his name was real, the Jones half; Rudolfo was a nickname he had acquired in graduate school with a double major in computer science and Italian. In his late 30s, he was scruffy-handsome, his body slim and muscular. His unique name added an exotic air to his already formidable charm because when he looked at me, he made me feel like the center of the universe.

We met at the late summer party of a good friend of mine, a psychiatrist who talked with a husky cigarette voice and wore expensive, large, and garish muumuus. She pointed him out to me. I had arrived as he was leaving and heard him saying his good-*bahs* to guests. Rudolfo could not say *bye*. He was from Nebraska and had a slight accent, but every farewell sounded like an affected bleat from a southern sheep. At least he was consistent, or maybe just consistently affected. I thought it endearing.

My doctor friend beckoned him and said to me, "That is Rudolfo. And didn't you just light up." And so I did (told you so), at the music of his name, not with celestial awe like the first time Tony heard the name Maria, but with interest in the package sauntering towards me. Like any gift, I was excited to know what lay within the pretty bow and paper.

"Good-looking, charming, boring, religious, and childish," the doctor whispered in my ear. "Beware. He'll make you weep."

Just as Rudolfo walked up to us, the caterer with blond highlights and a Slavic lisp rushed up, flailing his arms, exclaiming he was out of crab cakes: "Vath to do, vath to do!" The doctor employed her deft calming techniques and headed to the kitchen, leaving us to ourselves.

"Well," I said, "let's hope they find more crab cakes."

"Lordy, yes."

"So Rudy"—I decided to call him Rudy—"You seem to know a lot of people here."

"I was saying good-bah to my ode dancing gents."

That was another speaking anomaly he had: Any word with *old* came out *ode*, as though the syllable had no letter *l*, yet he had no speech or sinus impediment. I thought that endearing, too. More consistent affectation? I was a goner and didn't care.

In the light of torches and the fragrant breeze of a summer night, Rudy smiled at me, his dimples at maximum squeezability. He searched for more crab cakes, but found another rum cocktail. "My fourth," he said and laughed. "But who's counting?"

We compared our days living in San Francisco, but Rudy was not out of his closet at that time.

"This gay stuff is all new to you?" I asked.

"Lordy, yes, about a year," replied Rudy. "I haven't learned all the games yet."

"Don't," I said.

"It doesn't feel good, standing around bars feeling like a troll."

"You are definitely not a troll."

"There's no accounting for taste."

"Are you saying I have bad taste?"

"No," said Rudy. "Let's say looking at you, you don't have to be so desperate." I laughed, perhaps a little too loudly. "I'm going two-stepping tonight at The Corral," Rudy continued. "I have my cadre of little ode men I dance with. They appreciate me. Do you country dance?"

"No, but it looks like fun." I hated country music.

"Holding on to someone is very fun," said Rudy, "and I'm sure you would be."

"How can you tell?"

"I can tell."

"So, you want to add me to your cadre of little old men?"

"You don't qualify. I'll start a new regiment, only for you."

"Are you sure you haven't learned the games?"

"Lordy, no," said Rudy. "I've been in my Cleopatra phase for too long, you know, queen of denial."

He always got the biggest kick out of that hackneyed phrase as though he had coined it and no one had heard it. I offered to drive him home if he'd had too much to drink.

"No need," said Rudy. "I better get going. Will I see you at The Corral?"

"Only for Patsy Cline's comeback tour."

Rudy laughed, kissed me on the cheek, and left. "Bah!"

He never did find more crab cakes.

***

The next time I saw Rudy was at a poker game with some *ode* men—He and I were decades younger—who had started a strip poker group when their bodies were hard and hot. When muscles and skin began to sag, they kept it to only penny antes and socializing. The host lived in an ugly Victorian house with a dilapidated patio and disintegrating trellis, which was where we had started playing. The weather turned stormy, driving us inside and blowing the first faint smell of fall.

Rudy talked to his gents, sympathizing with their aches and pains and lovers who stayed or didn't, died or didn't. He laughed at their bad jokes and complimented them on their gaudy jewelry. In return, they adored him and thought him charming. I couldn't tell if he was genuinely interested—That's the problem with charm—but he made me feel cold-hearted. I decided to have a cocktail and relax.

The conversation turned to birthdays, and I didn't want to divulge mine because it was the following week. The host, whose toupee slipped further down his forehead the more he drank, demanded I tell, so I did. Rudy said he'd take me out for a birthday dinner; he'd save the spanking for afterwards. Everyone's laughter made me red and hot.

On the last hand, all the players folded except for me and Rudy, leaving us to battle out the bet. I was on my third martini, very dry.

"I see your blurry nickel, and raish your ten."

"Nobody here knows how much Rudolfo can raise," said our host.

                                              American Queer

Amidst whistles and catcalls, it was Rudy's turn to blush, confident charm abandoning him. "You don't want to go there," he said.

Eye to eye, I dared him, "And where would that be?"

"To heaven, honey," said the host. "To heaven!"

All the ode gents laughed again, and I blushed again.

Walking to our cars, Rudy said, "Don't mind them; they're just having fun." Then he hugged me and kissed me on the lips. "Yummy," he smiled. "That one was for you. This one's for me." And he kissed me again. "I just went to my happy place," said Rudy, "and you were definitely there."

For the first time, I felt like the center of someone's universe. I, too, went to my happy place, and Rudy was definitely there.

I again offered to drive him home.

"Perhaps you're the one who should be driven home," said Rudy. "You must think I have a disease or something,"

"Funny you should mention that," I said, "because I do." I told him all about it. I'd learned that ripping off the band-aid was easier than lying.

Rudy paused, then said, "Not a problem."

"Really? Right now, would you like to take advantage of me?"

"Like to? Yes," replied Rudy, "but will I? No. I have to give you something for your birthday." He grabbed a belt loop and yanked me close. "I have a few ideas. Dinner for starters." He smiled so sweetly when he said that. Charm. It's deadly.

We exchanged contact info and, luckily, arrived home safely.

***

My anticipation had been ratcheted up so high, I froze. I didn't contact Rudy, and he didn't contact me, until a week after the poker party. It was my actual birthday, so I thought he was calling to make good on his offer of dinner (and spanking?). But no, he needed the psychiatrist's phone number. I gave it to him, then blurted out an invitation for a meal. It was the first night we shared sleep.

American Queer

When Rudy arrived at my condo, he admitted bolstering his courage with two rums—for what, I wondered—and that he intended to buy me some flowers but didn't want to be late. I would have preferred a bouquet over punctuality but let it go. I also refrained from saying anything about his eating habits. I had made a nice dinner. (Rudy confessed needing a recipe to make toast.) He ate one food at a time, never taking a bite of anything else until he finished the portion he was eating: first the salad, then the zucchini, the chicken. Rudy passed on the fresh Italian baguette; he was allergic to wheat. I thought he might separate the strawberries from the custard, but he didn't.

We moved to the couch, and conversation veered towards discovery. Rudy worked as a computer technician, so nebulous a title, I had no idea how to even fake interest. He said his ideal job would be as a programmer in Italy, so he could use his double degree. He ached a lot, back and headaches due to a childhood disease. His mother and father, then a string of his mother's boyfriends, abused him and his younger brother for years. Rudy's excuse? "She was lonely." I suppose abuse could be considered a disease.

Rudy took a long drink. "One night my brother and I were being rowdy, and to teach us a lesson, Momma's boyfriend of the month, with her in tow, drove us out to the middle of a wheat field. He told my brother and me, 'The boogie man gets little shits who don't behave.' Then he yelled, 'Get out!' and they drove off. Maybe that's why I'm allergic to wheat. I don't remember how we got home. Our grandmother was given custody and raised us. I remember hugging Grams one time. She pushed me away and said, 'Stop it. You're too lovey-dovey for a boy.' I stopped hugging my Grams." Rudy took another long drink. "I'm going on vacation, Key West."

"Really."

I strove to be a good sport, reeling a bit from the change of topic. His childhood didn't seem open for discussion. His vacation was an exploration of this new life he was embracing at the end of the year by himself, but he was nervous about staying at a *clothing optional* hotel.

"So stay at a different place," I said. "I'll find you a different place."

　American Queer

"That's OK," said Rudy. "Heck, if some handsome tourist from Sweden named Lars is there, it would be my civic duty to make sure he had a good time in our country—wink, wink."

He thought his quip was very funny. I wanted to give him something to wink about all right, but I laughed, too. Such a good sport.

"I love this blue glass," said Rudy as he filled it again with rum. He came back over to the couch, sat next to me, nuzzled my neck, and said, "Mmm, you smell absolutely edible."

Over two years of celibacy had made me anxious that first night in bed, when heaven fell, when I learned what Rudy could raise for the titillation of his poker gents, not that I'd ever share. Rudy was mostly fun, mostly. I loved his soft hair, the weight of his body, his squeals and moans. We initiated a pair of dark green silk boxers a dead friend had given me to wear when I was with someone special.

Before we shared sleep, I gave Rudy a present. I was planning on giving it to him for his birthday, but I didn't know the date and couldn't wait.

"Close your eyes," I said. "Trust me."

"You've got my attention."

I opened Dante's *Paradiso* to the last lines and whispered,

"'A l'alta fantasia qui mancò possa;
ma già volgeva il mio disire e il velle
sì come rota che igualmente è mossa
l'amor che move il Sole e l'altre stelle.'"[20]

Rudy rolled onto his stomach. "Your pronunciation needs a little work." He read my inscription, smiled, giving me a peck on the cheek, and said, "I guess time will tell. Thanks. I

---

[20] Dante Alighieri, *The Divine Comedy*, trans. by Geoffrey L. Bickersteth. Cambridge, Mass., 1965. p. 768-9.
The high-raised fantasy here vigor failed;
but, rolling like a wheel that never jars,
my will and wish were now by love impelled,
the love that moves the Sun and the other stars.

owe you dinner." Was he referring to his gift or my birthday? I couldn't tell, and it didn't matter.

We sat up in bed, candlelit, draped in a blanket, and drinking wine. I fed him an ice cream sundae, scooping up the chocolate chin dribbles with a spoon and licking what I missed, the dessert unaffected by his peculiar eating habit. We joked about nuts and bananas of a different kind.

Rudy said a lot more that night: that he never wants to hurt me, that he's good boyfriend material, that my health concern is no concern to him. I believed him, and that he'd find no Lars, no one period, in Key West. Silly me. Yes, it was *my* birthday, and to me, Rudy was a gift.

He showered, his fresh, soapy smell permeating the bedroom, his wet hair falling naturally sexy. Sitting naked on the bed with his back to me, he told me about a recent meeting with his estranged army father in Nebraska, how he had tried to re-establish a relationship that, according to him, had never been established in the first place. His father had a new family and wanted nothing to do with the one from his past.

Rudy said, "My father was so happy he had a new son. He said, 'You're spineless and spermless. You could never give me grandchildren.'"

"Because why?"

"Why do you think?"

"Oh, right, forgot. Being gay means automatic cowardice and sterility."

"He never even mentioned his other son, like he never existed."

"Where is your brother?" I asked.

" I don't know," answered Rudy. "I've tried to find him, but ...."

"I'm sorry. And I don't know about your vertebrae, but I can definitely disprove your father's latter allegation. If that helps."

Rudy got under the covers next to me and continued his biography. A few years ago, he had declared his sexuality and resigned his position as a minister. His church preferred the term *excommunication*.

"Really." I'm not sure how high my eyebrows arched, maybe off my forehead. "You must be happier away from the church."

"No, relieved," said Rudy. "I got tired of the pressure to be like God. Happiness had nothing to do with it."

"I doubt God is happy," I said, "too grumpy."

"Disappointed more likely."

Rudy seemed disappointed, and bitterly stubborn about his god's condemnation which resulted in mutual abandonment. I suspected this self-imposed estrangement to be the cause of many internal battles, and as it turned out, external battles.

"I'm married. Fourteen years. We're separated."

"What?" Eyebrows up again.

"I know the meaning of the word commitment."

"Should I get a dictionary?" I asked. "You're still married."

"Technically."

"So technically, you know the meaning of the word *commitment*."

"Not once in 14 years did I ever cheat on her."

I lifted the covers. "Yep, you're naked."

"She and I are not together, haven't been for years. Lordy, she may not have known where I was, but she didn't have to worry either." Rudy must have sensed my eyes roll because he added, "Mary is content with our arrangement."

"Great," I mumbled.

"What?"

"Now she has a name."

Pillow talk is not all it's cracked up to be. And why he was telling me all this stuff, I couldn't answer and didn't want to ask. It was a lot of information, confessional almost. I turned my back to him.

We shared sleep, though it was restless.

The thing about sharing sleep with someone is that during this intimate time we bring all of our past to our new present. When you share a night of sleep with someone, you're both inanimate, unconscious souls escaping the bounds of gravity and earthly shells. Maybe you travel together, maybe not. Little matters in the end, for when you share sleep with someone,

    American Queer

the eyes of awake-world are blind compared to the eyes of sleep-world where you discover new stars. Or maybe you just zonk out; what do I know.

Tossing and turning, I was constantly affirming this man's presence next to me. At times it seemed as though some unconscious part of him had fled the bed. Of course, physically he was there because hard as a rock, he'd press tightly against me like he couldn't get close enough to me, like he wanted to escape his own body and climb into mine. I don't flatter myself that he preferred mine. Anybody's body but his own would have sufficed, but you can't share everything during sleep.

Like dreams … I was sitting amidst the dense foliage of a forest, hiding from a hunter with a bow and arrow who wanted to kill a fawn I cradled in my arms. I could see the archer's black shadow move against the rays of golden light streaming through the tall, green trees, smell the moist brown earth and thick air. The archer saw me and the fawn. I froze, unable to shout or run as he aimed for an eternity and released in slow motion the arrow that struck my hand and pinned me to the fawn. We twitched slightly, the fawn and I.

So did Rudy. And I awakened.

***

On our second night of shared sleep, I went to Rudy's apartment located near a park. I brought Chinese take-out for dinner. First, he ate a bowl of rice, then of spicy beef. He drank no liquor, which I hoped predicted lots of bouncing on his four-poster waterbed three feet off the ground. I felt I could sail on that soft floating raft forever with its billowy comforter, oversized pillows, and firm waves. We watched TV while eating dinner. I wanted to bite something besides bok choy, but instead of passion, Rudy gave me a peck on the cheek. "I'm exhausted," he said. "In the morning I'll spread some of my syrup on your honey-cakes." Corny, but my heart sizzled like ice thrown on fire.

We were lying on the undulating bed face to face when I asked Rudy, "So what's your real name?"

Even in the dark I sensed Rudy shutting his eyes tightly. "Bob. Bob Jones."

American Queer

"Robert's a nice name."

"Lordy, no," he corrected. "Plain Bob. That's what my parents put on my birth certificate. Grams told me they got drunk one night at a bar away from the army base. They had a good laugh over the joke." Anticipating my next question, he added, "And no, no middle name."

"Why not Roberto then? Why Rudolfo?"

Rudy sighed. "I was a freshman; it was Christmas break, and I didn't have anywhere to go, so I worked in the computer office. One day, I drank a few rum eggnogs, went to the lab, spoke Italian to the students, you know 'Buon Natale,' etc. I had caught a code, my nose was red, and somebody called me—"

"Rudolfo, the red-nosed reindeer." I laughed.

"Everyone thought it was hysterical, and it stuck."

"Geek humor."

Rudy rolled over, and with his back to me, I moved in closer, nuzzled his neck, and threw my arm over him. He patted my hand. "Go to sleep," he said.

A faraway train whistle broke the silence in the dark, early morning. A versatile sound, the train whistle: forlorn, or whimsical like a childhood toy, or the promise of adventure with an uncertain return. A fitting accompaniment—

—because I dreamed I was chasing a train as it was pulling out of a station. Dead friends poked their heads out of windows waving me on to run and catch it. I ran and ran and ran. Finally, I grabbed a handle and hoisted myself onto a step, grinning with achievement and panting so heavily I thought my lungs would burst. One dead friend put his hand on my shoulder, and I jerked awake.

I turned over; Rudy followed, clutching me tightly. "You ok?" I broke free, threw off the comforter, said I was hot. I moved away from him to the gentle bouncing of the waterbed.

Before getting ready for work, we breakfasted on his syrup and my honey-cakes.

***

Our third night sharing sleep—which turned out to be our last—Rudy showed up drunk at my condo. I asked him why.

"I'm afraid you'll leave me."

"Keep drinking."

"And from my brief encounters with other men—"

"You're seeing other men?"

"In the past. Lordy, they say they'll call, but they don't."

I told him lots of platitudes, that learning the rules of the game comes hard to everyone, that I wasn't like other men, none of which seemed to matter.

Thinking pasta would sober him up, I bought him dinner at an Italian restaurant run by friends I knew from my hotel days. (He did not separate the fettuccine from the alfredo sauce.) Leaving me out of the conversation, Rudy talked to the owners in Italian with cultural animation and nuance. My plan backfired. They repaid his charming impression with complimentary bottles of wine. Cin Cin!

"Can I spend the night?" Rudy asked, vino-inspired and all lovey-dovey, which I hated that I loved. "It's going to snow."

The weather was oddly balmy for this time of year. "It's over 60 degrees," I said.

"My shoulder aches. It'll snow."

Apparently, a few months prior to his Italian baptism, Rudy had broken his clavicle, and ever since, a shoulder ache predicted rain or snow. I told him it would be a shame if he froze his cute ass off.

"Why, sir," said Rudy, grabbing me about the waist and pulling me in close. "So kind of you to share. I look forward to repaying you somehow."

We watched TV on my couch, I with my head in Rudy's lap, Rudy stroking my thighs, caressing my face, petting my hair. He took his time undressing me and loved my tighty-whiteys. I was in a very happy place.

And amazed how all the alcohol didn't affect his performance. After a very good time, I felt Rudy's warmth sliding up behind me, his arm wrapped around me, his body pressed against me like a separated Siamese twin trying to re-conjoin itself. I heard sweet Italian nothings whispered in my ear, a grocery list for all I knew. We finished sharing each other again. I licked my lips with warm satisfaction and sighed, "You can be so lustily wicked."

Rudy tensed, disentwined his arms from around me, and lay on his back. "'For the wrath of God is revealed from heaven against all ungodliness and wickedness.'"

"What?"

"Romans 1, 18. Paul says God gives up on people with lust in their hearts."

"Then God's given up on this whole goddamn planet."

He may not have been a minister for years, but Rudy could still quote chapter and verse about how man shall not lie with man. "Verse 27," he continued. "'Men committed shameless acts with men and received in their own persons the due penalty for their error.'"

"Shameless? Penalty? Error?" I sat up and said, "You think I deserve my disease."

"Lordy, don't be silly. God does."

"You agree with Him."

I tore back the covers, slipped on sweatpants and a tank-top, and went out on the balcony. The temperature had plummeted. A few minutes later, Rudy came out and stood behind me.

"Come to bed," he said.

"It's not that you think you'll catch my disease," I said without turning around. "You want to catch it. And since you can't from me, I guess this is it."

"It's freezing. We'll talk about it tomorrow."

"Your god is cruel," I said. "That doesn't mean you have to be. It's not my fault you can't handle the fact I think you're good."

"Say it about yourself." He gave me a chance. "Say it."

"The cold feels good on my bare feet."

Rudy made no effort to comfort me or himself. He might as well have been a ghost. Out of the corner of my eye, I saw him rub his shoulder.

"Snow by morning," he said.

City lights lit the approaching, low clouds. A few stars fought to share their brilliance with anyone who cared to look. I looked.

"It's code," said Rudy. "Come to bed."

     American Queer

We didn't share much sleep. The humps of his hips and shoulder and head lay inches from me like a silhouette of foothills in a dreamy glow. I woke up with his legs and arms weaved around me, again feeling like he wanted to get inside of me hoping to find himself. I ended up on the couch.

You see, the tough part about shared sleep is that even though you both begin a new day, one of you always wakes up before the other, to live a life without the other, leaving the ship of sleep with its tossed blankets and indented pillows for the other to cling to as pointless rafts.

I woke up from a dream in which I was drowning inside a sealed waterbed.

The next morning, snow dusted the ground as though daubed with a powder-puff. When Rudy got up, I told him we should just be friends. He didn't say a word. He left for work. I vomited.

I called my office, said I was sick, and took a personal day. (Aren't they all?) The only thing on TV worth watching was the movie *Quo Vadis*, a 50s Roman spectacular tale of the Christ. Lordy, give me strength. A friend of mine called and said her boss had a heart attack. I think I had a kind of one myself, so I availed myself of her semi-sympathetic ear. She knew Rudy. "And he's nothing like what you've told me you're looking for." She worried about me and warned me about him, but she never liked other people's happiness. "If you're hungry for a burger and go to a Chinese restaurant," she said, "you'll leave hungry and disappointed." Her fortune cookie blurb didn't make weighty sense. So now I hungered for egg rolls, so what?

***

The holidays passed. I knew better than to expect a call or visit from Rudy, and I wasn't ready. When he finally did call, he wanted something. He told me he'd had the flu the past month. He was fine now, and then mentioned his departure to Key West the next day. I offered to take him to the airport. Why I saved him from asking I don't know. He pooh-poohed the offer and made excuses like, "It would be out of your way; I can drive myself and find some park-and-ride; I'm not worth the hassle."

"Fine."

                                        American Queer

"Of course, if you want to … "

"That's what friends do," I said, the words leaving an icky taste in my mouth. Lovers do other things.

I picked him up on a rainy and foggy morning. In the car Rudy exuded the aroma of menthol. "What's that smell?"

"Lip ointment," answered Rudy, shutting the door. "Lordy, can you believe it? Of all times to get a code sore. No one will come near me."

"Wait until it's dark," I said. Rudy shot me a dirty look. "I guess Lars will have to wait."

"Who?"

"Never mind." I smiled, knowing he'd forgotten his patriotic duty to befriend Scandinavian tourists.

During the ride to the airport, a radio newscaster talked of another religious battle that had turned deadly. Rudy went off on a tangent. "Lordy, they're all bunk. You have your God who is the head honcho, then you have Jesus who is subservient to God, and then you have the Holy Ghost who doesn't have a name at all. Lordy, they're bunk."

I looked at him like he was speaking in tongues. "What are you talking about?"

"The zealots who can't follow the basics. They're crazy."

"Speaking of crazy," I blurted out, "I can't do this."

"Do what?" asked Rudy.

"This friend thing." I pulled up to the curb for departures near his airline. "I miss your sleep."

Rudy grabbed my chin and made me look at him. "It's hard to keep my hands off you, too," he said.

His gesture was nice, but I shook my head and said, "That's not all of what I mean."

"Need I remind you—"

"Nope, no need." I didn't remind him that he had said nothing that night, not one word to combat my idiocy.

Rudy put his hand on my shoulder and pointed to his lip. "I'd kiss you but not with my—"

"Leaky lesion?" I smiled.

Rudy looked annoyed. "Anyway, consider yourself kissed."

 American Queer

"Go. You'll miss your plane."

"Lordy!"

He offered to take me to dinner when he got back. I never collected on the first two. (Third time's a charm?) Not sure why I was keeping tabs.

And not sure why, as we exited the car, I held my camera, calling to him as he headed for the airport entrance, "Smile!" He made time to pose (he's naturally sexy). When he turned, I snapped a picture of him from behind. I had to have a picture from that lovely angle, proof of the man with whom I had shared sleep.

Rudy called back over his shoulder, "Bah!"

***

Then he disappeared. Which didn't bother me until I realized I was pretending like a queen of denial. I tried calling him, asking the poker group, our psychiatrist friend, but no one knew anything. I even went to The Corral to ask his country dance gents. That friend who had given me the fortune cookie warning thought she had seen Rudy at a bar singing karaoke with a bleached blond number, a foreign caterer (which rang a bell). Though she achieved her desired effect of upsetting me, I never confirmed her claim. I thought of contacting his wife, but stunned by my bad idea, I gave up. No, he was gone.

Maybe Rudy had met some Lars and moved to Miami or even Malmö, preferring to share sleep with him. Maybe he had thought his flu and cold sore were the beginning of something much worse and blamed me and my condition, consciously or not—which was ironic, because he was safe with me. He had said he could handle it, but he couldn't, my condition, that is, and so much more. I still think at one point he had wanted the disease as a way out. Maybe he had moved back to Nebraska. I exhausted my few resources to end my worries, and eventually, they both disappeared, too.

***

A few years later, around Thanksgiving, I attended a candlelight vigil commemorating the death of a young man who had been brutally and mercilessly slain on a desolate dirt road in a neighboring state. (The rancher thought he'd found a grotesque scarecrow hanging on a fence.) The gathering also mourned a city civil rights bill and state amendment changing marriage laws. Both had failed at the polls. The night was freezing cold. People held candles; breaths floated like untethered cartoon balloons. And then, there he stood.

"Lordy," said his beautiful face, smiling with squeezable cheeks.

Everything rushed back to me, time travel in a scrapbook of mental postcards. He seemed delighted to see me, but with charming people, you never know for sure. "Rudy."

"How are you?" he asked.

"Right now," I said, "I feel ashamed."

"I know."

"And I despair."

"Don't look to me to take it away."

"I wasn't."

"Can't rid myself of my own."

"And how are you, asshole?"

Rudy stared at me, then chuckled with his sexy smile. "Doing the best I can." He looked down at the dead grass. "Which was never quite good enough for you."

"Your drinking sure wasn't."

"We were hardly together."

"Glad you're okay," I said. "I'm going to stand over there."

Rudy grabbed my arm. "I'm sorry."

"No, you're not."

Rudy cocked his head. "I still read the book you gave me. Your inscription came true."

I looked confused.

"What you wrote in my *Paradiso*. Don't you remember?"

"Of course I remember." I had no idea what I'd written. "Knew it would."

The tinny microphone made speaker after speaker— politicians and preachers with useless thoughts and prayers— sound like rubbed sandpaper. Surveying the crowd and placards and banners and media, Rudy said, "All this."

American Queer

"Yes, all this."

"Makes me think of my little brother," he said. "Think it will ever end?"

"Nope." I had to ask. "So where the hell have you been?"

"Oh, you know," said Rudy.

"No, I don't know. No call, nothing."

"I'm in the middle of divorce proceedings."

"Hmmm," I said. "Not easy I hope."

"Lordy no, not easy," said Rudy, staring into his candle that illuminated something deep within him. "That kid could've been me. Or my brother. I should have protected him more."

"What do you mean?"

"Back in that wheat field. Or at home."

"You were a kid yourself. You did well to get him home."

"I suppose so." Rudy looked up and said, "I never lied to you."

"True," I said. "You honestly treated me like shit."

"And what kind of a friend were you?" Rudy could tell by my look he had asked the wrong question. "Maybe we could have dinner. I think I owe you one."

"Making four," I said, laughing. "But who's counting?"

"Four what?"

"Never mind."

The crowd erupted into shouts and applause over what one of the speakers had said.

"I'm code," said Rudy.

He turned to leave, stopped, came back, pecked me on my cheek, and wrapped his arms around me. I rested my head in the crook of his shoulder. He didn't let go for a long minute. "Good to see you. Take care of yourself."

"Oh, Rudy," I said, caressing his cheek. "Nothing else to do."

He turned to leave again, raised his hand in farewell and with his back to me, said, "Bah."

I like thinking it wasn't charm that made Rudy hug me; it was certainly endearing. I shouted, "I still think you're a good

   American Queer

person," but wasn't sure he had heard me. Was it wrong to feel that way? Probably futile.

Next to me, a little girl wearing a knit hat with kitty ears and sitting on a man's shoulders cried for me, for all of us, that night.

Later at home, I cried for myself. I drank out of the blue glass Rudy liked, imagining my lips pressing his, and then dropped it. My psychiatrist friend had warned me Rudy would make me weep. (I'll never tell her; she'd gloat.) I threw out the broken pieces along with the cologne he had liked (*Mmm, you smell absolutely edible.*) A whiff always conjured his image.

***

Once in a blue moon, I come across a picture of a man taken from the back at an airport, faded and worn. He's like a lovely, *ode* song, forgotten, until a few notes rise out of nowhere. And I remember.

Funny, how life can cram so much in so short a space of time. Even the shortest periods of love, so maddeningly random, are fortune's shine. Being the center of someone's universe, no matter how briefly, is the reward for the thousands of insignificant days and nights that meld into a life. I had been happy. I know I only fooled myself—we're all experts on that—like Rudy finding his God. As his confessor, I hope he does someday. For me, when that muscle in your chest breaks, how much more divine can a human be?

I don't dream much anymore, but now and then, the man lying next to me—with whom I share sleep—wakes me up from his.

Images Will Be Disturbing

2018

originally published in
OFM (OUT FRONT magazine, print) October 17, 2018

Beady, red eyes zeroed in on his head; razor-sharp claws reached and clenched towards his eyes, and as serrated teeth were about to bite his throat, Joe woke up, crying out, his eyes boinking open like a cartoon. He sat up, gasping, shaking, squinting from white fluorescent light, its electric hum buzzing in his ears. He tasted blood, shivered from the cold air, smelled its stale nothingness.

What the—then Joe remembered: a van of creatures, his escape to an airfield, a long flight on a private jet, but nothing else after celebrating with vodka and caviar. Hated those damn fish eggs, he thought, but wait, the stewardess. Joe vaguely remembered a tall, beefy gal, odd looking, who wore lots of red. Why does my butthole hurt? Did I have a lap dance? Or? "No, no, no!" And then remembering the gang's mission, he laughed. "Libtards, gone for good!" He laughed again, hard, but stopped from a double ache, head and stomach. He struggled to focus, looked around. This was not the situation he had been promised. And why was he shivering? He was supposed to be on a beach with babes. Lots of big breasted babes.

Instead, he found himself in what looked like an operating room with white tiled walls—one with a large, mirrored window—and a floor that sloped to a drain in the center. He sat on a gurney; loose straps wound about him like leather snakes. A hose was coiled in a corner. Stainless steel cabinets and medical lamps encircled him. All was bright and white and shiny and sterile.

On a metal table sat bloody towels, a tray with a razor, a clipper, a steel bowl with clumps of dirty hair. His hair. He felt a

American Queer

peculiar draft on his face, his head. He stood up, felt hungover, nauseated. He staggered and stumbled, crawled to the sink, hoisted himself up. In a mirror, his bloodshot eyes stared at his scalp, face and neck, all baring scabbing cuts and scrapes. He thought of the ditty "shave and a haircut, two bits." He snorted, then grinned, exposing grody teeth, because he still wore his favorite t-shirt, stained and ripped, over his kind of six pack, a PBR beer gut stuffed into hospital pants. *What happened to my Wranglers?* he wondered. He was starving and thirsty, turned on the faucet, cupped his hands, gulped, coughed, choked.

A scratching noise made Joe jerk his head towards the windowless door. The scratching stopped. He limped to the door, cautiously opened it, peered into a hallway of steel and concrete. Incandescent tubes seared the ceiling like lane markers on a highway.

"Hello!" A soft echo. "Anybody here?" No answer.

His feet were freezing. He looked for shoes and socks, but didn't find any. Bare pads slapping the cement, he started down the hallway, so cold he exhaled puffs of vapor.

Joe came upon another hallway, then another and another, some with doors, all locked. Some dead-ended; he'd pivot and retrace steps. All corridors had cameras high in their corners. He wondered who or what there was for the eyeballs to ogle; the place seemed abandoned. "Where the hell is everybody?" The quiet was unnerving.

At the end of one hall, a spotlight pinpointed a silvery dish. He slowly approached it, knelt down, sniffed, and so famished, he devoured the clump of hard, yellow cheese. Joe wretched, but kept it down.

He limped and turned left, right, round different corners so many times the dull, flat walls began to blur, all the rectangles becoming hallucinatory. The monotony broke when he came upon an open door. He entered a warehouse filled with large cages. Hundreds. Doors eerily open. All empty. Of what, Joe knew. "So, this is where—" But he quieted himself quickly. Somewhere among the cages, he heard a scurrying noise and the click of claws on concrete. Joe stumbled backwards, ran as best he could, heard faint sounds, hobbled towards them. He opened another door.

     American Queer

A blast of loud, incoherent babble roared in Joe's ears. Above a console of switches, knobs and sliders, a bank of television screens lined one wall. Some were labeled with weird alphabets or foreign words, some in English with logos of recognizable networks. Monitors displayed sitcoms, cop shows, cooking contests from all over the world. Some screens were black, reflecting the room's glare, or flickered with strips of interference, or displayed the multi-colored rectangles of a no-signal screen. His favorite channel, Faux Noise, was the only screen that displayed digital noise at full volume, static like a billion gnats.

A woman entered. Joe jumped. They stared at each other.

"Velcome home, Comrade Joe," said the woman in a deep voice. She wore a short, white medical smock. She was tall with teased red hair, heavy charcoal eyeliner, thick flesh-colored makeup. Her lips were smeared with red lipstick; her fingers ended in sharp red nails, her feet in red stilettos. She liked red. Her hands and feet were big. Really big.

Joe followed her long legs that went from here to way, way up there. He thought she looked familiar, grunted, and grinned. This might not be so bad after all, he thought. Pain changed his mind. He grabbed his stomach, doubled over, sat down hard in a chair. What was in that cheese I ate, he wondered. The woman turned a knob on the console lowering the volume.

"Where am I?" asked Joe.

"Vhere ve take good care uf you."

"Am I in a hospital?" Joe panicked in pain. "Oh, God!"

"God ees not here," said the woman. "I am. I had to shafe your face and hair. Vere you sinking of joining zat band, how you say, ze ZZ Top? Zees vay, Joe, no more lice babies."

"You know my name. Who the hell are you?"

"*I*," said the woman, stressing the pronoun and locking onto Joe's eyes, "am *Dr.* Deek. Dr. Deeva Deek. I will take care if you. Ve never leave our comrades behind enemy lines."

"Enemy lines? I'm supposed to be on a hot beach with hot girls!" shouted Joe. "Not in a hospital with some, some—"

"Somewhat?"

　　　　　　　　　　　　　　American Queer

"Let's just say, you're not the ride I was promised."

"You didn't complain on ze plane."

"Is that why my—no, no, no!"

"Relax, what can I say," said the doctor. "Change of plans. Be wery glad you are not in Chernobyl. Zat's vhere ve get our—my English not so good—varmints so furry with ze sharp teeth. Da? Ees correct? Besides," said the doctor, her eyes crinkling and her voluptuous red lips smiling, "You got your vish. Ees not zat glorious?"

"What veesh?" Joe asked mockingly.

"You forget already? I show you."

The doctor flicked switches on the console. All the screens except a libtard network Joe hated blacked out. Its video was striped and jumbled, the audio hissy and garbled. The doctor mumbled something that sounded like curses and fiddled with a few knobs. "Reception wery bad up here. Zees snow, eet neffer stops," she said. "So much guddamn snow." She smacked the console. Joe jumped. The screen and audio cleared up. "Sometimes you heff to boss ze technology."

A talking head spoke in mid-sentence. "—brutal attack on the White House leaves many questions unanswered." The announcer stopped, his hand pressing his earpiece, then hung his head before resuming. "This just confirmed. President Ronald Dump has died. Vice President Spike Dunce, Senate Majority Leader Snitch McKuntul, Speaker of the House Saul Pyon and Secretary of Education Mitzi Depuss, are also dead. Attending the celebration, the president's favorite pundits Nan Poulter, Dora Graham, and Chucker Charleston have not survived the slaughter. Our thoughts and prayers go out to all the families. Many other cabinet secretaries and members of the president's staff and fans have not been identified as bodies are too disfigured. The following video of yesterday's massacre, retrieved from security cameras, provides a horrific testimony. No audio accompanies the video. Images will be disturbing. Parental guidance is advised."

The screen cuts to the broad perspective of a camera high in a corner. In the meeting room voiceless conversations appear animated, attendees smile. Silent laughter follows the president's moving mouth. People stop laughing, their attention

    American Queer

drawn to some commotion off screen. A door flies open, whams the wall, and a horde of deformed creatures rushes into the room, leaps onto the attendees, chomping their faces and necks. Mouths open in mute screams, bodies scramble over furniture, over each other. The president climbs on someone, grabs and hides behind someone else, but is overwhelmed by the creatures kissing his mouth with razor teeth, gouging jagged claws into his neck, locking strong jaws onto his small hands. He tries to escape through another door, but there is no escape. For anyone. The beasts leap onto backs or heads, blood squirts on white walls, gaping eyes are soon blinded, detached limbs get tossed in the air. Secret Service arrives and shoots only to be attacked themselves, succumbing to the horrific talons and gnashing fangs of giant rats with repulsive lesions, beady red eyes, spiked long tails.

The video feed ended, and the talking head returned. "As disturbing as these images have been, the American public needs to know the truth. Escaping the bizarre ambush is HUD Secretary Ken Larson. He had been napping in his office during the devastating bloodbath. He is under Secret Service protection, and according to constitutional law, may be sworn in as our nation's next president. No word yet as to what happened at Faux Noise affiliates around the nation. Simultaneously to the attack on the White House, all Faux Noise stations went dark." A commercial with cartoon bears and toilet paper followed.

Joe uttered retching sounds, bent over, vomited. "The president—dead? No." He wiped spittle from his mouth. "No. That's not what was supposed to happen."

"I tell you before," said the doctor, "change uf plans."

"They told me—supposed to kill fuckin' libtards!" Joe staggered to his feet.

"Dey lied," said the doctor. "Ve rescued you."

"I ain't been rescued."

"Suit up yourself."

Joe roared and leaped at the doctor. She stepped aside; he fell to the floor, delirious, squealing, weeping. Lifting Joe like he was light as a babe, the doctor put him back into the chair. "Now be quiet," she said, "I want to hear."

The newscaster returned. "—gruesome carnage began when an unknown man drove a van near the White House and opened its back door, releasing the horror of attacking animals. They wore a collar with a flashing light as though following some radio beacon. Our zoology experts describe the beasts as mutated rodents most likely from genetic manipulation and/or radiation. The whereabouts of the driver are unknown. He is considered armed and dangerous. When found, his name will be added to the deplorable list that includes John Wilkes Booth and Lee Harvey Oswald, American traitors, American assassins." A picture of Joe flashed on the screen. He wore a mullet, long scraggly beard, his favorite t-shirt.

"No, no, no, I'm a patriot," screamed Joe, "the best fuckin' patriot ever!" Joe started to snivel. "No one's better than me."

Another picture appeared, of him grinning and drinking shots with a short, foreign autocrat, muscular and bare-chested.

"What the—I never, never—that, that, that's a fake! You can't—"

"But ve did," said the doctor. "Looks real to me."

"No, this can't be happening." Joe knew he had to get out, escape, set the record right. He rose, limped as fast as he could from the lying TV monitor, the lying doctor. "You stay away!"

"Where you going? You big hero," said Dr. Deek, "and ve haff your money."

Joe ran down more cold hallways, pivoted more dead-ends, tried more locked doors teasing him of escape. Joe heard high-pitched squeaks, scurrying clicks. At the end of a hall he saw a stainless steel entry and above it, a sign in white letters lit on a green background. An exit sign, he hoped, in strange letters. In a frenzy, he rushed towards it, leaned on the slick door, slid to the handle, and heard faint footfalls.

The doctor's sing-songy voice echoed faintly. "Comrade Joe, come out, come out, vereffer you are."

Joe turned the handle. It gave, but the door was blocked. He used his aching shoulder to push hard. The door opened a crack. Icy wind and the whirr of a blizzard whooshed in. He pushed harder with all the strength he had left—"C'mon, goddammit!"—until finally the door gave way, and he plunged into a massive mound of—snow. Biting flakes blasted his face, clogged his nose, froze his breath and toes. He climbed to the top of the white heap, and through the stinging needles, he could barely see a horizon flat as a line without tree, rock, coast, river, hill. Nothing but endless white, wind, and bitter cold.

Joe backed inside, collapsed, then crawled and scrambled deliriously through the labyrinth until he wound up back in the room where he began. He knelt on the floor, hanging his head, and except for his panting, silence enveloped him. The clip-clop of high-heels broke the quiet. His eyes saw red stilettos and followed a pair of legs that went from here to there.

The doctor looked down on Joe. "I brought your hat." She placed on his head a red baseball cap with *Make America Great Again* emblazoned on its crown.

"What—" Joe rasped, "—what are you?"

"Vat you sink, eh?"

"I—I don't know."

"Your fairy godmother," said the doctor with glee. "Da, I granted your vish."

"What have you done to my country!"

"Vat do you care?" the doctor replied. "You got your vish."

"What *vish*," Joe asked. "I never *vished* to be—"

"Da," said the doctor, spitting her response. "But you deed."

Joe shook his head, frowned in confusion.

"You're vearing eet." Dr. Deek was losing her patience. "Your t-shirt so feelthy. I keep tellink you. Your vish, your vish."

Joe did not have to look down. It was his favorite, in big letters: *I'd Rather Be Russian Than Democrat.*

"Velcome home, Comrade Joe," said the doctor.

Joe lurched. "You bitch!" He missed, fell again.

"No, Comrade Joe," she corrected. "Dr. Deek to you. Dr. Deeva Deek."

Joe heard a scratching noise getting louder, closer. He fell back and crab-crawled backwards into a corner. Something large with beady red eyes and sharp fangs and crescent claws

   American Queer

rushed towards him, leaped upon him, ripped out his throat, his flung voice box trailing his last scream, "MAGAAAAAAaaaa!" as it faded into the frozen void.

Man Shoots Ghost

2024

Her prognosis was inevitable; not even bio-bots would eat her disease, a kind that leaves the mind sharp while the body disintegrates. In other words: hell. She had endured a physical recently, tele-watching the results with her physician, who suggested a cryovault but no immediate change in outcome.

"I've got to have some life," Madalyn said, determination in her plea. She wanted one last adventure where she had no history, where she could be her uncensored self, and, she delicately confessed to her husband, one that did not include him.

"Do I not matter any more?" asked John.

"Of course you matter," said Madalyn.

"Are you so lonely?"

"It's more than that."

Madalyn felt wretched, but this was her life, what was left of it. And she knew, deep down, how fortunate she was to have John because, quite simply, he loved her.

They had always wanted children. Despite all the biotech advances, her husband could not conceive, and since the big virus scare, adoption had been banned worldwide. John was the only man she'd known intimately, and she wanted to know someone completely new, not to conceive, but to live.

Madalyn felt hopeless until, when watching the mini-IMAX, a holo-grAD caught her attention.

"Try a Tech-date with REP-lic-8!

What have you got to lose but your loneliness."

She paused the screen, and a hologram sales rep explained their services. REP-lic-8 was an international AI relationship firm that formed companions for many types of connections. She had zero interest in the app forming a child—that would be too heartbreaking—nor did she want the apps forming parental replacements, endearing girlfriends, or aunties. She wanted an app called the Lover.

Madalyn told John about REP-lic-8. Convinced the Lover would fulfill her desire, she begged John for her last chance at happiness. That particular app was their most expensive product, he argued. A human companion would be cheaper.

"But John," said Madalyn, "it won't be for long."

"What?"

"I consulted my doctor."

"Please, not yet. Don't leave me."

"Soon."

His wife obviously knew more than she wanted to share, but John had learned when to pursue further, and this was not one of those times. "I wish we could, honey," he said, "but that kind of money is out of our reach."

"You'll find a way, yes?" said Madalyn. "Please, John. I don't expect you to understand."

But he did understand. John still loved his wife even though she behaved little and looked even less like the vibrant, beautiful woman he had married decades ago: athletic, sexual, with ivory-tinted skin and thick black hair. Now she was confined to a hover-chair; her skin sagged; her hair was luster-less. Sex was long ago avoided. And though Madalyn's condition was not contagious, its draining care exacted a toll. John knew his once good looks and trim body showed wear and tear: thin, graying hair, watery blue eyes, and a growing paunch. He didn't blame her for excluding him.

John was no Adonis, but he loved Madalyn and knew she loved him. In sickness and in health, so it goes. Life deals crappy cards sometimes, he thought, so how are we going to play them?

They both investigated REP-lic-8 on News-Net and discovered miracle stories on social junk feeds about models curing people's loneliness, of course, but also their physical afflictions. John had read on his version of News-Net those questionable healing rumors were an advertising ploy perpetrated by the company itself, leading to multiple lawsuits, two involving wrongful deaths. Madalyn was unconcerned, and her pleading continued unabated.

Though John felt Madalyn's clinging to her wish took courage and was admirable, he was conflicted. The price for this avatar was enormous. Despite the sales pitch, there was no guarantee she would experience the adventure she wanted. Is her hope misplaced? And short-lived? Because when Madalyn said "soon," how long was that? Days, months?

And then, how to pay for what may turn out to be an expensive indulgence, a glorified sex worker? More than that: a failure and a loss. John knew ways at work to divert funds and circumvent security protocols existed. That was his job. What if he got caught? He would lose a lot more than crypto-credits. Prosecution and plasti-clink would be guaranteed. Madalyn would be alone, if only briefly.

When you love someone, thought John, you do what they ask. Madalyn wants one last passion, one more proof she's alive. Then she shall have it.

As the primary interactor, Madalyn had to undergo an evaluation with a Mr. Steven Jeel, REP-lic-8's psych-tech engineer and salesman. The results were immediate: She passed. Jeel then offered the Rayners a deal: buy a new experimental model—called the Entity—with the latest advances at a huge discount, and allow the company to monitor behaviors. His insistence he would work twice as hard for his meager commission charmed Madalyn, who felt sorry for his sacrifice, but repulsed John, who thought him greasy and his fee greedy. Mr. Jeel assured the Raynors the Entity was safe.

John initiated creative bookkeeping, praying his accounting wizardry would go undetected by his employer. He hesitated before applying his digit-sign, then clicked "BUY" and downloaded REP-lic-8's costly app. When he told Madalyn, she wept.

John set up the boudoir to meet the program's specs. The room had been their entertainment center, but when Madalyn couldn't ride the esca-step to their bedroom, the transition of the room had been crucial for her well-being. He decided to splurge on an upgrade—At this point, why not? He purchased cushy hover-furniture she had chosen, renovated the immersible bath-pool down the hall with fully accessible, and pricey, VoIP control, all to make Madalyn happy. With the Lover due to arrive, she renamed the room the boudoir, thinking the descriptor in sync with her anticipated guest. John said nothing.

When the mini-pod of equipment containing the foto-lasers and plasma pyramid control arrived, John, being tech-savvy, installed the devices himself and saved a few crypto-bucks. Stepping off the hover-stool, he finished bolting the last foto-laser in the corner of Madalyn's boudoir ceiling. Finally, everything was ready.

"Are you ready?" John asked his wife.

"How do I look?" Madalyn asked her husband, trembling a little.

He nodded and smiled. "Beautiful."

"Then, I'm ready." She took his hand and kissed it. "Thank you, John."

The sun was setting. Prior to engaging the program, he checked the angles one last time, making sure the four foto-lasers were precisely aimed at the tip of the pyramid. Because the boudoir faced the street, John lowered the window-shield. The plasma pyramid control on the flo-table required a bio-i.d. He touched its point, an on/off switch after the install; verification, instructions, and fields appeared in air-scripts synced to a virtual mic. He activated the REP-lic-8 software, coordinating it with his tele-watch, then verbal-cued the choices his wife had given him, asking her if she was sure about them. She was.

"There's one field left," said John. "*Name of Entity*, and there's an instruction: *If left blank, app refers to the person as Entity*." Person? he thought.

"Call him Ilya," said Madalyn.

"Ilya?"

"Yes."

"Why Ilya?"

Madalyn didn't answer. John entered the name.

It was time to birth *Ilya*.

Obeying instructions, the two put on dark-spex. He pressed "CREATE" on his tele-watch, then again, placed his finger tip on the point of the pyramid.

                    American Queer

A hum vibrated the air and grew louder. Madalyn covered her ears. The walls, ceiling, and floor shook like a scared dog. An electric current tingled every cell of the couple. Beams of white-silver light shot from the foto-lasers like electric swords, sparking and fizzing, each meeting the others at the point of the pyramid, snapping more sparks and spitting more fizzes. Within seconds, a finger formed, a tip-to-tip mirror of John's. The shape extended into a being, first as a mesh frame covered in a flesh-like glow, translucent, as though its essence would waver if wafted by a breeze. Then, it morphed into a recognizable visual, taking space in this world and, much like an Adam from an ancient fairy tale, its first breath. Body parts shed pinpoints of light. Motes of cosmic dust crackled like oil splatters in a hot pan. After a few final hisses, the noises subsided, and the boudoir was silent. John and the Entity separated, each crying out and falling to the floor.

John stood and shook his head. The Entity had curled into a shivering, fetal position. Eventually it awakened, stood, a bit unsteady for a moment, searching for familiarity of which it had none. *Ilya* was perfectly formed, a Greco-Roman athlete coming to life in minutes in a coded, algorithmic yield that would have taken Praxiteles years to sculpt. But there was nothing marmoreal about the Entity's unblemished skin, nor glacial in its warm breath.

The wife and husband removed their dark-spex to see more clearly this immaculate birth.

Astonishing, thought John. It looks nothing like me. "It's beautiful," he whispered.

"*He's* beautiful," whispered Madalyn.

And naked. John shut his mouth. Suggested in the vid-guide, he held a robe ready to drape over the Entity.

"Not yet," said Madalyn.

The Entity looked around, saw John, and cocked its head. "Madalyn?" Automatically, its voice was a rich baritone, perfectly attuned as an echo of its physical beauty. The head moved to its right, passed Madalyn, jerked, and returned to her. "Madelyn?"

Tears ran down her cheeks.

"There, there, my love," said Ilya.

   American Queer

"Leave us," said Madalyn.

John said, "Don't you think—"

"No, I don't."

"I'll make dinner."

"I require no sustenance," said Ilya.

"I wasn't speaking to you."

Ilya returned a stare, but there was no warmth in its eyes, and a smile, but there was no mirth in its curve. "I sense—"

"A chill." John threw the robe at Ilya. His catch was quick and nimble. "Put it on."

It did as it was told.

John hid his amazement at how advanced the Entity was to don a tangible object. He surmised, as the vid-guide informed, that it was quickly familiarizing itself with their user profiles, and trillions of environmental variables. It was making decisions with access to the universe.

Ilya gazed at Madalyn. She shut her eyes and reached for him. John slid the panel-door down, leaving the boudoir and the happy couple in it. A ring-tone announced his mail would arrive by air in 53 seconds.

Mrs. Nettle lived next door and had been walking Bluebell #3, a clone of her beloved doodle-dog, on the neighborhood conveyor-walk. Rounding the corner to come home, she and her pretty girl heard popping noises and saw bright streaks coming through the slats of her neighbors' front window-shield. Bluebell thought the disturbance was a squirrel, yanked Mrs. Nettle onto the green, mock-turf, and beelined for a molded rosebush that sprayed scent next to her neighbor's fab-house. The oddities soon ceased. The closed window-shield puzzled Mrs. Nettle because it was down only when her neighbors watched the mini-IMAX screen. And that was only in the evenings.

Behind and above her, a postal drone descended. She tried to drag Bluebell away from the blooming bushes and back to the conveyer-walk. The front panel-door rose, and John retrieved his mail from the drone, startled to see his neighbor.

"Mrs. Nettle!"

"Hello, Mr. Rayner," she said. "I am so sorry; Bluebell ran away from me and I was just pulling her back home.

    American Queer

Bluebell, now stop it!" The dog strained her invisi-leash, tempted by smells in the Rayners' home. "Really, she has a mind of her own."

"Yes, you do, I mean, she does."

Mrs. Nettle giggled. "Is your wife all right? I haven't seen her for a while."

"She's fine."

"Poor dear." Like her doodle-dog, Mrs. Nettle attempted to peer past John through the open front panel-door. "Please tell Mrs. Rayner I'm thinking of her. I could tell her myself, if—"

"She's resting, Mrs. Nettle."

"Maybe tomorrow. I could bring cookies. I bought a new solar-wave, they bake in 60 seconds. Best ever, really, the cookies."

"She doesn't have much appetite, but thank you. Good-bye, Mrs. Nettle. Good-bye, Bluebell," said John, adding, "you naughty girl."

Mrs. Nettle giggled again, not knowing if her neighbor referred to her or her pretty girl. The doodle-dog sniffed, sneezed, peed on the rosebush, and then pulled her mistress homeward.

After dinner, John heard laughter through the closed panel. Oddly, Madalyn's was a sound he had not heard in a long time. To him, it was like a musical trill. Maybe this exorbitant indulgence will satisfy Madalyn, he thought, and some of her old self will return. He scoffed at his feeble hope and misplaced faith in REP-lic-8's self-marketed testimonials of healed customers.

About to knock and check on Madalyn, John heard *his* laughter. Full and throaty, masculine, such as an opera singer might perform, lovely in timbre and tone. But it lacks life, thought John. Belongs in a heavenly choir, if heaven was Antarctica. And since the continent had been reduced to icebergs, he grinned, picturing it stranded there. John rapped on the panel. "Madalyn," he called. The laughter stopped. He tried to open it. Locked. "Madalyn?" he called, "are you all right?"

"Yes."

"The panel-door is locked." No response. "Madalyn, let me in."

She unlocked the door and slid it up. "You need to leave us alone."

John looked for Ilya. He sat on the floor, cross-legged, his robe open, like some yogi or guru. His long hair had been pulled back into a pony-tail. The glint of something shiny caught John's eye: a ring on his left hand. "You're all right?" he asked his wife.

"Of course I'm all right, now go away."

Which John did. He slept restlessly by himself, as he had for many nights …

A ghost appeared. "Father," whispered the naked man with a lifeless smile on his handsome face. Like a neon chalk drawing, the figure glided toward him, above him, moved into a decumbent position next to him on the hover-pad and whispered one word: "Us." The aroused specter threw back the covers, pulled down his shorts, moved between his legs and—"Nuh!"

John sat up violently, panting, searching the dark, seeing nothing, no one. His shorts lay bunched down around his ankles. He pulled them up; they were sticky. His back was sore. Out of the corner of his eye, he saw a white chalky figure exit his bedroom with a faint, echoing laugh.

On the carpet, he found a ring.

John rushed to check on his wife. "Leave us alone" was her muffled answer between giggles through the locked door.

Worried, he descended to the ground-garage where he opened the safe with his ocu-scan, found a keycard, and put it in his pocket. He also retrieved his electro-gun, then secured it to a charging dock, checking its gauge, making sure it registered full, and was set to max. He returned to the boudoir and attempted to slide open the panel. It was still locked.

"Madalyn, if you don't let me in," said John, "I'll unlock it myself."

No answer.

"Madalyn, I mean it."

"Go away."

"Madalyn, please, let me in. I'm worried about you."

"Don't be, John," she moaned. "Don't be."

"But that ghost thing, whatever it is, could be dangerous."

Soft laughter.

"Oh, Johnny," sighed Ilya, "You purchased the pleasure program. Remember? Or do I need to remind you?"

John stepped back. Ilya's mocking voice was far from the electronic neutrality of even the most sophisticated 3-D players he'd encountered.

More soft laughter. More sighs and moans.

"We'll have a surprise for you soon," said Madalyn. "Don't ruin it."

"I have a surprise for you," said John, "now."

He held the keycard against the red-eye, unlocking and opening the boudoir's panel-door, then entered. Madalyn sat on the banquette, Ilya on the floor between her legs. She was brushing his long, luxurious hair.

"I'm deactivating this thing tomorrow."

"No!" screamed Madalyn, "please, John, you can't."

"Look, darling—"

"Look, darling," repeated Ilya.

John ignored him. "I don't trust it."

"He's not an *it*," said Madalyn.

"*It's* a ghost."

"He's real to me."

"It's not alive."

"I'll die without him."

"You will anyway!" shouted John. "Oh god, Madalyn—"

"

She turned away.

"I didn't mean it."

"No, you're right," said Madalyn. "I'll be gone soon."

John recalled her recent physical. "No, no, darling," he said.

"No, no, darling," repeated Ilya.

"I am so sorry."

"I am so sorry," repeated Ilya.

John tried to hold his wife's hand. She refused. "I need to lay down."

"Yes, darling," said John.

"Yes, darling," repeated Ilya.

Who winked at John, who thought his grin alarming and who immediately contacted their salesman, Mr. Jeel.

Wearing a yellow poly-papyrus suit with a solar-neon tie (purple today), he arrived early evening and sat at the kitchen flo-table. He waited for his host to pour coffee from the nuke-pot, his hair color (decided this morning) as silver as the pot, and solar-generated, too. "Thank you for the coffee, Johnny."

"John."

"John, yes," said Mr. Jeel, dipping his spoon into a bowl. "Real sugar. You've gone overboard. Sweet-oil is all I can afford." Mr. Jeel sipped from a green plastic cup. "Delicious."

"Helps flavor Imitivo coffee," said John.

"True fact, sir," said Mr. Jeel, "true fact. And that is exactly what I'm here to discern for you, your wife, and REP-lic-8. True facts. We usually wait a week for things to settle. You tele-watched and I answered, all part of REP-lic-8's guaranteed super service. I'm more than happy to evaluate your wife. And that's a true fact," said Mr. Jeel, chuckling.

After a pause, John asked, "Aren't facts always true?"

"Excuse me?" asked Mr. Jeel.

"It's that ghost thing that needs evaluating."

"We prefer the word *Entity*, as instructed; it's neutral, accurate."

"This experimental model is not working right," said John. "When formation was complete, we were both knocked to the floor. If you were monitoring it properly, you'd know."

"We do, my dear sir, we do. After formation REP-lic-8 and its engineers monitor the test models 24/7. Maybe there's a few kinks—the Entity packed a punch we had not anticipated—but please take them in stride. Remember you're getting a great deal. But REP-lic-8 wants to make sure you and your wife are 100% satisfied. Take this Imitivo coffee, made from tree bark—a true fact—a brand we love and buy and drink because of another true fact: the cataclysm that happened in the southern hemisphere. Point is, we take it in stride. We adapt," said Mr. Jeel, "which is what the Entity is doing. We created it in our own image. It's doing what we do."

"And we die." John stared at his coffee, then looked at Mr. Jeel. "I want it to die."

"It's not that simple," said Mr. Jeel.

"Death is very simple," said John. "It's not even alive."

Mr. Jeel was about to say something, but changed his mind. He entered information into his projection file, then scanned the air-script for an answer. "So how is Mrs. Rayner, Madalyn? How is she taking to her new, shall we say," said Mr. Jeel smiling, "relationship?"

John told his rep he preferred not thinking of the ghost thing, "excuse me, Entity," as half a relationship. He never believed an app would bring him and his wife closer, but he didn't think it would widen their gulf either. Madalyn had been behind the closed and locked door of her boudoir all day yesterday and was today. He could hear laughter and, well, sighs and trills, even groanings.

"Without meaning to sound insensitive, John," said Mr. Jeel, "what did you expect? You contracted for the Lover."

"It's alarming," said John, "that's all."

"We often get jealousy issues when one of a pair is excluded," said Mr. Jeel.

"Me, jealous of an artificial app?"

"You ordered that model; you've been excluded, they are consenting adults."

"She is, but it's only an adult *it*. How could *it* consent? *It's* a result of ones and zeroes, strings of code, and massive multiple choices," said John. "This was a mistake. Nothing good will come of it."

"Is Mrs. Rayner happy?" asked Mr. Jeel.

"What little I've seen of her," said John, looking to the ceiling, "from appearances, I guess so."

"Then good has come," said Mr. Jeel. "There's your true fact."

"Hardly." John rolled his eyes. "Her feeling is not a result of anything real."

"Who's to say? They are her feelings. You love your wife, don't you?"

"Yes, of course."

"Want to see her happy?"

"Yes."

"Do anything for her?"

    American Queer

"Anything, including protecting her," said John, "which is why I want to terminate our contract. I've tried to ignore REP-lic-8's lawsuits and deaths for Madalyn's sake, but—"

"Now, now," said Mr. Jeel, smiling and waving his hand, "don't believe everything you read on News-Net. I'll let you in on a little secret. We've made astonishing improvements."

"Such as?"

"I'm not at liberty to say, but if you knew, you'd be amazed at what this new model can create. But we still monitor the app. We just need more data. The Entity will revolutionize relationships. You and your wife are helping us do that for the happiness of future REP-lic-8 clients who are lonely and in need. Remember, there are true facts, and then there are true facts."

"Here's one for you," said John, leaning closer, as though someone was listening. "Your Entity—like a glimmering shape, an outline, transparent and filmy—visited me in my bedroom."

Mr. Jeel's face betrayed concern for the first time. "But that's impossible. The app's formation is confined to the circumference of the pyramid control. You must have been dreaming."

"I was not dreaming." His ecstasy proved that. "I found a ring."

"A ring."

"It—and don't correct me—wore the ring earlier in the day."

"Where did the ring come from?"

"Madalyn. And it gave the ring to me."

"So." Mr. Jeel leaned back in his chair. "He really is getting to know you."

"Delete that thing today, now."

"But Mr. Raynor, be reasonable, they've been together less than two days."

"I don't trust it with Madalyn."

"If the two lovers are happy, REP-lic-8 has delivered its promise."

"They're not lovers!" shouted John, pounding the flo-table and causing their Imitivo to slosh on the counter-top.

"Here's another true fact: Terminate the contract, or I tele-watch News-Net."

Mr. Jeel sat back, defeated. "Very well, Mr. Rayner." He would conduct a psych eval of Madalyn and a tech eval of the pyramid control and the Entity. He insisted on John's absence.

"Fine," said John.
Am I the only one with any sense in the world?"

Negative, Mr. Jeel answered to himself, knowing the excluded party usually needed a psych eval more than the included party. He dictated a few notes and instructions to his projection, swiped it, then accompanied John to the boudoir.

"Hello Madalyn, good to see you again," said Mr. Jeel, entering the room. "My God," he whispered in amazement. "And who's this handsome fellow?"

Mr. Jeel closed the panel-door and latched it securely. John leaned against it and heard three muffled voices but no words, maybe a small scream from Madalyn, a long, deep groan—from Ilya, he presumed.

After about an hour, Mr. Jeel exited the boudoir, shaking his head and scanning another air-script. "Your wife took it very hard, as did her lov—Ilya."

"What?" John frowned with incredulity. "My wife, yes, I'm sorry for that. But *it* took it hard? *It* doesn't contain one cell of organic material or neuron of consciousness."

"Our entities are very sophisticated, Mr. Rayner, and very sensitive."

John snorted. "Excuse me, I must take care of my wife."

"Do, because your wife is in a fragile state," said Mr. Jeel, "I've given them another week—"

"A week? No, today, now. I told you to cancel—" John stopped himself. "What do you mean, *them*?"

"The Entity, Ilya, needs time to adjust, too," said Mr. Jeel, "before the system shuts down. I'll collect the pyramid and foto-lasers then, at no extra charge, of course. That's my evaluation. We have a right to protect our assets, Mr. Rayner, and you don't want to precipitate a character crash. That could prove expensive. If rushed, entities never recuperate rightly; they get testy. No matter how thoroughly we scrub the code, something human remains, regret or depression, longing. They

　　　　　　　　　　　　　　　American Queer

are much more than zeroes and ones, quaint of you to think so, but true fact." He shut down his projection in preparation of leaving. "Be aware, Mr. Rayner, Ilya may not like it."

"That, Mr. Jeel, sounds threatening. So, Madalyn is in danger."

"You are both perfectly safe. You have REP-lic-8's promise, and our engineers report no abnormalities. Though Madalyn's, shall we say, rapport with the Entity may not be real to you, their connection is very real to them, as real as yours is with your wife." The front panel-door slid up. "Perhaps even more real," added Mr. Jeel. He turned and entered the night air.

John went to the boudoir. Madalyn lay on the cushioned banquette crying. Ilya sat next to her with a hand on her shoulder.

"I'm going to the bath-pool," said Madalyn.

Ilya said, "I'll join you in a minute."

"That would be lovely," said Madalyn, "if only you could."

"I adapt," said Ilya, winking, "Soon, I won't need the foto-lasers."

John frowned at the Entity. It's got to be lying, he thought. Madalyn looked at him with a mixture of hate and regret, then guided her hover-chair to the bath-pool.

"You told that evaluator a story," said Ilya, softly with a frown.

"How do you know that?"

"You shouldn't have done that."

"Or what?"

"You lied."

"Then, what's this?" asked John. He placed the ring on the flo-table.

"Oh, that. Ha! Madalyn give it to me. I give it to you."

"I don't want it."

Ilya pouted. "I am quizzical," said Ilya, "why this you are doing?"

"I don't answer to you," said John.

"For Madalyn you care muchly?"

"I love her."

Ilya received John's challenging stare and returned a scream. "She loves me!"

John blinked, and in that second, Ilya stood in front of him. John yelped and staggered back, falling onto the banquette.

"I learn!" shouted Ilya. "Terminate me? Me? You'll regret it. Madalyn won't like it. If I suffer, Madalyn will suffer. Then suffer you will!"

Ilya raised a hand and lurched, but John scrambled to the pyramid and touched its tip, Ilya freezing in a blur, a tall, smudged statue in livid mid-action. John was panting and sweating and shaking.

He heard the bath-pool draining. Rapping on its panel-door, he called out, "Honey?"

"I know what you did. Turn him back on. Please."

"He's not good for you, Madalyn. He's dangerous."

"I hate you."

"I love you. Does it, he, love you? Can he love?"

"You don't understand. Together, we have something special. I was saving it—I wanted to be sure—but we're planning a surprise, John."

"Me too, making your favorite supper: cutlet-synth and veggie-fleurs with rhu-berry pie."

John ate alone. He scraped the leftovers on his plate into the sink's composter, turned it on, then off, thinking he had heard a disturbance over the loud grinding. All was quiet.

The boudoir's door was open. John looked in and saw Madalyn asleep on the banquette with pillows and coverlets, breathing evenly. The ghost thing had rewound itself and sat on a cushion near a soft light. His hair was once again bound into a ponytail. But even without current, Ilya shivered, its eyes darted, and it groaned.

"Daddy," said the Entity, "kiss your boy good-night?"

"Tomorrow," John whispered, "you disappear forever."

He touched the pyramid tip again to make sure the ghost was powered off, and left the panel-door up just in case. He felt Madalyn was safe. He rode the esca-step to his bedroom, undressed, stepped into his hover-pad, and struggled to get comfortable and warm the cold sheets. He stared into the black, wondering what kind of husband he was to deny his wife her happiness.

John dozed off when sounds like falling furniture awakened him. He quietly opened the top drawer of his nightstand and pulled out his electro-gun, flipping its switch so it emitted a faint hum, and ran down the esca-step.

The boudoir panel-door was closed and locked. John tapped his keycard on the red eye and ran in to see Ilya rushing towards Madalyn. He pointed his electro-gun at him and yelled, "Touch her and I shoot!"

"John, no!" screamed Madalyn.

"Don't worry, darling," said Ilya. "He can't hurt me."

"How did you—?" asked John. "I turned you off."

"You forget, I'm the new and improved generation. If you'd read the vid-guide, you'd know I learn exponentially."

"I know you're fake. She thinks you're real."

"*Thinks*?" said Ilya.

"What else?" asked John. "You can't touch her; she can't touch you."

Ilya teased with a lilt in his voice. "Are you sure?"

"You don't feel; you're not conscious."

"I'm as real as she wants me to be," said Ilya.

"You don't bleed."

"Oh, I bleed," said Ilya, "the blood of a superior type fills my veins."

"Stop it, both of you," pleaded Madalyn. "Ilya has helped me, John, he really has. Our surprise is because of you."

"That ghost thing is dangerous," said John.

"You're not listening," said Madalyn. "My miracle is for you." Her eyes glistened, and she cleared her throat. "This will be hard to fathom, John, but you know how I, we, could never have children? Well, that's changed."

"Changed? How could it?"

"I think I'm pregnant."

John's face and body didn't react, remained frozen.

"Isn't this miraculous?" said Madalyn. "Say something."

John emerged from his shock. "Impossible. This can't be. You're imagining—"

"I'm not! I know it sounds incredible, unbelievable, from another world, but I can tell. You must believe me. We're going to have a baby."

"Stop talking like that," said John. "Your age, your illness—"

"When I asked for this adventure, I never expected such happiness."

"But Madalyn," asked John, "who's the father?"

"Hello?" said Ilya, smiling. "And in less than 24 hours."

"What did you do to my wife!" shouted John.

"He gave me life!" cried Madalyn.

John ran toward the pyramid control.

"No!" Ilya checked him at the flo-table, blocking his grab of the device and knocking the electro-gun out of his hand.

John was stunned. "How can you—"

"Told you I was a quick learner," said Ilya. "I'm the future, John, best get used to it."

"Best get out of my way!" John took a swipe at Ilya's jaw, but he nimbly ducked, and John fell to the floor.

"That's not very nice," said Ilya, raising his fist.

"Ilya, don't!" shouted Madalyn.

"Not so benign, after all, is he?" John faced her and said, "This is crazy. You don't really think—I mean, you can't believe—"

"But I do; it's true; it's real," said Madalyn. "Just think, John, a child."

"But what kind of a child?"

"A child of our own."

The mother-to-be braced herself on her hover-chair, as though to stand.

"Let me help," said Ilya.

"No. I want to do it on my own." Madalyn let go of the arms, took a step and another, smiling widely, looking at John who was stunned by her movement. "Another surprise, darling, I can—"

"Oh my god. Madalyn!" Tears fell down John's face.

Ilya watched the couple. Was that love? He knew—as much as he could know—that he expressed emotions, their automatic hormonal variations and body chemistry. To him, there were too many. Body performance was his specialty. Yes, quite the stud. He wondered if the engineers knew. That Jeel fellow would start counting the crypto-credits today. But love? What was love? It didn't matter. He was real. If not, then who was thinking? Did he not know jealousy, anger, threat? No, he was human. So what if he couldn't express love.

Madalyn took another small step towards John, then lost her footing and staggered forward, crashing into the flo-table, Ilya rushing to her, John shouting, "Stay away from her!" picking up the electro-gun, and shooting. The fireball went through Ilya first, wiping the smirk of invincibility off his face to be replaced by a look of horror. He had moved between husband and wife, and the deadly shot struck her in the chest.

"No!" John ran to Madalyn, knelt, and cradled her head. "No, no, no!"

"I can—walk, John," said Madalyn, " … my other miracle … for you."

"It's a beautiful miracle."

"This is real?"

"Yes, I'm real."

"I so wanted to be a mother and make you a father. Love you?" she said in a weak voice, then she said no more.

"Love you, too. Oh, Madalyn," said John, one arm still holding her, the other aiming the electro-gun at Ilya. "You bastard!"

"You know that won't hurt me," said Ilya. "I'm sorry. Good times Madalyn and I had in a time so short. This isn't my fault. You're the one holding a weapon. It's just us two. Madalyn loved me. I called her Mother. Now you can love me. Please. Father."

"What? You think—?"

"I know."

John aimed the electro-gun at the pyramid.

"No! You can't afford to replace it, especially if your employer finds out about how you've been stealing—"

"Shut up!"

"And since you've already paid for me, think of the other night. I pleased you, I know exactly how, and I always will and can, and will never wear out. You could love me. You should love me. That's what I'm for; someone must love me."

"You can't love back."

"I can."

"You're not alive."

"Who are you to say? I am alive. I'm different, and I live." Ilya continued to advance toward John. "I need to be loved. I beg you, Father, Love me, PLEASE LOVE ME—!"

The fireball passed through Ilya's abdomen—he looked so shocked, memory and code trying to compute—then it smashed the plasma pyramid, igniting the device in a swirling electrical short circuit. Cracked open, it no longer contained the lightning storm. Jagged arcs discharged their voltage, exploding the foto-lasers in each corner, frying the air in a frenzy of zapping bolts and flowering fireworks, erratic and volatile.

Ilya lurched at John, but his running legs and reaching arms moved sluggishly. His shouts sounded like a disc on a too-low speed with words dragging in a voice an octave lower. His beauty began to fade; sparks flew from his image, his expression changing from horror to sadness to blank oblivion.

John dropped the electro-gun and activated his tele-watch.

"911. What is your emergency?"

"I—"

"Yes? What is your emergency please?"

"I've shot a ghost."

"You … shot a ghost? Sir, you said you shot a ghost?"

"Blood … "

"What is your address? Where are you?"

"How can that be?"

"I've locked onto your location. The ambu-coptor will land in 73 seconds."

"So much blood."

"Stay with me, sir."

"Ghosts don't bleed … do they?"

The pyramid gurgled and flickered, then came alive as a white neon chalk figure stood over the two humans.

With her pretty girl tethered to its invisi-leash for their nightly stretch before beddy-bye, Mrs. Nettle strolled on the conveyor-walk. Bluebell's ears perked up. Much sooner than her owner, the doodle-dog heard the faint wailing of a siren and whapping of rotary blades growing closer and louder. They both saw lights zigzagging behind their neighbor's front window. Bluebell growled and yipped, then pulled her mistress toward the strobing beams.

Mrs. Nettle didn't see her neighbors, but then saw what Bluebell saw, neither making sense of a vague outline. The form was white-silver light, disintegrating into parts of a body—leg, arm, head, was that a ponytail? The glowing, electric shapes shot off sparks and flares. Even through the window, mistress and doodle-dog heard the flying glitter of the forms sputter, snap, and fizz, fading motes of cosmic dust floating into extinction. A final hiss, and it was nevermore.

Bluebell whined and peed on the rosebush.

A Million Pieces of Shell

2024

In the Beginning

Before the great empires conquered the land between two rivers, before Darius and the Greeks, when Ur was a coastal city, a wild-haired priestess with facial tattoos holds up to heaven a rough-hewn fertility goddess, a primitive Venus—the modern name twenty thousand years to come. Inside a dark and damp megalith, using pre-language cries, the priestess begs Great Mother to ease the agony of a writhing woman about to give birth on an altar of fleece and fur, her feet in stirrups of bone and branch. The mother curses and grunts with the roots of future words; she coughs, and her eyes burn from the smoking tree-sap of a primeval forest. The priestess places the idol in the mother's hands which curl upon her chest.

The Venus, carved from a soft stone no bigger than a fist by an artisan centuries before, portrays womanhood with a large head of plaited hair, bulging breasts and belly. A deep navel hole and v-gash complete the trunk etched above heavy hips and thick thighs. The fertile juices of many mothers have stained every pit and crevice. She has witnessed many births, but she is a blind witness, for the Venus has no eyes.

Still, like thousands before, she observes another as the priestess again supplicates Great Mother—deliver the child alive! Between the human mother's splayed legs, a bulge emerges, a crowning bloody and gooey. After tense moments— the babe is born!—announcing his arrival with wails shrill and strong. Abandoned from the warmth of a watery womb and exiled to an indifferent world, he cries for the comfort of mother's milk, but as the mother loosens her grip on life, she loosens her grip on the goddess. The Venus falls to the earth; the cries cease, both lives so short as to have never existed, yet witnesses to a beginning of our world.

Warriors, shouts, screams! Blades slice flesh, blood flies! A soldier grabs the effigy, sacred to his tribe, protects it in a bag of brown hide, then falls from an enemy's iron thrust. The Venus, trampled deeper into the wet, red sand, awaits her next mother, her next birth. For many millennia she lies dormant in darkness, covered in the packed earth of shifting plates, impermanent constructions, men's futile battles over who owns the sand blown from one side of an imaginary border to the other.

At long last, the sun rises on the day the Venus sees the light of another age, an age of mothers and children who, despite modernity and midwives, survive little better than they did long ago. Using tools and techniques similar to the icon's time of creation, a peasant farmer digs his field to lift what he thought was an odd potato. Its value to him was worth more as part of his crop than as the icon it turned out to be, but the discovery makes him famous in his local village and at universities around the world. Archaeologists argue about the date of the artifact but agree it accompanied a celebrant's laments and incantations of ancient fertility rites. The goddess moves to a museum to be locked in a glass case with a cool temperature. The sleeping beauty reclines on a triangular stand, washed, displayed, unused.

Then, in an advanced war amidst the exploding fires of Vulcan's terrorists, an elder in the museum under attack grabs the Venus and gives it to a soldier to save from destruction, or worse, being plundered to fund the fanatics' future. The soldier wraps the figure in a rag and hides it in his kit. He promises to preserve this relic of an ancient people whose heritage is a cradle of civilization, a blasphemous history to the terrorists seeking to obliterate it, to replace it with religious tyranny and hypocrisy, their chaos, and wrath.

And so, the soldier fulfills his promise. Months later, he pays dearly for this honor.

Again, the Venus disappears and the secret of its dark locale and its extraordinary value lights the greed—political, religious, monetary—in those who will seek to possess it.

The Captain

A military captain arranges to meet with a mother whose son had served under his command. Upon his punctual arrival, he immediately expresses their government's grief over the loss of its soldier, her son. The abruptness sets an awkward tone. The captain becomes visibly upset. Officer and private had seen combat together, had shared—but he cannot continue. He clears his throat. He loved her son—a good captain loves all his boys—but he was special, a fine soldier. The mother agrees and says, "Aren't they all?"

With delicacy, the captain informs the mother he also seeks a statuette, known as a paleolithic Venus, and shows her a picture. He says a long time ago, the effigy was used in fertility rites to ensure healthy births. This particular figurine is crucial to the political future between their country and the country where her son served. He may have taken it, may have hidden it, may have given it to her or someone else. No questions asked, the eternal gratitude of a nation given.

The mother stares at the picture, thinks the squat and bulbous stone ugly, really rather creepy. It does not possess the beauty of the Venuses she remembers from school, the one with no arms, nor the one emerging from a giant shell in a sea of blue-green. Its mottled and pockmarked surface, she feels, must be filled with the goo of birth. She remembers that, too. And its value, she asks the captain, is to be compared with the life of my son? That country halfway 'round the earth has his blood. Is that not enough? The captain looks down at a brown carpet. No, says the mother, I know nothing of this thing. All I know is my son is dead.

The captain reports his soldier sent his mother packages. She confesses the receipt of silks and ceramics, Persian walnuts, dried apricots, and figs. Also, his ashes in a plastic box. She replaced that with a beautiful onyx urn to contain her son's remains. The captain is welcome to sift through it but, embarrassed, he declines.

The captain thanks the mother, salutes, and leaves empty-handed.

The Attaché

From that country on the other side of the world, a cultural attaché calls upon the mother. The woman wears a scarf and never removes it. On behalf of her nation, she expresses its sympathies for the mother's sacrifice. (The mother does not react to her sympathies.) The attaché states her real reason for visiting (she does not say that out loud): Specifically, she seeks the statuette of an ancient fertility goddess, and thinks her son might have had it in his possession. It was probably given to him by the capital city's museum director. Why bother me, asks the mother, ask him. He was beheaded, answers the attaché, when the terrorists raped women and pillaged homes. The black market for artifacts is how they hope to pay for their guns and bullets. We want to prevent what they didn't destroy from financing their war. The relic is important to restoring my homeland's heritage. For millennia she's been the silent, detached observer of my country's terrors and triumphs. She embodies a spiritual quality intrinsic to my people.

The attaché shows a picture of the figurine to the mother, who comments it's the same one her son's commanding officer showed her. (The attaché does not react.) The mother does not have it. She would never have such an obscene thing in her home. She says, If this pitiful lump is so important and magical, why didn't it protect him, save him? (The attaché does not react.) After silence, she states her government wants the Venus returned. The mother wants her son returned, the hell with her government. All she has is her son's urn of ash and flag of stars and stripes. (The attaché resists reminding her that many mothers do not even have ashes.)

She acknowledges the mother's pain because she is a mother, too, but also a steward of her nation's relics. She says, I want my daughter to know about her ancestors' place in humanity's humble beginnings. The mother asks, What about my son's humanity, ended before it had barely begun? (The attaché does not answer.) The furious mother breathes deeply and says, That eyeless witch is an abomination to the holiness of life, just like your evil religion. You're all heathens who want to destroy the world like you destroyed my child. The mother holds her

head high, daring a contradiction. The attaché meets the
mother's eyes and says, I'm sorry you lost your son. Sorry, yes,
replies the mother, Sorry.

The attaché knows she will leave empty-handed, and
why mothers suffer the most. As one herself, she remembers the
birthing like it was yesterday. Again, she expresses her sympathy
and heartfelt gratitude for the soldier's ultimate sacrifice. The
attaché offers her hand. The mother takes it—a spark flies—and
she inhales a gasping sob

the fat man

Claiming to know her son, a fat man convinces the
mother to meet with him. He says he is an antiques dealer, that
they knew each other over there, he and her son, in that god-
forsaken land, a million miles from civilization with an
indecipherable alphabet and unpronounceable names. Funny,
says the mother, my son never mentioned you. Wasn't that just
like the boy? says the fat man. Only I have the right to call him
that, says the mother. With unctuous charm, the fat man bows
slightly. Quite right, he says, forgive me, madam, my apologies.

The fat man wonders if he, the son, had sent her, the
mother, any articles of that country's culture. In particular, he
seeks a small statue, no bigger than a fist, known as a fertility
Venus, called that by scholars and curators to define prehistoric
statues of the feminine figure. He shows her a picture. Odd, the
mother thinks, it's the same one the other two scavengers
displayed. It was carved eons ago, the fat man continues, by a
primitive artisan with a style the modern world reveres and pays
for dearly. In fact, he would be willing to oversee its auction, of
course, sharing the profits with the mother. The statue's value is
incalculable, he says, and a private sale might prove even more
lucrative. Such a small item. Just goes to show size doesn't
matter. The fat man smiles, gets a blank look from the mother,
and moves on. Imagine the largesse an appreciative collector
would bestow upon the agent. Who knows, maybe you could
find a sponsor and fund a scholarship in your son's name.
Pointing to the picture, the mother asks, Why is such a ghastly
thing so important? It's not even pretty.

                                                      American Queer

Madam, answers the fat man, this Venus fires the imagination and fuels desire like all women have since man began breathing, like all treasure has since man began collecting. There is sublime beauty found in the crude brutality of the prehistoric, and nothing exists like this queen. Through her miraculous longevity, we connect to our first ancestors who battled the saber tooth tiger and wooly rhino. In her rarity, the goddess personifies perfect imperfection, mystery, and history, the divine feminine at its inception. The fat man breathes excitedly. Surely, he says, you can understand such passion. For over twenty thousand years, the Venus has survived an unforgiving world. And our world loves survivors.

My son did not survive, says the mother. Do you imply the world no longer loves him? I do not require an answer.

The fat man looks relieved. The mother asks if the figure would be considered stolen loot. The fat man squirms and mumbles something about how the artifact may have been a gift, the necessity to keep the story small, tracking its challenging provenance. According to him, art connoisseurs pay extravagantly for discretion and privacy. The mother asks if the figure would give grand meaning to the dreams of small people? Indeed, madam, says the fat man, leaning forward, sweat on his upper lip, thinking at last he has persuaded the woman. A scholarship, you say? she asks. Yes, absolutely, he replies, and I'll be a donor, the first and most generous. No, she says. I have nothing. Nothing for you. Sighing, the fat man leans back in his chair. Oh, dear lady, he says, how you crush the splendor of my dreams. Imagine mine, she says. Before leaving empty-handed with slumped shoulders, the fat man gives her his card, and almost whispers, Should you, shall we say, madam, discover anything hidden.

The Venus and the Mother

The mother closes her blinds, takes the onyx urn of ash from the mantelpiece, and places it on a drape of purple silk. She unscrews the silver top, removes a red velvet bag, and gently pours out the ashes, more like a million pieces of shell than dust. A tiny cry of awe escapes her mouth. Buried in the remains of her son is the ancient Venus. She delicately brushes bits off and runs her fingers over its cool, bumpy surface. She stares at its faceless head for some revelation. Nothing arises. Maybe someday. She wonders if her son thought safeguarding a hunk of old rock was an honorable way to die. Maybe long ago in a different lifetime, he had defended this statuette that appears ripe to give birth. She imagines it held by flesh and blood mothers, pregnant with life so long ago, the stars defined different constellations. Maybe through a strange link across time and space, he had defended it again as the son she bore and knew. Maybe somewhere, someday, he will defend it again.

For today, the mother lives within the secret and cherishes the fertility goddess, maybe the last earthly thing her child touched.

How dare anyone think it belongs to them. She is its fearsome guardian now, priestess to the idol of her idolatry, the blind witness of her son's history.

The mother lies on her back on the sofa and spreads her legs as though positioned in stirrups. Her hands, curled upon her breasts, cradle the Venus—more the shape and size of the human heart she feels. The mother embraces this moment of unbearable loveliness, wondering why it is, wishing it would end, hoping it will last her eternity.

Acknowledgments

Writing is a one-person job that relies on many others to succeed.

My partner, Neil Stock — I trusted him with early drafts and myriad final drafts, "One more read!" and "This is it!" my rally cries. Thanks for your love and support. (Check out his fabric creations at SingularStock.com)

My muse, Miran d'Muse, aka Miranda Patterson — As a professional writer, she embodies the word *pithy* (not to be confused with citrus fruits), and for over 40 years has tried patiently and encouragingly to imbue within me her sacrosanct values of brevity and clarity, using the relentless drum beats of example and suggestion, rhythms I sometimes adopted and sometimes did not, this paragraph an accurate example of the latter. Pithily, I exclaim, "Thanks!"

My publishers, Addison Herron-Wheeler and Maggie Phillips — Though generations younger, they connected with my OK, Boomer words and I with their youthful vigor and encouragement. With these young women in the publishing world, there is hope for the printed and electronic word. Innumerable thanks for your belief in my words.

Russell Bush — When I was at Brown University to receive a prize, a friend no-showed and failed to reserve a hotel room. And when a room was unavailable at the inn, Russell graciously shared his. Later, he published *Affectionate Men*, a beautiful and historical photographic record of male relationships. The story *Testaments* was inspired by one of the pictures, which he has generously granted permission to include. Thank you!

John Johnston — This superior photographer and videographer graciously did a shoot twice for the author photo. He also engineered the recordings for the audio book. Thank you for your time, generosity, expertise, and for making the recording fun and a joy.

High school teacher, Miss Holly Hart — In the 70s, she tried to teach me the humor of Shakespeare ("Good Mistress Accost?" Funny? Really?). But more importantly, she explained *Boys in the Band* to her 17-year-old English student, a crucial episode of my coming out story.

American Queer

Tom Mills — Whatever success I may have as a writer will be due to his friendship. He demanded and dared me to "WRITE!" So I did. He led a ragtag group of guys, myself included, to come out more and more. Thank you for teaching me the amazing fun of being gay and for encouraging me to write even on your deathbed.

I have received the cheers of brother Lee, friends (and fellow bridge fiends) Maggie Kulik and David Goldberg, Mark Smith (Oscar to my Felix), Michelle Rokavec somewhere in the world, and many others through the 50 years it took to create this collection.

I also benefited from the wonderful public school systems in Ft. Lupton and Brighton Colorado, and at the University of Northern Colorado in Greeley. My exposure to the world was aided by many wonderful teachers who had little to no fear of retribution from selfish parents, craven politicians, and board lackeys.

Mom and Dad — well, you know … I'm lucky, blessed, grateful.

Readers — **THANK YOU!**